THE LIBERTINES AND ME

FOR THE LOVE OF A WOMAN

NOMIS

PARTRIDGE

To order additional copies of this book, contact
Toll Free 800 101 2657 (Singapore)
Toll Free 1 800 81 7340 (Malaysia)
orders.singapore@partridgepublishing.com

www.partridgepublishing.com/singapore

CONTENTS

Prologue...vii

Chapter 1 1
Chapter 2 7
Chapter 3 16
Chapter 4 36
Chapter 5 49
Chapter 6 83
Chapter 7 94
Chapter 8 117
Chapter 9 159
Chapter 10 174
Chapter 11 195
Chapter 12 226
Chapter 13 258
Chapter 14 287
Chapter 15 299
Chapter 16 307
Chapter 17 319
Chapter 18 350
Chapter 19 375
Chapter 20 399

Chapter 21 428
Chapter 22 442
Chapter 23 456
Chapter 24 465
Chapter 25 477
Chapter 26 495

The Wedding 593
New Chapter 617
Conclusion 631

PROLOGUE

T he 'Sarah' was a 172 foot luxury yacht, one of the top one hundred megayachts, docked in the quiet waters of Monaco bay. It was truly a splendid luxurious vessel.

John was laying in his bed in the master suite, sweating and delirious with fever. Kim was looking at him. She was perspiring in the arm chair next to his bed. Kim was a twenty-five year old blonde with green eyes, truly a rare beauty.

She gazed into the eyes of this man, whom she learned to admire, and slowly fell in love with him secretly. He had dark brown hair, brown eyes, a strong body, and six feet tall weighing two hundred pounds; very shy, gentle and reserved in nature. The doctor had said to her, "Take water and mix it with alcohol and massage his body; that will relax him, and will lower the high fever."

She had already done it, picking up his pants that she took off him in order to fold it and place it on the sofa.

A ring of keys fell from his pocket. She bent down to pick them up, her eyes locked on a particular key on the key holder.

It was made of gold. She knew that it must be the key to the secret room.

John had a special room in the yacht that no one was allowed in, not even the cleaning crew. He did that all himself. Suddenly, curiosity won over Kim's sense of right and wrong. She even came to suspect him of possibly being the serial killer still loose, murdering beautiful women, mostly models. They were found dismembered, especially cut open from their private parts, and their breasts removed, but they were not raped.

She began thinking about the possibility of he being that murderer.

John never had sex with her or touched her. She even thought that he might be gay. She found herself standing in front of the secret private room.

Her heart was beating hard and fast, and she feared her worst nightmare of what she might find in there.

This is all how it started three months ago ...

CHAPTER 1

In a luxurious office building of downtown Monaco, John was sitting in his spacious and luxurious office with two of his lawyers. David. was John's long-time good friend, and so was Peter, who were both from the United States.

DAVID: "John, finally the whole transaction was concluded with the German and Chinese governments. You are now officially the richest man in Planet Earth. Congratulations!". They shook hands and embraced, tapping their backs mutually.

PETER: "Now you have to fill all your pledges that you made last year when you still were hanging in the balance to lose everything."

JOHN: "I do not forget, Peter, and mostly this.", he said as he pulled a picture out of his pocket of a semi-naked gorgeous blonde, laying on her stomach, her head raised, resting on her folded arms. She looked like the goddess of love, Venus de Milo. What a beautiful creature indeed she was.

John had found her last year. He had shown the photograph to both and Peter and had said, "One day, if I can collect these bonds from the German and Chinese govermnents, I will look

1

for her." He did not know her name, or where to find her. The picture was taken out of an adult magazine, but time had gone by and they could not recall which magazine it had come from.

John had written to many such magazines, but none gave him satisfaction. Their response was always the same: "Give us the issue number or date." John did not have a clue.

DAVID: "Don't tell me that you are still obsessed with this girl."

PETER: "I can't believe it! John, you are the richest man in the world! You can have the most beautiful girl in the universe, even a rincess."

Peter meant one of Monaco's princesses. He had admiration for this proud royal family. Peter put the picture back on the table.

DAVID: "But John, she might be a dumb blonde, and the moment she opens her mouth, you might get nauseous!"

JOHN: "That's it? Did you say everything you had to say? Well, I still want her!"

DAVID: "But why here?"

JOHN: "I know why, please don't argue. Can you help me out or not?"

DAVID: "All right, I have an idea. I can scan her picture in my computer in Miami, and put an ad on the Internet. It will

state, "Looking for this woman: if you know her, or it is you, your luck has changed. Please contact the law offices of David D. and Peter S., esquires, at 1-800-761-0000 or through this e-mail address: xenus@ix.netcom.com"

JOHN: "Great! It's a beginning, but please do it the moment you get through. This is what you should tell her if she contacts you … "

With that, he handed David six typewritten pages. David read them silently and subsequently handed them to Peter for him to look over as well.

DAVID: "Well, John; I see that you had your idea all planned out for quite awhile. Tell me thoughtfully, John, didn't you ever have doubts that you would succeed in putting this deal together?"

JOHN: "I trusted G-d alone, having lost all of my fortune and having suffered eight years. Now it is our turn to enjoy life, and to help others enjoy it with us. Here is something for you David, and for you Peter."

John handed each of his friends an envelope which they both opened.

"Wow!", David exclaimed. "All of this for me?"

Peter had the identical reaction.

John answered, "Yes, guys, you deserve it, as well as having brought me luck. Enjoy it with your families. Let's go celebrate!"

They all left the office, and went down toward the harbor and onto the yacht, where a sumptuous party was being made ready. John had purchased the yacht "Sarah" two months earlier. He fired the previous crew, and hired a female captain and assistant. In fact, all sixteen of the crew were beautiful women, from Sweden, England, Italy, France, Denmark, Iceland and Holland. A Bell 52 helicopter waited surreptitiously on the roof of John's office building and flew them directly to the heli-pad on the top landing of the yacht. John had purchased the helicopter separately. He paid seventy and one-half million for the yacht, and one million seven hundred fifty thousand for the aircraft.

The party was exquisite beyond comparison, and all of "Who in the World" were invited, including the apex of royalty and of the rich and famous. The yacht was all inundated with bright lights, and streams of fireworks were fired off the main deck. John had already taken his place amongst the aristocrats of the world. He was well known and highly respected in all circles, including the decision makers of many governments, even though he emerged from a past which had been tainted by a rough period during eight years that came and went. He had survived the plot by certain United States officials to bury him, and he emerged stronger and more powerful than ever as a guiding force on the planet. In a way, this terrible period had taught him difficult lessons and strengthened him, teaching him who to trust. His wife of nineteen years had sadly divorced him.

John, now far wiser, was respected by all, as the saying goes: "Money talks, bullshit walks." It was John who was now talking, and everyone listened intently, including heads of state.

John desired above all to help his country to be self-sufficient and self-sustaining, no longer dependent upon other nations for financial aid and assistance. In a stellar way, John rose from the ashes of the forgotten man and came of age to influence political thinking and viewpoints in his country.

That evening, David was dancing with a beautiful blonde Italian girl, who was six feet tall with green eyes. David was well suited for her, being six foot two inches tall, and 34 years of age. He was having the time of his life. The champagne was flowing like water.

Peter was five feet four inches tall, sixty-one years old, but looked much younger with his black hair, well-defined body, although he was dancing with an Swedish brunette almost a foot taller than him. They were both incredibly drunk. Peter held her by her butt, and his face was buried between her prominent breasts. He loved it. He felt as if he were in paradise.

When the music stopped, Peter led his companion and both sat on the hand rail of the outer deck. John said, "Peter, be careful. You could easily fall."

Peter, trying to be valiant in front of his lover, released his hands, and began moving as if he were dancing. But the expected happened, as he lost his equilibrium and instinctively tried to

hold onto his girlfriend, and they both plunged backwards, falling overboard in a big splash fifteen feet down.

John, David and a few girls from the crew quickly jumped in to rescue them. Peter and his lady friend were both so drunk they barely realized their peculiar situation between the fish. One of the girls quickly jumped on the zodiac and picked up everyone. Peter had inadvertently swallowed some water. Once back on the yacht, he vomited his heart out.

The situation finally turned out to be quite a joke, and all of the guests were jumping into the water, some into the swimming pool and others into the bay, throwing champagne bottles and life vests to the swimmers. With it all, the night went well, and approximately three in the morning, the guests left the yacht with the exception of David, Peter, John and the beautiful ladies of the crew.

David and Peter went to their cabins with five of the girls, and had a wild orgy until the early hours of the morning. John returned to his suite, alone and sober. He never made a pass at any of the crew, or to girls in general. The crew suspected him of not liking women.

CHAPTER 2

John woke up around nine o'clock in the morning. After taking a shower, he checked in on David and Peter. He could barely see them under the pile of beautiful naked bodies of the crew. He shook the two men, and when they finally opened their eyes, hung over from so much drinking, John said, "Your plane leaves in two hours. You should be getting ready!"

David mumbled something, and tried to find his legs between twelve sets of legs. Peter fell asleep again, But John pulled his arm, causing him to fart.

When they finally were ready, they had breakfast together in the third deck. David and Peter drank four cups of black expresso coffee just to wake themselves up. John said, "All right guys, I'll take you to the airport."

John suddenly looked around the room. "Did you take the photograph I gave you of the girl?"

David replied, "Yes, John. I have it. Don't worry. It will be the very first thing I will do when I return to my office, I promise."

JOHN: "Peter, don't forget the contracts regarding the trailer houses for Israel and call the King of Jordan for the heavy equipment we are offering for sale."

PETER: "I will, John, and I am also going to send him a list of all the specials we have in army surplus to all our customers, including the inventory of the ships and planes. Have no fear, I'll be completely sober in a few hours."

John drove them to the International Airport in Nice, France, about thirty minutes away from Monaco, where they boarded a T.W.A. jet to New York, and from there to Miami.

John returned to Monaco, and went first to his office building that he had purchased for his home base in the business district. It was a high-rise structure, one of the few in the city. Quite striking, it was a modern, all dark glass building, with his executive offices conveniently located on the forty-fourth floor with a panoramic view of the coastal paradise.

These rooms comprised all of John's central offices for Europe. He had a vast empire, including holdings in real estate, commodities, garments and military items. He generated between One hundred and fifty billion dollars profit a year from this conglomerate. By anyone's standards, this was a colossal amount, becoming one of the largest expanding business in all the world.

The main reason for his success was that nothing was purchased without his direct approval. Then it was relayed to his lawyers, and finally to his buying experts all over the

world. Most countries preferred to buy from him than directly, because he could get a real bargain price on the equipment they were looking for, since he bought in extraordinarily great quantities and paid cash.

Anyone in need of hard cash would come to him to elicit his business, and were willing to sell anything. Nevertheless, John was a tough buyer and seller, and was blessed with the gift of turning garbage into gold.

Many wealthy industrialists and corporate giants tried to push their daughters onto him for the purpose of marriage. "A good merger" was what they all called it, but John was always courteous and polite in his refusal, and gave them equally the same answer: that he had a fiancee in the United States who would soon come.

Everyone who met him enjoyed pleasing him and serving him in some way or another. Not with standing, he was never arrogant nor proud of his colossal fortune, nor vindictive with people who had hurt him in the past.

Once David was back in his office, he placed the advertisement on the Internet by uploading it onto his web page and throwing it onto all of the computerized search engines at once using a "submit-it" device which he found at http://www.submit-it. com on the world wide web. It showed a picture of the gorgeous blonde and read as follows: "If this picture is YOU,or you know this young lady, you will be doing her a great favor by contacting her. Her luck has changed, and a very promising life is being offered to her. She has to contact the law offices

of David D. and Peter S., esquires. Telephone number (800) 761-0000 or write to 1201 Brickell Avenue, Suite 2201, Miami, Florida 33131-3207, or send a fax to (305) 564-0000."

David faxed a copy to John for his approval. The next day, David was at his office, preparing certain contracts when the secretary buzzed the intercom. "Mr. D., there is a Miss Kim W. on the line, and wants to talk to you."

DAVID: "I do not know any Miss Kim W."

SECRETARY: "She says it is regarding the add that you placed on the Internet about."

DAVID: "Oh, yes! What line?"

SECRETARY: "Line 27, sir."

David picked up the phone with heart-pounding anticipation and said, "Hello, this is Mr. D. Can I help you?"

A sweet and sexy voice answered, "Yes, sir. I read your add, and may I know what it is all about?"

DAVID: "Are you the person in the photograph, miss?"

KIM: "I am the one. It is a picture of me from last year's magazine."

DAVID: "Fantastic! Miss Kim, where may I ask are you located? I mean, in what city?"

KIM: "L.A."

DAVID: "If I send you a first class ticket, could you be here tomorrow?"

KIM: "Here WHERE?"

DAVID: "Miami."

KIM: "Miami? Can I know what this is all about first?"

DAVID: "Well, I am employed by the richest man in the world, and I am serious about that. Bill Gates is a pauper compared to him. The fact is, he is currently at his offices in Monaco. We have an employment offer for you that we should discuss in person. This is a unique opportunity, so would you come?"

Silence fell momentarily on the other side of the line, and then, from out of nowhere, she said, "Well, you might say I'm the curious type, so, why not … I'll come."

DAVID: "Great! Could you hold on for a few minutes?"

KIM: "Certainly. I don't mind making AT&T rich." David called their in-house travel agency and inquired about the following morning's flight from Los Angeles to Miami, and subsequently returned to the line with Kim.

DAVID: "Well, there's a flight leaving L.A. at 7:30 A.M. tomorrow. A first class ticket will be waiting for you at the ticket counter of Delta. You will be arriving at Miami airport

at 3:30 P.M. local time, and a limousine and driver will be waiting for you with a sign which has your name on it."

KIM: "What a mystery with such elegance! I'm looking forward to it. Life is a series of chances we take to live it to the fullest. I just hope I don't wind up getting kidnapped and sold into white slavery in Turkey or Afghanistan."

DAVID: "You have an amazingly positive outlook. And your safety is fully assured and guaranteed. Thanks so much for calling and for your cooperation."

KIM: "No problem. By the way, what's the weather like in Miami?"

DAVID: "Hot, I assume."

KIM: "No big deal. I'll check out the Weather Channel, throw my toothbrush in the dishwasher and It be ready on time. Bye."

After David hung up, he immediately dialed Monaco to reach John.

DAVID: "Good news! The girl you wanted called, and she is flying in from L.A. tomorrow to talk to me. Don't worry, I'll convince her."

JOHN: "Fantastic, Dave! And remember, she is off limits to everyone, capish?"

DAVID: "Don't worry John, I'll guard her with my life."

They both laughed and hung up.

In Los Angeles, Kim lived with her mother, her younger brother Mike and her younger sister Jenny. Her mother, a former tap dance teacher named Iris who turned into a withering old chain smoker, sat in her torn bathrobe combing the hair of her French poodle named Fluffinonkey while she flossed her teeth with some navy blue sewing thread while a Tiny Tim record was playing loudly in the background.

IRIS: "What on earth was that all about, dearie?"

KIM: "You're not going to believe this, Mom. The richest man in the world wants to offer me a job, and I am flying first class tomorrow to Miami, to meet some lawyer of his. He's going to explain to me what the job is all about."

IRIS: "I thought Bill Gates lives in Washington State. Are you going to work for Microsoft or something?"

KIM: "This guy is richer than Bill Gates. He's from Monaco, where that actress Grace what's-her-face married that prince or something."

IRIS: "Where Grace Kelly married Prince Rainier? The one who died in that accident? You know it might be a hoax, or dangerous, baby. What kind of work are you going to be doing? Working on your back? I thought I raised you to be a lady!"

KIM: "Mom, I am not stupid! I am twenty-five years old. I already checked out the law firm. It is one of the biggest in

Miami, with offices all over the world. I called my boyfriend Henry ... you know he's a lawyer, and he couldn't believe that this firm was looking for me."

IRIS: "You mean he's letting you go?"

KIM: "Of course he doesn't want me to go. He's mad as hell, jealous as can be. We had the worst argument today, and if I didn't stop talking about the trip I thought he was going to slap me around like he did the last time."

IRIS: "So don't go, baby. You might lose him. Where are you going to find another guy that's earning three hundred thousand a year handling accident cases? Plus you know how many of your best friends want to sleep with him. Men are under a lot of stress today. They hit their women once in a while to let off steam. If you love him it won't mean a thing. Your father used to punch me in the stomach every week and look how long I stayed married to him! You have to look in the mirror and see how pretty you are. Any man will be insecure about those looks of yours."

KIM: "If Henry doesn't trust me, I don't think there is very much future in our being together, period. Look at my horoscope on the Internet, mama."

IRIS: "It says "Your luck is about to change."

KIM: "That's just about what they had said. And this big boss, he's in Monaco, in Europe. I wish they send me there! I'd love to go. I've never left the country, except that time I had my high

school prom and that bozo geek on steroids I was dating drove me down to Tijuana and tried to get me in bed in a Mexican farmhouse. Yuck! But this guy is in Monaco! Imagine me hanging out with the rich and famous!"

JENNY: "Stop dreaming, sis. It might just be another modeling job, another grueling day on the set, having to take your clothes off and put them on fifteen hundred times."

KIM: "So what? If it pays good, I'll take it, especially if I get to travel all around the world."

That night Kim could not sleep a wink, since she was so excited and could not believe her luck. Henry called her, and started screaming at her.

"You're going to turn into a real tramp if you go on this trip", he screamed. "You belong to me, bitch and you're not going!"

This made Kim even more upset.

"I'm not one of your possessions. I'm not your piece of furniture", she cried as she hung up on him.

Great things were in store for her and she was not about to be convinced of the contrary.

The high rise tower was very impressive, even for Kim, who had seen much of the business section of Los Angeles known as Century City.

Kim was astonished that David's law office occupied the entire floor. She counted no less than seventeen secretaries working in their concentrically shaped cubicles, with magnificent views of Biscayne Bay surrounding all sides.

Moish the driver advised a blonde lady who seemed to be the head secretary or possibly Mr. D.'s personal executive secretary that Kim had arrived. She didn't even have enough time to sit in the reception area and read the latest issue of Vanity Fair when David rushed out to greet her.

Of course, when David saw Kim, he was mesmerized for a long minute, thoroughly engulfed and submerged by her beauty. She was dressed in raven jet black slacks and a white satin lace blouse which even further enhanced her ravishing appearance.

DAVID: "Kim? What a pleasure it is to make your acquaintance.

Please come into my office."

Kim smiled and shook his hand and followed him inside. The room was exceedingly spacious, luxurious, and decorated ultramodern.

He offered Kim a comfortable chair and motioned for his secretary to bring them both some freshly squeezed Hawaiian

pineapple juice which had arrived that morning from John's pineapple plantation in Maui.

"Florida pineapples don't compare to this", David said as he offered Kim a glass.

"I didn't realize this state had any", she replied curiously. David went to sit behind his desk, thinking about her answer.

DAVID: "Finally we meet. I truly thank you for coming. I do hope to interest you in the job offer I have for you."

There was a big picture of John on the wall. Kim was intently gazing at it in awe. As if he were reading her mind, David said: "Yes, this is John, Chairman of the Board and owner of International Trade and Finance, the largest corporation on Planet Earth. He is also the founder."

The man in the picture looked in his forties, with a serene and perhaps a shy expression, brown hair and deep brown eyes that seemed to penetrate the very soul of whoever looked at the photograph, and beyond that, the eyes in the picture had the mystical quality of looking anywhere one turned to. He also had the countenance and expression of a wise man, complete with all of the knowledge life has to offer, and above all else, one who could be trusted. Nevertheless, sadness could be detected in his quasi-smile and penetrating eyes, suggesting remnants of a painful experience, but he did not under any circumstances look arrogant because of his wealth.

David continued, "You must be puzzled as to what kind of job we brought you here to offer you."

"It sort of crossed my mind", Kim laughed innocently.

"Let me give you a little background of Mr. John. He is 46 years old, divorced after nineteen years of marriage, and has two daughters who live in Miami. He stays mostly in Europe, but travels extensively all over the world. He is well known and sought after by wealthy industrialists, kings, princes and presidents, because of his money and influence in the world of business and commerce. All of these opinion leaders and power builders want to marry him off to their daughters and nieces."

"How did he ever stay single?", Kim uttered in amazement.

"John doesn't like spoiled rich kids", David explained. He has been telling all of them that he already has a fiancee that he is going to marry soon, just to get them off his back. However, the pressure put on John continues to be insurmountable, because no one has ever seen him anywhere making public appearances with a woman up to this point."

Kim had that funny look in her eye, as if she were thinking that she was about to be offered a husband. However, David picked up on it and quickly remarked, "Don't worry, Kim. We are not trying to do matchmaking here. The days of 'Fiddler on the Roof' are gone. John does not know you, nor does he know your entire name."

"Then what is this all about?", Kim questioned, trying to understand what she had to do with any of this.

"John said to me, go forth and find me the most beautiful girl in the world and hire her!", David smiled. "So you see, I came across this picture of yours", as he reached for a magazine clip that portrayed Kim laying on a fisherman's table, with her derriere and breasts naked, and her head resting upon her hands assuming an upright position. The photograph highlighted her luminescent blonde hair and face, doing poetic justice to her expressive almond-shaped green eyes. Essentially, by the standards of mankind, she was a knockout. Kim blushed a little as she felt embarrassment at David seeing a picture of her undressed.

DAVID: "Incredible! I did not know that there are girls out there who still blush!" They both smiled.

KIM: "I took it last year, when there was a recession in the modeling business and I needed the money because my mother had just come out of the alcohol rehab and …"

DAVID: "No need to explain! There is nothing more sacred than images of the human body when it approximates perfection."

KIM: "Well, still, I'm not wearing anything..

DAVID: "That's what makes you such a treasure. But anyway, John needs you to accompany him everywhere and to act as his fiancee for, let us say, six months. Then, if you don't mind the

job, you can continue another six months and so on by mutual agreement."

KIM: "You mean of all the possible women to choose for an escort, he picked me?"

David continued explaining the arrangements, allowing Kim to calm down and digest the situation.

DAVID: "You will live on a megayacht that he owns in Monaco, known as the 'Sarah', and you will experience all of the trappings of wealth and fame."

Kim interrupted, trying to get a word in edgewise.

KIM: "But will I have to live with him as … husband and wife? You know what I mean, right?"

DAVID: "Of course I understand, but don't worry. He won't ask you to sleep with him or have sex with him, if this is what you are referring to. The job is strictly for you to be seen everywhere with him, at palaces, casinos, opening night at the theatre, in restaurants, simply holding hands and at the very most sharing a kiss in public."

KIM: "I don't know about that."

DAVID: "Please be patient and let me finish. He is a gentleman. You will sleep in the second cabin, next to his. The only thing that you will be required to do is to enter your room through his, because of the crew, who are sixteen magnificent women from all over the world who are dying to sleep with him. The

only item you might find inconvenient is the kiss, but first, I want you to hear your salary. For the first six months, you will be paid two and a half million dollars. The second six months five million dollars, and then from that point on it will be between you two."

Kim was overwhelmed and dumbfounded. She never had heard such amounts quoted as a "salary." Kim was trembling, about to faint.

David continued, "Plus he will buy you the most expensive clothing and jewelery in the world. Whatever you want and need will be yours. You will live like a queen. At the precise moment that we sign a contract, you will receive the first two and one half million dollars that we will deposit directly into your account, free of all taxes, because we will pay the taxes. Well, what do you think of this arrangement?"

KIM: "I'm stunned. It seems like too much money, just for a companion. What if he doesn't like me?"

DAVID: "Oh, don't even think about it! I know his taste. And about money, he is very generous. I do not know any other human being quite as generous. Working for John, I have accumulated enough money to buy my own third world country! But most of all, he is very gentle, patient, shy, and extremely respectful to everyone, most especially to ladies. He is unique, a rare gentleman. He would die before ever disrespecting you."

Kim looked at her hands shaking. She was so nervous. It amused David to see her in such a quandary so he originated an idea.

"You know what", David began, "let's call him up on the video phone and speak with him, okay? That might just break the ice."

"Wait, what should I say to him?", she mumbled. "Well, okay, let's do it."

David dialed, and a few seconds later, John's voice came through on the other end of the line.

JOHN: "Hi, Dave. What is new? How is your family?"

DAVID: "Everything is okay, John. I have here Ms. Kim, the young woman you requested that I hire."

Looking towards Kim, he shot up from his seat and asked her to come toward the phone and say hello to John, in order that he might be able to see her on the monitor.

"I'll be right back", David whispered. "You two have some things to discuss, so feel free to ask him any questions."

David left his office, closing the door behind him.

Kim stood and approached the desk timidly, and sat in front of the video phone. John was the first to speak.

JOHN: "Hi, Kim. It's a pleasure to make your acquaintance."

KIM: "The same here. I ..."

JOHN: "I know it is a bit of an awkward situation, but once here in Monaco you will understand it better. David did not do you justice. You are infinitely more beautiful than your picture."

Kim blushed again.

KIM: "Mr. John, I ...

JOHN: "No, please! Call me John."

KIM: "Okay. John, I like the idea of being in Europe, but I am a little.., let's say confused about kissing a man I do not know."

John smiled unobtrusively and acquiesced, saying "I can appreciate that. I myself have the same dilemma, and I even told David about it. I am overly shy in nature, and I perhaps might feel embarrassed kissing a total stranger. If you are apprehensive, and have doubts, maybe we should call it off, because it also puts me in a weird predicament."

KIM: "I did not say I do not want to go ahead with it. Maybe we should rehearse it alone first, and see if we can be comfortable enough with it to adjust to the newness of the situation."

JOHN: "Great idea! I'll arrange that when you get here, so we can spend some quality time together just to achieve a comfortable rapport between each other. As to me, I have no diseases of any kind. I am not the typical male who runs after

skirts. I do not have time for that. First of all, I forgot to ask you, are you compromised, I mean, in your love life?"

KIM: "I was, but we broke it off. I am also free of all diseases. I don't sleep around, if you know what I mean."

JOHN: "Well, that is good to know, since you are my fiancee!"

They both laughed, and the ice was broken. She felt more at ease to talk to this empowered stranger. Though astonished by the vast scope of his empire, she liked his simplicity, and the thought just kept dancing around in her mind that she was in fact talking to the richest man in the world!"

KIM: "Well, what do I do next?"

JOHN: "My private jet has arrived in Miami an hour ago. Would it be terribly inconvenient for you to come to Monaco today?"

Without thinking, Kim said, "Of course, yes, I guess so."

She didn't even know what she would tell her mother or how thoroughly extemporaneous the situation was. But somehow, she knew that she liked this man, and was fully aware subconsciously that she could trust him.

JOHN: "Well, I am glad that you accepted my invitation to meet with me. When you arrive, if for any reason you don't like the situation, or me, or both, I will send you back and fully compensate you for your trouble."

KIM: "That sounds very fair, and you seem very nice. Thanks for being so understanding."

JOHN: "Okay, I'll see you when you get here. Bye, Kim."

KIM: "Bye, John."

They both hung up. Kim had a smile on her face a mile wide, and slowly her fears seemed to subside a little.

Ten minutes later David came back, and this time Peter was with him. David introduced Kim to Peter and asked, "So what's your verdict?"

Kim laughed and said, "I'm traveling tonight to Monaco and I'm going to talk to him personally. He said that his jet was here in Miami."

DAVID: "Bravo! I knew you two would get along splendidly. I compliment you on your insight. Would you like to notify your family?"

KIM: "Yes, because I don't have enough clothes to wear. I only brought one suitcase, and my mother can pick out some of my outfits and ..."

DAVID: "Nonsense! My secretary Rachel will take you shopping temporarily and then John will accompany you personally in Monaco to buy you a complete wardrobe. I'll call ahead to one of Princess Stephanie's clothing designers and they will set up a fashion show luncheon in your honor so you can actively participate in the selection process. You will

have beyond the best of the best. As you are well aware, money is no object. By the way, are you hungry?"

KIM: "No, I ate too much on the flight."

DAVID: "Then why don't you call your family, and Peter and I will be next store arranging for your appointment for the clothing designer." After they walked out, Kim dialed home and her sister answered.

KIM: "Hi, Jen. Where's mama?"

JENNY: "Kim! How was the interview?"

KIM: "Put mom on the phone so I don't have to repeat it twice." She picked up the other line after Kim yelled upstairs for her. Kim could tell that her mother had a cigarette dangling from her lips and she could tell her mother had been drinking a little again.

IRIS: "Kimmy, where are you? When are you coming home?"

KIM: "Mama, its a dream come true. I'm leaving for Monaco to meet my new boss. I spoke to him over a video phone. You just wouldn't believe it. First, a brand new Rolls Royce picked me up at the airport. Then I am being paid two and a half million dollars for the first six months and five million for the next six months to go out to dinner and parties and meet heads of state with hint He's flying me over there in a private jet. I couldn't wait to give you the news"

IRIS: "Damn it, Jenny, your sister is high on LSD. Kim, you swore up and down that you never took any drugs. What kind of cockamamie bullshit story are you giving me, sweetie pie? Here you dumped Henry who made a damn good living as a lawyer just because he gave you a couple of love taps and now you're higher than a kite on some kind of dope. You tell me where you are and I'm going to call John to fetch your little ass back over here. The last thing I need today are these crazy pack of lies. Give me some intelligence for something, Kim! I wasn't born yesterday! What are you trying to do, sell snow to the Eskimos here?"

With that, Iris began coughing her lungs out, since her Camel unfiltered cancer sticks were just about getting to her.

KIM: "Mama, are you all right? Listen, I'm not lying to you. You've got to believe me! You can check it out, call these lawyers where I'm at. It's for real. Jenny, tell her I'm not making all of this up."

JENNY: "Well, it does sound like you're on something."

KIM: "I swear on Grandma Elionor's grave that this is no made up story."

IRIS: "Give me a break, darling. Why on earth are they paying you that much? Who did you have to screw to get a deal like that? Come on, Kimmy. How many millions of dollars to go where? Out to dinner and to visit some kings? I knew I should have sent you to a psychiatrist that time when you were eight years old and you caught your father sleeping with your

baby sitter. I knew that would have an effect on you. I read somewhere that kids make up all kinds of stories when they have a traumatic experience."

JENNY: "Daddy did that?"

IRIS: "Oh, shut up and bring me upstairs a new bottle of Cuervo Gold with some ice and a sliced lime swizzle."

KIM: "Are you drinking again, mama?"

IRIS: "Who wouldn't be with my oldest daughter flying around the world pretending she owns it, your brother Mike smashing up the Mustang again and Jenny sneaking out of the house at two in the morning to be with that Puerto Rican boyfriend of hers again, at fifteen years old. I think I'm about to lose my mind! If there's the slightest truth to your story, who is this lunatic anyway? Why would he pay you so much money? Nah, this is all too much for me. I don't believe a friggin' word of it. I need a cigarette."

KIM: "Mama, you just HAD a cigarette. You're going to die of lung cancer. You remember the doctor told you if you keep it up you'll need oxygen tents next to your bed."

IRIS: "Well, for seven and a half million dollars, you can go buy me gold plated ones! Really, such a load of crap I never heard of in my whole miserable life! Jenny! Go do something with that dog. He just shit on the carpet again!"

KIM: "Mama, he's the richest man in the world. He is in every business magazine and newspaper. He wants me as his personal assistant, to go with him all over as part of his entourage. The rest I'll find out when I meet him tomorrow morning."

IRIS: "Just make sure he doesn't give you AIDS."

KIM: "Now stop it, mama. This has nothing to do with sex. It has to do with image."

JENNY: "Does he look old and fat like all rich people? Does he slobber and drool when he speaks? Or is he some kind of nerd?"

KIM: "No, on the contrary, he is well built and seems to take very good care of himself from the way he appeared on the video phone. He is forty-six years old, very distinguished and respect. I already like him."

IRIS: "But how can you leave me? You think your brother and sister are going to take care of me ill get sick? Nobody can make peach mocha tea the way you can, baby."

JENNY: "Stop thinking of yourself so much, mom. Kim has a chance to be someone, to make something of her life. After all, models get old and twenty-five is almost over the hill for fashion models, and Kim hasn't even hit it big yet. You don't really think she'd be better off with that creepy lawyer, do you?"

KIM: "Look, all of you, its my life, and I've made up my mind. Fm hanging up now because I am going with the secretary to the airport. I have to stop along the way in Coral Gables and get some quick clothes just until they get me the rest of my wardrobe in Monaco."

JENNY: "You're getting paid millions AND all the clothes you want? Ask that guy if he wants to date your sister too. And see if they have a Marilyn Manson T-shirt while you're in Miami. I love that band."

KIM: "I don't have time for any of that right now. I've got to go. I'll call you from there. Love you, bye."

David entered with his secretary.

DAVID: "This is Rachel, and she will accompany you shopping. Buy her anything she likes. Use the Barnett Bank account. There's fifty grand in there. I' she needs anything more, here's my Visa gold card. Now Kim, Rachel is the only other person who knows about this arrangement besides myself and Peter, and of course John. You must agree not to discuss this with anyone except your family members, and tell them not to talk about it the next time you speak to them. The news media is always trying to find out things about John or his private life. The paparazzi even followed him into a men's room in Milan once and took a picture of him in front of a urinal. John values his privacy. This is a very confidential, delicate matter, and anyone knowing the contents of this arrangement could potentially place him in a very uncomfortable situation with a great many people."

KIM: "I understand. You can rely on my discretion."

DAVID: "Here is a folder that contains your contract, and another file on John's personal life. Study it on the plane, so that you will learn everything you need to know about him in case people talk to you."

He handed her the documents, which she put on her lap.

KIM: "Don't worry, I'll guard these with my life."

DAVID: "I want to wish you luck and have a pleasant trip, and I sincerely hope you two agree on whatever you decide and work well together."

They shook hands and said goodbye, after which Kim followed Rachel out to the limousine, where Moish the chauffeur greeted them. In the Rolls Royce, Rachel said, "You know Kim, you are the luckiest girl on Earth. I wish I had been offered the chance you have. I would leave my husband for him, even though he does all the cooking, cleaning, and takes out the garbage twice a week." They both laughed.

Once in Coral Gables, Moish parked on Miracle Mile at the corner of Ponce De Leon Boulevard and Rachel took Kim to a few very chic stores and bought very expensive garments that suited Kim as if they were made for her. Then she bought Kim eight pairs of shoes and matching handbags, a set of Louis Vuitton suitcases, a sable and sharkskin jacket, some exquisite jewelry, and much more. The final bill for these temporary items was a paltry fifty thousand dollars.

CHAPTER 4

Kim sat in the luxurious cabin in a very spacious reclining chair. The plane was decorated in sleek shades of pastel, with tufted velour yellow and peach color pillows thrown generously across the large twenty foot sofa in the lounge area. To the rear of the plane was John's personal Mile High Club Suite, with a round fined water bed across from a filly operational hot tub and spa which was large enough to accommodate eight people quite sparingly. There were fourteen silk monogrammed robes bearing John's initials, one of each color of the rainbow, hanging on cultured pearl and ivory hangers adjacent to the hot tub. Kim had never seen anything quite like it.

Captain Harry Sebakovitch was one of the Soviet Union's finest manned-spacecraft astronauts and flight engineers, and when he retired he was quickly hired by John. Mylo Canderian, the co-pilot, was a twenty- year veteran aviation instructor from the University of Brisbane, in Australia, and could not resist the five hundred thousand dollar a year job on the aircraft known as Modesty.

They both came out and bowed in ceremonious greeting toward their very special guest, after which they proceeded to return to the cockpit and began preparations for taxiing down the runway. Felicia the stewardess returned to the main cabin.

She was another knockout, a sumptuous brunette with azure blue eyes which could melt a molten iceberg just with a casual stare. Felicia helped buckle Kim up for take-off in the gray ermine belt with smoked alligator trim that was fitted into the lounge chair.

With her permission, Felicia stowed Kim's briefcase in one of the overhead compartments.

"Where did John get such a plane as this?", Kim asked Felicia.

"This bird cost sixty-three million dollars, but John didn't pay a penny for it", she answered.

"How can that be?", Kim inquired with perplexed eyes.

"He won it in a Baccarat game at Monte Carlo from its former owner, the Emir of Khazakstan, and the funny thing is, John doesn't even enjoy gambling that much and he is rather new at Baccarat", she explained. "The whole of Monaco has been talking about it for over a year."

KIM: "Outstanding, in every way."

FELICIA: "Is it all right if I keep you company during the flight?"

KIM: "By all means, please do."

Felicia sat down in a chair opposite Kim and fastened her own belt. The plane was approaching lift-off.

FELICIA: "You are very beautiful, Miss Kim. My boss is very fortunate to have such a lovely fiancee. But between us girls, you are very lucky too. He is so marvelous. I always take care of him when he flies all over. It is strange that I have never seen you before."

Kim thought to herself that Felicia was on a fishing expedition, trying to find things out. But she caught on to it immediately, and said, "I know. I was in college finishing my degree in Business Administration. John came to see me all the time. I love him very much."

Admitting such a thought made Kim feel good to put Felicia in her place. Nevertheless, she enjoyed being shown so much attention and reverence.

After several minutes when the plane was high above the Miami skyline, the seat belt light was turned off by Captain Sebakovitch. Felicia stood up and retrieved Kim's briefcase for her.

"You are welcome to take a bath in the hot tub if you like. I normally set the water at 105 degrees Fahrenheit, and I have Epsom Salt crystals you can sprinkle in the tub to allow you to float more easily in case of turbulence. I can bring in the Sevrugian Beluga Caviar and Gruyere finger dip toastettes if

you are ready for a snack. The sauna, steam room and shower are in the closed cabin in back of the robe closet next to the hot tub if you'd prefer. And, I am also a licensed nurse and masseuse specializing in Trager massage and Reiki meditation. I take good care of the boss and he just loves the touch of my fingers. Would you like one, Kim?"

KIM: "I wouldn't mind actually if it's not too much bother, miss … "

FELICIA: "Please call me Felicia. Let me show you to the bedroom." Kim followed her to the elegant private quarters of John. It was beyond comparison!

FELICIA: "Why don't you take a shower and put a towel around you. I'll pull out the massage table and change clothes. I'll be right back."

Kim followed Felicia's advice and took a shower. It relaxed her and made her feel refreshed after so much she had been through in one day. Felicia came back, dressed in white shorts and a tank top T-shirt. Five foot eight inches tall, Felicia was quite ravishing in her own right.

She placed a thick pleated towel from Neiman Marcus down on the massage table and directed Kim to lay on her stomach, which she did. Felicia opened the towel unraveling Kim's incredibly beautiful and firm body. Her derriere was palatably prominent and invitingly sensual.

Felicia poured oil on her back and began massaging her from the neck down, very professionally.

FELICIA: "You have a great body. Do you do aerobics?"

KIM: "Yes, every day without fail."

FELICIA: "No wonder you're in such good shape. He must be crazy about you!"

KIM: "Yes, we love each other very much."

Felicia was massaging her lower back and buttocks. Her hands lifted one of her thighs and spread them, in order to be able to reach all the way up from her thigh to her lower cheek.

Kim felt her strong and smooth hands, up and down, grabbing one cheek at a time, her hand sliding in between them, down to her womanhood, all the way down to her thigh. Felicia was giving her a great massage, but it also aroused her each time her fingers passed through her lower lips and derriere.

Felicia then continued to her legs and feet. Then she quietly said:

"Please turn around", to which Kim graciously complied. Felicia whistled, "Wow! You are a real beauty! Are those real breasts or are they silicone?"

Kim laughed hysterically. "No, these are mine, and they are real ones."

Felicia poured oil on her legs first and worked them into the massage mode. Then, when she got close to Kim's most intimate parts, she lifted one of Kim's legs toward her shoulder and began to massage her all the way.

She felt Felicia's hands touching her lower lips each time she went up. Felicia, noticing Kim's embarrassment said:

"Don't be up tight. I am a nurse, and I do it to the boss too. You'll enjoy it so much better if you relax. Of course, if there is something I do that you don't like, please say so. I am here to please you for your benefit, and for no other intention."

Kim: "I am sorry. I'm just not used to such an intimate massage. But please continue, because I am enjoying it."

FELICIA: "You're on your way to Monaco. That's a swinger's town. Anything can happen over there, so you've got to be prepared. People living on the Riviera are far less inhibited than we American girls. You've got to be prepared."

KIM: "The world may see me as a glamorous fashion model, but I'm still plain old Kim from Van Nuys, California. I'm just from a working-class suburb of Los Angeles, and my mom was always so strict with me. I'm not used to women being so forward and ..."

FELICIA: "I think it's time to sample some of the gourmet delicacies from the kitchen. Enough talk about innocence."

She retrieved a tray and placed it on the bed. Kim had covered herself with the sheet, up to her arm pits. Absorbed deep in thought, she looked at Felicia and asked, "Can you tell me how my fiancee acts around his employees, especially the knockout drop-dead-gorgeous women?"

FELICIA: "Oh, he is the most wonderful boss, so polite and courteous. We are all afraid of losing our jobs. He pays us more money than we would earn in the Mafia. He has great retirement benefits and major medical coverage at one hundred percent because he owns several health insurance companies and the underwriting companies that assume all of their risks."

KIM: "Okay, okay. But what about sex? Does he cheat on me? Please tell me the truth. I swear I won't say a thing."

FELICIA: "John? Cheating? You must be joking. Each time I gave him a massage, I tried to make love to him, like with you. He stopped ate instantly, but extremely politely without offending me. One time I think I succeeded in exciting him, but the only thing he let me do was to give him a blow job, but I knew his mind was somewhere else at the time, probably on you."

KIM: "How rare a quality it is for a man to be so discriminating and so loyal. Normally, when a man's dick gets hard he can be easily distracted. It takes a lot more willpower to stay focused, especially since you are so pretty, and he surrounds himself with magnificent looking females."

FELICIA: "I thought it might be that he didn't like me in particular, but when I spoke to the yacht's crew, which is comprised of incredible beauties from so many countries, it seems as if all had the same results with him. Until you arrived on the scene, I thought that he might be gay. But seeing you, I truly can understand why. I don't normally look at women, and heaven knows I would never touch one, but you are the most gorgeous creature 1 have ever seen. He must be spellbound and fixated on you. But above all, he is a wonderful person, so kind and unpretentious, and we all love and adore him."

Kim scratched her chin and thought to herself:

"Maybe he is gay after all, and wants me to dissipate the gossip. After all, Michael Jackson married Lisa Marie Presley to improve his image, and he still chased after little boys. And Mr. D. said I was safe with him. The whole extent of our "relationship" would be kissing in public. It makes sense, but why me? And why is he paying me so much money? I guess one day I'll find out"

FELICIA: "A penny for your thoughts."

KIM: "Where's the penny?", she laughed. "No, I was just thinking about what you said."

FELICIA: "Can I ask you two unpleasant questions?"

KIM: "If! can, I 'will answer."

FELICIA: "First, are you really in love with him? And secondly, from one to ten, would you share with me how good of a lover he is?"

Kim smiled, chuckling to herself.

KIM: "I see you are very curious. But to answer your questions honestly, yes, I adore him body and soul. From one to ten, he is an obvious twelve."

FELICIA: "I knew it! He is strong and has big muscles, but when you touch his hands or he touches you, one melts just from his delicate and silky-smooth touch. I am sorry to admit that not only me but all the girls who work for him have wet dreams about him. Now, don't misunderstand me, I love my husband and I would never cheat on him, not with anyone. But I would drop him for John in a heartbeat. He is a very interesting man, so powerful and intelligent. By the same token he is humble and polite, the idea of every woman's dream come true. Every time he sees one of his women workers carrying something heavy he jumps to help and take it away from them. So you can imagine how we all see him as a knight in shining armor."

KIM: "With not even a spot of rust on the armor. It is so hard to fill the shoes of the lover of a perfect man without faults. He not only walks on water, but he purifies it at the same time. That's my John! Sometimes it is all so exasperating. But love conquers all, isn't that what they say?"

FELICIA: "How did you ever get so fortunate as to have everything?"

KIM: "I must have either been pretty damn good in my past life, or else I suffered a lot and I'm making it up in this one. But one thing for sure. John is the best thing that ever happened to me, so lovable and so sweet."

Kim finished eating, and so Felicia took the tray from her, and after checking with Captain Harry Sebakovitch, she reported to Kim that they would be arriving in Monaco in less than two hours.

FELICIA: "Do you need anything, Kim?"

KIM: "No thanks. I just need to study some documents."

Felicia left, closing the door behind her. Kim opened her briefcase and reviewed the file containing everything that she could possibly learn about John.

The first item she found was a recent picture of him. He looked young and gentle. The second page was his Curriculum Vitae or biographical sketch generated by one of John's three public relations and marketing companies. It read:

"John G, born December 18, 1950, . Parents: Manny and Sheli. Five brothers, from eldest to youngest. Ya' akov, age 50; Joshua, age 48; Ari, age 41; and Avi, age 37."

John was the middle son. Quite intrigued, Kim read some more.

"John served in the Israeli army, finishing as a Captain in the paratroopers, ranking highest in his platoon. He received thirteen medals, most of them for bravery and courage, one of which for saving an entire town. He married his ex-wife Mazel three years his junior while studying architecture, and had two daughters. John finished his career as an architect in 1976 when he was twenty-six years old."

The reading continued on and on for pages about his accomplishments, his business, troubles, and his shocking divorce in 1990, two years after he had lost a colossal fortune, some seven years ago.

Somehow it did not state why Mazel divorced him.

"Maybe she discovered that he was gay", Kim hypothesized.

The dossier had nothing in it for the years between 1990 and 1996. Then it revealed that in 1996, be began to reacquire his wealth, and only eighteen months later he became the richest man in the world.

"There's some missing data here", she concluded silently.

She read about his hobbies: "Fishing, weight lifting and martial arts." And then, she saw a page dedicated to his vices, or rather one vice: "Sweets."

She sat spellbound, absorbing the rest of the information in the file.

"He is some interesting man!", she thought. "He went from riches to rags to super-riches again, with no mention how or why. It is such a shame that he probably does not like women."

Suddenly there was a knock at the door. It was Felicia, who entered the bedroom quarters of the aircraft with a portable phone in her hand.

FELICIA: "Hi, Kim. We are landing in twenty minutes, and the boss is on the phone for you."

Although Felicia gave Kim the phone, she did not leave the room. Kim said "Thank you, Felicia", as if to indicate that she needed some privacy. Reluctantly, Felicia left, closing the door behind her. Kim picked up the cellular phone.

KIM: "Hello …

JOHN: "Hi, Kim. Did you have a nice flight?"

KIM: "Oh, it was very stimulating."

JOHN: "That's great. Listen, when the plane lands in eighteen minutes, stay in your cabin under the pretext that you are not quite ready to disembark the plane, that is, until I come to get you personally, because the press is here following me around like flypaper and we should prepare ourselves by meeting before we have to deal with encountering the media."

KIM: "I understand. Anyway, I am getting dressed and Felicia is helping me make my debut, so the excuse is valid since I am running a bit late after my nap."

John said good-bye and hung up the phone.

CHAPTER 5

The door of the plane stood open as Felicia and Captain Sebakovitch stood there. Felicia was the first to greet John.

FELICIA: "Welcome, sir! How are you?"

JOHN: "Good to see you, Felicia, and you Harry. Where is Kim?"

FELICIA: "Sorry about the delay, but Miss Kim is not ready yet."

JOHN: "That's okay. Harry, how was the flight?"

CAPTAIN HARRY SEBAKOVITCH: "Very smooth sailing, highly uneventful and very little turbulence."

FELICIA: "Sir, congratulations are in order. Miss Kim is so beautiful and gracious. She is still in her cabin getting ready to see you."

John thanked Felicia and rushed to the back of the plane where the bedroom suite was. He knocked and entered, closing the door behind, Kim was standing there, an alluring vision of

unsurpassed beauty, certainly a dream of perfection in her red skirt and jacket.

Her hair was combed in a fluffy style to one side of her head, leaving four fifths of her face exposed in a rare quality of magnetic attraction. Her almond-shaped green eyes radiated a deep look.

Kim's lips were well defined as if they were woven out of silk brocade. She did not use make-up, nor did she need any. Well prepared was she, because Kim had read it in the sheets of Shawn's preferences.

John stood there for a moment mesmerized without saying a word, thoroughly stunned and paralyzed by her essence. To Kim, the moment of silence seemed like an eternity. His gaze embarrassed her a little. Finally, John shattered the quietness by extending his hand to shake hers in a warm welcome.

"I am John", he said with the utmost of dignity and decorum.

JOHN: "I am terribly sorry that I wasn't prepared for such a beautiful sight. The faxed color picture sent to me and your image on the video phone does not do you justice. I did not mean to embarrass you, as it was not my intention."

He held her soft and long, pale hand in his.

KIM: "It's all right, sir. It is a real pleasure to make your acquaintance. I read everything I could about you and know it by heart", she boasted as she pointed to the file.

JOHN: "Splendid, I thank you for that, Kim. Please sit down. You see, I didn't want you to meet me in front of everyone where it would have been more awkward for you, and we would have had to … you know … kiss before actually having met each other."

John blushed, and for the first time in history, he was almost at a loss for words. Kim was amazed to see a man so powerful turn red like a teenage schoolboy.

JOHN: "I wanted to be prepared first before asking you to go out there. The press can be one's most fervent ally, but there is also a cruel, unfeeling side to the media mob. But for your personal information, I assure you that I have a hundred percent clean bill of health, and I know you have too. I have no hidden diseases. Today, with the terrible curse of AIDS, it is a problem, and possibly a death sentence, so I can't overemphasize how we can't take enough precautions. My solution to this dilemma has been celibacy."

Kim looked at him without saying a word. John glanced right back into her eyes, and then started profusely blushing again.

JOHN: "This is an embarrassing situation, but we have to … kiss here and see if you can manage it. I know it is not customary to kiss before even our first date, but for me it is no problem because I get the good side of the bargain, as you are so marvelous that anyone would kiss you, even your feet, but for you, you don't exactly get your Prince Charming."

Kim blushed so much she almost matched the color of her dress.

KIM: "Do not say that, sir. Every one of your lady employees would cut off their right arm to have you. Can I ask you an impertinent question, sir?"

JOHN: "Please begin by calling me John, or "my love" because you are supposed to be my fiancee. Second, please, by all means ask any question you wish."

KIM: "Why did you choose me? And why pay me so much money?"

JOHN: "First, David chose you. He said that you looked wonderful, and as usual, he was absolutely right. Second, with regard to the money, no amount of money is worth not having a companion like you. But mostly, you are going to be very careful not to tell anyone, and the bad part of the bargain is that you can't have a man, you know to have sex. Of course, if you need to, I will fly you to Los Angeles once a month so you can do whatever you want in secret. Monaco is one big gossip mill. The press is all over me. The rich dowagers and all of the eligible single women are scrambling to marry me. One even divorced her husband in the hope that I would give her a tumble. I have never encouraged any of them. On the contrary, I chased them all away, saying that I had a fiancee whom I was about to many. Then, after a while, the press, and even business associates were asking, "Where is your fiancee? Can we see a picture?", and so on. Finally I made a decision to materialize her, or in this case, you. Now, in order to show

why I was not cheating on my fiancee, she had to be the most beautiful woman on the planet, and that's where you come in. Believe me, David did a great job in finding you. I couldn't have done it better myself."

Kim overwhelmed by the flattery and continued blushing to epidemic proportions.

JOHN: "Well, the hard part is right now. We have to try and see, and I will do everything that I intend to do to you in front of the press and of those blue-blooded royalty nuisances right here and now. I guess the best technique to approach this is to imagine kissing the man you really love and not me, and do so in different ways, so we know how we are with each other and there are no unexpected surprises. The first kiss is always special, and I even made sure that Felicia did not serve you any garlic or onions for lunch, nor did I have any myself."

They both laughed.

John then offered his hand to Kim, which she took and stood up to be nearer to him.

JOHN: "G-d, this is a weird situation. I feel like I did when I was nine years old and my mother sent me to dancing school and I was the last one of the boys to ask a girl to dance."

KIM: "And all of the pretty ones were taken, and you got stuck with a real dog, right?"

JOHN: "No, just the opposite. There was a little girl so beautiful, in the dance class that none of the other boys had the courage to dance with her. She was last and therefore she became my dancing partner. She was my girlfriend for many years after that, and then.., she died in the Six Day War. Her house was blown up by Arab guerrillas."

KIM: "Oh, how sad that must have been for you ..."

And with that, Kim clasped her hand in his, as John touched her face very gently and tenderly, holding her cheek in the palm of his hand, closing his eyes. Slowly, he put his lips against hers, just as she had closed her own eyes as well.

Kim's lips were soft and silky-textured. Willingly, she made the second move, opening her mouth and accepting his tongue, which he inserted tenderly, tasting the fragrant honey of her sensual mouth. He then softly caressed her upper lip between his own as if to savor every aspect of it.

Gradually he moved down to her lower up, surrounding himself in her oral delights. As perfect as Kim seemed, she had one silver filling in her upper left molar which was a result of a cavity stemming from her former addiction to lollipops as a child, but John wasn't thinking about that right now.

His heart was beating like a thermonuclear reactor, and hers did too, in complete synchronicity with John's. Then, releasing her delicious mouth, he kissed her nose, holding her tight as she felt a big bulge between his legs. Her eyes were next in line for kissing softly.

Kim felt his lips burning her face. She could feel his heart beat on her lips. That was no pencil in his pocket she was feeling pressing against her. Kim became uncontrollably aroused. Felicia was right. She was easily sexually excitable.

John continued his survey, pushing her long blonde hair backward, and kissed her face with an incredible dedication. Kim became instantly feverish from his passion.

When he kissed her under her ear lobe and neck, she began to moan. She was tense, like a lynx ready to pounce. He held her in his arms and continue to press her body against his.

John felt her pointing breasts against her chest, and she felt his manhood pressing against her abdomen. "This guy sure isn't gay", she laughed to herself, amusingly. She knew he got real excited, just as much so as she was.

He immediately realized that he was getting too carried away and he slowly released his embrace, closing his jacket to cover his bulge and his embarrassment.

Kim had her head still arched back, enjoying his kisses. Feeling that he had stopped, she returned to her senses and opened her eyes. Her face was red, burning from the heat of her embrace.

JOHN: "Well, that was an example of everything you will have to put up and suffer from me. I hope it wasn't so hard to endure. I really …"

Observing his insecurity, Kim suddenly intervened and said, "You went well beyond my expectations I had of you. No one has ever kissed me like that before in my entire life. You are actually a great kisser, and maybe I should be the one paying you for thrilling me like that!"

They both laughed hysterically. Then, returning to serenity, he said:

"Let us go, and please hold me as a fiancee would."

He held her by her shoulders and she leaned slightly toward him as they exited the bedroom suite. Felicia saw their faces still red and holding each other quite cozily. She asked, "Is everything all right, sir?"

John smiled and answered, "Things couldn't be better, now that Kim is here. And, oh yes, Felicia. Thank you for everything you have done to make Kim's journey more pleasant."

Felicia was startled by that remark and dropped some napkins she was carrying. Noticing that the stewardess was nervous, John turned to Kim and asked her, "How did Felicia treat you, my princess?"

Kim looked at Felicia, whose eyebrow was twitching, but all she could think about was how John had held her and called her a princess, and for that moment, she actually felt like one.

She instantly tried to recapture the ecstatic feeling she had when she had felt his muscles surrounding her, but she soon realized that she had to answer John's question.

KIM: "Oh, she was great! She gave me a fantastic massage that thoroughly relaxed me, and afterward, I slept for nearly the rest of the trip."

JOHN: "You are so right, Kim. She really does give good massages. Thank you, Felicia."

John caressed Kim's face with the back of his hand. Felicia looked on, analyzing everything, seeing how much in love John was with his fiancee. Alter summoning his driver to fetch Kim's luggage, he and Kim expressed their farewells to the crew, and proceeded to descend the stairs, arm in arm.

A flood of reporters ran toward them, besieging them at every turn in their incessant hunt for gossip. In all of the excitement, Kim missed a step and twisted her ankle. The photographers wasted no time in getting pictures of Kim stumble, since they above all are parasites of bad news. Kim uttered a scream in pain.

JOHN: "What is it, my precious love?"

KIM: "Oh, I am such a klutz! I missed a step and sprained my ankle."

"Let me see", John said, as he kneeled and touched her where she was injured.

"Ouch!", she cried.

Like a brave and gallant knight rescuing a damsel in distress, John stood up and lifted Kim in his arms, as if she were as light as a feather. The crowd cheered at his chivalry and the cameras clicked away like there was no tomorrow.

"No, darling", she said. "I can walk."

"Nope, now you be a good girl and let me handle this!", John responded with the voice of authority. The press tried to stop them and ask questions, but he did not allow that, saying "Sorry, but my fiancee is hurt, and all interviews will have to be conducted another time."

He quickly carried her into his car where his chauffeur Bashir was waiting. Bashir, a former camel driver, was a poor unfortunate soul who John had found in the bowels of a Syrian prison, where he was serving a twenty year sentence for stealing someone's sandals. Mysteriously, Bashir had heard about John in a radio interview with the Asian Wall Street Journal, and wrote him a letter in rudimentary, broken Arabic and pleaded for his help, even though he had never met him before.

John was so outraged at the inequity of that unfair sentence, and was so moved by Bashir's eloquent letter begging for mercy, he paid off a corrupt Syrian official with fifty thousand American dollars and took Bashir out of that dungeon, educated him, and then hired him as his very own personal driver. Bashir promised he would never steal again, and now he is one of John's most trusted employees. According to Bashir, John has

a heart of gold, always willing to give an underdog a second chance.

Bashir was faithfully waiting with the bags. Felicia noticed that Kim had fallen and rushed from the plane followed by Captain Harry, who were fussing over Kim and trying to exercise crowd control at the same time.

"Don't worry, John", Kim smiled. "I don't intend to sue."

"Kim, are you okay?", Felicia shouted.

"Yeah, it's no big deal", Kim replied. "But you know how overprotective John can be!"

Kim had her head on John's shoulder, and felt like a kid in her father's arms, very comfortable and secure.

Bashir opened the front and the rear door of the car for them. John said, "Please, Bashir, go drive the crew in the Bentley and I'll drive my car to the yacht. You guys follow me."

"Yes, your excellency", Bashir answered, always elevating John to new heights with his esteemed and unparalleled respect.

John placed Kim very carefully into the vehicle and closed the doors, including the back one, and then came around to the driver's seat. Kim looked at the interior and remarked, "This is a beautiful car. I have never seen anything like it. What is it?"

JOHN: "It's an Aston Martin Lagonda, made in England. There are very few in the United States."

KIM: "Is it very expensive?"

JOHN: "Not really. It's only around four hundred thousand. It's made well, and certainly worth every penny."

KIM: "Wow! I could buy a house with that kind of money."

Without hesitation, John said, "Keep it. It's my welcome present to you. I'll just buy another one. This is last year's model, and I really wanted to order a 1997 with an automatic map tracking guidance system built in. Now I have a good excuse."

Kim looked at him, dumbfounded.

"But why?", she exclaimed. "It's too much money!"

John looked at her and adoringly reminded her, "For you, my dearest love, there is nothing that is ever too much money."

It was then that John noticed his entourage directly behind them, so he said to Kim, "Place your head on my shoulder as two normal lovers who haven't seen each other for a while would do."

She did, resting her lips on his neck, and began kissing him. She sensed his virile smell as he advised her.

"Thank you, that was sweet, but I don't think they can see your kiss from where they are, now that we have accelerated. When we are alone you don't have to pretend, only when we

are in public. As long as they can see two outlines of our heads nestled together, that is fine enough."

But she felt scorned and saddened, and he immediately picked up on this, and remarked, "Oh, please don't take it as an offense. On the contrary, I am trying not to impose upon your good graces and generosity too much."

Kim started to wonder whether John might be "gay by preference", even though he got excited with her in the airplane. She kept quiet, trying to get a better grasp on where John was truly coming from, but he broke the deadening silence.

JOHN: "When we get to the yacht, I'll take care of your ankle by putting a cold compress and an ice pack on it. I know how to heal it immediately, having studied paramedical life support in the Israeli army."

KIM: "Don't worry, John. It's easing up a bit. I'll be all right." They finally arrived at the marina where incredible giant yachts of all the kings and princes of Europe were docked.

"That's it, coming up … This is ours", he explained. The entire crew of the 'Sarah' Fleet was there to greet them, and each of the girls had a bouquet of roses, each one of a different color, in order to give to the new first lady. A big banner was strung across the yacht's entrance which said, "Welcome, Miss Kim!"

Kim felt like she had just stepped out of a storybook novel either into someone's well-written fantasy or it was an April Fool's joke that everyone forgot to tell her about. She felt a

pinch in her heart, remembering what David had said to her. "You'll be treated like a queen and live the life of the rich and famous." She was swooning from the attention and the adoration of everyone.

"How gorgeous is this yacht!", she exclaimed to John. "And what a warm reception, I love it so much!"

John exited the vehicle and went around the side to open the passenger door, beaming as he took Kim in his arm to lead her onto the magnificent yacht. Meanwhile, the other car carrying his entourage stepped behind them, and Bashir proceeded to take out Kim's luggage from the trunk of the yatch. Kim, who was getting delirious from all the "oohs" and "aahs" coming in praise from the crew, said to John, "I'll walk, it's embarrassing."

But John was resolute in his decision to assist the object of his desires. "Sorry, my love, but you are my responsibility now", and carried her over the threshold of the boat effortlessly.

Each of the girls greeted them personally, presenting Kim with a bouquet and inquired into the status of her accident, which Bashir had radioed ahead to the control tower of the yacht.

Each crew member was more beautiful than the next. She became thoroughly overwhelmed after she thought about her seduction.

Felicia: "How was she going to avoid making love to all these beautiful women, some even more beautiful than herself?"

And then another ghost of fear came over her. "How could John avoid making love to them all? Or was this really his harem, and was he the Sultan of the Sarah in disguise ..."

They boarded the yacht, followed by their procession of attendants.

John carried Kim directly to his suite and sat her on the bed, saying, "I'll take all of your pain away in a minute."

Kim was marveled by the opulent luxury of the yacht, and of his suite with the most radiant onyx bathroom she had ever seen. Come to think of it, she never saw an onyx bathroom before of any kind!

"Is this my room or yours?" she asked cautiously, not wanting to make a fool out of herself with presumptuous dialogue.

John smiled and said, "Yours is straight though that adjoining door. You will have to come and go through this room so no one will suspect that we sleep in separate quarters. My room is off limits to everyone. I would have given you my room, but then I would have to pass through yours all the time, and in this way, you will have more privacy."

Kim shook her head and protested, "But this way I'll be bothering you!"

"You can't bother me at all!", John responded. "I'm a heavy sleeper. Take your jacket if you want and make yourself at home."

She did, under which she revealed a white silk blouse, leaving her shoulders and arms uncovered, which gave rise to John's deep unexpressed appreciation for her supple, sensuous breasts.

He kneeled, took her shoes off as if she were Cinderella and he was the real Prince Charming in the fable, and then he held her ankle between his hands. He closed his eyes and concentrated, like a mythical mystical Tibetan monk. She could swear that he was generating a tremendous heat, and not just from his groin.

John's knowledge of meditation and super-concentration coupled with his awareness of chiropractic folklore soothed the ever so quickly. He delicately and slowly twisted her ankle bone very slightly, until it made an inaudible click, which indicated to John that the muscle was put back into its regular upright and locked position.

John then opened his eyes, took the ankle, and placed his open lips on it, and began kissing it.

Kim appreciated the gesture and was elated with his expertise in home health care.

"I can also twist your arm!", John said in a joke.

Kim looked at him in utter amazement. The ankle felt completely normal.

"I use the same doctor as the royal family, but he charges too much for house calls", he continued with his sordid attempt at subtle humor. Kim burst out laughing.

John asked, "How is your foot now? Let's see what happens when you try to walk." Kim hesitated but to her great surprise there was not even the slightest remnant of pain.

"Astounding!", Kim exclaimed. "You healed me! Was the kiss part of the healing or …"

Before she could finish her question, he replied, "Yes, my touch and kiss are transmissions of my energy as they come from my deepest emotions. Sit down, and let me treat you one more time, just to be on the safe side."

Kim was distracted by a newspaper that was scattered on the bed. It was in French, and although she could not understand a word, she saw pictures of eight separate women in the article. Just to satisfy her curiosity, she asked, "What is this article about? Who are these women here?"

John sadly raised his gaze and said, "Alas, these women were murdered, each on a different day and place by a serial killer. He kills them, cuts them up in pieces, and throws them away. Each time there is a different piece of the women missing. They say he must be gay and has lost all touch with reality. He never raped them. He seems to collect different souvenirs for a reason unknown to the civilized world. So it is better that you do not travel alone, and always have company with you, preferably mine."

Kim was petrified.

"Oh, G-d! It's horrible!", she cried out. "Is this maniac in Monaco?"

JOHN: "We assume he is, but the murders were committed between Nice and here. So the best thing is to be careful and not take any chances. By the way, are you hungry?"

KIM: "I ate just an hour ago on the plane. I am flit!"

JOHN: "Oh, I forgot to tell you. The Royal Family of Monaco have prepared a gala night to welcome you."

KIM: "For me? Wow! They sound like real nice people!"

JOHN: "All the women who tried to get me to put a ring on their finger will be there. The reason for the celebration is the curiosity of the elite and the press and of course to gain favor in my eyes, by honoring my beautiful bride to be."

KIM: "But one thing puzzles me. I understand that one okay. When I finish my job here, how will you explain my departure?"

JOHN: "By the way Prince Charles and Princess Diana did it, although in my opinion they were amateurs, since they let the media control them. In Monaco, the press eat out my hand like pigeons, even like stool pigeons. We will create some extravagant excuse, such as the fact that I started snoring and we could not sleep in the same bedroom or something."

KIM: "Do you?"

JOHN: "I did once upon a time. But I hired the best surgeon I could find to do a root canal on my sinuses and now I sleep like a pre-natal child in the womb of life."

KIM: "How poetic! You bring tears to my eyes when you move my soul like that with such imagery."

JOHN: "Besides which, I hope I can persuade you to renew your contract for a long period of time."

Kim smiled. She liked him already. "Felicia and David were right", she thought to herself "He is a real gentleman, very well mannered and delicate."

JOHN: "Would you like to make a tour of the yacht?"

KIM: "Oh, yes! I would love it!"

John stood up, taking her by the hand. Kim followed him, holding tightly to his arm. He had taken his jacket off, so she could more fully appreciate his muscles. His polo, thoughtfully, had short sleeves.

All the crew stood at attention to be acknowledged, and each one gave Kim their name, a salute, and a description of what she did on the yacht. It took forty five minutes to inspect the boat on all of its levels. On the top deck she noticed a Bell Helicopter parked on its launching pad, and she told John that such a sight on a yacht was indeed very impressive.

The crew were in the glee of admiration over Kim, flaunting her with adorable congeniality and pleasantry, naturally smiling as if nails were embedded in their cheeks, and inwardly appreciating her beauty. If any were jealous of her relationship with John, they failed to show it. However, Kim felt the women gaze at her as if each one wanted to have sex with her.

She achieved that special status of being magnetically attractive to all humanity, men and women alike.

"I hope I can produce enough estrogen", she prayed devotionally.

John was holding Kim by her naked shoulder, and unconsciously she loved his soft touch.

He kissed her on the cheek from time to time, and on her forehead tenderly. She closed her eyes each time, in order to feel the warmth and the passion with higher intensity.

The last room which Kim visited was her own suite, adjacent to John's room. It was exceptionally spacious and had a large king size bed, and an enormous marble closet the size of two standard rooms put together.

A large bouquet of roses in every color imaginable was on top of the dresser with a lace card engraved in 22 carat gold stitching, next to a bottle of Don Perignon Champagne, vintage 1787, said to be the rarest bottle in the world. She looked at the card, which read, "Welcome to my Adorable bride."

She smiled and thanked him; and for the first time, she wished that it were true. This was the story of "Cinderella the working girl", she feared, as John, never willing to offend her, said:

"I'll leave you alone to rest, to take a shower, and to get used to these humble surroundings."

"I can't believe I am really here in the middle of all of this opulence!"

Kim expressed in a sigh of gratitude. Looking at his watch, John said:

"In about an hour, three dozen fashion models will be arriving aboard the yacht to show you a few sun dresses, bathing suits, and ready-to-wear outfits from Paris, Milan, Lisbon and Barcelona. It's okay to mix and match them. If you wish to hire one of the models as your servant to help you dress every day, please just pick one. And if you want all of the clothes, just take them. Do not worry about the cost. If you spent five hundred thousand dollars a day on clothes and jewelry, it would only amount to one half of one percent of my daily income. So indulge yourself, besides, it's your job to spend money."

John opened her dresser and revealed a safe behind the drawers and opened it, pulling out various exquisite jewelry creations from it. He took out a ruby necklace, and put in her hand.

"This is an antique", he began.

"It used to belong to Julius Caesar's second wife. I paid thirteen million dollars for it at Sotheby's Auction. It would look great on you if you wear it with that scarlet satin see-through bathing suit in the closet when we go swimming or to the beach."

"Thirteen million dollars?", she gasped.

"Yes, and I overpaid too", John confessed.

"I didn't realize until after the auction that I was bidding against one of the jewelers I had hired to buy it for me. That was the first and last time I ever made a mistake in business. It's only worth eleven million five, so it is very special to me. You are the first person I have ever allowed to wear it."

"I am stunned, flabbergasted and overwhelmed!", she replied. "Is this for me to wear? Are they real?"

"Of course they are real!", John insisted defensively.

"These are investments. Even the overpriced necklace is worth over fourteen and a half million by now, although I consider a ten percent increase in value a pretty bad deal, comparatively speaking."

And her eyes nearly popped out of her head when she saw all of the other necklaces, bracelets, watches, earrings, clasps and brooches, some with so many diamonds on them Kim needed sunglasses. There were amethysts, emeralds, pearls of every size, and every variation of gold, silver and platinum imaginable.

She especially loved the gold Rolex ladies' watch with the hundred diamond bracelet. John told her that there was a matching necklace inside the safe, but it must have been buried beneath the fifty pound bag of uncut South African diamonds laying in there from the Oppenheimer mine. Kim tried to lift the bag but it was too heavy.

"Well, I am sure you will pick out something appropriate, and wear whatever you feel goes with the dress you pick out from the models", he suggested.

"Meanwhile, rest up a little, and if there is anything you want, I am right next door. Don't hesitate to come in. If you knock and I don't answer, just come in and make yourself at home. I might be out, in the shower, or dreaming about you, so don't hesitate. We have to live as "roommates" for a awhile."

Kim was marveled, and she couldn't even acknowledge all of John's generosity and compassion. He caressed her chin with the tip of his index finger, smiled, and left. Kim, returning to reality, shouted "Whoopee!" and jumped on her bed, happy for her good fortune.

"And to think my mama didn't want me to go into modeling because she thought I would turn out to be a tramp!", she laughed to herself.

"She must be shocked out of her cigarette-coughin' mind!"

Thinking about what she would tell her family, she drifted off into a deep sleep. An hour later, John knocked but there was

no response. Kim was out like a light, dressed the same way he left her. He sat next to her, shaking his head, amusing himself and admiring her captivating image. She reminded him of Sleeping Beauty, a real marvel, a jewel of humanity, worth infinitely more than all of the diamonds and gold in the safe. Unlike the other furniture and tangible assets, she was alive.

John took Kim's hand between his, stroking her gently with his right thumb while his left hand caressed her cheek. Finally, she moved, moaning "Hnimnim … "

She opened her eyes, and encountered his gazing into them. She was startled, and jumped.

"Oh, did I fall asleep?"

"It's normal after a thirteen hour flight, and jet lag, and all of the excitement of coming here", he analyzed.

"I am sorry to awaken you, but the models are here, and they have congregated in the central hall waiting to enter the living room salon once you have arrived."

"Oh, G-d, the models … That's right", she replied groggily.

"They will display theft dresses while wearing them, as the world famous fashion designer Gaston Sere De Rivieres wants them presented that way. Come, let us join the entourage", he coaxed.

As they left the master suite, John locked the doors with a key. On the way out, she noticed a room with a double door, which

to her seemed very large from where she was standing. She didn't remember seeing it before on the tour, and accordingly, she told

Kim: "John!! I believe we missed this room when you showed me around."

John became serene and said, "No, my love. We did not miss this room. It is off limits to everyone but me. It is my personal study, where I do my thinking and build my empire."

Kim felt like he had reprimanded her, but he quickly calmed her down and said with a smile, "Within that room are all the secrets of my success and life. It's just a space surrounded by four walls, that's all. Insane asylums are full of them."

With that joke, they both laughed and Kim forgot about her curiosity. They walked outside on the deck, as the weather was superb beyond belief, as if the daylight was made for them alone.

When they arrived at the living room, a multitude of incredibly stunning French women wearing garments fit for a queen in metallic red, white, gold and blue were waiting for the elegant couple.

They walked around showing off their garments to up beat production music piped in the background, taking the top jackets off, exposing their bare shoulders. It looked as well rehearsed as a Parisian fashion show could ever be. The demonstration and choreographed dance took about an hour.

John was beginning to exhibit signs of impatience. "So?", he indicated.

The lead fashion designer, a flagrant homosexual named Barry Friedman who was oddly enough wearing a sweatshirt engraved with fake rabbits, became a little offended when he saw that Kim was having a difficult time deciding what she wanted.

"Now listen, Deane", he began with a lisp, "we sell to royalty and to the richest people in Europe and America. If you think these threads are not high and mighty enough for you, I'll tell all of these swishy ladies to pack it in and we'll be off to the races."

KIM: "I am overwhelmed, Mr. Friedman. Please do not be offended. I just do not know which to choose! I like all of them!"

JOHN: "Fine, we'll take them all then! Friedman, have your alteration assistants measure Kim for everything."

Kim was thoroughly astonished and so overjoyed, she wrapped her arms around John, jumped to his neck, and kissed his lips which took himcompletely by surprise.

FRIEDMAN: 'When you're done, honey, let me kiss him next because I just love all this business!"

KIM: "Thank you, my love. It's too much! I do not need so many beautiful outfits!"

John smiled, then retreated to the back of the room quickly as Friedman moved towards him.

FRIEDMAN: "Oh, this sweet savage is afraid of me, even though I'm the most famous designer in the world. Missy, you've got one hell of a man there, so hold on to him!"

KIM: "I know. Mr. Friedman. I truly love him. And John, I thank you from the bottom of my heart."

John: "You are welcome, Princess. You will certainly need these clothes, because we will be traveling a lot, visiting kings and presidents, and I wants you to be the envy of all theft wives and daughters. No doubt you will need a lot more."

Kim moved toward John once again. Her face was close to his, as he kissed her nose and forehead. She took his hand and placed it on her chest in a warm embrace. Although it was spontaneous and sincere, he thought she was simply playing the part very well.

The models undressed right there on the spot, seemingly unbothered by John's presence. They all wore tiny panties which barely covered their vaginas, and naked breasts plentifully abounded in the room. All of that stimulation went unnoticed, since John and Kim could not take their eyes off each other, and all Barry Friedman could think about was his six hundred and forty-five thousand dollar order and his fantasy of jumping into bed with John.

Trying to quiet his shattered nerves, he surreptitiously popped a Lithium and a Thorazine, regained his composure, and asked Kim to select the dress she would like to wear for the evening, asking her to please try it on. She chose a white metallic lustrous gown made of thousands of tiny cultured pearl shavings from the Caspian Sea.

Kim was a little embarrassed to undress right then and there, but she did, uncovering the body of Venus, the goddess of Love. All the models whistled from admiration, and some from lust.

"How beautiful!", they echoed in French, as Barry Friedman waddled over to them, hissing at them and demanding that they shut up.

"Don't flirt with the customers, you silly geese!", he reprimanded, his rectum swishing and swaying in a hundred different directions.

Meanwhile John could not take his gaze off Kim's miraculous body, and admired her with an intensity as if she were sculptured in marble.

He was serious, lost in the dream of her vision, and one might say that he looked shocked having seen her perfection in the flesh for the first time, if only for an instant which seemed like an eternity.

Kim noticed John and looked at him, wondering if he had been hypnotized. She approached him, allowing her casual clothes

to drop loosely from her palm as she made her way toward John, almost totally naked with the exception of a mini-bikini covering the key to her inner sanctum.

Even so, her derriere was totally visible and he was lost in the admiration of it, totally submerged in her uniqueness.

"Can you help me with it, love?" Kim said, referring to the white gown, although for a moment John thought she was referring to her buttocks.

As John took the majestic dress from her hands, Kim observed two drops of perspiration on his temple. His demeanor was slightly nervous. She lifted her arms as he slid the dress on her slowly, her breasts almost touching him, and the heat from her nipples shooting invisible lasers of passion into his soul.

Remarkably, the dress was perfect and did not need any kind of touchup or alteration. Kim continued trying on the others, but John excused himself:

"I have to make a phone call to David and Peter", he said apologetically. "I'll meet you in our cabin, baby."

He kissed her lips and disappeared. She thought that he was offended by her nudity, but she shrugged her shoulders unwittingly and did not let it bother her.

She tried all of the outfits, gowns and dresses, trying to find some flaw or reason to give something constructive to the seamstresses, who were standing around her like pigeons in a

park, waiting for some direction or activity. However, it was to
no avail, since every single one of the garments was a perfect fit.

She was so exhilarated! Barry Friedman curtsied as he left the
room, taking his entourage with him. Several of the crew girls
came rushing in and helped Kim carry away all of the dresses
and accessories, including the purses, jackets, and four pair of
mink shoes in various matching colors.

Loaded to the max, Kim and her attendants made their way
toward the master suite. She opened the door. John wasn't
there. She entered, followed by her helpers, who busily began
hanging up the dresses in the triple armoire chest inside the
huge walk-in closet where John's three hundred and seventeen
suits were hanging and arranged according to the colors of the
rainbow.

Kim thanked the crew girls and they left.

John had been taking a shower. He entered the room
completely naked, unaware that Kim was there. John had a
towel in his hand and was drying his hair. They were both
surprised and gasped. Kim saw his penis, and began staring
at it. John, blushing the color of hemoglobin, quickly covered
himself with the towel.

"I am so sorry!", John exclaimed, not knowing what to do as
the towel fell out of his hand.

"I should have knocked!", Kim screamed.

"Oh, what have I done! I thought you were out. The girls helped me bring all of the dresses and accessories. Should I pick up that towel for you?"

Kim started to bend down, with her face less than six inches from John's third arm. John backed away and ducked down, grabbing the towel and modestly putting it around his waist as if the entire incident did not even happen.

"Well, I guess we know what we look like in our birthday suits!", Kim laughed, frying to relieve the tension in the room. Then, changing the subject, she asked, "Why did you leave the room when I was trying on the clothing?"

JOHN: "I thought you might be embarrassed so I left."

KIM: "I wasn't actually. You forget I am a model. But, thanks for the thought. Anyway, I'll let you get dressed, and I'll go take a shower while you are doing that and I'll get ready for this evening. And as for what happened just now, let me tell you that you don't look so bad without anything at all."

John did not know what to say as he watched Kim smile and turn to enter her suite. At nine o'clock John was ready in his tuxedo, prepared to make his grand entrance. He knocked on Kim's door.

"Come in, it's open!", she said loudly.

Suddenly John's jaw dropped as he gazed upon the stunning sight which the events of the day had created. Kim was wearing

the white metallic dress, which molded around her like a supple glove. Each facet of the gown showed her inimitable curves and assets.

"You look exquisitely marvelous, Kim", he uttered in amazement.

"I love it. Did you choose some jewelery to go with it?"

"I need your personal opinion", Kim replied.

John took out a ravishing necklace of Zainibian diamonds from the jewelry case in the wall vault and quickly walked behind her, locking it gently around her precious neck, taking a brief moment to inhale the aroma from her hair.

The necklace was stylish and graceful, despite its hundred and eighty thousand dollar price tag, and covered just enough of her bare skin to knock out anyone who came within a ten mile radius of her. The seven carat pear shaped diamond which eclipsed the center of the design rested in the cleavage that divided her fantastic breasts.

"You truly look like a queen", John whispered, as he adorned her with matching diamond earrings, the bracelet, and the ten carat diamond ring.

"So many stones!", Kim remarked. "It looks like you've cornered the market on them!"

John laughed silently, knowing that he genuinely had!

"You look incredibly beautiful, just like an angel!", he told her as he felt his throat feeling very dry from hyperventilation of the libido. He quickly turned his gaze and placed the mini-jacket on Kim's naked shoulders. The dress, of course, was strapless.

"Shall we?", John said suggestively.

Kim smiled and answered, "Yes, my fine prince, let's go."

She held his arm and they left. They truly looked like royalty. A Bentley limousine was waiting for them, with John's faithful camel driver Bashir behind the wheel.

"Is this jet yours too?" Kim asked.

"Yes, Princess, and now it is yours as well. Feel free to use it anytime you like. Bashir will take you anywhere you want to go. Just don't ask him to drive you to Syria, because he is homesick and he hasn't had a vacation for a while. He only goes home to his wife once a year."

"Why is that?", Kim wondered.

"Well, Bashir's wife Chamor is very fat, and I think he has lost interest in her. You would have to see her to believe it", John explained.

"Poor Bashir", Kim sympathized. "That's why I exercise every day and try to stay in shape, so I will never look like that!", Kim explained.

They walked toward the car, arm in arm, under the admiration of the crew. She loved when he called her 'Princess'. Perhaps that was because with John, she actually felt like one.

And so she was destined to live two lives, one in public with his full attention, warmth and kisses, and the other in private, alone and with his indifference, with neither love nor passion. In other words, Kim was falling for him.

CHAPTER 6

A t the palace, the baroque music radiated onto the street for blocks away. The parking lot, located a half-mile behind the two hundred thousand foot greenhouse and plant nursery, contained more Lamborghinis, Ferraris, Bentleys and Rolls Royces than the eye could safely count. Bashir stopped at the main entrance of the palace and two valets dressed in white satin uniforms opened the door of the limousine. John came out first and extended his arm to Kim in order to gracefully help her out. Once inside, the major domo announced "Mr. John and Miss Kim."

All activity ceased, even the music, as if they were rehearsing an old E. F. Hutton commercial. Gazes of the hundreds focused upon them with whispers abounding, as some known to the couple began approaching these two perpetual guests of honor, entrenched in the pillars of the high and mighty Monaco elite.

The Royal Family was the first to greet them.

"Your Highnesses", John began, "this is my future wife Kim."

Prince Rainier took Kim's hand, kissed it, and said, "Indeed, John, she is most beautiful. You were right. No wonder you are so much in love, my boy."

The Prince then turned to Kim.

"It is such a pleasure to finally meet you, my dear", he spoke to Kim softly.

"The pleasure is all mine", Kim smiled, with a curtsy of dignity. Many of Monaco's most eligible young lathes came toward them out of the intense curiosity that comes from jealousy and rivalry among the females of the species.

After all, Kim won the lottery. They lost. John, or let us say his enormous fortune, was the prize.

The music resumed. It was a Viennese waltz. John took Kim's arm in order to rescue her from all of the drooling men undressing her mentally and the cat-eyed ladies who were glaring at her and touching her as if she were an alien from another planet.

Everyone followed suit and began dancing, but the stares of the entire room were fixated upon Kim's powerful beauty. Vibrations of admiration and envy flooded Kim's aura but she reflected all of it outward like water running off a duck's back as John held her like an exquisite piece of fragile but priceless porcelain.

Kim was angelically poised on the dance floor, like the dancing choreographer of heaven itself. And even though Kim's neurotic mother Iris was always told that she had two left feet, Kim was nothing like that, and if I have to say so myself, she danced quite well.

Even though John was twenty years her senior, he danced like a young handsome acrobat, swinging her in places she never felt before.

"You look very dashing and debonair this evening", Kim said, trying to sound even more sophisticated than she was.

"I could sense the hostility in all of these jealously-spoiled palace prawns. They are all so envious of me. How can I ever repay you for saving me from them?"

"By dancing with me all night", John replied, completely mesmerized by Kim's allure and perfection. He could see her lips moving and the only thoughts that consumed him is how badly he would have wanted to kiss them.

He barely heard what she was saying. Yielding to temptation, he reached for her appetizing lips and consumed them in a very delicate, dignified and yet quietly passionate kiss. Although taken by surprise, Kim responded to his kiss, offering her deliciously sensual tongue which he immediately pressed between his lips in order to suck the juice out of them, and then, realizing that everyone was dissecting his every move, he politely offered her his own lips to devour tastefully.

The curious maddening crowd could not stop watching their every move. Nevertheless, for John and Kim, no one else existed. Even amongst the multitudes, they were quite alone by choice. And perhaps the reason for this was how well they stood above the masses.

Even members of the Royal Family felt like peasants around this outstanding couple, meaning of course no disrespect.

John held Kim tight against him and kept dancing, and slowly led Kim toward the grand terrace, until they were safely out of the line of sight of the ballroom. Kim held his hand as they walked amongst the rare tropical plants which the Prince had imported from Zanzibar to adorn the terrace.

Multicolored spotlights planted into the ground gave an almost holy glow to Kim's countenance. Her eyes shined through the evening mist like laser diamonds.

"You look marvelous, a real gem", he added poetically. Thank you so much for accepting this job. I could never find a more suitable companion than you."

John held her by her naked shoulders. Kim listened to his wordsand wished deep inside that it could be so much more than just a "job" or "companionship." It was hard for her to be reminded of reality when she somuch preferred to feel like a princess who was genuinely loved by her prince.

"Thank you, John", Kim sighed.

"I am grateful to have accepted too, and I truly appreciate this unique opportunity. I feel like Cinderella and that you are my prince."

"Well, then you'd better not lose your glass slippers", John joked.

Suddenly, Kim through her arms around John's neck, approaching his face and exclaimed, "the witches are watching us", and proceeded to seal her silky lips with his. He responded to her gesture and held her by her waist, pressing her against him.

The kiss lasted for ten good minutes, but in actuality, no one was watching. It was simply Kim's ruse to kiss him. When John released her lips, he continued by kissing her lovely chin, and as he did so, she rolled back her head, offering him her sensual and deliciously long velvet-like neck, which he kissed with an open mouth, sucking the spot where her Adam's apple would have been.

He continued with extreme thirst and desire, rising to the side of her neck, going on up to her ear lobe, tantalizing it with his tongue. She gasped with excitement and released a long sigh.

"Is he faking it or not?", she thought with perplexity.

Finally, John held her lovely face with his two hands and kissed her eyes, then her nose, thereafter completely covering her cheeks with tender kisses, causing her to burn with desire for him.

He leaned on the railing, almost sitting on it. She turned her back to him, grabbed his hands, and put them on her stomach and laid her head against his. As if on cue, he kissed the back of her neck tenderly, his lips spreading fire within her.

Proving that passion travels faster than the speed of sound, a dozen young women came into the garden toward them, sniffing the love and romance in the air. One brazen petite thing extemporaneously asked, "John, can we borrow your lovely fiancee for a few moments?"

Kim was hoping that he would say no, but instead, he consented, and said, "All right, I'll go talk to the Prince." Kim was devastated, although she did not show her feelings outwardly.

Kim was now the center of attention, although this was not her idea of a good time. She would have preferred to continue to ignite John's passion. The horde of the envious females began stroking Kim's long, fluffy hair, touching her face, saying:

"Oh, what lovely skin you have. What brand skin cream do you use? Is it Nutrogena?"

One bold wench even touched Kim's breasts, remarking:

"Wow, these are not made of silicone. Are they really real?"

In the next instant, a third girl began feeling her butt. She felt as if she was besieged by reporters, who asked the most impertinent questions.

"Are you marrying him for the money? Is he good in bed? Do you really love him? How many times an hour do you have intercourse? Do you think of other men or women when you are having sex with him?"

This grilling went on and on.

The Baron's daughter, Lady Celeste, who everyone thought would be the one to many John, was an exquisite redhead with green eyes.

"Here in Monaco we have private gatherings between us girls",

Celeste began: "Where we enjoy some seductive times together ... real nice times."

"You must be so delicious!", she continued as she pinched Kim's chin.

Kim felt rather intimidated by her, because of her rare beauty. This reinforced her fear that John was probably either gay, impotent, self-sufficient, or had been traumatized in some way by women.

Mother, young lady, who was a thin flat-chested brunette approached Kim in her ear and whispered:

"We have some great sex toys and gadgets, including electric vibrators with clitoral stimulators, and we girls spend a lot of "prime time" together to keep from getting bored."

Kim looked at her in amazement as she stooped down and started caressing her derriere, announcing to the group:

"She's got nice firm buns! Great!"

An older couple approached them. He was Monaco's Chief of Police, Captain Koenig, a tall phantom of a cross-eyed bald man with an ugly conehead and a square chest which resembled Frankenstein on a bad day Lady Celeste asked him: "Any more details about the serial killer?"

Captain Koenig began recounting all of the murders down to the smallest detail in order to impress Kim, since he obviously was not going to impress her with his looks. However, it did just the contrary.

Kim felt like vomiting as she was thoroughly nauseated by his descriptions of how the murderer would cut up the vagina or slash the butt or hack off the breasts.

This madman never raped any of the women. Captain Koenig said the most he would do was to sweat on the bodies of his victims, most likely from tremendous sexual excitement and post-traumatic stress.

"I figure he's got at least fourteen sets of tits mounted on his wall by now", the Captain boasted, as he picked his teeth with a thorn from a dead rose bush loosely hanging on a limp vine in the garden.

"You girls better start carrying some mace and learn karate so you can kick him in the balls!", he added paternally.

John came back outside and overheard the last part of the tale, and immediately excused himself and rescued Kim from that tense scene.

Seeing her pale face, he asked, "What is wrong, my precious adorenment?"

"Oh, GA!", Kim gasped, catching her breath. "That horrible policeman was making me nauseous with his stories about the murders. It turned my stomach."

"Are you sure it wasn't Prince Rainier's hors d'oeuvres? They weren't Kosher", John explained, trying to lighten things up with a joke.

"John, I would like to leave", she demanded. "I've had enough of the palace."

John understood.

"Yes, princess, we will go now", he said tenderly.

"We must first excuse ourselves from the Royal Family and leave."

She held his arm, and followed him. They made their exit without too much fanfare, as a lot of attention was being paid to Princess Stephanie who was getting drunk on Anisette and

Wine Coolers and was making a spectacle of herself in the corner of the ballroom.

John quickly waived to a few phony petty millionaires who were always trying to get inside information out of him and hastened Kim out of the main hall when they were both accosted by Lady Celeste who was holding a glass of Gibley's Gin and Grapefruit Juice mix in her hand.

"I expect you both for my Tuesday morning tennis party at my place",she insisted. "John knows where it is. And I won't accept no for an answer."

Slightly tipsy, Celeste grabbed John's face and kissed him on the lips, then suddenly she squeezed Kim's ass, drawing her closer, and gave Kim a hard French kiss on the lips as well.

"Bunch of nymphomaniac lesbians", she thought to herself. "But she sure knows how to kiss!"

John and Kim walked through the palace doors and John called Bashir on his cellular phone. He had just gotten through screwing one of the palace chambermaids named Gitaine, and had a big fight with her because Gitaine's dog, a Doberman Pinscher, insisted on sniffing and licking Bashir's balls during intercourse, and Gitaine accused Bashir of putting too much peribme and after shave lotion on his ass which had gotten the dog excited.

Bashir slapped her and took the money he had previously paid her for sex as he zipped his fly and ran out to the limousine to pick up Kim and John.

"You stinking bitch!", he screamed at Gitaine. "Next time I see your dog I'm going to strangle him."

"You cheap bastard!", Gitaine replied. "Give me back my money!"

"Filthy tramp!", he shouted, wanting to always get the last word.

Five minutes later, Bashir had pulled himself together, driving the limousine to the front gate.

"How was your evening, John?" Bashir inquired.

"They were a little rough on Kim", he sighed.

"And what did you accomplish?", John asked politely, trying to make conversation.

"I just spent another quiet evening admiring nature", Bashir explained.

"Nothing really exciting ever happens around here."

"Yes, it's just a palace", John said with total empathy for his good friend.

"When you've seen one you've seen them all."

Kim slumped in her seat, anxiously awaiting to get back to the boat so she could take a triple-strength Excedrin.

CHAPTER 7

At the yacht all were asleep, with the exception of Debra and Antoinette, two girls guarding the top deck, dressed in army-fatigue bikinis carrying machine guns. Security girls had a four hour watch.

They worked in pairs as part of the crew, and all were expert in martial arts, kickboxing, and handled their weapons like pros.

Well, they were pros, actually, although each one had specific duties aboard the ship.

When John and Kim entered his cabin, John majestically opened Kim's door as if he were playing the part of Sir Galahad of the Mossad, and Kim stepped quietly in her room, which was lit with beautiful translucent neon night lights that were subdued and intertwined amongst the baseboard of the floor. John stared into Kim's watery eyes and said, "Kim, I ......"

Kim waited an instant and replied, "Yes, John?"

He did not answer immediately, just scratched his head in internal contemplation and said, "Good night, my princess."

She thought he wanted to kiss her, but as usual, she was disappointed.

Kim went to sleep, zonked out from the events of the evening and all of the plastique royalty babes she sifted her way through all evening long in order to stay sane and in character.

John went to have his shower first, then laid in bed to read a financial report for the morning's meeting. The Iranian Ryal was collapsing again due to the pending war with Iraq, and John held the largest short position on that currency in the world, and he was making money at the rate of sixty two million dollars per hour.

The report put him to sleep. He knew what he was doing and Peter's reports were always so thorough but boring.

An hour later, while soundly counting Iranian sheep jumping over suitcases of cash, John heard a frightening scream coming from Kim's room. He jumped out of bed, and ran toward her door. She was jumping and hollering in the bed. John quickly held her with all of his might as she trembled.

"Shush … ", he comforted her. "Kim, darling, what happened here?"

"The killer! He cut me! He slashed me with this knife!", she panted, hardly able to describe what she had seen.

"You had a nightmare, my precious angel", John sighed.

"No, no, Kim insisted. "He was here, look!", she screamed once more as she lifted her nightgown, uncovering her vagina.

"He put his knife through there and slit me wide open!", she continued wildly, pointing a finger between her vaginal lips in order to show John.

She was shaking from head to toe. She was all wet, drenched in the most sweet-smelling sweat he had ever experienced.

"It was only a nightmare", John consoled her. "I'm afraid whatever slit you had down there you've always had before. There is no blood, not even from a menstrual cycle. Calm down quietly, my dearest. Shush, calm down now."

He held her in his arms, as she hid her face in his neck and cried hysterically. John kissed and massaged her face gently with his lips.

"I am here, my love", he reassured her. "I am here with you, and no one can hurt you. You see, nothing is wrong. Try to go back to sleep, baby."

Kim was still shaking and shivering, her teeth tapping against each other as a reflex action beyond her control.

"No, don't leave me", she begged. "Hold me. I can't be alone."

Obligingly, John carried her in his arms to his room and sat on the most comfortable arm chair he could find, holding her on his lap, pressing her against him tightly. She was still soaking wet.

"Let me get you something to wear instead of these drenched clothes. You are wetter than a drowned cat. You are liable to catch a cold", he explained.

"Please don't move!", she cried out.

"Don't go anywhere."

Undaunted, John took his pajama jacket that was on the dresser, and said:

"Here, take your gown off and put this top on. It's very soft mongoose flannel and was a birthday gift from Count Andreyovitch from East Vladivostok. I promise I won't look."

Kim was so visibly traumatized by the nightmare she didn't pay any attention to the pedigree of his pajamas at all. She changed into it like a robot, while John kept his word and looked the other way. He suddenly felt the burning skin of her derriere in his lap.

"What's this warm business?" he thought to himself. He was in sheepskin boxers and enjoyed sleeping like that without a shirt. She finished putting on the jacket, and laid her head against his chest.

"Hold me, please!", Kim sobbed sadly. "Hold my hand." John complied, replying, "Oh, G-d, you are burning up with fever."

He put his mouth on her forehead. "You are not feeling very well, my princess. Let me get the thermometer."

He ran to the first aid closet in the master bathroom and brought it to the armchair. Kim grabbed it and put in her mouth.

"It doesn't matter", Kim cried as she spit the thermometer out onto the carpeted floor.

"Just don't leave me, John! Please hug me!", she uttered in exasperation as if she were over-acting in a soap opera.

However, she truly meant every word, and sensing this, he willingly hugged her, with her beautiful behind burning a hole on John's lap.

He picked up the phone to call Josiane, the Chief Medical Assistant on the yacht, as he shoved the thermometer up her ass in heartfelt tenderness. Interestingly enough, it went up unassisted, needing no Vaseline. Apparently her anxiety made her inner lining lubricated.

"Now maybe we can get an accurate temperature reading", John said with the utmost of sweetness in his voice.

"Josianne, this is John!Please call Doctor Michelle to come to my quarters immediately. My fiancee is on fire with fever, so please hurry!"

John hung up as he pulled the thermometer out, holding it up to the light shining from the master bathroom. The thermometer read a scant 99.3 degrees Fahrenheit, which indicated more of a nightmare than a fever. John breathed a

deep sigh of relief. Nevertheless, Kim continued clenching her teeth and crying slowly.

"It was so vivid, so real!", she described. "I felt the knife cutting my stomach open. I begged him to stop, but he laughed. He wanted my vagina, my butt and my breasts to take with him."

Restimulating the dream, she began sobbing again to no avail. John kissed her face, cleaning her tears away and held her tightly.

"Shush, little girl", he soothed. "I am here. I love you and I will protect you, and no one would ever dare to lay a finger on my adoring princess."

Suddenly, Kim stopped crying and said, "Am I really your little princess? Do you truly love me?"

John was caught off guard.

"Of course I love you", he answered. "If not, why would I be holding you? My duty is to watch over you and guard you until you return home. I love you like a companion."

"Oh, shit!", Kim thought to herself, disappointed once again that her hopes had been dashed and turned to shattered illusions.

However, under the circumstances and evidencing his tenderness, she decided not to care. She kissed his chest endlessly.

Responsively, he caressed her lovely face, and assumed that she was confused and needed love and tenderness in her moment of fright. She moved her backside against his loins, in order to excite him. There was no doubt about it.

She wanted to make love. He felt her burning desire, and the perfect roundness of her incredibly firm derriere. As bad luck would have it, he was getting a very stiff erection when there was a loud knock at the door.

"Come in!", John acknowledged.

Josianne and a middle-aged woman wearing white shorts and carrying a doctor's bag entered. John explained to Josianne and Doctor Michelle that Kim had a nightmare as a reaction to the incident at the palace when she heard Chief of Police Koenig describe the serial killer.

"Josianne"

Doctor Michelle took her temperature again, this time with an oral thermometer, and this time it showed that Kim had a reading of 104 degrees Fahrenheit.

"How could this be?", John asked, showing Doctor Michelle the thermometer.

"Isn't this the thermometer Bashir used to take the temperature of the limousine's water pump?", Josianne observed.

"It's broken, and it should have been thrown away. How did it get back here?"

"Get rid of it!", John commanded as Josianne ran out of the room to throw it overboard into the Mediterranean Sea.

"Josie shouldn't do that", Doctor Michelle complained, nodding her head negatively. "Things like that pollute the entire ocean."

"Look, I don't give a damn about the thermometer!", John yelled, nearly losing his temper for the first time in years. "Do something to help Kim! She's nearly delirious."

Doctor Michelle took a stethoscope from her bag and opened her jacket and listened to Kim's heart, which was beating very fast. John courteously looked the other way.

"Nice fits", Michelle mumbled to herself in French, too low for anyone else to hear.

"Look, John", she explained in a didactic tone of voice.

"Your lady's scare caused the onset of post-traumatic stress syndrome, which triggered the high fever. Purely psychosomatic, John. There is nothing medically wrong with her. I'll put her on some Prozac, Ritalin and Lithium and one or two anti-depressants. She'll be just fine. I'm also giving her Codeine Elixir to lower her heart rate, and some Procardia to open up her arteries. I don't want this young lady to get a stroke, and I don't want to give her anything else because I don't believe in overmedicating anybody. That's how Elvis died, you know."

"You're the best, Michelle", Josianne echoed.

"Cut the crap, dollface", Michelle said to Josie."

"I were really the best I'd be working the palace." Josianne rolled her eyes.

"Now listen here, John", Doctor Michelle said with the authority of Marie Antoinette: "I want you to take some of this Yankee rubbing alcohol you got here in the medicine chest and mix it with luke warm water, and massage her body all around, and get this G-d damn fever down. Big boy like you can handle that, can't you?"

John, trying to restore a little decorum to the room, thanked Doctor Michelle politely. "How gracious of you to come so quickly", he said.

"So quickly?", Michelle laughed. "My cabin's two floors down and straight across the hall. That's what you pay me those big bucks for. Imagine getting a half a million a year and I work less than a day a month? If it weren't for my VCR and all one hundred episodes of 'Pee Wee's Playhouse' I'd be bored shitless. I've memorized every medical book I could find at the University. What I need is some more patients!"

"I would be eternally grateful if you look in on Kim every day for me" John replied with the understanding wisdom of a prophet.

"Well, all right then, cool!", Doctor Michelle smiled.

"Here, Josie, get all eight of these prescriptions filled. If Bashir is out screwing around, just take my car. It's the only 1952 Studebaker parked on the dock."

The two members of the ship's medical contingent left the stateroom.

"Interesting doctor", Kim remarked, indicating that she was feeling a slight bit better.

"A bit eccentric, but she was at the head of her class at the Sorbonne", John explained.

"Originally she's from Texas, which accounts for her unpredictability. She's also a licensed veterinarian, like most of the doctors that work in American prisons."

Kim wasn't paying attention to anything John was saying. She felt exceedingly comfortable in his arms, having left her right breast uncovered. She was playing like a spoiled child for all of his attention and love.

"Why is your heart beating so fast?", Kim asked with those big innocent eyes. "Do you need some of that crazy medicine too?"

Embarrassedly, John whispered, "It is just that I am so worried about you, my pet."

"You are?", Kim replied, staring him right smack dead in the face.

She took his hand and said, "Feel my heart, how fast it is beating." Kim slowly dragged his hand to her uncovered breast but he softly hesitated and resisted her advances.

"It won't bite, you know", she giggled. "I just need to feel your hand on my heart, to calm me down."

Overruling his polite withdrawal, she pressed his hand on her pointed, proud breasts, her chest panting a mile a minute with momentary excitement, covering it fully with the wide palm of his hand.

Suddenly she moaned, "Oh, it feels so good, John. You have a very soft touch. … That's it. See? I told you I wouldn't hurt you. I am a woman and I need tender care, especially now, far away from home."

John appeared frozen in space and time.

"Are you repulsed by me", Kim asked, showing her deepest insecurity.

"Now what kind of nonsense is that?", John argued. "It is just that I cannot in good conscience take advantage of a confused girl, and I signed a contract that I would not seek any sexual favors from you. Legally, if I violated it, you could sue me for breach of contract!"

"That's what you see me as, a contract?", Kim snapped in exasperation, tired of being rejected twenty-four hours a day.

"My beloved", John began. "You do not even begin to see the flawed soul of the male species. You are the most gorgeous girl in the entire world. Who would not want to love you?"

"Apparently you don't!", Kim replied.

"You say I'm the most gorgeous. Some men prefer brunettes. Whatever. So what, even if I were that amazing, I still need your caresses. I promise not to do anything else. Just squeeze my breast with one hand and my butt with your other. It would please me very much and comfort me, not as a sexual favor but to calm my nerves. Please! I can't believe I have to beg you for this ... I don't want you to simply put me on a pedestal and leave me high and thy. I want to be touched!"

Seeing the writing on the wall, John once again gave into temptation and began gently brushing her breast and caressing it, touching it with the tip of his fingers. He was sweating from nervousness.

Concluding that John was too shy for the human race, she took his other hand and placed it in the middle of he ass, gliding it between her cheeks, and asked him, "Do the same thing here, please."

With the tip of his fingers, he also brushed from the top of her valley very smoothly all the way down to her torrid zone which seemed to emit steam from every aspect, pushing further up to her vagina.

He repeated this motion over and over, while his other hand massaged and squeezed her tantalizing breast, his fingers totally spread around the base of it, gently closing down to her nipple, immediately hardening it.

"You see!", Kim said with commanding reassurance, "it doesn't hurt at all and you are pleasing me. Just don't forget about my other breast. It gets lonely once in a while. Just between us, I am happy, okay? I like this. Forget about contracts and lawyers. What does Peter know about love? He's an old man! Someone like me would give him a heart attack."

Instantly she observed something.

"Wow, John!", she exclaimed. "Your heart is beating a little too fast. Are you all right?"

Actually, she was teasing him and loved every minute of it. She spread her legs a little more, took his left hand and passed it between her thighs, directing his fingers all the way up her orifice, pressing his fingers even more savagely in order to make them feel the velvet pink cushion between her cheeks.

She felt tingling on her rear entrance, and then smoothly amidst her heavenly vaginal lips. She was guiding his hand, moaning,

"John, oh, John, what a great gentleman you are!"

John thought for a moment that he was guilty of not being a gentleman, and tried to pull his hand away, but she did not let

him, clawing her nails into his skin deeper and deeper, forcing him to continue as if he were her very own sex slave.

"You are such a gentleman", she continued pseudo-mockingly, "to attend to your very neglected princess in distress."

She swooned around to his forefront and began kissing his breast, her tongue lashing and tickling and teasing his right nipple. Overwhelmed, he was thoroughly drenched in a pool of sweat.

She had it down to a science, my friends. She knew he was totally confused. She felt his penis against her ass, covered by his hundred and fifty dollar boxers.

Meanwhile, Josianne came back from the pharmacy with Jackie, the saladmistress of the yacht's kitchen. Josianne and Jackie were roommates on the yacht and went everywhere together.

They were almost alike in manner and speech, except that Josiatme was a curly blonde and Jackie was a long-haired brunette. Josiamie knocked on the door, but Kim and John were so engrossed in their own excitement, they never heard the knocking.

Concerned about the safety of John and Kim, Josianne barged in, only to discover themselves right in the middle of the couple's tender scene.

"Jackie"

"Oops!", Josie gasped, realizing what she had done, excusing herself a dozen times while Jackie just froze in fright, expecting to be fired from the yacht for such an inexcusable intrusion. John was even more embarrassed than they were, and tried to take his hands off Kim, but she did not let him move a muscle.

"Continue, my love", Kim proudly announced, astounding everybody. John, who was completely perplexed and so unaccustomed to being caught in a compromising situation, even with his supposed fiancee, stumbled across his own words and just said, "Thanks a lot, girls."

Then mustering up some composure, he added, "Josianne, would you do me a big favor and mix some of this Lavacol brand wintergreen alcohol with some water from the water purifier in the bathroom in a small basin?"

Josiame complied in a hurry, trying to make light of the situation. Jackie was still looking at them in half-shock, although John pretended not to notice, having his back toward her. Nevertheless, Jackie loved the tenderness John displayed with Kim, never having seen the intimate side of him before.

After all, the most time she ever spent with John was in dicing Sevrugian Beluga caviar for his Caesar salad tableside. Secretly, as did all of the girls on the ship, she had dreamed of him making passionate love. But it was nothing more than a wet dream, because the only bed partner poor Jackie ever had for sexual fulfillment was her roommate Josie.

"Kim, my precious", John interrupted, "Josianne will give you a nice rubdown now."

Kim closed her thighs on his arm and with her hand on her breast on top of his hand said, "No, my love. You'll do it!"

She was like a sweetly stubborn little girl, unwilling to give up the attention he was giving her.

In order not to arouse any suspicion amongst the crew girls, he agreed.

Following the doctor's orders, Jackie took some codeine elixir from the prescription bottle and poured it in a platinum tablespoon and directed it to Kim's mouth.

She held a cup of purified ice water in her left hand. Kim smiled at all of this royal treatment and drank the syrup and then the water, and said, "Thank you, Jackie."

Josianne returned with a large basin of water and poured the entire bottle of Lavacol wintergreen alcohol into it. She fluffed up a goosefeathered towel onto the bed and helped Kim to lay on it. Insecure about what Josianne planned to do next, Kim abruptly held up her hand and said:

"Thanks, Josianne. John will massage me."

Seeing that this was their cue to leave the room, both crew girls got their things together and started to leave.

"If you like, I can prepare you a nice chefs salad", Jackie offered.

Kim looked at her in amazement.

"Who needs food when I've got my man here", she laughed, ushering them out the door with a wave of her hand.

Kim unbuttoned John's pajama top and let it fall on the carpet, leaving her totally naked like a dream come true. John tried to turn his gaze from her but was unable to do so. He gawked at her in stunned astonishment, not believing that any creature of this planet could be ever so beautiful.

He told Kim to lay on her stomach, to which she gladly complied. He brought a matching towel from the bathroom suite, folded it and covered the middle of her butt.

Kim chuckled but did not say a thing. "More shyness", she thought to herself. John took one of his monogrammed wash cloths, wet it, and passed it all over her body. She moaned with pleasure. Who would have ever believed a wash cloth could feel that good?

Pleasure turned into ecstasy when John massaged her from head to toe with his bare hands, repeating the same exotic ritual with the wash cloth and towel.

Every time he touched her butt, she imprisoned his hands on her cheeks, saying, "Harder, my prince!" Accommodatingly, he massaged her longer in there. His heart was about to stop from excitement. Seeing that she had moved him, she pulled the towel from her body, slowly sliding it, bearing all.

Swallowing his saliva and choking on his own words, he reminded her, "The alcohol is going to burn you there."

"I am burning up much more than alcohol could make me feel", Kim replied like a wildcat in heat. "Pretty please!", she added coyishly, loving to tease him. He came close to throwing caution to the wind, but not totally. As you may have guessed by now, John has more willpower than ten priests at a live sex show. When he massaged her very tightly up and down, she decided to shift her derriere downstream on the bed so that he was forced to touch her vagina.

Finally, he said, "Please turn over." She did, hoping he would devour her right then and there. But alas, he turned his eyes away and covered her nudity with an empty pillowcase and her breasts with two small hand towels.

He continued massaging her within the confines of the same ritual, but she threw the two small towels onto the floor quite angrily and deliberately uncovered her breasts, very annoyed that he had hidden them from view.

"Don't pretend that you can't see these firm old things", Kim mocked.

"I want you to massage me, please. I don't need a Saint right now. I need a hard-handed masseuse."

John was gentle, ignoring her demands without demeaning her honor. It is not easy to be gallant and chivalrous when you have two beautiful tits staring at you in the face. His sweat

was pouring onto her body Kim could see the beating of his temples.

He continued to massage her breasts very gently, as she moved and moaned like a cat at her master's touch. Fearing that he was about to ejaculate into his boxer shorts, he changed his position and continued massaging the rest of her body.

Wise to his defenses, she played right into his hand and shoved her deliciously shaved vagina into his two middle fingers.

John was bleary-eyed and swooning as she forced his hand against his will on her eternal triangle and made him massage her, pressing on his hand to feel his grip on her.

Then she slowly opened her legs, letting him admire her immaculate vagina, totally inviting him into her holy den of iniquity.

Kim reached for his head to push him toward her burning offering, her other hand busily grasping in the direction of his loins. He almost acceded, but then stopped, as if some demon of righteousness was preventing him from having a grand old time.

"You promised me not to turn this into a love scene, my darling", John said patiently as the fumes of lust were flying out of his eardrums.

Kim made a childish frown-like expression, as if someone had stolen her toy. She felt humiliated inside but she collected herself and took a deep breath.

"Sorry, my prince", she sighed. "You are right. We hardly know each other, and I'm such a mixed up little girl. Please forgive me." John smiled gently at her, touching her nose with the tip of his finger and covering her with a silver satin sheet.

She looked at him and said, "This is the first time in my life that 1 have begged for love, selfishly, all the way around. I acted impulsively, wanted to be satisfied and fulfilled without the slightest consideration of your feelings. You have to forgive me. I just feel like taking control and stealing some sexual gratification and power sometimes. I suppose I have never grown up."

John laughed out of deep love for her. "You are a marvelous child. Please don't take this as a rejection. It is not you, but me. I wish I could explain, but trust in me that one day I will, and in fact, my whole existence depends upon it."

Kim looked at him with such sad eyes, her womanhood still burning from unsatisfied desire.

"I know you have a secret, John", she answered, "and I will respect that."

Literally breaking the ice, John went to the refrigerator and took out some ice cubes and put them in two plastic bags. He picked up the two small towels that Kim had thrown on the

carpet, and surrounded each bag of ice with them, placing one on her head to cool her off a bit.

He then lifted the silver satin sheet and put the other ice bag under the curvature of her feet.

"It's cold!", she shivered.

"Yes", John acknowledged, "since the blood circulates from the feet to the head, the ice cools the blood, and the important part is in the cooling of the brain. We have to keep the heat away from it." "Yeah, I guess I got some hot cells up there", Kim laughed. "Did Doc Michelle teach you all that? You are so smart, it slays me sometimes!"

Before John could answer, she took his hand and kissed it tenderly, saying, "Thank you, you are so gentle and kind. I know you are actually respecting me, treating me like a child."

"You are a great child!", John responded flatteringly. He also kissed her hand with the delicateness of a summer shower of mist.

"Aren't you upset staying awake all night?", Kim asked in wonder.

"Not in the slightest bit", John answered. "And I intend to stay up as long as it takes, at least until your fever goes down."

Kim motioned John once again to come towards her.

"Please come and lay down next to me. It will do wonders for my temperature. I want to put my head on your chest and fall asleep. Is that too much to ask?", she whimpered.

"Of course if you don't want to, you can say no and I won't be insulted, not much!"

John appeared to be embroiled deeply within this dilemma.

Then he smiled, and commented, "What the heck. We will behave like sister and brother. We are two civilized adults, and above all, friends. Okay?"

"Thank you, John", she replied with unceasing gratitude. He tiptoed around the bed, lifted the sheet and crawled underneath beside her. Faithful to her promise, she put her head on his chest and obligingly he put his arms on her bare back. He had forgotten that she was laying there totally naked.

Kim turned toward him, putting her right leg on top of him. He felt the inferno of her burning body against his, and could not help but sigh. His intimacy did not escape her.

"I used to sleep like that with my younger sister Jenny", she smiled, reminiscing of her plain life back home in California.

"I just need a place to put my leg. You make a great leg-pillow, John. I feel so at home and secure with you that I can just about do anything under the sheets with you. Are you comfortable?"

John kissed her hand and said, "Yes, sleeping beauty, more than you realize. It's about time to go to sleep now, sweetheart.

I will guard your nap with my life. No more nightmares, and no more worries."

He stroke her hair back and forth, gently. Within a minute she was in a deep sleep.

John sensed her soft breathing on his torso, and once when she moved closer, he felt her burning vagina against his hip, her leg firmly situated on top of his loins. He smoothly moved a little away from her in order not to be in contact with her inviting cavern and shifted her leg from the shaft of his penis. He drifted into an equally deep sleep, fall of a theatre-fill of wild dreams and fantasies of his beloved Kim.

CHAPTER 8

T he phone rang.

John looked at his watch. It was 4:00 AM and the dawn of a new day so he picked it up effortlessly. He looked at Kim's head on his chest and once again feeling the wetness of her vagina on top of his thigh.

"Hello?", he answered.

"It's David! Sorry to wake you up, I know what time it is over there", David apologized. "Here it's 11:00 P.M. I need some decisions from you regarding the hostile takeover of TCNN News Network."

Kim drowsily awakened at the sound of conversation on the phone, looked at him with one eye closed, kissed his chest and dug into it with her chin. John glanced at her and smiled.

"David, how much TCNN stock do we have between all our corporations?", John inquired.

"You own 31% of the company, John", David rattled off like an adding machine on overtime.

"Great", John laughed. "Let's dump 2% during the first hour of trading and every hour thereafter, rotating the stock owned by each corporation. Keep your chin up; we're going to make a fortune on this one."

"When should I stop selling?", David asked, sounding alarmed.

"What about later in the day?"

"That's easy!", John reminded him. "Remember how we took over Frankfurt Electric? Just before the close, if you see a mad rush to sell TCNN stock and the price drops below 25% of yesterday's close, have my brokerage firm in Monaco buy up everything in sight. I'm going to teach Sheik Mechmet Ali Kusemach of Abu Dhabi a lesson. I know he's behind all this!"

"Yeah, John. That kook has been a pain in your ass for years", David replied. "Meanwhile, how's the little mermaid doing?"

"She is right here and very naughty", John told David as he looked at her, stroking her nose and smiling as she made funny faces at him in order to make him laugh while he was on the phone.

"Say hi!", David said loudly so Kim could hear. Kim giggled mischievously, saying, "Hi, Dave!"

"David, I need you here next week and bring Steve with you", John told him. "I need him to stay here for awhile, and you know for what"

"I know, okay", David replied. "Listen, John, don't overdo it with this young angel. She'll wear you out! Ha! Ha! Ha!"

"That's very funny, David", John protested. "I'll tell her", he added, afterward hanging up.

"Tell me what?", Kim joked as she tickled John under his chin.

"That I am naughty? Is that it? Well, if you're going to spread rumors about me, I might as well act the part!" With that, Kim took his thigh between hers as if she were riding the saddle of a motorized bull, putting her breast on his and rubbing his chest with it.

"Oh, John", she complained, "you don't like me too much. You think I'm this spoiled California brat like these horny crew girls here, except I'm not sure which sex they all want. But I am just a normal girl with natural female urges and a thirst for love from a man, I mean, this man, yo!"

She began moving up and down on his thigh, humping John like apanting dog in heat, making sure that he felt her vagina all over him.

"I'm going to get you to respond to me if I have to pin you down and rape you!", she screamed. John looked at his watch, except he wasn't wearing it.

"Listen, little girl", he whispered poetically, "it is five in the morning, and I have to go to work at 7:00 A.M. Would you like to come with me, and I'll show you my office building, and then I'll take you to lunch in the city of Nice, France. You'll meet a lady who was my first girlfriend. Her name is Orly."

Kim stopped for a moment and while kissing his chin, said, "Oh, I know you are still madly in love with her, otherwise you wouldn't be dogging me in bed. That's it. Anyway, what kind of a goofy name is 'Orly?" Does she get up 'Orly' in the morning or is her hair too greasy and 'Orly."

John started laughing uproariously.

"Oh, no … ", he corrected. "She is happily married, has children and is a gynecologist. She is just a good friend. I am still going to present you as my adorable fiancee."

"Oh, I get it", she rationalized as if a light bulb turned on in her head.

"You want her to check me out to make sure I don't have any sexually transmitted diseases before sleeping with me. Well, I don't, so that's cool."

John just nodded his head in utter amazement, neither confirming or denying her suspicions. Rather than speaking, he simply kissed her forehead, which made her continue to get excited with his thigh, but she did not dare touch his penis, knowing that he would predictably pull away or get mad, or at least that is how she sized up the situation.

"I am so hot from you, Kim admitted. "I don't know how I will survive like this, with you kissing me and exciting me in public, and when we are here alone I feel so horny. And yet you don't want to quash my fire. I know you for two days, but I've learned so much about you before meeting you, from Felicia, Bashir and David, that I feel I know you my whole life. I know I am bothering you with my needs, but let's face it, buddy, they exist, and I can't hide them anymore."

John stroked her lovely face as he pulled up her chin to look into her super-sensual deep green eyes.

"Okay, look … I'm going to share with you a secret but it has to remain a secret", he blurted out. "Do you promise?"

She suddenly jumped up, stopped teasing his body and sat next to him, all ears ablaze and her eyes cast fixated upon him, her heart beating rapidly, not having a clue as to what to expect from this very private man who controlled his feelings and sexuality like a puppet-master. She assumed he was going to finally tell her why he didn't have sex with Josianne and Jackie and all the rest of the beautiful girls on the ship, but all she could answer was, "Yes, John … I promise."

"Well … all right", he said with some hesitation. On this ship there are five girls who are very special. No one else knows their secret, no one except me, and now you. I hired them because they are quiet, very serious, they keep to themselves and do not mingle with the other crew members. They work security on the ship, mostly."

"I don't understand", Kim exclaimed in puzzlement. "What is their secret?"

"They have very special qualities", he continued slowly, not wanting to overwhelm her. "They are self-sufficient sexually between themselves. They are hemaphrodites."

Kim looked at John with the most intent curiosity. "You mean, with two sexes?"

"Yes, exactly, and it was no easy job finding them. They look radiant, with great bodies, breasts, behinds, and vaginas; but additionally they have a normal penis. To the best of my knowledge they can bear children but their sperm can make a woman pregnant."

Kim was stunned.

"Beautiful girls with normal penises?" she laughed in amazement.

"Yes, my darling", he winked. "Bashir checked them all himself, and he would never lie to me. He has a natural talent for finding the unusual."

"Damn!", she exclaimed. "My mama would never believe this, that's for sure."

"And that is the reason they keep to themselves, since they don't want to" he elucidated.

Suddenly a light bulb went off in Kim's head.

"So why are you telling me this, John?", she asked suspiciously.

"Do you like to have sex only with them?"

John burst out laughing. The thought was a bit more than he could take.

"Oh, No! Ha! Ha! Ha!", he roared. "No, I told you because you asked me a question about how you can quench your thirst for sex and lust. So, at my request, they will give you a full treatment of sex that would satisfy any woman in the world, even a frigid goose. This way, you can keep everything you do a secret."

"And you wouldn't be jealous or mad ill wanted to have sex with five men?", she questioned insecurely.

"Five women!", he corrected her.

"They are as feminine as they could possibly be. They were born with a slight abnormality, but they use it to their advantage, and I'm not just talking about their legal right to walk into the public rest room of their choice. That is not the reason that I hired them or asked Bashir to search the ends of the earth for them. These ladies are experts in martial arts. They also don't bring men aboard the boat. I couldn't feel safer with these ladies. I would rather have them protecting me thanArnold Schwartzeneger, Sylvester Stallone and Steven Segal all put together."

"But don't they bother the other girls in the crew?" she asked, trying to sort it all out.

"No, they are all gay. Jackie, Josiame, all of them", John smiled.

"They don't require men at all, although they keep trying to get me in bed because they think I am different. They enjoy trying to seduce me, but they never succeed. I also hired them for detective work. They have private investigator's licenses in every country in Europe, the Mideast, and in the United States."

"So what you are telling me is that they will fuck me all together", Kim inquired philosophically.

"Don't take the romance out of it", John reprimanded. "They are here to serve you, to make love to you, to satisfy you, not themselves. You are an intruder, an interloper to them; but for me they will do whatever I ask."

"You are a very strange man, John". Kim sighed, throwing her hands up in the air.

"Here I offer myself to you, and instead of taking me on, you give me a present of five men trapped in the bodies of women. How would I ever explain this to my psychiatrist?", she said jokingly but with unnerving frustration.

"I wish I could understand what is going on in that unreachable mind of yours. They say geniuses are on the edge of madness. Yet you are a great kisser, very sensual, a more-than-perfect

gentleman, and still inside you there is a very deep dark secret which prevents you from having sex with the woman who you kiss and adore all thy, like a real pro. I know that you desire me. I felt your magic wand standing erect against my stomach and butt when we kissed in the plane, in the palace, and in your bed. You might be the best actor in the world, but you couldn't make that thing stand up straight if you didn't feel anything, so I know you are not impotent."

John kept laughing as if he was being entertained by a bunch of clowns.

"Oh, no; I'm not impotent. Perhaps this analogy will answer your question."

"What analogy?", she replied, just staring at him like he was on display in a zoo cage.

"Can I hire a graduate from the finest university and put him in charge to run my empire on the first day he comes to work for me?", he asked. "Can I trust all of my life experience, work, wealth and secrets during the first week he starts working?"

"No, of course not!", Kim snapped. "But ..."

"So you have your answer handed to you on a silver platter right there", John explained, quickly interrupting her. "I can't tell you everything I have in mind for you or what you are or represent to me, any more than I am telling you right now. The only thing I ask is that you be patient, let me learn to know you, watch me feel your trust in me, until I can bring myself

to tell you more. My confidence is something that has to be cultivated like a little flower, blooming in the desert. I hate to be abrupt or blunt, but you will just have to earn it."

Kim was thoroughly confused.

"Are you telling me that you could be my real dad or something? That you are?"

John laughed so hard he nearly pissed in his pants.

"My funny little princess, I love you so much", he said, kissing her beautiful nose.

"You really love me?", she repeated, as if his words were oxygen she could breathe.

John took her adorable face between his wide hands, gazed into her eyes for awhile and kissed her lips passionately. She closed her eyes tightly, and entered the deepest level of trance from that kiss which he had put his entire heart into as he tasted and savored the honey flowing from her sensual mouth, sucking gently on the heat emanating from her incredibly silky lips.

When he released her, she had her eyes closed and was in a trance-like state, almost dreaming, with her head rolled back. John kissed her chin and tasted her velvety throat savoring her neck, which caused her nipples to get hard as a rock.

"Wow!", she said. "That is a kiss!"

"Think nothing of it, my sweet", John said majestically.

"But John!", she protested. "I felt a very deep feeling from you, right down to my groin, and I could also feel your heartbeat within your lips. I ... I know, I can't ask anymore. I have to trust you. I'll take your advice. If I am excited, I'll go relieve myself with the girls. What are their names?"

"We call them the 'sisters'", John laughed. But they are Janice, Michelle, Debra, Antoinette and Gladys.

"They are quite an experience. Of that I can assure you, judging by what I have seen, but nevertheless they are very delicate."

"Penis women", she laughed, shrugging her shoulders. "That's a tough concept to swallow."

"They will give you all the sex you need when you need it, my love", John uttered like the grand patriarch of flulfihlment he was pretending to be.

"It will last for three to five hours, depending upon your needs to be serviced."

"In five hours I'm just getting started". Kim joked, although John mistakenly took her seriously.

"All the more reason why it will be kept secret", he rationalized, "Because even the other girls on the yacht do not know. You can bring them to your room, and if you are not satisfied with that, then I will fly you to any country you like for a few days and you can invite one or two intimate friends from the states."

"You are turning me on, John honey", she answered, pawing him slightly.

"Let's just say that I'll be very content going wherever you go, anywhere and everywhere. Strange how life is, though."

"Why is that?", John inquired.

"You kiss me and excite me, and then they have to finish the job!", she blurted out with more honesty than anyone should have to tolerate. John thought before answering.

"Let us say that is what we are dealing with for the moment", he concurred. "And I need one more favor from you …"

"What is it, my beloved?", Kim asked, not knowing what other cataclysm was coming, if any.

"Try not to be naked around me, or walk around the suite naked, please!", he exclaimed with a supplicant voice.

"Why?", Kim snapped. "Do I excite you too much? Does it drive you crazy?"

John's eyebrows dropped and he suddenly became far too serious. Kim looked at his mood swing and said, "Okay, okay … I understand;no more questions. But now I need one more favor, and that's another kiss, and it better be one of your best ones!", she said with a childish expression.

Obligingly, he took her in her arms, thirsting of her beyond belief, pressing her wonderful body against his, and in

desperation, kissed her neck, face, while his hands grabbed her backside, his mouth finding its way onto one of her breasts. Then, as suddenly as he started, he stopped, and ran into the master bath to take a cold shower.

"Shit!", she said to herself, every bit of her quivering for more.

"What passion, wow! Why do you always have to exercise so much damned self-control! Can't you just let go and take me? This game where you reach from me and withdraw from me makes me desire you even more, as if you are playing me like a flute! What can your terrible secret be where you can't have sex with me?", she sobbed, whispering to herself in agony.

She felt the remnants of his burning lips all over her face, neck and breasts which were hotter than a witch's tits holding firecrackers on the Fourth of July. His strong hands had left a lasting impression on the delicious cheeks of her bun. She was so aroused that she began touching herself as tears of isolated frustration flowed from her almond-shaped green eyes onto her flamingly exquisite red cheeks.

She wanted him more than life itself John came out of the shower whistling an Israeli army tune, his hair still wet and a towel wrapped around his waist. He didn't even look at her, still kneeling and naked in the bed, the same way he left her.

Finally, he said, "I am so sorry, I shouldn't have done this. I was so wrong for making you so hot. But if we make love now, it could end my life in many ways. That's why I have decided that

if everything goes right, I will tell you everything you want to know in three months."

She looked at his soul as if she were peering through the window of a lockdown ward of an insane asylum.

"Sorry", he added flirtatiously.

"This man is going to drive me out of my mind", she told her inner self. "I'd better chill out."

Like a robot, she wrapped herself in the sheet and went toward the shower. When she was done, she found a note on the dresser.

"I'm going to my office", he said dispassionately. "If you wish to join me, call Bashir on the intercom and ask him to drive you there. Goodbye."

Trembling, she was still consumed with rage, desire and overwhelming sadness. She knew that he desperately wanted her, but some dark secret was keeping him from consummating his need for her special love. Undaunted, she got dressed and went to the top deck to have breakfast.

On the verandah, she encountered Kathy, the yacht's Director of Personnel and Efficiency Expert, who was laying out on the sun deck in a see-through blouse with a silk brown sash draped over her backside.

"Morning, Miss Kim", she said as she gazed at the yacht's first lady with a curious glance.

"How are you feeling? Some of the girls said you were pretty sick last night."

"I feel a lot better now … ", Kim answered, trying to recall her name.

"Kathy", she smiled.

"I'm the one who gets things done around here, where perfection is a way of life rather than an unattainable goal, which reminds me that your hair needs to be combed out in the back."

"I just got up", Kim replied, excusing herself. "Did my fiancee leave?"

"Actually, yes, he left in a hurry", Kathy laughed.

"But certainly you would know that! He looked so very sad, the poor precious thing. Is everything all right? No trouble in paradise, I hope."

Kim got the feeling that Kathy was a bit of a troublemaker with an attitude. Nevertheless, she maintained her composure.

"Oh, we couldn't be happier!", she gloated pretentiously in a distant manner.

"He is just very concerned about one of his business deals, and did not want to wake me up. He is such a good-natured considerate love."

"I know all about him, my dear", she snickered. "Now, would you like some breakfast? It would be my honor to serve you."

"Just some dry toast and decaffeinated tea", Kim winced.

"I don't believe in eating heavy breakfasts. It puts weight on in the wrong places. By the way, could you phone Bashir for me? I need him to drop me off at John's office."

"He's never up this early, but for you, Miss Kim, I'll wake him", she promised as she waved her arm in the air in a condescending gesture.

"Ever since Bashir has let Serpentina move into his cottage on the dock, he never gets up on time, and if it were up to me, I'd fire him and replace him with a billy goat."

"Who is Serpentina?", Kim asked her, unfamiliar with a name like that.

"Oh, she's the snake lady at the Monte Carlo circus", Kathy explained. That's not her real name, and Bashir just calls her Tina. She wears this yellow body suit and always has a rattlesnake with her. Gladys, one of the sisters, told me that she saw Serpentina French-kissing the snake. Bashir must really like her to put up with a snake in his bed."

"I'm going to have to find Bashir someone normal to go out with", Kim said.

"Some nice girl without any weird pets or sexual hang-ups."

"Normal? Who wants 'normal'?", Kathy scoffed. "Normal is boring!", she added as she left the room to call Bashir.

Kim scratched her head. "Yeah, I keep forgetting where I am … On the ship of fools with a bunch of hermaphrodites and buildikes and a sweet but secretive guy who likes me but won't touch me!", she said to herself, shrugging her shoulders once more. "What a madhouse!"

As Kim was finishing her toast, Kathy came running back up to the top deck, out of breath and all agitated.

"Sorry, Miss Kim, but I'm going to have to ask Josianne to drive you. Bashir was rushed to the hospital. The snake tried to swallow his balls and they had to call an ambulance. I hope they don't have to castrate him."

"Oh, how horrible!", Kim cried. "Don't worry about me, go see if you can do anything for Bashir. Does he need anything from his cottage at the hospital?"

"Just a new set of nuts!", Kathy screamed as she ran downstairs in a wild panic, mumbling something about who was going to drive the limousine until Bashir got better.

"Tell Josianne to take her time", Kim yelled down the stairway.

"It will take me twenty minutes to get ready anyway."

Kim turned around, feasting her eyes onto the harbor, which is always such a beautiful sight.

"Monaco Bay on a day without clouds, where the water was shimmering as if it were oil; what could be nicer than such a vision", she thought silently.

She adored how the cool breeze from the water's mist refreshed her face. Loving it, she breathed in deeply, filling her lungs.

"What a delightful morning, except for what happened to poor Bashir",she said.

"John, John. … What a sad disappointment I could not have you when I awakened;would still be in your arms."

Kim shook her head sadly.

"I won't despair", she advised herself. "He will fall in love with me. I know he desires me."

She went to her suite and dressed herself in white shuns and a pink blouse with short sleeves. She looked exquisite, as always. Josiatme met her at the bridge of the boat and Kim followed her.

"I don't have Bashir's keys to the limousine", Josie apologized, "so I'm afraid we'll have to make do with the Rolls Royce."

"Hey, it's cooler looking than the Dodge Dart I drove in high school", Kim answered.

And indeed it was a stunning cherry red Corniche convertible with pearlized leather seats and a custom ivory trim instead of the standard mahogany.

"I guess they had to kill a herd of elephants to make this dashboard", Kim commented studiously to Josianne.

"Actually, John requested that the ivory be extracted from older pachyderms that died of natural causes", Josianne explained.

"John is a genuine humanitarian who loves animals and would never take an elephant's life just for the ivory."

"I bet he won't have that many kind words for the snake that got Bashir", Kim said.

"This car has such a great leather smell! I love it!", she added.

"It's brand new", Josianne replied. "The boss bought it yesterday for you. It was supposed to be gilt wrapped in a white bow but Bashir forgot to do it, and now you see how fate paid him back."

"He never said anything about it", Kim said in semi-shock.

"I saw him this morning before you got up", Josianne said. "He looked pretty sad, but he told me to give you the car after breakfast as a token gesture of his affection. He left a card in the car for you."

Josianne took the card from the glove compartment and handed it to her. It had a montage of dehydrated rose petals in every color of the rainbow inside.

"Rose petals actually smell a lot better shortly after they die", Josianne originated proudly.

"That's a morbid thought", Kim analyzed to herself as she read the card.

"To my beautiful princess and future wife", John had written, gorgeous as all of the roses in the world together. Please accept this small present as a sign of my love ... John."

Tears flowed freely from Kim's lovely eyes as she read his proposal. "Is everything okay?". Josianne asked.

Kim looked at her and wanted to share her joy. She decided to hand her the card. Josianne was only too curious to read it.

"I didn't know that the boss was so romantic!", she exclaimed.

"He must love you very much, and you are so fortunate, because he normally never confides in anybody. You are so lucky to have his trust."

"I never tell secrets, that's why", Kim bragged.

Josianne sat in the passenger's side of the Corniche, just daydreaming as Josianne drove off, with tears of both joy and sadness freely intermingling down her perfect cheekbones. She wiped them dry first with the back of her hand, and then with one of the crimson monogrammed handkerchiefs which she found neatly stacked in the glove compartment. is not my initials", she protested. "It's K.W."

"That's Kathy for you", Josianne laughed.

"She's such an economist. She did not want to bother ordering a second set after you marry John. She's our efficiency expert, you know, keeping everyone from going over budget."

"Oh, yeah", Kim realized. "That would be a waste of money."

Josianne stopped the car at the main entrance of a tall glass office tower. In giant letters made of bronze, it read: 'The J.K.E. International Building.'

"What does the name J.K.E. stand for?", Kim wondered curiously, asking Josianne.

"I don't have a clue, although the joke on the yacht is that the letters stand for 'John Kisses Everybody', although you might not find that so very funny", Josie snickered.

"I've asked him various times, but as usual, he was evasive. Maybe you can pump it out of him, Miss Kim. No one else has had any success."

The doorman opened Josianne's door first.

"You should have opened up the other side, Pierre", she scowled.

"She's the princess, I'm just the Chief Medical Assistant, which is nothing more than a glorified nurse."

"Hello, Pierre", Kim said politely.

"Be careful how you park this thing", Josianne waned him. 'This belongs to Miss Kim here, the boss' fiancee."

"Oui, mademoiselle", Pierre answered, not understanding any English at all.

They took the elevator to the penthouse floor. The door opened to an atrium salon where at least twenty well-dressed secretaries were working on word processors. Suddenly, Josianne clapped her hands to get the attention of the secretarial pool.

"Say hello to Miss Kim, the boss's fiancee!", she shouted, which was highly embarrassing to Kim, who did not expect such a fanfare. They all stood up and came toward the elevator in single file to shake hands with the most famous lady in Monaco.

Each one feasted her eyes on this rare and unique American beauty, complimenting her excessively. Within moments two of the girls brought bouquets of flowers to her, showering her with more attention.

Josianne had called in ahead and told them to expect Kim's arrival, and Kim had no idea this was going to happen.

"What do I do with all these gladiolas and geraniums?", Kim asked Josie, as by now she was slightly bewildered.

Josiane snapped her fingers and three other secretaries grabbed the flowers and carried them behind the procession as Josianne led her through an inner chamber of four more exotic looking secretaries; thereafter entering a very spacious antechamber room where John's personal secretary worked.

She was typing on one of John's Pentium super-computers, and without looking, she asked, "Yes? Can I help you?"

"Hi, Gina!", Josianne said cheerily. "This is Kim, the boss's fiancee!"

Gina jumped out of her chair, and nearly out of her skin. She was an exquisite brunette, with blue-gray eyes and a body to die for.

She was about six feet tall, with prominent breasts which and a round shape. The freckles on her nose and cheeks only enhanced her beauty, although they were barely visible to the naked eye.

"Gina"

"Gina, this is Miss Kim", Josie proudly announced.

"Oh, welcome. I have heard so many delightful things about you from my cousin Felicia. It's a real pleasure to finally meet you."

"The pleasure is all mine. And Felicia is so very lovely too!", Kim said with glee, frightened inside as to how much Felicia had told Gina.

"You look a lot alike, and both so beautiful", Kim added.

But there was tension with Gina. There was an instant jealousy between the two women, as Kim felt very insecure about such a magnificent creature working so closely with John, and Gina

couldn't stand the thought of John engaged to anyone else but herself!

"It's only his secretary", Kim rationalized to herself.

"I shouldn't be so worried", she thought silently.

"Still it is such a mystery to me why John did not choose one of these outstanding female creatures who work so close to him, these goddesses of beauty and grace. Why did he choose me from a naked picture in an adult magazine? He can have any girl he wants, being the richest man in the world. It's probably a mystery to Gina, to Josianne, and to all the secretaries in this office, but here I am, and that's it!"

Gina tiptoed to her switchboard and called over the intercom, "Mr. Miss Kim is here."

There was no response.

"He's probably in the conference room with his guest", Gina replied, making excuses as only she knew best.

"He must have forgotten to tell me."

"Don't worry, Gina", Josianne reassured her. "We will wait there."

Without waiting for approval from Gina, who was starting to resent their presence tremendously, Josianne opened a very impressive double door made out of gold and silver metallic electroplate.

Inside, John's office was colossal, measuring 108 feet in circumference, being entirely round. In the center of the salon was a ruby drinking fountain statuette in the shape of a flamingo which sported purified Zephyrhills drinking water. On the north side of the office was a wet bar containing four hundred bottles of Manischevitz, Mogen David and Cannel Almog vintage wines from the 1940's.

The bar stools were covered in foxfire sable and adjacent to the bar was a mother-of-pearl grand piano with a diamond Lucite candelabra which Sharron had bought from the Liberace estate. There was a gigantic one-way mirror that overlooked the Executive Conference Room.

Kim observed that there were a lot of people in it, and John was right there in the middle of them all, as big as life, explaining the contents of a video which could be seen through a giant 42 foot screen, although I could not understand what it was all about,

"Can he see us, Josianne?", Kim asked.

"No, this is a one-way mirror", she replied. "We can only see them."

Kim watched as John picked up the telephone, looked at the mirror, and excused himself to everyone, giving the floor to an old woman dressed in a hand-woven sweater, wearing a Linny basket hat with a pink rose on it. Everyone applauded when she started to speak.

"Who is that?". Kim asked in surprise.

"That's John's Aunt Yetta, the lady who taught John everything he knows about the world of business and finance", Josianne said.

"She's seventy-seven years old, smart as a whip, and runs nine of John's companies and is his partner in thirty-six of them. Believe me, Miss Kim, that's the one person you've got to impress around here, because if she doesn't like you, there is no way in the world you'll ever get to marry John."

"Aunt Yetta"

"I can't wait to meet her", Kim replied, rolling her eyes sarcastically.

"She's a tough old battle-axe", Josianne said comfortingly.

"She likes to chew everybody up for breakfast. But John is the apple of her eye. If anybody ever tried to hurt him, she'd carve them a brand new asshole."

"That wouldn't condescendingly feel too comfortable", Kim responded Suddenly Kim recognized one of the people in the conference room. It was that beautiful catty witch, the Baroness Lady Helena-Celeste, the one who had invited her to the tennis party.

She did not like her at all, and especially not so close to John. Kim wanted John all to herself and was extremely jealous of her.

John walked to the back door of his office, which was open. Kim ran to him, as if she had not seen him in a long time. Immediately she embraced him, wrapping her arms around his neck and offering him her appetizing lips which he gladly accepted.

"Thank you, my love, for the beautiful card", she cried. "It was more precious to me than the car itself. I will love you forever for it."

Mother kiss convinced him of her sincerity.

"That was a very tasty kiss, my darling", John acknowledged.

"You are very, very welcome!". Kim answered rather seductively.

"Josianne, where is Bashir?", John asked. "What are you doing here?"

"Bashir is in the hospital with an unfortunate accident", Josianne began.

"He was bitten by a snake ... well... sort of"

"We don't have snakes in Monaco!", John yelled. "That is ridiculous."

"I'll explain later, honey". Kim interrupted. "We'll visit him in the hospital this afternoon and cheer him up."

"Well, Josianne, thank you for bringing Kim to me". John said as he calmed down, "I'll take care of her from here. You drive

the Aston Martin back to the yacht because it is in the tower garage."

"I'll treat it like a baby", Josie promised as she walked towards the exit.

"And have twelve dozen roses delivered to Bashir's hospital room", John ordered as he opened the door for Josianne. Kim admired John's gentlemanly and courteous habits.

Even though Josianne was just another employee, he treated her like an important person and like a lady.

Once alone, Kim took his hand and kissed it.

"I am sorry about this morning", she said apologetically.

"It won't happen again. I'll be patient and wait until you are ready to open up to me. But know this with certainty, that every day I am learning to love you more and more. I have never met anyone quite like you."

John invited her to sit on a sealskin couch that had been a gift from Boris Yeltsin.

"You don't have to apologize for anything, my sweet love", he reassured her. "I am the one who should say I'm sorry due to my impulse of the morning. I lost my head. Please forgive me."

He took her hand, gently turning it and brought it to his lips and presented her with a long, warm kiss. She caressed his hair with the other hand.

Suddenly the door burst open and there was Aunt Yetta, waiving her umbrella at John.

"Decided to take the day off?", she asked with a gleam of terror in her eye.

"So this is the American shiksa you are all hot and bothered over!"

"American what?", Kim asked, looking at John.

"It means a Christian girl", he answered quickly. "Aunt Yetta, this is my beloved fiancee Kim, my pride and joy."

Yetta looked her over like she was a piece of meat in a butcher shop.

"Can you cook him a meal?", Yetta inquired suspiciously.

"Aunt Yetta, we have a complete kitchen and galley staff on the yacht", Shirnon argued annoyingly. "I didn't fall in love with Kim because of her culinary skills."

"Actually, if I may say something, ma'am", Kim interrupted, "now that you're asking, I can put together a meal of pork chops and potatoes that will have you begging for seconds!"

"She eats pork!", Aunt Yetta said disapprovingly.

"I can make fried chicken if you'd rather have that", Kim offered affectionately.

"You don't fry chicken you boil it!". Yetta screeched.

"Then you throw some carrots and matzo bails into the pot. Didn't your mother teach you how to cook? Where are you from, anyway?"

"Van Nuys, California", Kim answered. "Ever been there?"

"What kind of family do you have? Have they accomplished anything?"

"Not a hell of a lot", Kim snapped, fighting back.

"My brother is sort of retarded, my sister is a nymphomaniac who likes to screw anybody she can get her hands on, my mother is a drunk who has been married a bunch of times; and she smokes cigarettes all day and watches soap operas. My father is a gambler and a drifter who used to punch my mother in the stomach and I haven't seen him since I was twelve. Oh, and we also have a French poodle that's trained to piss on the rug. And my background is probably as white- trashy as you can get, but I pulled myself out of that mess, got an education, got into modeling, and this year I'll be earning more than five million dollars. I know I don't have the proper pedigree, but there's no one in the world who is better for your nephew here, and we are going to get married with or without your blessing!"

Yetta looked at John and smiled.

"She stood up to me. I like that!", she admitted.

"Of course!", John interjected.

"She insists on being treated with respect."

"You still better learn how to cook", Yetta warned. "John's not used to hillbilly food and he doesn't eat pork!"

"Well, one day when you are in a better mood, you can teach me a few of your favorite recipes", Kim said, offering her an olive branch.

"I used to look as good as you fifty years ago", Aunt Yetta told her.

"Now I'm an old dried up prune, but I can still run this businesses and I can certainly put together a nice Jewish meal. Eventually sex and lust dies, and a woman's crotch turns gray and gets dust all over it from not being used. You'd better learn what's important to John, because sometimes my favorite nephew here can be a real big pain in the ass. A man's heart is through his stomach, and if all you can feed him is a good lay in the sack, you'll wind up being nothing more than part of his harem on his wacky boat, or some figurehead in his trophy case."

"Enough unsolicited advice, Aunt Yetta?", John asked, trying his hardest not to be disrespectful.

"Look, I can talk to you like that, John", she continued. "That's because I love you. I used to stand him up on the toilet seat when he was three years old and wash his nuts with a hot cloth so I can just about tell him anything, what's your name again, girlie?"

"It's Kim", she answered.

"Kim, that's a Korean last name". Yetta blabbed on. "Who ever gave you a name like that?"

"It's short for Kimberly", she explained.

"Oh, Kim, Kimberly, what's the difference!", Yetta scowled.

"The point I am making is that you can't monopolize John's time. He's got an empire to run. I'm not going to live forever. Why don't I have my driver take you back to the boat and I'll send over some recipes for chopped liver. John always liked that, but you'll never make it as good as I do."

"With all due respect, Aunt Yetta", Kim quipped, "I fully intend to be the driving force behind my man, accompanying him not only to social events but to business meetings. Now I have a role model to look up to, and that's you, so excuse us because John and I have customers to greet in there."

Yetta winked to John.

"She's not a wimp like your ex-wife Mazel. When she talks back to me and makes sense, she scores one notch higher in my book, even if she is a shiksa. This one has promise", she decreed to John.

"Anyway, I've had enough excitement for one day. I'm going over to the commodity broker. I'm short 200 contracts of live hogs and they are down the limit for five days in a row so I'm

going to take my profits and run like hell. You get in there with your cutie pie and handle the business, John. I'm out of here."

Yetta left, calling for her driver on her cellular phone.

"Interesting lady", Kim observed. "She won't eat pork but she trades live hogs. I've got to write that one down in my diary."

"She made a lot of money trading pigs", John explained. "And more importantly, I think she likes you."

"Somehow, you shouldn't have put those thoughts in the same sentence", she whispered to herself.

"Now that you have survived your first meeting with my lovely aunt, I want to introduce you to the people in the conference room. They are very important customers of mine", John said.

"Is the Baron's daughter also your customer". Kim inquired enviously.

"Actually, she is", John admitted. "Lady Helena-Celeste spends most of her time here and gives me all of her business."

"She wants you, not what you are selling", Kim suggested.

John smiled.

"In a sense you are correct", he agreed.

"But I am not interested in her in the least. Are you telling me that you are a bit jealous?"

"Possibly", Kim said. "She is very beautiful, in a plastic, transparent sort of way. Why is it that you haven't pursued her?"

"You are once again asking very personal questions, my princess", he warned.

"Maybe I can get a straighter answer out of your Aunt Yetta!", she blurted out in an exasperated tone. But then suddenly Kim came to her senses, and her facial expression restored itself to normal.

"No, I'm not using the right approach, John", she stated gratuitously. "I'll be nice to her, don't worry. I won't come between her business dealings with you. I'll try to be her friend, okay?"

"That's my delicious girl", he beamed, kissing her invitingly thin nose.

"Let us go."

"I'm not going to kiss her ass neither!", Kim thought to herself, not expressing her anxiety to John.

"I'm not dressed properly for this business meeting", Kim questioned.

"I look too casual."

John lifted her chin with his finger and said, "My loveliest of lovelies, you look simply divine in whatever you wear, or

even when you are wearing nothing at all but a sheet draped around you."

Kim loved his compliments, in fact she sustained herself and thrived on them. She slowly kissed his finger and said, "Thank you for being so supportive of me, and for defending my honor in front of your Aunt. That must have been hard for you to do, since she is such a powerfbl lady and you respect her so much."

"She's my buddy", John laughed. "I can confide in her about anything. We have no secrets from one another. We are family." Ignoring the implication of that remark, Kim took him by the arm and held it with her two hands, and jointly they entered the conference room. Everyone stopped chattering and looked at the two of them as they graced the room with their grand entrance.

"Ladies and gentlemen". John announced, "this is Kim, the lady I intend to marry."

Everyone stood up and applauded. John and Kim walked around the large royal blue onyx oval conference table and shook hands with everyone. When the Baroness' turn came, Lady Helena-Celeste said to Kim, "Hi, love. You look wonderful today", and kissed Kim on her cheek.

"It is simply marvelous to see you again too!", Kim replied, trying to conceal her contempt as much as possible.

"I am expecting you Friday at my villa for a tennis party", Helena- Celeste said to Kim.

"Oh, not this Friday", John interrupted. "I am flying Kim to Paris to meet some more of my family."

Kim was quite relieved.

"I'll take a rain check for another day, all right?", she responded, trying to smooth things over.

"I don't know how things are done in America", Helena-Celeste scoffed, "but here in Monte Carlo, we don't play tennis in the rain."

"You should build an indoor tennis court on your property, Baroness",

Kim answered combatively. "Then it can snow for all we care."

"Oh, how adorable", Helena-Celeste acknowledged mockingly.

"I'll tear down the servants' quarters and start building it brick by brick right away."

Seeing she was going nowhere fast, Kim simply ended the conversation, telling her that she would not miss another opportunity to play tennis next time.

"I will be indeed looking forward to it", the Baroness answered with a fake smile, after which they both exchanged fake hugs and sneers. Needless to say, the men's tongues were hanging out like junkyard dogs as they mentally undressed John's angel in disguise. Predictably, John sat Kim next to him, and then took over the meeting.

"I now have acquired total control of the factories needed to produce all these special computer chips in Israel's silicon valley. I intend to provide the highest quality and service at the most competitive price. Do not forget that even our competition, the United States and Japan are ordering from us. Buying from me means buying from the source. The only viable supplier in the Mideast is Sheik Mechmet Ali Kusemach of Abu Dhabi, and his technology is three years behind mine. He is still making chips for 486 computers and he charges forty-five percent more than I do across the board."

Everyone nodded theft head in vast approval.

"You have in front of each of you a file listing the latest products and services in my conglomerate", he continued. "You will see that I have spared no expense for research into new and innovative technologies. I humbly request that you study these documents, and if you have any questions, please contact my lovely Aunt Yetta Blashinsky, who as you know is my Operations Manager and Chief Information Officer and accordingly is imminently qualified to answer any of your questions, inquiries and requests. Kim and I thank you all for coming, and for your continuous business and support."

John stood up, and everyone followed suit, applauding like there was no tomorrow. With Kim in hand, John left through a rear door. The Baroness rushed after them, first kissing Kim the way a crow kisses a worm, afterward stealing a kiss from John, sandwiching his lips in hers in a moist, wet kiss. Kim was boiling but just smiled.

"I have some mouthwash, my darling", Kim whispered to John gracefully. Lady Helena-Celeste pretended not to hear Kim's remark, and instead turned toward John and said, "Thank you for the delightful presentation, my love. I hope to see you again real soon. You too, Kim." She followed the others out, lifting and swaying her butt in order to keep John's attention fixated upon her. But John was looking squarely at Kim, and laughed hysterically when he noticed her facial expression.

"Oh, how I hate that bitch!", Kim cackled, grinding her teeth. Still in plain sight of the Baroness, who had turned around once more to look at John, Kim hugged him tightly with her two arms, and kissed his chest, as if to say:

"You're mine". John took her out of the building, suggesting that they have lunch in France in the town of Nice.

"We should visit Bashir first in the hospital", Kim reminded bàn.

"Good thinking", John agreed, as they drove over to the Monte Carlo Medical Center Complex where John maintained his own private wing of the hospital. Dr. Anatoly Ukutchikokoff was the finest surgeon of urology that money can buy.

Formerly the Chief of Staff at the University of Providenya in Eastern Siberia, he was known the world over for his grandiose invention, a do-it-yourself circumcision kit, and had been.

The personal physician of Soviet President Gorbachev, performing six prostate operations on him alone during a six

month period. Acclaimed as well beyond a genius, John always felt honored to discuss medicine with this great healer.

"It's so good to see you, Dr. U.", John smiled as he hugged him.

"I heard you received that multi-million dollar grant I arranged for you. I saw you were on the cover of the European Journal of Medicine for the first successful sex change operation ever done on a dog. And now it's great to know that you have been taking good care of my faithful driver. How is Bashir, by the way?"

"He's in a lot of pain, my Mend", the good Doctor answered. "We were able to save one testicle. I'm afraid the snake got the other one."

"What a tragedy!", Kim said, quite in shock at the news.

"Dr. Anatoly Ukutchikokoff, can we see him?", John asked patiently.

"Yes, he's resting comfortably in there, John", Doctor U. said as he pointed toward the suite at the end of the hall.

When they entered the room, Bashir was crying his eyes out. "Oh, John, I am in such pain!", he whimpered.

"You'll be all right", John comforted him with reassurance. "I'm sure you will feel much better in a couple of days."

"I can't feel a thing down there", Bashir corrected him. "They shot me up with pain killers. That's not what I'm crying about."

"What's wrong?", Kim asked.

"Police Chief Koenig shot the snake, and Tina got so mad at me for that she left me forever. I love her so much!", he explained.

"Plus, somebody sent me dozens of roses and I'm allergic to them. I've been sneezing my head off!"

Kim left the room to call a nurse in order to have the roses immediately removed.

"You know it's the law in Monaco to kill an animal when it attacks a human being, Bashir", John sighed.

"Koenig had no choice."

"I know, John", Bashir wept. "This operation was dreadful. Do you think I can ever have children?"

"Well, maybe not twins", John joked.

"Lots of people can manage with just one ball. But tell me, how did this happen?"

"I was jack-hammering her", he started to explain.

"You were what?", John asked, unclear as to what he was talking about.

"I asked Tina to stand on her head against the wall, and then I began pumping her upside down. In Syria we call this the

jack-hammer position. It's really quite pleasurable for the man. For the woman, I don't know. Maybe, because all the blood rushes to her head. So there I was, having the time of my life when all of a sudden her snake thought I was hurting her and attacked me without warning from behind, tying to swallow my nuts when I screamed and passed out! Kathy said she will see if this accident can be covered by workman's compensation."

"I don't give a damn about the money!", John yelled. "I just want you to get better! You might not be the same for awhile, perhaps with less

"But I was the best in bed!", Bashir agonized.

"What woman will look at me now?"

"Don't worry!", John promised.

"We'll pay one enough to look at you!"

"Ah, you're the greatest friend anyone could ever have, John", he admitted.

"I know", John said.

"And I brought Kim here to cheer you up. Snake charmers are a dime a dozen. We are your family. Always remember that."

Kim returned into the room with three handymen who removed the flowers.

"You are such a sweetheart", Bashir told her

"I feel so bad that I can't drive you all around town right now."

"You're going to take the whole month off with double pay and that's an order!", John insisted.

"And if this circus witch is blaming you for the dead snake, we can assure her. Better yet, I'll have her exiled from the entire country!"

"I just want her back in my arms", Bashir cried.

"Very well", John reluctantly agreed, throwing up his hands and scratching his head.

"Kim, get Gina on the phone, and tell her to buy Bashir's girlfriend ten snakes, and make sure they are exotic ones. But I want you to promise me as a brother that you will never sleep with any of them again!"

"May Allah bless you forever", Bashir prayed in deep thanks.

CHAPTER 9

K im called Gina and told her to order the snakes.

"Is this a joke?", Gina said suspiciously. "Where the devil am I going to buy them?"

"You're the executive secretary; you go figure it out!"

Kim snapped as she slammed the phone down hard on Gina's ear. Gina was fuming like a hot lava cauldron as she sat at her office desk moping and seething.

"She is the lucky winner of the biggest fortune in the world", she said to herself.

"What does that blonde bimbo have more than me?"

Obviously Kim was besieged with a lot of jealous competition. Women like Gina, Kathy, and Helena-Celeste smiled to her face, but hated and resented her. They concerned themselves with one thing alone: money, not John's body nor personality.

Kim new better. John was a super-nice person, not a hunk, and not someone a girl would fall in love with at first sight.

Knowing him very intimately made the difference. Seeing how he respected her and did not take advantage of her when he could have, that is what attracted her to him. The money enhanced his personality, but he did not flaunt it to extremes.

Upon leaving the hospital, John handed Kim the keys to the Corniche.

"I already called Orly in Nice", he said.

"She is going to meet us for lunch with her husband, who is a dentist; a very nice guy. You drive, baby."

"I don't know the roads!", Kim pleaded.

"Plus I never drove your car before."

"This is your car, Kim darling", John reminded her. "I trust your driving, and I'll show you where to turn."

With that vote of confidence, Kim drove off, quite happy about her new car, especially that she was alone with the man who gave it to her.

"I feel I know you all my life", she said.

"I know a lot about you too, my princess", he replied.

"You had a boyfriend Henry, who is a lawyer. I know a great deal about your family, your work, your studies, your friends, and even your childhood and teenage years. I know everything."

"You don't know everything!", Kim protested in surprise.

"But how is it you know as much as you do?"

"A man with my assets has many resources", he explained.

"I have detective agencies who work for me on retainer. Before I brought you here I found out all about you, even that you broke off your relationship with Henry because he was abusive. I can't say I'm sorry when in tact I am glad."

She pinched his thigh and smiled at him.

John picked up the cellular phone, dialed it and gave it to Kim.

"What's this for?", she asked. "Who did you call?"

"You'll see!", he laughed. A voice on the other end of the line said

"Hello." Kim's eyes were wide open.

"Mama, is that you?", she asked, all excited.

"Kimmy!", Iris said.

"Why did you take so long to call me? You about ready to pack it in and come on home? Where the hell are you calling me from anyhow? I hear a lot of noise in the background. Are you at the bus station?"

"No, silly!", she laughed. "I'm here in my car."

"Your car is right here in front of the house, dummy! It's as rusty as ever.", she argued.

"Are you on some kind of medicine?"

"No, mama", she interrupted.

"You don't understand. John bought me a brand new red Rolls Royce convertible today. It's a Corniche, and we are on our way to have lunch in Nice, France."

"Yeah, and I'm sittin' here with President Clinton, Hillary and the poodle, sippin' tea", she mocked.

"Did you call me up long distance at six in the morning just to yank my chain, Kimmy?"

"Oh, that's right! It's six hours earlier there! Sorry!", she realized.

"But honestly, I do have my own Corniche."

"They got you workin' on your back in a French cat house?", Iris asked in wonder.

"Have a little more faith in me than that, mama", Kim complained. "I just wanted to share my happiness with you. It's like I'm living in a dream, like some fairy princess, and I'm afraid to open my eyes for fear that I will awaken soon."

"Yeah, I heard they got plenty of fairies over there in gay Paree", his acknowledged. "You stay clear of them or you'll catch a death sentence that all the money in the world can't cure."

"It's not like that at all, mama", Kim continued. "I'm in the south of France, and Paris is way to the north. I've been to the royal palace and there is just too much for me to tell you right now."

John took the phone away from her and said, "Hi, Mrs. Wyndmere. This is John. How are you?"

"Wyndmere is Kim's name", she grunted, coughing her head off from the stench of unfiltered Camels. "Her daddy was my fourth husband. My name is Snodgrass. Iris Snodgrass."

"Oh, my apologies, Mrs. Snotgrass.", he quickly pleaded.

"Snodgrass, not Snotgrass!", she screamed. "Call me Iris. You foreigners can't hear what I'm saying too good over long distance. It's easier to pronounce if you speak English with such a thick accent."

"Yes, I've got it, Iris!", John repeated with an air of righteous indignation. "Anyway, your daughter is doing very well."

"You know, I've got nobody here to wash the dog. My back is out and the damn thing is getting fleas all over the carpet. I'd sure appreciate it if you sent my baby home so she can get her chores done."

"I'll do the next best thing", John proposed. "You give me your address and I'll send in a professional dog groomer to wash the poodle and to clean the carpet too! One of these days when you are up to it I will fly you out to Monaco to see your lovely daughter."

"Kimmy will give you the address, unless she forgot it already living in storybook land", she coughed, spitting all over the telephone receiver.

"Maybe I'll take you up on that trip of yours, John. I'll see ill can get my passport renewed. They took it away from me in 1968 for drunk driving, and it wasn't even my fault. I used to guzzle a lot of gin back then, but three quarts wasn't enough to affect my driving. That stupid deer walked right in front of my car and I know I was on the right side of the road. I can drive home from that roadside bar blindfolded."

"Well, you take care of yourself, my dear", John said politely as he tried to end the conversation. "Meanwhile please don't be concerned about Kim. She will live the life of a princess as long as she likes, and I promise to keep her safe, and fly you out here when you are ready."

"Just try not to knock her up", Iris advised compassionately. "I can't afford to pay for abortion like I had to fix Fluffmonkey.

"Like who?", John asked.

"That's my little poodle", she groaned. "I couldn't stand puppies all over the place. One even took a piss in my shoes. They were

my dancing shoes, but shit, I can't go dancing anymore. I'm too old, I've got emphysema from these stinkin' cigarettes and my back is killing me. Maybe those fancy French cigarettes are better for my lungs. Send me a carton, will you, honey?"

"I'll send you ten cartons!", John promised. "Meanwhile here is your daughter back. Nice talking to you."

"Same here", she mumbled, her cough thoroughly out of control.

"You okay, mama?", Kim asked.

"Yeah, I should stop smoking one of these days, probably after I'm dead", she choked. "So you like this guy, Kim? He sounds nice enough for a refugee."

"I'm in his country, mama", she corrected. "And I not only like him, I love him! He's a great guy. I'll call you later on from the yacht. Meanwhile, you put out that nasty cigarette, get some sleep, and later give Mike and Jenny a big hug from me, okay?"

"I can't sleep once you woke me up!", Iris yelled. "You oughta know that by now."

"Well, you take care, mama.". Kim whispered.

"Hey, can you send me any money?", Iris asked presumptuously.

"I'm nearly out of oxygen tanks, there's no liquor in the house, and I ran out of dog food and I can't keep giving him Big Macs to eat every day."

"I'll send you ten thousand dollars tomorrow, mama", Kim promised. "That will keep you going for a while."

"I'll believe it when I see it", Iris nagged. "Just send me five hundred, that's all I need."

"Don't worry about a that, mama", Kim sighed. "You take care. I love you."

"Bye", Iris said as she let the phone drop.

John glanced at Kim with a big smile.

"You love me?", he beamed. "Is that true? Or do you think you love me because of all the attention I get from all the girls that hover around me."

"Sugar, if you only allowed me to prove it to you once and for all, you'd be convinced!", she said mischievously.

"I don't doubt it for a minute", John laughed.

Two hours later, they arrived at an elegant restaurant in Nice. John's friends were there, anxiously awaiting them.

Orly was a brunette, 5' 5", and quite cute for a middle aged lady.

Her husband, Pierpont, was about 5'10", half-bald, and most likely in his late forties pushing fifty.

Orly was so excited to see them, she screamed with delight!

"John!!"

In mediocre English, Orly said, "Why John, she is such a cute baby, and so gorgeous!"

Her spontaneity and facial expressions were sincere. Kim liked her immediately.

"You are absolutely right, Orly", John agreed. "Kim is twenty-five and was a model for an elite magazine. She is driving me crazy, and makes me feel like a teenager all over again."

Kim beamed with joy at all of the flattery.

They ate at a Kosher restaurant called 'Yizkor's Place', where the food was excellent. It was the first time that Kim ever ate boiled cow's tongue on rye, and she loved it, although she told John that it would taste a lot better with cheddar cheese and Hellman's mayonnaise.

Two hours later they were on their way back to Monaco, after having invited the couple to come to visit on the following Friday and spend the weekend on the yacht. They were exhilarated at the prospect.

On the way back, Kim said, "I like Orly a lot. She seems sincere. But I have one question for you, John. Did you love her very much?"

"Well, I was fifteen years old", he reminisced. "It was puppy love. She was my first. We barely touched hands and a kiss on the cheek was as far as we went. That was thirty years ago,

can you imagine, but I kept good memories of her. You never forget your first love."

"You are a very special man, John". Kim sighed with unfulfilled passion stinging the air.

"Knowing you intimately makes me realize how very little I understand about love and people's hearts", he concluded. "My entire life has been geared toward business by aggressive influences like Aunt Yetta. In a sense I have led a very sheltered life when it comes to women."

"I know even less, but I do know how I feel toward you and it is like walking on air", Kim answered.

"Do you think I am a good man or a good match for you?", he asked in wonder.

"Oh yes!", she smiled. "I am sure of it!" John scratched his chin, analyzing her every word.

"Let us say that I met you in a club and you did not know me", he proposed hypothetically, "and I invited you to dance. Would you have accepted? Just answer sincerely."

Kim thought about that one long and hard.

"Probably not", she said. "First I'd want to know if you were a good dancer or if you had two left feet. Secondly, I think I would be scared to death of you because of your power, wealth and fame. And third, I don't speak five languages, I just know one."

"You know two", John corrected. "You have a master's degree in body language."

"I'm talking seriously!", she complained.

"Enough with the jokes! Today, even if you lost all of your fortune, G-d forbid, I would still love you and want you just the same. I truly mean it. It's the way I feel about you."

John's face was serene, and appeared totally confused at her answer.

"What's wrong?", she inquired in a startled manner. "Did I say anything wrong, my love?"

John caressed her face with his left hand and whispered:

"On the contrary, your words have warmed my heart tremendously, but there is still so little you genuinely know about me. Nevertheless, one day, I promise you thithftlly that you will know everything, and I hope then you will have the same opinion of me and not run away to the end of the earth as fast as fate can carry you. Some of us have rather large skeletons in our closet. Right now you are under no obligation to love me, but only to fake love in front of the world. If you pretend to love me as much as the photographer's camera as the glamorous model you are, I would be intensely satisfied. Therefore, you can be completely sincere with me all the time. Your contract is good for six months, with an option to renew for another six months at your discretion. After that, it will be totally up to you whether to stay or to leave. I don't want

you to answer now. It is far too early for you to know how you really feel. Later, in a month or two, you will find out more about everything. Then and only then you will know what you truly want."

"But will you ask me to leave after a year?". Kim asked, exhibiting the height of insecurity.

As if he were insulted, John barked, "Never! It will be solely your decision."

"I like that!", she smiled. "That gives me some hope. By the way, can I ask you a question regarding what you spoke to David about today concerning TCNN in America?"

"Sure!", John replied with enthusiasm.

"Why do you want to take control of a TV news station?", she wondered. "Why is that so important to you?"

"TCNN has the power to brainwash people around the world, and they are doing a great job", he explained, "They are left-wing radicals who are not presenting news to the general public in a fair way. They have the ability to destroy countries by turning public opinion against them, simply by propagandizing one side of the coin, hiding the truth on the other side totally. Half truth is not the whole truth. This station hates my native country, Israel. When I buy it or take control of the company that runs it, I'll fire all of the leftists and all of the political puppets who are in the pocket of the Palestinian Liberation Organization, and other terrorist enemies of my country like

Sheik Mechmet All Kusemach of Abu Dhabi. The sheik is a major financial contributor to TCNN, along with Colonel Khaddafi of Libya, Saddam Hussein of Iraq, and Yassir Arafat of the P.L.O. With TCNN in bed with these gangsters, they poison people's minds and promote racism and anti-Semitism. So for me, this is war; a war of power, psychology, economics and the mind."

"You sound like a Prime Minister!", she exclaimed. "I'd vote for you in a heartbeat."

"If there is anything I can do to stop the spread of hate and bigotry, I will do it at any cost", he promised.

"Anyway, if I didn't, Aunt Yetta will whip my ass, because she feels as strongly about this as I do, being a holocaust survivor. Kim, my darling, over the years I discovered the reasons for things, the cause of what moves empires and alternatively makes them crumble. TCNN is being subsidized by Lybia, Iraq, and Syria with hard currency and with gold bullion. They sponsor terrorism all over the world. The money they pay this network is used to spew venom to naïve audiences who accept the newscasts as uncontested facts. That I am against. It's my war, Kim."

She was stunned to sense so much emotion.

"Wow!", she reacted. "I saw fire coming out of your eyes, and felt the strongest energy emanating from your frustration, John. I like what you said and I am with you all the way, even if I don't know much about the politics involved. After

all, in Van Nuys, California, the most we have to deal with is which dogcatcher is running for re-election. I only voted once; for Ross Perot in the 1992 presidential election, and when he lost, I sort of gave up after that. If I can help, let me know what to do. Behind every powerful man there is always a remarkable woman", she admitted modestly. John bent toward her, and kissed her neck tenderly. She moaned from the heat and intensity of his kiss.

"Oh, I liked that!", she panted. "Can I have another one? Except, please wait until I stop the car because you almost just hit a kid on a bicycle."

John complied, after parking the Comiche, and kissing her cheek that had turned red from his passion.

After some heavy petting and the tell-tale implanting of a hickey or two, they arrived at the yacht.

"Go ahead up without me", John suggested. "I have an important meeting in an hour. Relax for the rest of the day. I'll be back late tonight."

Kim made a childish expression, showing her disappointment.

"Can't you take me with you?", she pleaded. "Don't leave me alone with all these oversexed gay women."

"I can't, my princess", John answered quietly. "It's very important. Please let me go, okay?"

Kim was thoroughly disgruntled, looking sad and despondent.

"I was hoping we could have spent the afternoon together, and that you would kiss me a lot, rekindling the fire in me."

"Sorry, my sweetness", John said as he moved away from Kim slowly. "I'll be back as soon as I can."

He kissed her gently, got into his car that was parked adjacent to hers, and departed into the city after planting one final kiss upon her forehead. On her way up to the master suite, Kim bumped her head on a fire extinguisher that was swaying to the movement of the boat as it was docked.

"I don't need you!", Kim yelled at the fire extinguisher. "I've got John to put all my fires out!"

CHAPTER 10

I t was four in the afternoon when Kim arrived back on the yacht. She waved to Kathy and went up directly to John's room and laid down in his bed, emotionally saddened that she could not go with him on his business trip. Exhausted from the day's events, she fell asleep. Sometime around six o'clock there was a soft knock at the door, which awakened her. It was Josie.

"Sorry to awaken you, Miss Kim", Josie apologized, "but the boss called but your phone was busy."

"This phone?", Kim replied curiously. "How is that? I didn't call anyone."

Suddenly she noticed that the phone had fallen off the bed onto the floor, undoubtedly having knocked it over in her sleep.

"What did John say?", Kim wondered.

"Just that he will be back around 2:00 A.M., and that you shouldn't wait up for him", she answered.

"That's it?", Kim asked, slightly confused.

"Yes, and he also told me to give you dinner", Josie said accommodatingly.

"Thank you, Josianne", Kim sighed, "but I am not hungry. I'll watch some TV for a while and then go to bed. Do you know if they have 'Melrose Place' in Monaco? That's my favorite show."

"What is 'Melrose Place'?", Josianne asked.

"An American night-time soap opera", Kim explained.

"You will find that this entire boat is one big soap opera, with steamier scenes than you get on TV", she laughed. "I'm afraid I don't know if we get the show or not."

"Well, I am tired anyway", Kim yawned.

Josianne smiled at her, and said "Good night, Miss Kim. Call if you need anything", emphasizing the word "anything." Josie's tone was sexually oriented, and Kim felt a sudden excitement, a sensation of lust between her thighs.

Kim smiled back at her and said, "Thank you, Josianne. You are sweet. I'll keep this in mind."

Josianne then kissed Kim on the cheek and left the room. Kim was immediately aroused and awakened with heightened female hunger. She thought about the "sisters", the hermaphrodites on the boat. As she laid in bed, all sorts of fantasies about the five girls crept into her head.

She picked up the phone, and dialed the cabin of the "sisters", which John had written down in the unlikely event that Kim got lonely.

The phone rang and one of the lathes answered, "Hello!"

Kim remained silent and then finally hung up. She felt ridiculous, not knowing what to say.

"What am I supposed to ask them: Come fuck me?", she asked herself.

Bored and no longer sleepy, she switched on the television. There was a movie playing, which of course was all in French, and poor Kim did not understand a word of it. Undaunted, she looked in the dresser drawer but did not find any interesting videos to watch.

The videos John had were all shareholder's reports on failed oil and gas limited partnerships.

"These really suck!", Kim screamed, throwing them all over the place.

She called Josianne on the house phone.

"Sorry to annoy you", Kim said, "But the TV is all in French and John's videos are the most boring things I have ever seen in my life. Are there any nice romantic movies in English on the boat that I could watch?"

"Let me see what I can find in the library", Josianne offered. "I will bring you whatever I feel you might like."

"That would be great!", Kim answered, much relieved.

Ten minutes later, Josianne knocked at the door, and came in with her blouse nearly all open, showing her exquisite breasts.

"I found these", she replied, handing three videocassettes to her.

"Thank you very much", Kim said, very grateful to Josie's kindness.

"Listen, if you're bored and need some company, just call me, okay?",Josianne replied, again with a seductive glance on her face.

"I like you a lot and I would love to be your close friend."

"I really like you too", Kim acknowledged.

"I might go later to the pool deck for some fresh air, and I'll look for you. You can count on it."

Josianne could not have been more than twenty-two years old. She looked cute and delicious, but Kim did not feel like she wanted this type of company right now. She wanted John, and only John.

His presence made her feel good, safe and primarily she loved his kisses and smooth touch. Consequently, she just said

"goodbye" and closed the door behind her. Kim put the video into the machine. It was a pornographic movie.

"Oh, shit! That's exactly what I need right now!", she growled. She tried all three titles and they were pretty much the same. Needless to say, she decided to watch one.

The plot involved a woman who made love to three men. The actress' mouth, vagina and anus were all being utilized at the same time. Kim became excited, and started masturbating to the video, moaning for John, who she wanted very badly.

After relieving herself she switched off the television and laid in bed, staring at the ceiling, trying to sleep, but to no avail.

Around 9:00 P.M. she couldn't take it any longer, and she couldn't take it any shorter either. She fantasized about being with the "sisters", making love to all of them.

"What would it be like?", she thought? "Should I or shouldn't I?" The debate raged on and on in her head.

"What the hell!", she decided.

"John knows about it. He even wrote down the telephone extension of their cabin for me to call them. So if he doesn't care, why on earth should I?"

Her nipples started to get hard just thinking about it, and her vagina became numb from mental frenzy.

Having made up her mind, she switched on the light and called the "sisters" cabin once again.

"Hello? Yes?", one of them answered.

This time, Kim was going to muster up enough courage to see things through.

"Hi ... this is Kim", she answered quietly. "I ..."

"Say no more. This is Michelle. I know what you need. The boss told us that you might be calling. Would you like me, or one of the others, or you want all of us? I think you might appreciate the variety and experience of something new and very pleasant. So what is your wish?"

"Michelle"

Kim stopped dead in her tracks for a moment, and with a trembling voice said, "Why not! Please come, all of you."

"Good choice!", Michelle responded with confidence. "We'll be upstairs in your suite in thirty minutes, after we all take a shower, take our aphrodisiacs and splash on some perfume. Or would you rather come here?"

"If it's all the same, this is a much bigger room with a great big bed and I think this will be far more comfortable", she suggested.

"I do have something to confess, Michelle. I have never been with more than one partner. I don't have a clue about what to do."

"Don't worry about it", Michelle reassured her.

"None of us ever have been with anyone outside of our little circle. We would do anything for the boss. Most of all, you are very beautiful and delicious. Go take a shower and relax for a little while, and we will all come upstairs. I know that you are very nervous. Don't be. We are all so very friendly, and we will do everything to please you. We will come up very soon."

Kim obliged and showered, but she was exceptionally uneasy, so much so that she wanted to cancel.

"I've never seen a 'he-she' before!", she muttered to herself. Kim was highly afraid of the unknown.

Suddenly, a knock at the door made her jump out of her skin. She opened it, with many excuses running through her head about why she cancel, but all that changed and fell by the wayside when she saw the beautiful ladies in front of her.

Thunderstruck, she was unable to talk at the sight of these lovely mutations of nature, but fortunately Michelle spoke first.

"Hi, Kim!", she said cheerily.

"I am Michelle. This is Janice, Debra, Antoinette, and last but not least, this is Gladys."

Michelle, Janice and Debra were blondes. Antoinette was a brunette, and Gladys had long, natural looking hair that wasn't one particular color or another.

"You are so stunning, Kim!", Michelle continued.

"We saw you when you arrived the other day. I see that you are trembling. Don't be nervous. You don't have to do anything. We will do it all. You just close your eyes, if you wish, and enjoy us." Kim was scantily clad in a white lace and gray satin see-through bathrobe. Michelle was the first to approach Kim and opened the robe very slowly. Janice took it off Kim's back, letting it drop on the floor. Kim shivered. The yacht's air conditioner blew a rush of cold air on her back. The five were drooling at Kim's sensational body. Kim was breathing so hard, she was ready to burst.

Michelle was the first to touch Kim's lips with the tip of her index finger.

"Shush, relax", Michelle smiled, as she tried to conceal her enormous erection. She brushed her lips on Kim's nose, giving Kim goose bumps all, over her body.

Then, with the fingers of her two hands, Michelle gently glided across Kim's face, very slowly. Janice did the same on her neck, descending upon Kim's soft shoulders. Debra and Antoinette followed suit by caressing her breasts with the back of their hands and dainty fingers. Kim's nipples hardened instantly. Gladys massaged and played with Kim's thighs in the same way.

Kim was trembling from so much excitement. Simultaneously Michelle motioned to the others with a subtle wink of her eye and at the same exact instant, all of their robes dropped to the floor, joining Kim's robe in one grand pile.

"You're so very beautiful, Kim", Michelle said. Kim's eyes were shut tight from the excitement, as droplets of female orgasmic fluid ran down her leg from her vagina.

"Open your eyes and look at me!", Michelle commanded. Kim did, but could not face her, because she was already in ecstasy and was slightly embarrassed.

"The party is just beginning!", Debra laughed.

Michelle lowered Kim's hand a little, which was partially covering her chest. Kim took a look at Michelle's amazing breasts and white silky skin, causing her to silently swoon. She looked downward at Michelle's lovely stomach, then focused on her penis, normal like any man's as it stood stiff as a soldier, already excited beyond belief.

"Please touch it, Kim", Michelle begged. "Don't worry, it's not going to bite you!"

Kim's hands slowly lowered, brushing up against Michele's thigh until she reached her destination.

"Ahh!", Michelle beamed with delight. "Now reach under my groin and tell me what you find there!", she giggled.

Kim obliged and found her vagina, as normal as can be, her hand fondling the lips of Michelle's hidden treasure, examining carefully the sensation of the wetness beneath them. Michele moaned with intense lust.

"You see!", Michelle reassured Kim. "We are just regular women, except we have an additional toy to make our lives more interesting."

In the meantime, Janice began massaging her neck down to her hips, applying some kind of exotic lubricant to Kim's delicious skin. Michelle and the other girls also applied the tangy oil to their hands. It smelled like violet roses, mixed with the aroma of boiled hibiscus flowers, which was exceedingly pleasant to breathe. Michelle continued massaging Kim's face, while Debra and Antoinette vigorously stimulated her breasts, as Gladys moved from Kim's thighs to her lower stomach.

Kim could feel the cheeks of her derriere massaged very slowly, in a sweet, penetrating sort of way.

Suddenly, Gladys' hand slipped in the middle and began rubbing Kim's cheeks up and down, stopping each time briefly to pay a visit to her rear entrance, sliding a finger inside it in order to introduce some of the lubricating jelly. Kim was overwhelmed by sensations she never quite felt before, moaning and shivering like it was her very first time. Gladys' finger played inside her, and at various times she compassionately added more lubricant to soften up the walls of her insides.

Debra and Antoinette started Kim's breasts while continuing to massage the outer perimeter of each, causing Kim to sigh little screams of passion from her open mouth, which Michelle seized with her lips and began kissing her with her tongue. Michelle continued to lick her palate, then pulling her tongue and gradually sucking it dry.

"Debra"

Gladys voraciously began licking Kim's stomach and hips, then slowly lowered her mouth to her perfectly shaved vagina, encountering on her way the interruption of Janice's busy hand on Kim's rear entrance.

Gladys continued repeating the same ritual, until the third time, she let her middle finger slide between the lips of Kim's vagina, causing Gladys to kiss Janice's finger by mistake. Kim moaned loud like a buffalo in heat. This did not deter Janice's determination one bit. Janice continued her massaging action until she introduced two fingers rapidly rubbing Kim's inside lining. In case you may have guessed, Kim had come already, not once but five times.

She felt her whole body in a state of frenzy, at the complete control of the five sisters. They all began licking Kim's body from head to toe, as the expert tongues of Janice and Antoinette did a dance inside Kim's vagina.

"Gladys"

The sisters did not miss a single spot with their tongues on Kim's body. "She is ready, Michelle", said Janice. Everyone knew what to do. Janice laid on the floor first, holding onto Kim by her hips, and directed her erect penis into the sanctified regions of Kim's magnificent clitoris. Antoinette and Debra helped out by spreading Kim's vaginal lips. Interestingly enough, Gladys had the largest penis of all, at least are from. Gladys moved the head of her extended equipment to the enticingly and inviting spread vagina, and suddenly shoved it inside her.

Kim felt a tremendous gust of pleasure which she never felt before, getting the royal treatment through her two passageways simultaneously.

"Antoinette"

Antoinette and Debra laid side by side next to Kim, their hearts pounding as they sucked Kim's nipples like it was going out of style. Their hands were all over Kim's thighs, keeping them spread and moistening lubricating jelly everywhere. There was no question that the bed sheets would have to be changed when the party was over. Antoinette and Debra were also getting hotter than a witch's fit.

Coincidentally, their penises wandered close to Kim's hands. Not wanting to leave her two sisters out in the cold, Michelle graciously took each of Kim's hands and gracefully placed them on her sisters' penises, which were very lubricated and ready for action. She coaxed Kim into closing both of her hands very gently and to very slowly masturbate both of them.

Kim felt the rigidity in her grip, and held on tightly without moving her hands until both of them started shaking and moving within Kim's exquisite grasp. Kim then proceeded on cue and started pumping them at the same pace.

Michelle threw caution to the wind and kneeled on top of Kim's head. "When I get into your delicious mouth", she whispered, "cover your teeth with your lips to make it feel pleasant."

"It's a good thing I don't have braces anymore", Kim reassured herself, shrugging a sigh of relief.

Suddenly Michelle took out a spray can that she had bought in a sex shop.

"I'm going to spray a little of this into your throat", Michelle said soothingly.

"It's a combination of hormone particles and absinthe. It will prevent you from gagging, even if I start throbbing down into your tonsils."

"I'm afraid of choking!", Kim replied apprehensively, never having been flicked in the throat before, even by her former abusive boyfriend.

"Don't worry, Michelle smiled. "I won't put my weight on you. I'll be holding myself up by my knees and elbows. This is easier than riding a bicycle. I'll do the 'in and out' thing. Just close your lips on my penis, so we can all enjoy each other and have

a good time." Kim did as she was told. After all, nobody gave her a rule book. She was winging it.

Kim flinched a little as she felt Michelle's penis penetrate her mouth, but as Michelle promised, the spray made it go down easy. Michelle began moving slowly in and out of her mouth. Feeling Kim's lips massaging her penis, Michelle went further and further down her throat without causing her the least bit of discomfort. It was like Kim was sucking on a big lollipop the size of a hot dog.

Always full of consideration, Michelle positioned Kim's head to have her throat level with her mouth, just like she was getting mouth to mouth resuscitation; only instead of oxygen, she had a dick to breathe with.

Finally, the entirety of Michelle's penis was well within Kim's deep throat, with the tip of it tap dancing with Kim's tonsils. And it was a good thing that Kim never had her tonsils taken out, because the way Michelle was pumping, she would have reached down right to the pit of her lungs. Kim realized how important it was to brush her teeth after every meal.

You never know what might pop in. Meanwhile, Janice began moving Kim by her hips, penetrating and exiting her at the same pace as Antoinette and Debra shimmied and swayed to the pace of Kim's hand rhythm. Janice was very experienced, and moved skillfully without hurting Kim.

Janice knew that all it would take was one wrong move with a novice like Kim and sister Michelle might wind up a castrated

eunuch. It was simply delirious. Kim couldn't control herself from tingling and shaking, her muscles vibrating wildly in a world of their own.

Gladys began moving in and out of Kim's vagina without laying on Kim; her hands massaging her triangle and teasing her clitoris close to Gladys' penis. She also moved at the pace of the same unsung song as Janice and Michelle.

Kim felt her insides erupt in the ecstasy of all the attention she was getting, so electrifying and wonderfully exciting. Antoinette and Debra motioned Kim's hands to stay with the rhythm and gently masturbate them. She did so willingly, pressing her closed hands on theft penises, going down to their groins and up to the head, repeating the motion over and over, savoring their rigidity.

Antoinette and Debra bent over during all this and started sucking Kim's breasts and softly chewing on her nipples, their hands still spreading the cheeks of Kim's derriere, massaging between her thighs each time as they pulled apart her vaginal lips, caressing them. They all repeated the same operation over and over, as if it were well rehearsed, which it probably was. They all moved in unison, an exhilarating scene, keeping perfect time at one incredible pace. Michelle kept dancing in and out of Kim's mouth as Kim pressed her lips even more firmly on Michelle's penis in order to enjoy more, and to help Michelle get the maximum stimulation out of it.

Accordingly, Kim felt Michelle's penis penetrate deep within her throat, where no man, woman or beast had ever been

before. What an experience this was for Kim, who felt so joyously invaded and possessed!

After two exact hours of this astounding foreplay, Michelle ejaculated directly on Kim's tongue, daintily ramming the rest down Kim's throat in a plunge of insatiable release, resting deeply within it, moving ever so slightly in order to ejaculate totally. Kim felt the warm liquid within her gullet, wondering what or who would come next. Michelle obligingly moved out a little, allowing Kim to finish sucking her off, making sure that Kim licked the head of her penis high and dry.

Gladys and Janice moved faster and faster at the same time, taking Kim's torso in a host of gyrations until they instantaneously stopped pressing hard against Kim's vaginal cavity and derriere. She felt their strong ejaculations fill her to capacity. Oddly enough, the two penises could actually feel each other inside the body of Kim.

Then, not by complete surprise, Antoinette and Debra ejaculated madly, pressing their penises against Kim's body, shooting waterfalls into the air and then lubricating Kim with their fallen sperm as they froze their mouths on her breasts, thoroughly engulfing them in their wide-open gasping faces.

Their hands gripped her thighs and buttocks for dear life. Janice took out her hands and swooningly caressed and toyed with Kim's face, with her lips, and with the remaining penis inside Kim's sensual mouth.

They all laid on the floor, thoroughly exhausted; panting like wild cats in heat for a good thirty minutes without moving a muscle. They were all sweaty, oily and greasy, and a casual observer would have said that they were having a 'bad hair day'.

Only Michelle released Kim's mouth to let Kim breathe comfortably. She kissed Kim in the mouth, collecting a few drops of leftover female semen between her teeth.

"You see my vagina?", Michelle asked Kim, pointing to it as she lifted her groins covering a pair of beautifully formed vaginal lips, protected all of these years by a set of intruding nuts.

"How lovely!", Kim responded.

"Please taste it", Michelle begged.

Not bowing how to say know to such a tempting offer, Kim licked it gently and then introduced her tongue to it. Lo and behold, it was a normal vagina, just like hers.

"So Kim!", Michelle exclaimed cautiously. "Did you like to be enraptured this way?"

"It was incredible!", Kim admitted, swallowing the scent of Michelle's tasty knish with the remnants of liquids still swishing around in her mouth. "I never quite experienced anything like this!"

"Are you ready to play some more?", Michelle coaxed.

"Yes!", Kim said, astonishing herself by her resiliency. During the last encounter, John arrived. He opened the door, but no one seemed to notice him. He saw the enrapturing scene, but always a gentleman, he retreated and left the room, and wandered outside onto the deck, breathing deeply of the night air.

It was 3:30 in the morning. The girls finally finished their last round. Michelle went to the bathroom, and filled the jacuzzi with bubble bath and incense soap with an alluring fragrance of minted pine nuts. Michelle ordered the girls to clean up the room and then wash Kim. Debra took all of the bath towels and linens to the ship's laundry, and brought back fresh new ones.

The others helped Kim to her feet, but the could barely walk. Her legs could not even support her. There was no doubt that Kim was thoroughly worn out.

In the bathroom, they led her to the bidet, gave her some Turkish douche beads, and proceeded to sponge and clean Kim's vagina and derriere with the thoroughness of a gynecological emergency room nursing stag repeating the cleaning twice, washing her inside and out, eliminating the last trace or residue of sperm from her body.

Then they picked her up and carried her to the jacuzzi, and quietly laid her in it. Each of the sisters took a large sponge in each hand, soaping Kim all up, down and over, washing her, and then drying her. They splashed gobs of perfume on her

which had cost John $1,375 an ounce. It was Amour Toujours Number 5.

Janice was busy making Kim's bed with the silky sheets that Debra had brought back from the linen room, and once she was done, she and the others all helped to carry Kim into bed, where she laid naked, looking every bit as pure as a virgin bride. They gently covered her with the glistening sheets.

There was no doubt about it. She received a queen's treatment. Only a fool would fail to mistake her for Sleeping Beauty. She exhaled an air and felt a total relaxation permeate all over her body. Amazing as it may seem, she wasn't even sore, as she had a body to the for that was built to last.

At most, she just felt relieved of sexual desires for the time being. Of course, no one really knew how long that would last.

The girls continued cleaning the room until it was spotless. Mary Poppins could not have done a better job. Then, when all the work was done, each one of the sisters came toward Kim and kissed her on the lips and said, "Good night; sweet dreams."

Although she was partially asleep, Kim thanked the girls, adding "It was quite an experience, I enjoyed it so very much."

"Anytime!", Michelle laughed. "Whenever you feel the need, just call and say 'come upstairs.' We will be here at any hour of the day or night. But as John has ordered, we can't come without you calling."

"Yeah, we have never been in this room before!", Antoinette remarked.

"It was always off limits for us. So it was quite an honor, for inviting us to be here.'"

"Pleasant dreams!", she said as they walked out, holding hands so they did not trip in the darkness, as Debra had shut the light a moment earlier. After they closed the door behind them, they noticed John sitting on a deck chair facing the sea.

"Hi, boss!", Michelle greeted. "Have you been waiting here very long?"

"About an hour", John replied nonchalantly, vaguely looking at his watch. "I saw you girls busy in there, so I decided to leave without bothering you. Did Kim enjoy herself?"

"Very much, John!", Michelle beamed proudly. "And we did too! She is so great. ... She has such a fantastic body!"

"Thank you, girls", John responded patronizingly. "I'll see you all tomorrow."

Each one of them said 'good night' to John and left for their cabin. John entered the room. It was 4:15 A.M. Kim heard him, but did not speak a word. She was embarrassed about what she had done, and she did not know what to say to him.

John undressed himself, took a shower, and entered the bed between the sheets. Looking at her delightful face, he kissed

her forehead and whispered, "Sweet dreams, my beloved princess."

Kim's breathing was heavy.

He knew that she was awake but decided not to ask her any questions. He assumed that she must be thoroughly confused about everything that transpired. He simply laid next to her, inhaled her exquisite perfume, and could not help but admire her tantalizing lifted his head to kiss her red cheeks and sultry lips, and then laid next to her to sleep.

Kim had tears in her eyes. She felt so humiliated about what she had done, as if she had betrayed the man who adored and trusted her so deeply.

CHAPTER 11

The sun danced through the port hole of the master stateroom at eight o'clock in the morning. John awakened with a profound squint in his eye from the bright light.

The sound of a sea gull saying his morning prayers pierced John's ear drum. He felt Kim's hot body burning his skin, as she had rolled over and fallen asleep on top of him, with her face next to his, and her bare breasts wrapped tightly against his, while her hands rested gently upon his stomach.

John looked down and noticed her vagina pressing against his upper thigh. He caressed her back and stroked her derriere. She had a velvety texture, so exciting and invigorating to behold. He began massaging her nervously, concentrating upon her angelic backside, as he kissed her lovely face.

He was thinking about how it would be to make love to her while she remained sound asleep. He was dying to do it. His hands were groping between her lower cheeks, feeling her treasures between his fingers. John's breathing became heavy. He reached for her lips, consumed with thirst for her.

Suddenly she began to moan. She was beginning to awaken. Paralyzed by shyness, he instinctively pulled his hands away from her supple buttocks and rested them listlessly on her back. She opened her exquisite eyes.

"Morning!", she yawned, afterward kissing his lips. She realized that she was on top of him, and that John was not smiling, so she apologized.

"Oh, I'm sorry!", she gasped. "I did not know that I was all over you. I probably moved in my sleep."

With that, she tried to roll over. However, John held her and said, "It's all right. I like it. It doesn't bother me in the least."

Images of her sexual escapade of the evening before came shooting back into her mind. Embarrassed, she turned her haunting gaze away from his countenance.

"Did you have a pleasant visit with the sisters?", John inquired politely.

"Yes", she said quickly. "It was different, I guess."

She blushed from head to toe. John raised her chin to stare into her deep green eyes and told her, "Look at me, my princess. You don't have to hide your feelings. It's all right. I entered the room in the middle of the party and I saw all of them making love to you."

"Oh my G-d!", she screamed.

"You were in such total ecstasy!", he continued, ignoring her exclamation. "So don't worry. There is nothing to be ashamed of.

They are just very sexually active women who admire rare beauty such as yourself"

"Women with dicks!", she thought to herself.

Kim lowered her eyes in shame. "What did you see ...?"

"I entered the bedroom but all of you were so engrossed in sexual pleasure that I left and closed the door behind me", he said truthfully.

"I waited on the main deck until you were done."

"Aren't you mad at me?", Kim wondered, rather confused.

"Me mad?", John jumped. "It was my suggestion to attend to your need for sex, remember? I said to you that I would prefer to keep it safe with these special girls so that no one else would learn about it, rather than becoming pregnant by a man who brag about it and tell the whole world. It would be far worse for word to get back to me that someone was saying, 'I flicked the girlfriend of the world's richest bastard', because that would injure my reputation and above all, that would make me insanely jealous."

Kim lifted her lovely face and said, "You said jealous! Really, you, jealous? That would be your reaction if I dated a man?"

"Of course!", John admitted. "I would be very jealous. That is a normal reaction!"

Moved by his sincerity, Kim kissed him hard and long on the lips, offering him her mouth-watering tongue that he savored so well. The taste of honey flowed from her jaws.

"So you love me a little?", John asked, seeking reassurance. "I love you very much", she replied quietly.

He kissed her eyes and nose and said, "One day … one day." Suddenly, Kim jumped.

"John!", she shrieked. "You have blood on the pillow. Let me see! Oh, no! It's a wound in your neck."

John touched his neck and felt a small burning sensation festering there. "It's nothing, my sweet pet", he laughed. "I cut myself shaving and the gash reopened.

"No, my love", she contradicted. "It looks more like a scratch. Let me go and clean it for you."

Kim was about to uncover herself, but John rapidly covered her with the bed sheet and reminded her, "Don't walk around naked, remember I told you?"

"Sorry, baby!", she sighed. "I know that you don't like to see the body of an ugly girl."

John shrugged his shoulders and said, "If you were truly ugly, then the word 'beauty' would have never existed."

She chuckled and disappeared into the bathroom, trying to assess his mixed signals. She returned two minutes later with alcohol and gauze. She gently patted down the wound and blew cool air from her sensational lips so that the sting would not hurt him.

John thanked her and then said, "Kim, my darling, you and I are going to Paris on vacation like two lovers, for a whole week."

Kim jumped on his back, careful not to injure the part of his neck that hurt him.

"Oh, that's fantastic!", she cheered. "I love it. Just you and I? No sisters or Aunt Yetta? When can we go?"

Looking at his watch, he said, "In a couple of hours. We'll go in my car. Why don't you get ready and pack a couple of things. I'll send up six suitcases."

Kim was all bubbly with the prospect of going on a trip with John alone. She accompanied John to the top deck where they had breakfast.

"I'm getting the hang of eating all of these smoked fish!", she said.

"What are these things?"

"Regular belly lox, nova lox, kippered salmon, baked whitefish, and carp", he explained. "All Jewish delicacies."

"I guess I've got to learn to give up bacon and eggs, don't I, honey?" she asked.

"Only half of it", John admonished her. "Eggs are fine." While John was in the bathroom washing his hands, Kim picked up the newspaper on the table. Again it had a picture of a young girl who had been murdered by the serial killer. Kim took a closer look at what it said. The girl had been murdered last night.

According to the article, there had been a struggle and the skin and blood in her fingernails indicated that she had scratched the killer.

"I hate reading the paper!", Kim said to herself "Always bad news." Meanwhile Josianne walked in and said, "Good Morning, Miss Kim. How did you sleep?"

Kim looked at her twice and said, "Great, thank you!", not knowing if she knew about her rendezvous with the sisters and was just being sarcastic.

Turning her head away, Kim glanced at the newspaper again, and remembered that John had been out until 4:00 A.M. and had come in with blood on his neck.

"Nah!", she said to herself "What a stupid assumption. A person so polite, so gallant, so gentle and sweet doesn't go around killing girls. Besides, he is the richest man in the world. He can have any girl he wants."

She threw the paper on a deck chair and put it all in the back of her mind. The sisters showed up after John returned from the bathroom and was saying a prayer over the fish.

"Hi, boss! Hi, Kim!", Michelle greeted loudly. "How do you feel today?"

Without looking directly at her, Kim answered, "Very well, thanks!"

John interrupted her.

"Girls, I want you to watch the yacht for this whole week. Don't leave the ship. I am going with Kim to Paris, so I entrust you with everything. Bashir is feeling much better today and just called me that he is coming back to work. He can go shopping for you and get you anything you need."

"You can rest assured that everything will be under control, boss!", Michelle promised. John excused himself to make a phone call.

"I was hoping we could get together tonight again, but you are leaving", Michelle said sadly. "Well, we will have fun next week when you return. We have many more goodies in our bag of tricks that will give you the experience of a lifetime."

"I'm flattered", Kim answered, blushing and smiling.

"You are such a great lover!", Michelle added, "and your body is so fantastic. If I were a man I could not crave you any more.

You know, I couldn't sleep a wink last night after I left you. I thought about you ever since that time."

"It's only been a few hours!", Kim remarked.

"Hours, minutes, seconds; who cares?", Michelle replied bluntly. "I want you!"

Michelle slid her hand between Kim's thighs under her dress. Kim breathed hard, as if she was burning once again with passion. Gladys came up from behind and glided her hands on Kim's breasts and said "You gave me the time of my life, honey!"

"Careful, someone will see us!", Kim warned them apprehensively.

"Don't worry so much!", Michelle squawked, as her finger penetrated Kim's vagina under her panties, massaging it there; continuing it in order to give Kim something to remember her by during her trip. She plunged her finger deeper, then pulled it out, and then slowly put it into her own mouth to taste Kim's juicy secretions.

They all kissed her and said, "Have a great trip! This is so you don't forget us! We love you!"

"I suppose insecurity is not an issue when someone is as beautiful as you, Kim", the mirror told her poetically as her mind began to wander in all different directions.

"Here he comes!", Antoinette warned Kim, "so have a safe trip and come back as hot as you were a few minutes ago."

"Don't worry about the boss!", Gladys said. "He is great. Remember, this was his suggestion."

"Bye, I'll miss you girls!", Kim said as she walked down the stairway toward John as he was coming up. John took a second look at Kim as he waved goodbye to the sisters.

"You have the native ability to make anyone lose control. Even the Pope would break his sacred vows for you. I'll bet a million dollars on it. Everyone melts over you. Even me."

She smiled ever so shyly. John kissed her on the cheek.

"Thank you, my love, for not being upset with me", she answered with a sigh of great relief "I too am easily influenced and lose control of my actions, but I never want to hide anything from you or lie to you, not ever!"

She wrapped her arms around his neck and hugged him with all of her strength. John started sniffing her.

"Hmmm ... delicious!", he observed.

Three girls were loading suitcases and a cooler into the trunk of the Aston Martin. It was Kathy, Josianne and Gina.

"Why are you picking up this heavy stuff?", John asked.

"We didn't want Bashir's stitches to come unglued", Gina said with dignity. "Anyway, we need the exercise."

John thanked them all by kissing them on the cheek, until he came to Kathy, the youngest one. Kathy was a sultry blonde with bedroom eyes, wearing a short skirt. He delayed the kiss a little, and when he came forward he landed on the side of her lips That strange move did not escape Kim. She noticed everything.

In the car, Kim asked, "Do you especially like Kathy in particular?" John smiled and shrugged his shoulders.

"Are you jealous or just very perceptive?", he answered.

"So is it true?", Kim demanded

John laughed his ass off.

"Oh, I love you, princess", he stated devotionally.

"Yes, I like her because she is the youngest. It is true that I treat her a little differently, but not in the way that you mean. She is an adorable child, nothing more."

Kim wasn't convinced. Disturbed, she put on a very sad face.

"There, there, now!", John replied, patting her on the back. "My princess is mad and jealous. Come and kiss me right now. The press is following us."

Kim complied and kissed his neck, although it seemed to be against her will.

John looked at her and asked, "What if I have an affair with her? Would you be annoyed?"

"I'd kill the bitch!", Kim said with a childishly angry expression.

"But you had five at the same time, invading you, nearly raping you, making love to every part of you they can find, and you don't see me getting jealous or possessive, do you?", John questioned hilariously.

"I made love to the sisters because you wanted me to, John", she protested, "but if you had wanted me yourself, I would have never gone with those sex maniacs, even thought I had a good time with them! I am just wondering why you would even ask about sleeping with Kathy, and not me, your so-called alleged 'fiancee', who you are paying a fortune to play let's pretend with every day!"

"You are a hundred percent right!", John concluded.

"But how can it be that you would prefer me over all the five wild sisters together? It just doesn't make sense!", he added, but this time, seriously.

Kim was looking at him in complete shock and amazement that he was so blind that he failed to understand her at all. John felt the tension and wasn't laughing any longer.

Frustrated as hell, she didn't answer. She simply lowered her head and put it on his lap against his stomach. A small tear fell from her left eye.

"What would you do if I took out your thing right here in the car and started to kiss it and do some other stuff to it?", she inquired in wonder.

John felt a heat wave all over his body, but he did not answer. She took his silence as an acquiescence. Kim opened his fly and unbuttoned his boxer shorts, freeing his instantly hardened equipment.

Immediately she started kissing John's penis all over. His heart beat began to accelerate. He couldn't say a word, although he was worried about what he would say if he got pulled over by a policeman.

"Damn it!", he thought to himself. "I should have let Bashir drive!" He felt her burning lips on his loins. Her tongue continued teasing him and playing with it. He could barely concentrate on the road.

This was the very first time that he allowed Kim to see his penis, let alone to touch it. She experienced it in her mouth. The one consolation that occurred to John was at least it was Kosher, unlike the sisters.

"Oh! Angel! Oh!", John moaned out loud in ultimate delight, not even bothering to think about what Aunt Yetta would say if she were along for the ride.

He felt the wetness of her mouth, slowly engulfing his member. She gently played him like flute with her tongue and lips. Starting to think like a real professional, she thankfully remembered the spray in her purse.

Without missing a beat or a stroke she reached for it, retrieved it, and then sprayed a gob of it down her throat, catching her sweet breath in the middle. She flung his dip. Back in her thirsty mouth, slowly encouraging more of him inside her, until she had all of it rammed down her throat. John was speechless. He couldn't utter a word. A trucker in a semi-tractor trailer passed him on the road and gave him a "V" sign for victory.

She opened his belt and pants and lowered everything to the floor in order to caress his stomach and thighs. Her hands reached down so she could squeeze his balls a little bit, in order to give him even more satisfaction.

She could feel his rigidity.

"At least he's not gay!", she thought to herself with the utmost of confidence. She finally succeeded in having him in some way. As Felicia had told her on the plane, the only thing she would ever get from him would be to give him a blow job. She was moving in and out, reaching down to his groins, repositioning her head to allow it deep within her supple gullet.

John shrieked tears of excitement! She felt his throbbing, so he released a little of it, in order to be fully able to wrap her lips around his tip, doing to John what Michelle liked so much. She never put two and two together, that John had thrown her in

with the sisters so that they could give her a few lessons and teach her lots of new tricks.

She made John shiver, sigh and moan, all at the same time. When she least expected it, his ejaculation erupted like Mount Vesuvius, completely flooding her mouth with his hot lava, then exploding all the way down her throat.

Ten minutes later when the sporadic discharges stopped, she began teasing it again with her tongue, pressing her lips forcefully around his penis, making him shiver and tremble with pleasure. He felt a profound relaxation and relief. Kim continued for awhile until she felt his hardness slowly die between her lips.

She kissed it, licking him all over like a mother cat, and wiping his stomach clean with her tongue. She finally took a Kleenex and wiped him thoroughly dry, covering his nakedness with her burning cheek, feeling his hot staff under her face.

"Well, I finally got something from you!", Kim finally said with a total sense of accomplishment.

"Are you going to punish me when we get to Paris? Does Kathy do it to you as good as I do?"

John caressed her face with the gentleness of a baby lamb.

"I suppose I should be mad at you for bending the rules and going off the deep end", John began in wary consternation, "but how can I be? You are my princess. I once told you not to,

but you are very insubordinate and extremely naughty. I have plans for you that I cannot divulge to you, even now, but with the passage of time, I will reveal more and more."

"Just tell me you enjoyed what just happened!", she demanded.

"Oh, it was fantastic!", he decreed. "Thank you very much for that unexpected surprise, but just don't do it again!"

Kim bit his penis, extracting a little scream from him.

"Now that is bullshit!", she argued. "Felicia told me that she used to do the same thing to you in the airplane, and you allowed her to do it again and again, sort of like a ritual. So why not me? You have no excuses!"

John faintly smiled.

"So, she betrayed our little secret and told you, eh?", he sneered.

"Maybe I should find another stewardess."

"Why, because she was trying to prepare me for you? I don't think so!", she said defiantly.

"Did Felicia make love to you too on that plane?", John asked.

"Never mind!", Kim roared. "I promised not to tell you anyway."

"Okay, so you didn't tell me. I figured it out!", he answered.

Kim was very aroused by the feeling of John's loins against her cheekbone. She began kissing the tip of his penis again, but this time he stopped her with a loud, emphatic "No!"

"I told you already, baby!", he reiterated. "No more! Besides, I don't want to get sperm stains all over the leather."

She sat up straight and took his hand and put it between her thighs and said, "Caress me down here. After all, I am also human!"

Kim pulled her panties down and pushed his hand against her snatch. "Please!", she begged. "At least finger me if you don't want to make love to me. I am burning with desire!"

Against his better judgment he obliged her. She spread her sensuous thighs in order to allow him to explore the cavern beneath her lower lips. She was crying and moaning with pleasure, enjoying the penetration of his hand even more than she did the entire episodes with the five sisters.

She also nonchalantly put her palm on his penis and began massaging it. She was moaning like a buffalo being flicked by an orangutan.

"Oh! Yes!", she screamed. It was incredible to see such a beauty being pushed to the limit. She laid her head on his penis again, locking it into her mouth.

With her right hand, she pulled up her dress a little higher and reapplied his index finger onto her clitoris. He complied

nervously and was taken aback each time his finger slipped into the crack of her wet womanhood. His hand covered all of her magnificent assets, creating extreme heat from his rubbing back and forth.

Don't tell anybody, but he was also in ecstasy. She felt him come her mouth, which she controlled skillfully, making him shriek with pleasure a second time.

"I'm going to get him addicted to this if it kills me!", she thought to herself. Kim was alive with oral pleasure, but could not express herself vocally, because she had a big dick in her mouth. His hand masturbated her so proficiently, that she came three times. John took a T-shirt from the back seat and cleaned her gently, wiping all of the dripping goo from her heavenly triangle to her precious vagina.

He kept stroking it all the while, making her exhale as if she were in labor. He massaged the flaps on her clitoris, the ones which led to paradise. Kim finally released his penis.

"Oh, that was flicking incredible!", she grunted quite tactfully.

"Your touch is worth more than fifty sets of sisters! What I really want is to have you completely; to conquer you and have you fuck the living shit out of me!"

John continued caressing her hard-boiled box and said, "Listen to me very seriously. If masturbating you will satisfy you for now, I'll accept it. It calms you down and I will know when the moment of your climax has arrived. We almost had three

accidents now. People in the south of France drive crazy and I am also one of them. You have the power to drive anyone wild, including me. But you and I will have too much to lose if we go at a faster pace. One day you will understand it all."

"Why wait?", she argued.

"Because just touching you makes me lose control. I don't want to be in that position. I can't be vulnerable, not now. It's impossible. I can't allow it."

Kim was more puzzled than ever, but she has heard John sing that song before, and resigned herself not to argue. Cars were passing them by, giving them the finger. John lowered her skirt and zipped up his fly. At that moment, the phone rang. He had caught the zipper on his pubic hair.

"Ouch!", he yelled. "Honey, please answer the phone while I straighten myself out!"

Kim sat up tall in the car seat and picked up the receiver.

"Hello, can I help you?", she asked.

The voice on the other side said, "Can I speak with John?"

"Who is calling?", Kim inquired.

"It's David."

"Oh, Hi, Mr. David", she said enthusiastically. "This is Kim. How are you doing?"

"It's nice to hear your voice again!", he replied.

They exchanged some small talk and pleasantries for a few moments, after which she handed the phone to John.

"Hello, Dave", he greeted. "What's new?"

"We got it!", he laughed. "We bought 53% of their stock. Peter and are preparing a shareholder's meeting in order to announce the takeover."

"My dream is finally coming true", he beamed. "Very well done, Dave."

"Are you putting Yetta Blashinsky in as Chairman of the Board?", he asked.

"Not this time", John said. "Aunt Yetta wants to take it a little easier. No, I have something else in mind. Make Kim the Chairman of the Board."

"Kim? You've got to be kidding. John, are you losing your mind?", David challenged, extremely worried and upset.

Kim also turned and looked at John as if he were nuts.

"Do you believe in me or not?", John stammered. "Have I ever made a mistake since my comeback?"

"Well, no, but … ", David began.

"Fine, then!", John interrupted. "I'll tell you why I am doing this when I see you next week!"

"What about me?", Kim asked, tapping John on the shoulder.

"Where are you putting me?"

John made a gesture instructing Kim to wait.

"Okay, Dave", he continued. "I'll see you Thursday in Monte Carlo. Bye."

Kim's eyes were scrutinizing him, and her face showed a worry.

"Where are you sending me? I am going no where without you."

"I am not sending you anywhere, but I just make you the chairman of the board of T.C.N.N." Kim thought that he was joking, then said "you're not joking?"

John caressed her face and said "No I'm not, I've never been so serious. You are a part of me, since you are American I'm not, you can be the chairman. The most sexy chairman in the world, you will travel there once every three months with me or David, we are your assistants."

Kim was incredulous.

He continued, "This is because you gave me a good blow job, he laughed."

She pinched his mouth "Please talk seriously, why me?"

John: "Okay you have a B.A. in business administration.

So you could be instructed as to what to do, you are not a dumb blonde, but a smart one. I trust you with the company, I'll give you in writing or tell you my instructions and I am sure that you can do it, that's simple. So the chairman of the board for T.C.N.N. is the fiancee of the richest man in the world. That's a good title, so everyone will give you respect and think that you are a dumb bimbo that is after my money. So I look bad like an old fool and you, like a black widow looking for the right moment to get rid of your old rich husband."

Kim smiled and said "You are doing all this for me? Oh my love, she gave him a hard kiss smacking his cheek and continued, "It means that you have plans for me for a while yes?"

John as if upset said "what was I saying all the time little girl? I am going to pay you millions just to keep me company? or just sex?"

Showing his pants he laughed. She kissed his hand, and sucked each one of his fingers sexually, he said "here she goes again" she smiled mischievously turned her head toward the passenger door, and laid on the seat face down, the lifted her dress showing him her incredibly sexy derriere.

She said, "I want to sleep for awhile, if you caress me it will help, you know I like that."

He swallowed his salive. His hand as if magnetized touched her wonders of wonders, she moaned "Oh John your touch kills me hum."

He caressed her soft velvety derriere his hand shaking from strong emotions. She extended her arm grabbing his hand and made middle finger brush the valley splitting her lovely ass, making her and him shiver. He was nervous massaging, feeling all of her cheek in his wide palm, clenching a fist to feel the flesh trapped in it.

She directed his finger to her rear gate and pressed it indicating him to penetrate and caress her inside. He began then immediately stopped "I am sorry love, I can't do that you are making me lose total control, I never did that before. This is the reason I became the richest man in the world. Now you little angel or little devil, making me lose my head, this could destroy my plans. No please cover yourself, if not I might forget what will do next," she sat and looked at him, he was all in sweat, he even had a nervous twit in his right eye.

"So I make you lose control, am I so sexy? I remarked that especially my butt drives you crazy because each time you touched it you become upset, is that it?"

John smiled and said: "All of you make me lose control, but your butt as you call it has especial powers, it is dangerous to my health."

She giggled: "Hum good to know next time when I want something I will threaten you with it, give me your money or

I'll show you my butt "she laughed a joyful and clear laugh with all her heart, he joined too.

He pulled her lovely face against his chest and said "Try to sleep baby, I'll sing you a song in Spanish, a love song okay?"

"Really? You sing too?"

"I use to have a musical band when Orly was my girlfriend. I was the singer and guitar player."

She let her lovely face rest on his chest, his arm around her shoulder and sang her a song. She liked it, and as predicted she fell asleep. They arrived finally in Paris, and he drove to the hotel, the valet came, opened the trunk and retrieved his luggage.

He motioned with his fingers not make noise, showing Kim asleep. He gave the keys to the valet, took Kim in his arm and carried her into the hotel. She was totally exhausted. He didn't care for anyone looking. The reservations were made for the "Presidential Suite," the valet called the elevator and they went up under the scrutinizing eyes of hundred of hotel guests and employees. He was happy to carry her like a child, or a baby in his strong arms.

He tipped the valet, once alone, he carefully undressed her, discovering her immensely exciting body, that could give a heart ache to any one. He couldn't help but kiss her lovely triangle, and then covered her. He went to the shower and relaxed taking a bath.

When he was finished he went and laid next to her. Millions of ideas and impulses made him think about jumping on her and make love to her, or drown between her thighs.

He took a deep breath and calmed down, turn the other way. He was so tired from driving, that he fell soon asleep.

When he awakened, Kim was on top of him, she had his penis inside of her in a sitting position and was moving frantically. John became rapidly aroused and begin devouring her breasts his mouth totally opened "Oh Kim you shouldn't haven't done it baby, you shouldn't"

His hands grabbed her formidable ass savagely Kim told him "You see I told you I will have you soon enough and I knew that no thing will happen. She was laughing loud and kept moving up and down. He was sweating and nervous. Suddenly she stopped and kneeled, she had her head down in the mattress offered him her succulent ass, totally spread for his excitement.

"Come now come and fuck me hard now I said, come, don't make me wait".

He rose behind her and penetrated her with all his strength in onesingle hush. Making her scream of pleasure and pain. "Yes that's it, yes, you see how you can."

His face turned blue, laid on her his hands reached for her throat and pressed" No what are you doing I can't breath, I cant, I told you not to do it, but you had to. You stupid now it's

too late." He kept pressing until she turned blue and stopped fighting her eyes totally open, lifeless.

He stopped and turned her, "Hey answer me princess, answer "he felt her pulse her beautiful eyes looked at him as if not understanding what has happened.

Suddenly John screamed loud "No. No."

He jumped sweating, "My love what happened you screamed very loud, you scared me terribly", he looked at Kim with disbelief and held her in his arms kissed her lovely scared face.

"Oh my princess, you're alright Oh G-D"

He kept kissing her all over her face hands and again embrace her, with all his strength feeling her warm body against his.

"Thank G-D it was a nightmare. I thought I lost you he lifted her and held her on his lap, her face against his, Kim calmed.

"I said you dreamed that I had some kind of accident?"

"Yes baby I thought I will die seeing you dead."

He had his face flooded with tears.

She begin crying too "You cried for me my big boy and you thought you will die without me! Oh John you love me so much?"

John kissed her face and grabbed her lips in a desperate kiss then took refuge between her two proud breasts that he kissed tirelessly.

Kim: "Calm down baby...shush ... it was only a nightmare. One thing I am happy about this bad dream, is that I know much you love me."

Then she looked around and couldn't figure out where she was.

"How did I get here? I don't remember coming here?"

Calmed down John said: "When we got here you were asleep so nicely I didn't want to wake you up, so I carried you in my arms from the car, through the lobby registration and the elevator, until we got here. Hundred, of people have seen sleeping beauty carried away."

She held his face looked him in the eyes very close, nose to nose and said: "You have so much love in you. I never felt like that my love."

John laid down holding her tight as if afraid to lose her. She kissed his chest and caressed his stomach.

She said "I'll give you a massage love, your too tense, turn around."

He did, she took some baby oil from their luggage and came back to him. She pulled his boxers all the way.

He wanted to stop her, but she said "Don't worry I won't rape you I'll be gentle". She giggled. She splashed oil on his body and began massaging his back for a while it was very pleasant.

John said: "You have wonderful miraculous hands, I feel better already." she continued to his derriere massaging each of his cheeks with two hands then to his thighs by the same token she would massage his groin. She finished his calf and legs and said

"Turn around big boy." He did, she appreciate his errected member

"Hum … do we take care of him too." She laughed. She massage his feet then to his thighs when she got to his penis she massage his groin and capture his manhood in her mouth making him tremble of desire. She again went for the spray and applied it in her throat and took his penis back into her mouth totally up to his groins.

He was moaning in ecstacy she will play with her tongue around it, then let it out and kissed it, pressing it against her lovely face taking his groins one at a time in her mouth, then emprisoning it again until she felt his throbbing. He couldn't hold any longer.

She moved to his tip pressing her lip tight around the head her tongue rolling around it, making him delay his ejaculation even though he thought to burst but her doing stopped it and his excitement hundred fold making all his body ache tense like a piano cord moaning "Oh Kim Oh... you're killing me."

She did faster and faster, the lips pressed on his tip, moving to the top then return to its neck back and forth not letting it burst her tongue rolled non stop. Then she release the pressure of her lips from the tip and in seconds she felt his ejaculation flood her thristy mouth her tongue. Then she moved deeper to allow his Penis totally in her throat feeling his warm flow directly into her throat.

When he stopped his sporadic releases. She sucked him up and down making him shiver. Electric current running through his spine. She skillfully massaged also his groin and then released them and kissed his relaxed penis laying her face agains it. A few minutes later, she massaged his stomach and chest and then neck and face.

She finally sat on his chest and said "So do you feel better?"

He caressed her lovely face and smiled: "Thank you my angel in disguise you were exquisite. No wonder all the girls are crazy about you baby."

He pulled her and laid her next to him and caressed her back with gentil strokes.

She said "The moment you will decide to make love to me I think I will have a heart attack from so much desire I have for you."

John looked at his watch it was 9 a.m. "My love do you want to have breakfast in bed or do we go to the champs Elysee?"

Kim: "I want to eat you not food and now. She took his hand to her vagina. He stroke it gently and said," love we have one week here. let's get up and I'll take you everywhere, you never been in Paris'.

Kim looked at him and made a childish expression "I want first a massage and a kiss there. I gave you one now I want to be payed nothing is free."

John: "Please baby let's get ready and we will do it later, pretty please?"

She agreed against her will. They finally got ready and went out all day. He drove her all around Paris, the Eifel tower, Champs Elysee, the Louvre museum and Le Palais de Verssailles.

They took the boat in la Seine, ate in a terrace of the Champs Elysee. They were holding each other like teenage lovers. They didn't care about the world around them. In a news stand a picture attacted his attention. He bought the paper. He was in the first page carrying Kim in the hotel the night before.

"Look" he said.

Kim couldn't believe her eyes. "What does it says: Mr John the richest man in the world carrying his sleeping future beautiful bride onto the hotel as if carrying sleeping beauty"

"Oh! I love you my Romeo the whole world knows about us now and mostly that you love me."

She jumped on his neck every one was looking at them. This evening Kim met John's cousin that lived in Paris. they had dinner in a fancy restaurant. At night back at the hotel the whole press was waiting for them.

He said "Hello!"

"Sir can we ask you a question. We heard that your company have purchased the majority of the shock of TWCNN. Can you tell us about it? When is the over?"

John said "Gentleman I am in vacation, my fiancee and I do not want to talk about business we are here enjoying our vacation. If you do not mind, when the time comes, we will anounce whatever there is to announce. Thank you".

They spent a beautiful and romatic week. He brought her everything she looked at.

"But baby I will have to put sun glasses so you won't see what I am looking at. What if I look at the Eiffel tower would you buy it for me?"

"Seriously?" he said, "You want it"?

She held his face with her two lovely hands and in front of everyone gave him a kiss that could have his hair grow instantly. Finally the moment to return came. they left happy the car filled gifts for Kim. They made love everyday with hands and mouths but not completely. He held his grounds.

His reasons must have been very powerful to resist this incredible beauty. Monaco was at the horizon Kim slept peacefully on his shoulder. It was dark when they got there 11 p.m.

The sisters were at gard that night and saw the car, park. They ran toward them. He motioned them to keep quiet, again he carried her in his arms and gave Michelle the car keys to help with the luggage and said: "Thank you, I'll see you in the morning, she is exhausted, she slept all the way to here."

He could see their happy faces seeing her. Kim could charm even a lion. He put her to sleep and he himself was so tired that he undressed and layed naked next to her.

Chapter 12

A beautiful sunny morning, she awaked first and smiled seeing him next to her she caressed his face then kissed his torso. Her hand covered his virility. She kept kissing his lips and nose until he opened his eyes.

"Hi lover it's 10 a.m. Friday. You better wake up your exgirlfriend is coming today with her husband remember? and again you brought me in your arms asleep my prince charming, I love you my sweet thing. Who else in this world can love me like you do?"

John smiled and realised what she had said. He was glad to hear it even if she didn't mean it really. She jumped on him covering his body with hers, I am starved let us have breakfast.

John: "Go ahead darling. I have to use the bathroom. Just ware your bikini, we will spend some time in the pool upstair, ok?"

"Yes my lord. Your desire is my command." She was so gracious, she put the bikini on and left. John took the phone and went to the bathroom.

He called Steve F.

"Hey Steve how are you doing?"

Steve: "Great John, you know that we are flying to you on Monday we will be arriving in the evening. Do you need anything from here?"

John: "Bring everything you need for the room in the yatch. Did David give you my message about you staying with me for a while. Is there a problem?

Steve: "It won't be a problem if you'll find a girl for me. John laughed one girl no but many yes. take the concord it is faster it takes half the time. Tell David so you have time for reservation. Also if you need more hard drive memory for our computer buy them."

Steve: "Ok John. I'll see you Monday evening and I will finally meet the beauty of yours."

"Bye Steve".

Kim met Josianne at the pool.

She said: "Hi Kim nice to see you back, we missed you."

Her eyes were devouring her."Do you want me to put you some sunscreen?"

Kim said: "Ok thank you."

She ran and brought a sun tan lotion bottle and said "lay down." Kim did and laid on her stomach. She spread the lotion

on her back then on her arm and in her barely cover cheeks. She applied it there longer with her two hands. Then she moved to her thighs all the way to her feet.

"Turn Kim, I'll do your front".

She turned. Kim looked at her lovely face, she put sun screen on her face. Josianne was bitting her lower lips as if saying "Oh how much I want you."

Kim felt a little uncomfortable. Her hands went to her breasts and spread the sun screen her fingers as if by accident will touch her nipples making them hardened. Then continued to her stomach and between her thighs touching with her fingers the uncovered space close to her lower lips.

Kim said "Thank you Josianne, I appreciate it."

"Anything." she said "Anytime."

"Oh I forgot John will be here in 30 minute can you tell the cook to prepare us breakfast?"

"Of course I'll do it myself." She was happy to serve her. Everyone was falling in love with Kim as well men and woman a real Venus.

After she left the sisters showed up. "Hi sleeping beauty we saw you coming last night in your prince charming's arms. You looked so comfortable. How was it?" Kim felt a pinch between her thighs.

"OH,great it was so romantic, I never been in Paris before. He made me fell like a queen."

Michelle said: "Can we kiss you? We couldn't wait any longer to see you. We miss you terribly, we were sad."

Kim look at them and said: "Why not" she stood up and they surrounded her and kissed her but without touching her they could be seen from the yatchs near by.

Debra said, "We have so many programs for you, you will love it, when can we get together?"

Kim said "Not this weekend we have guest this afternoon. For this whole weekend, she was John first love when he was 15 years old she is very nice. She comes with her husband."

Janice said "we are dying to touch you, you became like a drug to us. Escape later for just an hour, come to our cabin please? She looked at her lovely face, her eyes supplicating for her grace, a morsel of Love.

She said: "I'll see what I can do. I'll ask him after breakfast."

Michelle: "Oh, no the boss will get mad."

Kim said "Don't worry he won't."

Antoinette said "The boss will rest after his breakfast. I know that for a fact. Kim did not really pay attention at her statement. Michelle said: "Don't tell him anything please."

"Ok, Ok, Don't worry I won't."

Josianne showed up with a cart and two breakfast. John arrived just behind her.

"Hi, how was the yatch in our absence?"

"Oh good morning sir, all was great, no problem what- so -ever. Helena the baronesse came looking for you. She looked upset to know that you had left with Miss Kim for Paris. She seemed quiet disturbed, she that it was important and left in a hurry."

John: "Oh don't worry there is nothing in this world that can't wait."

Kim was upset already to hear her name.

Kathy showed up next. She saw her joyous childish face illuminate when she saw John, she walked nervously toward him and said:

"Welcome back Boss." She kissed his cheek touching his lips.

Kim already was in self defense and said, "Hi Kathy you kissed him only what about me?"

With a fake graciousness. Kathy came toward her and kissed her too.

"Nice to see you again Miss Kim, good to have you back."

Michelle showed up with two big glasses of fresh squeezed orange juice and gave one to John and one to Kim.

"Just squeeze it is chilled."

"Thank you "said John and they both drank it. "Oh delicious especially in this hot day."

They ate breakfast they was sweating. John began yawning.

"Oh!! baby I am sleepy. I'll better take a nap before our guests get here."

Kim looked at Michelle and understood what was going on. They gave him a sleeping pill, she was upset.

She said: "Darling let's go we will have a nap together."

They left to their quaters. John barely put the head in the pillow that he was already asleep. Kim looked at him sleeping peacefully.

A knock attracted her attention. "Come in." It was the girls.

Kim: "Who gave you permission to do that?"

"Oh please don't be upset, he does that from time to time. He will rest well for at least 3 to four hour. We would like to welcome you we were fantasizing about you. We have you under the skin. Please don't be mad at us, we beg you."

Kim said:" Ok, but no more games." The last girl closed the door behind them. They began undressing.

Kim said: "You are crazy here?"

Michelle: "Why not, he won't know". It's more exciting to have him next to us. Debra took her bikini down, and they all undressed in a blink of an eye. They began first by massaging her parts. Front and back.

Michelle made her open her mouth and sprayed her inside. Antoinette and Janice lifted her and tilted her upside down, her head close to the floor. Each held her by her thighs spreading them like a ballerine, they began massaging and kissing her vagina and butt. Michelle laid on the floor, paralel to Kim's legs, held her head and brought it to her making it slowly disappear in her mouth.

Michelle moaned "Oh, how much I dreamed of this moment. "Antoinette and Janice spread her cheeks. Debra came and penetrate her gorgeous ass, "Oh, yes your so good and hot inside."

She plunged totally up to her groin. Gladis came to her vagina and her, in one push. Oh you are a great fuck, the best ever. Antoinette and Janice massaged her butt cheeks and her vaginal lips. Michelle was busy moving her lower stomach to Kim mouth, her hands squeezing Kims breasts.

Debra and Gladis were moving inside her at the same time, touching each other's breasts and kissing in the mouth face

to face. Antoinette and Janice without releasing Kim's thighs they went behind Debra and Gladis and penetrated both in their vagina. It was very exciting for Kim it wasn't so too. She massaged their groins seeing Gladis penetrate her vigina each time; and felt the push of them four, two on the back and two on the front.

Michelle was coming, she said "Please now babe, now do it she did."

Michelle screamed: "Oh' Oh!that's it, yes." Her scream made the other ejaculate too, they lifted harder Kim by her thighs to press her vigina and butt against their groins. They were all in ecstacy. Without releasing her they licked all of her charm.

Michelle had her penis all the way to her throat releasing the part drop of her ejaculation. Her groins against Kim's chin pushing as much as she could inside her throat. Finally they released her, gently and all layed on the floor. One on top of the others, they all exclaimed "Oh Kim, you have a so great body."

They stayed in the same position 30 more minute to the last electrical discharge across their body. The girls kissed Kim all over, they stood up and lifted her in their hands in a horizontal position and licked all of her, especially her vagina and ass out of their ejaculation. They again washed her in the jaccuzi, dried her, perfumed her and layed her in bed next to John.

Michelle said, "I never seen the bosses Penis". She pulled his bathing suit and said, "Wow!, he is a good caliber."

Kim tried to stop her, but she already had her mouth on it, she did for a minute they all the other did the same, and they said, "Thank's boss for Kim and you. You're great, we'll see you tomorrow if possible if not after the guests leave."

Kim relaxed, "What an experience she thought." These girls are something else. They take me as their sex toy, but I enjoy it. They excite me terribly. She fell asleep on those thoughts. She was naked and John too, the girls did not put his bathing suit back.

Kathy was knocking at the door, no one answer. She was coming to tell them that the guest had arrived, the door was unlocked, she entered, and saw them on the bed naked. She became aroused and jealous. She shaked her boss, but no answer.

Kim seemed also passed out. "Oh, I need you so much, I missed you my big guy." She kneeled and captured his manhood between her lovely baby mouth. She was so young, she didn't even look 20 years old. Freckels all over her face. Kathy was from Sweeden.

John awakened finally to see Kathy giving him a head job next to Kim. He immediately stopped her.

He whispered "What's wrong with you? You do not see her, Kim? What are you doing here?"

She was all aroused, her pink cheeks looked gracious and cute nose. She looked like a 15 year old child. 5"2" but she was over

20. She made a sad face with a childish expression as if her daddy has scorned her. She blink her lovely blue eyes, looking at her hands.

John looked at Kim, she was deep asleep, her head next to his shoulder totally naked. He felt bad to have yelled at Kathy. He picked her up in his arms. She wrapped her arms around his neck and carried her to the bathroom, locking the door behind them.

He looked at her, she said, "I saw the sisters leaving this room without locking the door. So I knocked, but there was no answer. I wanted, to see you, I haven't seen you for a week. I needed you" she said childishly looking at her nails.

He smiled and took her lips with thirst, kissing her. He took her legs on top of his powerful arms leaving her vagina defenseless to his awakening desire penetrating her almost savagely.

Pressing her against the wall, then lowering his head to devoure her lovely firm breast like they were the last delicacy on earth. She moaned and cried, kissing his head, "Oh my boss, Oh!!How much I missed you Am I not your little baby anymore? You love Kim and you probably did sex with her already?"

John didn't answer, he was all excited moving in and out of her, making her little breast disappear one at time in his widely open hungry mouth. She was crying of ecstacy, feeling him, up

to her entrails. His powerful fingers invading her cute ass. He suddenly release her breast to emprison her mouth in a kiss.

She felt his throbbing and strong ejaculation. She moaned and also came at the same time, both kissing each others face with the despair of the moment. When he ended his sporadic release. On her young vagina.

He raised her in his arms straight and kissed all her body, shewing her little shaved bulge triangle. She loved it she felt like a candy. Then continue kissing her between her thighs. She knew already the ritual, she flipped over and he devoured her cute little ass, not missing a single spot.

She giggled and loved it. She was like his toy. Finally she ended seating on his shoulders, her cute triangle on his mouth.

She said, "Oh master I forgot why I came. The guests have arrived." John immediately lowered her to her feet.

"Get dressed baby and go. I have to awaken Kim."

He kissed her cute nose and went to the room to get dressed. After Kathy left, he caressed Kim breasts and said, "Love our guest are here wake up."

She looked like a vision, so beautiful as if a veil of mist or light covered her sculptured body. She finally open her eyes.

"Oh John, I am too tired. Hum." she said stretching herself arching her back. He felt like jumping on her and have her a

million times, but he couldn't as of yet. "Hurry up babe my guest are here."

She jumped on her feet, "Oh love I am so sorry I fell asleep. I was so tired."

John smiling, said "No wonder with the five making love to you. I wonder how haven't I noticed, I must have been very tired."

Kim looked down, but dressing at the same time. "How did you know."

"Just a hetch! You look all pink from sex, look at yourself."

She did, he was right, her cheeks were beautifully colored enhancing her already incredible beauty. "Are you mad?"

"Why should I, baby? you feel you needed it so do it as much as you want until you get tired of it. I hope that one day you will think differently and grow up."

She didn't say anything. They were ready in five minutes, of course they dressed on shorts, T-shirt and deck shoes. They went out. She graciously held him by his waist. Orly and her husband were given tour of the yatch by Josianne. John and Kim approached the guest.

"Welcome aboard! We fell asleep heavily the hours flew by like minutes."

He kissed Orly and shook hands with her husband. Kim followed suit and held Orly by her shoulder.

"Let's go, we will show you your cabin."

Orly: "John incredibly the long way you have come."

Speaking to her husband and Kim "I remember our group and John musical band as if it were yesterday. 30 years have passed by, incredible."

Once in front of the guests suit, John opened to a gorgeous suite with all the luxury closet and bathroom with jaccuzi.

Orly: "Wow!!! What beauty, i love it" talking to Orly's husband John said, "Let me have the keys of your car, so I'll get your luggage or bags."

He said; "Oh no, I'll go, I'll be right back."

John: "I'll come with you. "

They left together leaving the woman alone.

Kim looked at Orly and said, "John told me that he loved you very much. You are his first love."

Orly couldn't help but blush, "He said that? Well we were just kids in puppy love, you know. But we did not forget each other to long. It's nice but that's it just memories. But tell me, how did you two meet?"

Kim told her the story agreed upon by her and John.

Orly: "John has a good taste, your gorgeous"

Kim: "Thank you too look great. Do you need anything, like shorts or bathing suit. We could go shopping."

Orly answered: "Thanks, but we brought everything we might need for two days."

Kim sincerly said, "I wish you could stay for a week, we could have fun."

Orly smiled at her and said, "I would have loved it, but we both are doctors. He is a dentist and I am a gynecologyst."

Kim said, "Great, I have two doctors here, can I be your patient? In the states I check monthly with one."

Orly said, "It will be my pleasure. Can you come to my office?"

"Sure why not. I am sure any of the girls will drive me there, or maybe John."

Orly said: "Just tell me before you come to be sure to find me."

Kim: "I will, thank you."

The men returned, Kim said to John, "I have already a Gynecologist in Nice ... Orly"

John smiled, "Great, who's better!!!!Orly who would have believed that one day you will be my futures wife doctor?

Incredible. Okay, you two want to rest or you're ready for the pool, some drink and snack?"

Orly jumped first, "The pool for me".

John turned to Kim and said let them put their bathing suits on, we will meet in the pool on third deck. They left closing the door behind them.

They met again in the pool, the weather was fantastic, blue skies. And Monte Carlo was magnificent, the loud sirene of the yatch sounded. The yatch crew was releasing all it's rope, ready for departure.

Kim said, "Oh we are moving. We never did since I got here, love."

They could see all the girls running from one place to another. Moving the passarelle with the crane.

Kim hugged John, "Oh I love it. It's great."

Orly and her husband were delighted, they could see Monte Carlo slowly spacing away from them. What a beautiful sight.

Orly said: "Where are we going???"

"To Porto Fino Italy a two day round trip."

They were all excited about it. Josianne came with hors d'ouvres and various juices.

She said "Anybody want's a drink from the bar?"

The bar was accesible from the pool without getting out of the water. Everyone settled for a soft drink. They ate with hunger. The day went by fast. They watched the sun disappear on the mediterannean sea.

John was behind Kim hugging her and kissing her cheeks. Orly and her husband embraced, kissing and enjoying the beauty of the moment. Words were not necessary.

John said, "Let's go for a helicopter ride."

They looked at John, "But to where?"

"Just around the coast and we will be back."

Kim asked, "Who is the pilot?"

"I am baby, do you trust me?"

"Of course love." She turned around and offered him her silky lips in an ennebriating kiss that could shake a mountain. Orly and her husband smiled at their embrace.

John called Kathy that was nearby and said, "Listen, tell the captain and all of you that everyone is invited tonight for dinner. All dressed formal for 9 p.m. in the dining room. My guests, Kim and I, are going for an helicopter ride and will be back in an hour."

She gave him a sweet smile, "Yes boss."

He pinch her nose "Good girl." She turned and left. John looked at her lovely butt, while she walked away. Of course it didn't escape Kim. She pressed his arms as a sign of protest.

"Should we?"

They went to the top deck and boarded the helicopter. John ignited the switch and a blaring noise broke the silence of the evening. The blades began rotating a few moments later they were flying south. What a sight!!!They could see the light of the continent from far.

They approached it at great speed. John said speaking loud, "All this is the coast of Italy."

Kim said: "Oh darling, it's breath taking." she hugged him and kissed his neck. In the back seat Orly held tight her husband and was looking to their left the coast lights. The tour was great.

The Helicopter radio sounded "Hi, boss this is Kathy all your orders were fulfilled. We are ready when you are."

John: "Thank's kid. We are on our way back."

Kim express her jealousy and said to his ear: "I am sure you and this kid have an affair. The way you look at her, the way you talk to her, am I right?"

John said smiling: "I love your jealousy you look more beautiful. Kathy is another secret that I will tell you when the time comes!"

Kim didn't seem to be convinced and made a long face. John put his right arm on her shoulder and pressed her breast.

She jumped "I Iold your controls with two hands you scare me."

He laughed, but the other three were not amused, because the helicopter tilted slightly down to the right.

"Don't worry I am use to it" he said laughing.

They were approaching the yatch. John radioed "I am back to base. Please keep course steady"

John came behind the yatch and approached it very carefully. The three passengers were gripped with fear. It looked like the blades would hit one of the masts. Kathy stood outside, directing him with red fluorescent sticks, until they touch the deck.

John immediately cut off the turbo and the noise began dying slowly until the blades totally came to a halt. Outside John said:

"I am disappointed at you three.." I saw you all pale and afraid. I wouldn't take you if they were any risks or I didn't know what I was doing"

Orly's husband apologized: "It's not that. It is our first time and seeing the yatch so close. It looked like you were about to hit it."

John, "I am just joking. I know the first impression. Let's us go and get ready for dinner."

Kathy was dressed in a lovely expensive looking dress; forming her gorgeous curves enhancing her beauty, but the childish face was still there.

John said, "You look cute baby. We will be there soon. Let us say, in twenty minutes!"

They all left and separated at the door of the cabin. Kim said once the were inside the master suite "You probably brought her the dress, it looked very expensive."

John said, "I won't answer until we go for dinner. Then ask me the question again, okay princess?"

He kissed her exciting lips, but she protested turning her face away.

John smiled: "You are so beautiful when you're jealous. I wish you really were like that all the time. It will mean that you love me a little."

Kim did not answer and got undressed, totally naked. John face turned a little pale, and looked away, of course Kim noticed it in the mirror of the dresser. It puzzled her again, but thought maybe he is upset, because of her jealousy.

Once they were ready. Kim had a gorgeous long pink metallic dress made of thousands of little metallic circles. Moving

individually. Melding her fantastic body curves giving a good idea about what was under it.

The dress was open on both sides, up to half way to her hips, showing part of her sensual thighs. She was bursting in sexuality. John was dressed in tuxedo. They left the room, and when they passed by the couple's cabin, John knocked twice.

The husband opened he was in a tuxedo. "We're ready". He looked at Kim his eyes almost popped out of their sockets.

He was marvelled by her elegance and beauty. She was like a dream. Orly noticed his consternation and broke the silence.

"Kim you look incredible beautiful, my husband seem to have swallowed his tongue."

They all laughed and her husband was embarassed. Orly had a nice white dress, with a red belt enhancing her figure. They went to the dinning room. All were present. The captain was at the head of the table and all the crew around it. they look? like models or rich girls all wearing long superb expensive dresses.

Kim couldn't believe her eyes. All look different even the sisters. They looked so distinguished and gorgeous. their gaze made her feel as if she was naked. It was a little embarassing.

John noticed it, and whispered to her ear "You have the sisters eating from the palm of your hand."

Kim looked down blushing. "I owe you an apology for what I said of you and Kathy."

John said, "You were right in a way I did buy her the dress, but not only to her, but to the whole crew. I love and respect all of them."

All the ladies were devouring Kim with their eyes. The dress she wore melded her well, that even her sensual triangle could be defined when she stood rect. Josianne couldn't help but stare at her. She probably was secretly in love with her. Who wasn't? Even Orly's husband couldn't help but look at her, mostly her prominent round deffined breasts.

John said, "Ladies and gentlemen, I want to welcome my friends and all of the crew present. Let us seat and enjoy dinner. Captain, after you."

They all did. The food was already in the center of the table. Four of the ladies began serving around the table. Champaigne bottles were uncorked. The dinner was excellent, a real chef-d'oeuvres.

John gave a compliment to Gina, the chef, "She is a professional Cordon-bleu cuisine."

She stood and all clapped as a sign of recognition and thanks. She had a marvellous fitgureia nevus face, red hair and very large green eyes. She looked more like an actress than a chef. After dinner, they had tea and pastes. Then they moved to the living room and put slow music and danced.

John said, "May I have this dance Orly?"

She said, "Of course" and John led her to the center of the room. She blushed when she heard the song, "A whiter shade of Pale of The Procol Harum.." It was their song 30 years ago.

She said, "You remember"

John smiled, "How could I forget?"

Orlys husband timidely invited Kim. She gracefully accepted. He was sweating heavily from emotion not from heat. The air was cool, John said to Orly, "Your husband seemed impressed with Kim!!!"

Orly: "Yes I can see that."

She is a real jewel: "Thanks, she cause the same impression everywhere she goes."

Then Kim danced with John and Orly danced with her husband. The rest of the crew danced between themself. Kim was melding to John, she was terribly excited, she wanted him badly. But what excited her was the gaze of the sisters as if they were making love to her with their eyes.

Then John danced with Kathy, Kim with Michelle, she said, "Oh how lovely you look. I would like to undress you and make love to you now, here."

Kim said: "Be quiet someone can hear you."

She was looking at John and Kathy dancing and chating. Kathy was looking at him with admiration her little bands burried in his big ones. Everyone danced with everyone even Orly and her husband.

Kim said: "Let's enjoy the deck. It's a wonderful night. Let's take our dresses off and ware our bathing suits."

They liked the idea and all disappeared to return 10 minutes later in the deck. A loud speaker was connected and they could hear a slow music unto the deck. The conversation turned around any subject. John was talking with the couple, and Kathy, the sisters and Josianne were surrounding Kim.

John and the group were all looking towards the shores of Italy.

Kim: "I am going to the bathroom, if anyone ask, say that you seen me going toward the cabin."

Effectivelly John turning around said, "Where is Kim?"

Gladis said, "Boss I think she went to the bathroom, to your cabin.."

John turned toward Kathy and said, "Kathy go see if Kim is alright."

She did without asking any questions. John looked around to see if anyone else was missing. Just the captain. She could be seen in the pilot room.

Kathy found the room open, said "Hello".

She entered and saw through the open door of the bathroom Kim naked was cleaning herself.

"Sorry Miss Kim, but the boss ask me to see if you were alright?"

She was mesmerized at Kim beauty. To tease her, and see what she got and why John was attached to her.

Kim said, "Could you help me?"

Kathy without detaching her eyes from her nudity said, "Of course, what do you need."

"I feel a little wet inside, due that John and I made love. Could you help me with the intimate douche to clean my butt and here" showing her vagina. "Standing like this it doesn't work properly. It's better to bend for the butt and lifte my legs for my vagina, could apply it to me if it is not a problem for you?"

Kathy said: "No, of course not."

She approached Kim and took the douche from her hands. Kim bent over totally offering a beautiful derriere vue to Kathy that was confused. She slowly inserted it in Kim's butt. Kim said, "Now push it all the way in."

She did began pressing the plastic bottle to pour the liquid in her.

Kim said: "Good now let's do the other ... "

She went to the bed and layed her back down and spreaded her legs totally showing a wonderful charm to Kathy. Seeing Kathy confused, Kim said, "I am waiting."

She approached and tried to put the nozzle in her butt was doing it wrong.

Kim said: "Spread my lips, so you can see, are you afraid?"

"Oh, no."

Kathys little hands touched her afraid she was going to be burned, spreaded one lip and inserted the nozzle all the way in.

Kim moaned and said "Now press the bottle."

She did.

Kim grabbed Kathy's hand and said: "You have cute hands and body. Please caressse me around here." putting Katty's hands on her vagina and one on her butt.

"But … shush, it's alright."

Kathy did slowly the bottle still in her. Kim moaned and push the bottle further inside her and begin moving it, in and out. "Oh!!!"

Then she took it out pulled Kathy by her hands. Kathy did not resist and grabbed her head to push it to her inviting vagina, Kathy complied by licking and kissing her. Then Kim made her roll over the bed and pulled her bikini and looked at her

lovely shaved triangle. She wanted to see, what John liked in her.

The sight was delightful, a young triangle with baby fat on it. White like milk, conducing to a well defined vaginal lips and a cute clitoris.

She began kissing her and gently bitting her lower lips, splitting between them with her tongue. Kathy had tears and moaned loudly. Kims mouth was all over her bounty. Her finger pushed into her butt hole moving it in and out.

Kathy came fast into her mouth sighs of pleasure and ecstasy sounded between her little lips. She caressed Kim head and said:

"Oh that was wonderful, thank you … "

Kim kissed her more and gave her a final brush with the tongue, making her shiver.

She said: "Let's get ready. You and I have to get friends because we love the same man."

She was trying to make her talk.

Kathy said carefully, "Oh we all love him, he is wonderful."

Kim said: "Oh I know about you, he told me, don't be afraid. I'll arrange that we make a menage a trois would you like that?"

Kathy's face illuminated from joy. "Would you, you mean you don't mind?"

"Of course not baby", she kissed her lips. Let's make a surprise tonight. "we won't tell him nothing okay? You come around midnight … I'll leave the door open, okay?"

Kathy looked like a kid that was given her favorite cake.

"Yes. I'll be here."

At this moment John asked: "What took you so long?"

Kim said "Just chating. You were right Kathy is a great kid. We will be friends from on."

John was suspicious but said, "Great, that is good news. Go out, all are waiting to say good night."

Kim said: "Give me a second to use the bathroom."

She ran taking the empty bottle with her trying to hide it and sat on the toilet releasing all the liquids in here. Once outside all said their good night and went to their cabin, but the sisters that had to guard the deck, stayed.

In the cabin John took a shower first. Kim's sudden happiness as quite suspicious. Kim followed and took her shower, when she came out. John had passed out. She looked at him and said:

"Love are you awake?" No answer, she went opened the door. It was close to midnight, Kathy was there waiting, nervous.

Kim smiled and said: "Come in". She did. Once inside, Kim took the sheet that cover John off, then opened his boxer, incovering his virility, she said, "So what you normally do to awaken us thing."

She undressed and his penis between her lovely lips and began sucking it. Her hands skillfully massaged the neck of his penis, close to his groins. Kim knew for sure now, that they had sex together.

Kim moved her little ass and began licking it, circling her hole with the tip of her tongue, then made her kneel on top of the bed to be able to eat her lovely vagina, her tongue totally teased her clitoris and brushed her all the way up to the end of her butt.

Kathy was wet from excitement. She had succeeded in awaking John's virility.

Kim whispered: "What do you do next? Go ahead."

She kneeled around his waist and inserted his penis in her vagina, making her moan, "Oh my big boss, I love you so much."

She forgot about Kim totally, now Kim knew that was something that she couldn't grasp yet. He is not gay or at least he might be bisexual, because he fucks this kid.

Kim stood in front of her in the bed and gave her vagina to devour which she did gladly moaning it: "Oh that's great, Oh

yes. I feel him in my stomach. I love your lips Kim they are delicious, no wonder my boss is crazy about you."

"Oh, he also said that to you? What else?"

"Well he said that one day when you are ready, he will probably marry you."

Kim knew that this was the story he told everyone.

"Can I borrow him for a little and you eat my butt?"

"Of course Kim he is your fiance not mine."

For the first time Kim felt his penis penetrating her. She cried, her lips was shaking.

"At last. Oh, yes." she layed on him without putting her weight on him. Kathy was kissing her ass then her small hands opened her cheeks and began licking her from his penis to Kim's butt hole.

Kim was in ecstacy feeling her man finally, she desired him terribly, here he was in her. She moved faster and faster, breathing hard. Kathy's little mouth and tongue made her more excited until Kim finally came, but couldn't make him come. She kept him in her for a while longer, then she rolled over.

Kathy went and took her place and was in frenzy massaging her breast and moving in and out of his erect penis. Kim caressed her lovely face. She began touching her nipples and breasts all

the way down to her clitoris, that she rolled between her two finger making Kathy come, loud moaning laughing and crying came out of her mouth.

Kim pulled her face and kissed her face gently in her lips. She was real cute Kim said:

"Now I understand why he like you so much, you are very dedicated to him. He does he make love to anyone else?"

Kathy said: "Oh no, he barely do it to me, because he knows me longer and on top of it, I owe him my life."

"How is that?"

"He save me from a gang that was rapping me. He jumped in and almost killed the five of them single handed. I was in a bad situation, hurt and no where to go to. He brought me here and attended my wounds and cleaned me of their filth. Since then, I wouldn't leave him for anything. he many times talked about this fiance he had was waiting for her and they will get married. Mostly he would say it, when I wanted his caress."

Kim asked, "How long ago was that?"

About a year ago."

Kim seemed confused, she came into the picture three week ago, maybe it was the reason they got her to make believe the story he was telling everyone.

"So he make love to you?"

"Yes, rarely only when I see him sad or excited. I come to him and caress him all over. Kiss him slowly until I put him in heat, then you know like we did tonight."

"Did any of the girls made love to you before?"

Kathy: "Oh no, you are the first woman that touched me. Mostly because you are his girl and also you are very beautiful."

Kim caress her lovely face and hugged her, feeling her warmth and young body against hers.

Kathy said: "Can I?" Without waiting for an answer went between her legs and kissed her putting her lovely face against her triangle, and then kissed her between her thighs licking her lower lips.

Her hands went to his penis gently stroking it. Then rose her head and went capture his virility and sucked it faster and faster until reviving it anew. Then she motioned Kim to seat him on her ass. She smiled and did accepting him on her her butt. Kathy wanted to please her too. She, then spread her legs and liked all of her vagina gently biting and chewing it.

Then inducing her tongue in it. she felt his erection in her. Kim was breathing hard, this kid was really a marvel, no wonder he adored her. She took her clitoris and suck it, making Kim moan. She caress her lovely head, her hand reached for Kathy cute Butt and caress it between cher cheeks. They both had an orgasm.

"Oh Kathy you are a doll. You really care for both of us. Thank you. From today on, you are part of us. You better keep this in secret until we will make him accept to make love to the two of us."

Kathy: "Yes, thank you. Can I ask you a question Kim?"

"Yes please"

"Do you make love to the sisters? I saw you with them."

Kim said: "Making love. No, just coming out of here? I know about them I am the only one that knows anything around here. They have a double sex, you know!"

Kim said: "Okay I'll tell you the whole story" and she did and explain, about her and John regarding sex only, not the other arrangements.

She was not surprised, she said: "Well, he wants to keep you for the wedding. It's an old custom of his country. If you make love before you might not end up marrying him."

That made Kim shiver was this true or just a story for this cute child? Well one day she will know for sure.

"Go baby, leave before he find out you were here."

She kissed her lips and put her bathing suite and left hurriedly. Kim cleaned up his penis and rested her head on his chest and all the left side of her body on his and fell asleep tired from the long journee.

CHAPTER 13

"Good morning everyone, this is the captain. We have arrived at Porte Fino Italy. You should wake up to be able to enjoy a few hour ashore. It's 8 a.m."

John opened his eyes hearing the message on the loud speaker. He looked at Kim lovely sleepy face on his chest. Her hands on his neck and her leg on his stomach. He smiled and kissed this angel in disguise. The face of love. He kissed her nose, gently pressing it with his lips. Then her beautiful eyes and teased her lips with the tip of his tongue.

She moved: "Wake up princess we have to get ready to go ashore. It's a wonderful day!"

She took his hands and put it on her flat sensual stomach, white adorned by her belly button. He didn't want to look further. It might create love unrest. Kim put her burning lips on his neck.

He shivered: "Oh!! baby that was mortal."

She giggled. "You love it, I know. Hi my man, how do you feel this morning?"

"Well, seeing you happy I am too."

She remember, what Kathy told her the night before. Did he really want to marry her. She was dying to ask him, but refrain it might put him in an embaracing situation.

They took a shower and dressed in shorts and short sleeve shirts, all white with cops that had the yatch's name on it. Kim put it side-way, she looked adorable. A knock at the door.

John opened, "Hi Kathy" he said smiling. She looked at him with different eyes this morning.

"Hi boss, did you sleep well??"

At this moment Kim came out the bathroom, "Hi babe come in." she kissed her in the cheek. Kathy returned her kiss. John looked at both suspiciously.

They both laughed at his expression. Kim put a hand on his shoulder and one on Kathy and said, "We had a chat last night. I couldn't sleep so I saw her outside, I invited her in and we talked for a long moment. So we became good friends and voila."

John suspected ulterior motives behind her sudden friendship, but said "Great. I also like Kathy in particular. She is being with me longer than any in the crew. She is my mascot and lucky charm."

He stroke her little nose then bent and kissed it. He waited to see Kim's reaction. But to his surprise she smiled, "She is so cute John."

They left the room, Kathy said, "The guests are upstairs waiting for you in the breakfast area. We will be serving breakfast in 15 minutes."

Kim said: "You are coming with us ashore? Yes, Kathy?"

"Oh. I would have love to, but I have to work."

"Non sens, John please tell her to come"

John said, "Well Kathy she is my boss, you have to obey or she will fire both of us."

Kathy's face was radiant from joy. She hugged Kim kissing her cheek and said: "I'll be back very soon." I'll put a short and shirt, bye."

She left running happy. Kim looked at John face, he seemed pleasant at their sudden friendship. "I hope there, this is no conspiracy or you intend to play with her."

Her smile disappeared from her lips and for the first time she looked disappointed. "Why did you say that? Do you think I am so bad or I could hurt this child?"

John took her face in his hands and said: "No my love, I just can't comprehend your sudden friendship, when yesterday you were jealous of her. I can't allow anyone to hurt her, she was

badly hurt already. As I would get anyone in the world hurt you over my dead body."

Her beautiful almond shape green eyes smiled and said: "I know everything about how you helped her when she was being raped, so I also like her very much. She is very sweet. She is lucky to have you as a protector and of course you are mine too."

She landed a kiss on his lips.

"What else did she tell you?"

"You know, just her life and how you two got along, she adores you."

John didn't want to push further.

"Let's go the guests are upstairs."

They joined the guets. Josianne had served breakfast. The sisters showed up, "Good morning Ladies and gentleman."

"Good morning" answered all.

"Mr. John, who would be going ashore, so we know how many crafts to put on the water?"

"Well" answered John, "we are five including Kathy. Who ever want to join us is welcome. We have to keep someone in here to watch over the ship. So if everyone wants to join, you are welcome. We should put all the crews names on pieces of

paper and pull 4 out. So these will stay for 2 hours, then four will return and replace them. So it will be fair to everyone."

"Thank you sir, we will."

Michelle was looking and smiling at Kim and then left. Every time Michelle looked at her this way, she would imagine her penis in her mouth. She felt a little embarassed. the boats were dropped to the water. It was a little choppy the ladder followed John and Orly's husband went down first, to be able to help the ladies onto the first boat. They were then five plus Josianne and Gladis.

On the other two boats the rest of the girls ; four stayed in the yatch for the first two hours. Gladis drove the boat to the shore followed by the other two. The beaches were filled with young people some totally naked some half way and even older people. Many were the rich and famous. Beautiful yachts were docked all over the bahia. An incredible sight.

John hired a mini-bus for the four hours to take them to town.

They had stopped in a market plaza to buy souvenirs. It was a great morning. John bought all kind of things for everyone.

Orly said: "John you're spoiling us too much … "

John smiled: "Listen we have a 30 year friendship, so what?'

Kathy was holding hands with Kim, John liked it. She looked like a little sister. They took pictures all together. On the first row, Kim, Kathy, Orly, Josianne, John and Orly's husband one

at each end. John rose, when Kim returned to retrieve and put the chair back for her. As if nothing happened they continued their meal.

The two Italian girls were with two good looking young men. Probably their boy friends. They looked at Kim then talked to their guys which turned he to look. They admired the beautiful American. Kim blushed.

One of them threw a kiss with his lips and finger. The other just pressed his lips and rolled his tongue, as if he said, "Oh I want you."

They all had finished their meal and went to the market place to buy all kind of T-shirts and sooner. John was buying things for Kathy at one stand. Orly and her husband on another. Kim was in a small store full of beach clothing and towels, and other things. She was looking when she felt a hand on her arm. It was the Italian girl, then the other came to.

They talked, but she wouldn't understand a word. They pulled her by her arm toward a dressing room smiling and talking Italian. Kim tried to tell them no, but they were joyful. Inside by the two guys. Kim was surprised they were there waiting for her, each grabbed her she was about to scream, but one of the girls muffeled with her mouth pushing a tongue in her. One guy opened her shirts and pulled it down. They pulled their pants and tried to penetrate her from front and behind. The place was tiny. The other girl guarded the door. Kim was fighting them. She felt their penis pushed against her vagina and ass.

Their hands opening her lower lips and rear hole to direct their penis in them, with the other hands squeezed her breast, the girls opened her shirt, they were all excited like hungry wolves. She hit one on his balls with her fist and then the other with her knee and bit the girl tongue. They winced in pain, but Kim couldn't get away. Their hands were inside her vagina and the guy on the back had finger in her butt hole. They recuperated and they pressed her against them sandwiching her.

She felt them penetrating with their dicks pushing hard until she felt their testicles against her. She screamed but the girl put a hand on her mouth.

One of the guy said in English, "Don't play the good serious girl, you are a hore … "

They fucked her on and on slaming her each time between them each time they penetrated her completely. The guy on the back squeezing her breast and the other sucking her nipples. The guy in the front was pressing her butt cheeks with all her strength spreading them so the other could feel her all the way. The one in her butt was kneading her breast with rage, she felt their throbbing and ejaculation in her. Her beautiful face was flooded with tears.

The girl licked her face and tease her clitoris between her boyfriends penis and Kim's vagina.

Then they turned her over to take each her other side. The girls was keeping Kim's mouth muffled with her kiss. Then the other girl entered to replace the one inside. The guy on the

back took Kim from under her knees and lifted her legs totally touching her breast putting her feet against the wall in front of her on top of the guy, trying to get in her vagina.

The guy first held her feet, kneeling and devoured her succulent vagina, while the girl sucked her breast. The guy on her back also kneeled to lick her ass. After a few minutes they stood up and the back guy directed his penis into Kim's ass hole and pushed making Kim in the girl's mouth penetrating her up to his groins. The guy in the front spoke English then with his palm first kneaded her vagina closing his gripe.

Then brushed his penis between her vaginal lips without penetrating as if lubricating it. Then without notice plunged in her, pushing all the way in. Holding her butt with two hands and his friend her hips and fucking her at the same time, cursing in Italian. Their hands kneading on each of her body parts they touched. The girl massaging Kim between her thighs pinching her vaginal lips and biting her lovely lips.

When they had finished the guy said: "You're a good fuck. Here is my card and $100.00. Call me anytime we will arrange for another public place. You do a good job."

Kim put her pants back. Still with her shirt open ran crying until she founded John. Seeing her like this he worried: "What happen to you????"

Kim: "Two guys and the two girls inside have raped me."

She showed extending her arm in their direction. He looked and saw them still in the store.

"I'll be back."

Kim tried to stop him: "Please John be careful." But he wouldn't listen. She saw him approached them, and spoke to them. Kim was dumdfounded at what she saw. John was even smiling and shook hands with them., and returned toward Kim.

Kim angry said, "What was that all about???"

"Oh, I just invited them to the yatch, I told them that for $500.00 each they can have you for 2 hour, both couples together."

Kim screamed "What? Are you losing your mind?'

John suddenly turned serious, his eyes were sparkling a strange fire. She never seen in him before. She frowned.

"Do you trust me or not?" he said clenching his teeth and jaw, she nodded. He made a hand sign to them.

Couple as saying, "Great we have a deal."

Then John called Kathy, "Listen take care of my friends and bring them to the yatch in two hours sharp. We will be leaving, if they ask what happened tell them Kim didn't feel well."

Kathy looked at Kim's red eyes and without asking question, said: "Yes boss."

John and Kim left followed by the two couples in the boat that took them to the yatch John looked calm. The two guys sat next to Kim and tried to caress her.

But she said, "Not know, in the boat and when you pay. "She had a face.

Okay, Okay I knew that you were a high price hore, but I like you. You are a great fuck. I enjoyed you a lot."

They didn't see the strange dark gaze in John eyes, but Kim saw it and frowned in fear. In the yatch, John took them to one of the cabin's and said, "Well where is the money?"

They both took their money and gave him $500.00 each "Good." he said.

"Now get ready and undress she will go clean herself and will be right back."

Kim followed John, still not understanding what he had in mind. He picked up the phone on the deck and said, "Michelle come with your sisters to the control cabin, I'll be waiting outside."

In five minutes the five were there.

John said: "This 2 couple in there showing the cabin have hurt my Kim. They raped her in a store. So i supposedly told them that they could continue in here for $500.00 each. They are waiting for her, you know what to do. I'll be watching with Kim behind the one way mirror."

The 5 girls nodded, no questions asked. John took Kim by her arm and led her to a cabin next to where they were. It was small. Kim could see them through the mirror, but they couldn't see them.

John caressed her lovely face and said: "Go clean yourself in the bathroom there is everything you need there is also a vaginal cream that will prevent any possible infection or pregrancy. Do you need help?"

"I'll manage, thanks."

She looked at his severe face expression, she could see his jaws clenching moving as if we was chewing a hard stake. She kissed his hand and left. When she came back. The two guys and girls were naked. Suddenly the door opened and the five sisters came in.

John switched the microphone fire on: "Hey were is the blonde?. We payed for her."

Michelle said: "I know we are only for the warm up."

Gladis locked the door with the key and put it in her pocket. They were knock-out looking. The two girls looked at them as if they looked familiar. Michelle carried a bag.

She said: "Okay today we will give you all the best souvenir ever."

They took handcuffs from the bag and asked them to lay down facing the floor.

The guy asked: "For what?"

"Are you coward? We are going to give you the excitement of your life. Sex is our specialty."

The guy explaind the others. Reluctantly they agreed. She handcuffed them to each other forming a circle in the middle of the room. Once their hands were tide. The five girls shackled their legs one to the other's leg. So keeping all of them tight against each other. Their legs spread totally. They were worried by now. Gladis took from the bags, some rings with straps. Kim didn't know what it was, but she soon found out. She came caressed the guy who spoke English, kissed his face that was laying on his chin against the floor carpet made him open his mouth

"For what?"

"Please trust me and you'll see."

She licked his lip with her delicious tongue. Put the ring between his teeth stretching his mouth open around the metal ring covered with rubber and strapped it behind his head. It was secured so it won't fall.

When they wall with their mouth opened and secure with the "O" ring. John and Kim came around and entered the room.

John stood in the middle of the room and said: "So you have rapped my future wife. Called her a whore and payed her

$100.00, well my dear friend one thing I can say:You are Fucked!!!"

The face of the one that understood English his face turned green from fear. The other one's did not understood, but seeing the expression of their friend, they began making all kind of sounds of hysteria from their throats.

Their mouths were all strapped wide open and their eye wide open rolling from fear. Their eyes almost popped out when they saw the girl take their pants off then a stretched belt freeing their erected penis. They tried to move but they couldn't.

Gladis and Antoinette came to the guy that spoke English and said, "Since you are the one that speaks our language, we will start with you. So you understand us."

Gladis put a sand paper around her penis and tied it tight with scotch tape at the end. Leaving the rough part to the center. She made sure that all of them saw it. Their eyes rolling scream. Kim was laughing hard and crying, but John's face was very severe. Michelle and Debra did the same. Debra had sand paper and went behind the guys.

Gladis lifted the lutter by his penis to be able to push a hard piece of foam under to elevate his ass. Then she spread his cheeks, he tried to prevent it by pressing them together. Gladis say: "Oh, you want the hard way."

She took a black rubber stick and spank him ten times on his ass, and turning his butt blood red: "And next time, I will beat your balls with it."

She spread the cheeks put the tip of her penis in his butt hole. Then in one single push penetrate him all the way. He began crying.

"Ho! Ho! Ho!" Michelle said, "What are you Santa Close?"

She lifted his head and plunged her penis in the "0" ring. Keeping his mouth open and reached his throat.

She said, "You better suck with your tongue, before I do worst she felt his tongue moving fast like crazy."

His eyes were red blood. She began moving in and out of his mouth. Antoinette and Gladis did the same to the other guy, blood was coming out of their ass. They were rapped by their mouth and ass. Janice began rapping the girls also with sand paper in their ass. They were crying and screaming. Then lifted their legs and penetrated their vagina one at a time. Kim felt sorry for them even though they had raped her. Blood was all over the carpet.

Then Janice came and said, "Now you will suck my dick."

She took her head and plunged her penis in it. The five ejaculate at least three timed each in their mouth and ass. And the girls also in their vagina.

Kim looked at John and said, "It's enough they got the message let them go."

John looked at the sisters and nodded. They stood up, and took the handcuff from them, got dressed. The couples could barely stand up their asses bloody. They made an effort to take their clothing.

John said, "Nope." and kicked both with his foot in their balls making them wince and bend, from extreme pain. "Michelle throw them over board naked from the side of the sea, not of the beach. So no one will see them drown. They can swim back (whispering to Michelle) have a boat follow them without them seeing you, and make sure they do not drown, Okay?"

"Yes boss."

The girls took the couple to the back of the deck and pushed them overboard to the water making a big splash on the water.

John yelled, "Next time, I don't think you will rape anyone again" Turning to the sisters: "Pull the carpet from that room and trash it."

He took Kim by the hand and led her to their cabin. He filled up the jaccuzi with warm water and soaps and said: "Come on baby."

He helped her undress. She fell in his arm, crying and shaking. He conforted her.

"Shush!It's all over, just a bad dream."

He stroke her naked back gently and kissed her head. He carried her in his arm and sat her in the jacuzzi. She felt relief, he took a sponge and soap and wash her face, shoulders, breasts. She looked at him with love and respect. She kissed his hand.

"Please wash me from their filth in there, please. Only our hand can make their touch disappear."

She was sincere and not trying to excite him.

"No, problem baby. I will do it, if that is the only thing to alliviate your pain."

He released the sponge and reached in the water between her legs that she spread further and inserted his fingers in her vagina for the first time and gently caressed and washed her inside, she closed her eyes. Her lips were shivering, he kissed them, deeper she said deeper. He did. He then lifted her derriere with his other hand and reached deeper in her lovely vagina. She felt relief.

"Yes my love, thank you. I know now that what I feel there is your touch you have erased the others. Now my derriere if you may."

She turned a little to allow his hand, He was sweating and breathing heavily. He pushed his finger in gently and caressed her inside. She looked at him and feeling his finger caressing and massaging her inside tenderly. After 10 minutes stopped him.

"Thank you, my love. I know that it was hard for you to do this, but you did it for my peace of mind."

Without taking his finger, he lifted her in his arms and carried her to the bed wrapping her in a towel. She wrapped her arms around his neck. He layed her on the bed and retrieved his fingers from her exciting assets, he took a cream from the cabinet and pour some in his hand and massaged her inside and out, her vagina, then her derierre it was burning him, feeling the fire of her inferno.

He was sweating and fighting the desire for her.

She was all aroused and was moaning: "Oh my love, you have a great touch. Magical, I feel great already. Come here rest next to me."

He let himself go, she helped him out of his clothes and said: "I need to compensate your effort for cleaning my inside against your will."

John couldn't utter a word he was to excited, even if she made love to him all the way. He wasn't about to object. But Kim respected his will she just layed between his legs and kissed his erected virility, rubbing her face against it, her eyes her lips kissing all of it then his groins, sucking one at a time. Then capture his penis in her mouth stroking it with her lips covering her teeth.

Her hands massaging his groins. was in heat, his back arched his hands caressing her gorgeous face. She had all of it in her

mouth inside her throat too, her tongue licking it. It didn't take long to feel him throbbing in her mouth, she quickly enclosed her lips around the tipe's neck and made her tongue roll around it non-stop making him moan in ecstacy. her hand strangling the bottom of his penis to make him delay his ejaculation.

Her lips pressed on his tip in and out just on the head finally releasing her hands. He convulsed and ejaculated with all his might in her lovely and delicious mouth. At that moment Kathy entered and looked at them. John had his eyes closed.

She approached Kim and caressed her head. Kim looked, seeing her acknowledge with her eyes and engulfed all his penis, feeling his warm flow fill her throat and mouth.

Kathy caressed John face and left, he didn't even noticed her. Kim continued for a while until he pulled her next to him, to kiss her.

He said: "I don't blame people for wanting you, you are unique, but to hurt you that, I'll kill anyone."

She kissed his face and layed on him. He felt her two pointing firm breast against his and her loving stomach against his. He frowned, she understood and moved away. Tonight I have a special surprise for you. You'll like it very much.

John: "Can I have a hint?"

"Nope". She kissed him.

John said: "Let's get dressed, everyone is back."

The yatch began sailing. The ancre and the loud sound of the sirene sounded. There was a knock at the door. It was Michelle:

"Can I come in?"

John said: "Yes, please thank you for the treatment of the fuckers. Did they got back?"

Michelle: "Yes Sir … But they stayed in the water, because they are naked. So I think they have learned their lesson …"

John said, "Good. Michelle keep Kim company … I'll go see the guests. They must be worried, and he left.

"Don't worry Michelle, I'll be alright, it was just anger. I was upset because they forced me. I know that this sound crazy but if they had been more gently and less by force. I might had accepted it and maybe enjoy it. I don't know what is wrong with me, but I am frank with you."

Michelle caressed her breasts and was about to bend and kiss them. Kathy entered without knocking.

"Oh, I am sorry."

Kim said, "Don't. Come in (turning to Michelle). From now on Kathy will come with me to your parties."

Michelle said, "Oh no no one."

"So I won't come either. She knows everything about you all before I did, So??

Michelle: "Well if you put it this way, okay. Come here child."

Kathy approached her, Michelle put a hand between her thighs and with a finger penetrated her lovely vagina. She didn't move or make a sound. She continued until her finger was in her all the way. "Hum, ready, good okay, when?"

Kim: "Probably tomorrow night. Tonight. I have a surprise for John."

Michelle kissed Kim's mouth and left. Kathy looked at Kim, and layed her head against her breasts and said, "What did they do to you???"

Kim: "Oh don't worry, no big deal. I feel better. I made John put his hands inside me. That only was worth the whole trouble. Listen, tonight, after the guests leave. I'll be with John in the cabin. I want you to come. I'll ask him since he doesn't want to penetrate me. I want you in the middle and we both make love to you as if we did to each other. What do you say?"

"I don't think he will go for that." She said making a strange face expression.

Kim: "I'll take care of that he will be hot by the time you arrive. He won't object to anything I'll ask. Put a good perfume on you and dress in a gorgeous gown. Do you have one?"

"Yes he brought me plenty. I love you Kim." she said hugging her, her little mouth, kissing her breast, her hands caressing Kim's triangle.

Kim caressed her hair and said: "Me too, little girl, me too. Now before the guests come and could surprise us like you did."

Kathy sucked her nipples, one more squeezed, her hand on her vagina and left. Kim was smiling, she thought: "What is going on with everyone. They are all falling in love with me!"

She felt proud, stood up looked at herself in the mirror, touching and suveying her incredible curves. She took a dress and put it on.

At that moment John entered, "Are you decent darling?"

"Yes, baby who is it? It's Orly and her husband they want to see how are you doing."

Come in guys here she is.

Orly said: "How are you feeling, what happened?"

Kim smiled and said, "Oh nothing just stomach cramps. I think the fish didn't agree with my stomach, but I am alright."

They left all together and fot in the terrace, to enjoy the way back to Monaco, around 9p.m. They were dropping the ropes in Monte Carlo bay in the dock. Before letting the guest go, John took a small alongated box from his pocket and handled it to Orly.

"For me? Oh, thank you."

She opened it: "Oh my God, it's a diamond bracelet? I can't accept that, it' too much already."

Kim took it from her hand and braced it in Orly wrist: "It's John's pleasure and mine too, don't offend us!"

Orly kissed Kim then John and her husband shook hands and kissed Kim.

John said, "Now you know where we are, please come again soon."

Kim said: "I'll come to see you at your office for consultation, bye."

They left after thanking them gaciously. They all waived them good-bye and returned to the yatch, Kim and John holding each other by the waist and Kathy holding Kim's hand. Kim whispered at Kathy ear: "In 30 minutes. Good night Kathy," she said aloud and kissed her.

John said: "Come kids and give me a kiss, my fiance doesn't mind.."

She kissed him on the cheek and left smiling.

In the cabin, Kim said: "I have a surprise for you, you don't have to move at all, be quiet and stay standing here. I'll undress you."

He wanted to protest.

"Shush ..." She said putting a finger in his lips which he sucked. She began taking his shirt first, her hands caressed his strong chest, her sensual finger playing with his nipples and her lips sucking them after that. Then she began kissing and getting lower each time to his stomach.

He moaned and caressed her long blonde hair, she opened his short without stopping kissing his stomach, her tongue also wetting his bare skins. She dropped his pants to the floor. She could feel his erected penis against her neck. She continued kissing, then she caressed his penis with the tip of her fingers, making him shiver. She felt the door being slowly opened.

She said, "Close your eyes now."

She turned and made sign to Kathy to enter. She did. She looked beautiful in a pink gown. Kim stood up and took Kathy by the shoulders and stood behind her, putting Kathy between John and her. Just three feet from him.

"Now my love open your eyes, but you can't say a word promise?"

He nodded and then opened his eyes. Seeing Kathy, he was about to ask the meaning of it, "Shush! you promise ..."

She undressed Kathy slowly letting her gown fall to the floor. Uncovering her beautiful nakedness. John looked puzzled, but kept silent. Kim stood behind her, and with the tip of her fingers began brushing Kathy's face down to her lovely breast teasing her nipples hardening them. Then to her lower

stomach. Kathy opened her legs and let Kim's fingers caress her between her thighs.

The other hand on her cute lovely derriere doing the same job. It was visibly exciting John. Kim kissed her neck and then faced her to kiss her lips, gently going lower and lower to her breasts that engulfed with full mouth slowly closing until arroused her nipples. Kathy looked at John in the eyes tears of joy flooded from her blue eyes. Then rolled her head back emiting sighs, moaning with open mouth.

"Oh, I am so excited, Oh Kim … "

Kim had reached her vagina and with her drawn tongue licked her between her vaginal lips Kim stood up and stood behind Kathy, then walked with her toward John that was mezmerized by the sensual scene. She pressed Kathy's back to Johns body grabbing his penis and put it between Kathy's ass cheeks. Then went around and melded herself to Kathy's front and held John by his lips presing Kathy in between. You see my love, she will be the connection of our ove until the day you can make love to me. I'll be patient. She stole John's lips in a kiss.

Kathy was kissing Kim's breast with passion and desire, her small hands one in Kim's vagina and the other between the cheeks of her derriere, gently brushing her finger from bottom up, feeling her valley and brushing the rear entrance, circling it with the tip of her fingers.

Kim took her middle finger and inserted in Kathy's rear entrance up to the end moving it in and out a few times.

The other hand on Kathy's vagina that was already wet from excitement. Kim then reached for John erected penis and pointing to Kathy's rear entrance which she spreaded ler cheeks and push his tip in her then held John by his cheeks pressed it making him penetrated Kathy's lovely butt slowly all the way down into her.

The three of them in ecstacy. Kim's mouth was kissing John, the three connected, she said, "Now feel her ass if you were making love to me."

Yes, she was moving him in and out of Kathy's delicious ass. Kathy was devouring Kim's breasts, her hands masturbating her vagina and derriere. Kim's hand also masturbating Kathy's vagina and pushing her against John penis. Three of them were moaning until they reached an orgasm. Kathy felt John's throbbing and ejaculation fill her rear entrance, she cried between Kim's breast.

Then Kim turned of Kathy to face John after she gave him another blow job reviving it. He stood there memerized at Kim's dedication to please him for second time. She took his penis and standing behind Kathy, she lifted her by her thighs and said, "Hold him with your legs around his waist."

She did then Kim took his virility and inserted it in Kathy vagina. She stood to their side, one hand on Kathy's ass. She caressed and penetrated her lovely hole with her finger and the other hand held John by his derriere squeezing Kathy and him together her mouth devouring Kathy's breast. Then went behind her and to her lovely ass each time feeling John's penis

inside Kathy's with her tongue. They were enraptured with so much excitment.

From time to time Kim would steal his penis in her mouth lubricating it and toward the end, she ept it in when he ejaculated. She licked it dry.

John and Kim began caressing each other with Kathy between them as a both fucking her. She was more than delighted she loved both. Kim holding both and her lips on John face, Et Voila Menage a trois. All the ollowing nights were to be as one. In the morning when Kim woke-up, she saw John on top of Kathy, moving on her, his lips devouring hers in a savage kiss. She was emprisonned between his powerful arms fucking her faster and faster. Kathy girded him with her two legs, her eyes half open in ecstacy. He breathed heavily. Kim watched silently their love unrest, then he freed her lips to devour her lovely breasts.

She began moaning: "Oh yes, my big lover. I love you, Oh, yes more, harder. Ah!!!"

She cried loud. In a way Kim felt a little jealousy seeing them so in heat and her desiring him. Kim kissed her lovely face, and robbed her lips in a kiss. Her hand reached for John groins and massaged then until he ejaculated, convulsing on top of Kathy.

They were all in sweat. John rolled to the side and rested, leaving Kathy in the middle Kim kissed her all over then rose to the bathroom and filled up the jaccuzi with hot water and

soap with bubbles and perfume. She went took Kathy in her arms and put her in the tub.

Then went pulled John by the hand and made him enter, then she joined too. She washed both of them, delaying mostly in their private parts. She massaged John neck and sat on his lap, kissing him tenderly. Kim then washed the soap from them. John and Kathy looked at her dedication.

She told them, "Okay, out of here."

She took towels and dryed them like two kids. Then layed in bed tired and said, "Now it's my turn, you had plenty of fun."

"Now, I want a full treatment by you two."

John laughed: "Okay my lovely fiance you got it."

He layed next to her and began kissing her face, licking it continuing down until reached her precious breasts, were he drowned his face in them, sucking and licking them endlessly. Kathy between her legs did wonders eating her with full mouth. Then John decended toward her stomach, but stopped to the last moment and went back up to her breast and face. Then she began biting with her teeth Kim's derriere then vaginal lips making her feel her teeth gently sinking in. Kim was all convulsing trembling in ecstacy. She licked her again and again, chewing her thighs to return to sect her clitoris with full anxiety. John even though he had his arm under her knees, could easily knead her breats endlessly. He said kissing her neck and burning red face,

"Are you enjoying my beautiful princess??"

She cried, "Oh, yes. She is incredible down there. I wish you could too, the day you will eat me, I think I will faint from so much excitment."

John rejoiced at her remark: " I think I will too my angel in disguise, that day will be the day we will remember the rest of our day. together, I hope baby. What a question?" answered John.

Kim her eyes half open, thought maybe Kathy was right after all. He might marry me. She felt Kathy chewing her vagina harder and harder as if losing control pushing a second and third finger in her ass hole, moving faster. Her other hand began masturbating his penis just under Kim's butt faster and faster. Until she felt him about to burst. She put her mouth in the head of his penis and stroke her hand faster and faster and she felt his ejaculation again filling her mouth. She waited until he finished and poored the whole thing from her mouth into Kim's spread and excited vagina, making her come, seeing her doing.

She understood exactly what she was doing. Since he wouldn't do it. She did it for him. She spread it in her as much as she could, then rose to kiss her lips which Kim' licked, her lips tongue and face. Enjoying the flow of happiness of her beloved. Kathy returned to her vagina, kept kissing her wet ups spreading the sperm on her clitoris and with two finger rolled it, making her moan loud and cry of joy and ecstacy holding Kathy's wonderful mouth and face.

She then plunged her nose in Kim's vagina, her hands spreading as much as she could Kim's vaginal lips, her tongue licking her inside, rolling it feeling the continious flow of joy. They all was under a wonderful exhaustion. When Kathy lifted her sticky lovely with her freckels. Kim licked her completely. They stayed in bed and continued until lunch time.

CHAPTER 14

Around 1 p.m. the phone rang. John picked it, "Hello" …

David: "Hi John we just landed in Paris, is your plane here for us?"

John: "Of course were is Steve?"

David: "He is right here."

Steve: "Hi, we're almost there"

John: "Did you bring everything?"

Steve: "Of course, even more than you think. I have and new stuff in electronic, that will amaze you. I will tell you in person."

John:" I'll see you later."

They hung up. John turned toward Kathy that was between him and Kim, kissed her and his right hand caressed her lovely curves pressed his lower stomach against her, feeling her gorgeous little derriere against his. She was braced with Kim, a leg on top fo hers. they look cute like that.

Kim's incredible beautiful face. No wonder everyone wants her, then at a risk of getting hurt badly did the two couples. Her body drove John crazy, he would have given ten years to make love to her this minute in then their lives might split forever, he won't take a chance.

He extended his hand to gently brush his finger around her brows, eyes and nose, barely touching her long silky lips. He rose his head above Kathy taste her juicy lips with his. How much he loved her. She opened her eyes.

And they looked at each other, she didn't need words, his eyes expressed everything, she smiled, extended her arms and wrapped them around his neck in an enabriating kiss, squeezing Kathy between them.

Kim excited her lips trembling said, "Oh my love, how much I desire you, I need you desperatly, When? When??"

After getting a bath the three together, they got dressed and were ready to welcome John's three associate, friend. They departed for the airport in the limousine and followed by two pick-up trucks to pick up the packages that Steve was bringing from the U.S.Finally here they were, all smiling, rushing toward John and the girls. After friendly embraces. John welcomed them.

"Finally Steve, Dave, Peter. I was getting bored (turning toward Kim) almost bored." she made an angry face.

David:" Hi Kim, you have my body here like a teenager"

Kim:" Hi David, Mr. Peter, sir."

John: "This is Steve also a good friend."

Steve: "finally I meet you. I thought they were exagerating your beauty, but now I think they didn't do you justice. You are more beautiful than." Kim blushed

John: "Hey are you trying to seduce my fiancee? "They all laughed.

The luggage boys loaded all the boxes and suitcases in the truck and they departed.

Once in the limousine "You know Kathy?"

David, Peter: "Yes, of course, how are you?"

Kathy shyly said: "Hi, how are you sir."

Steve: "I haven't had the pleasure. I am Steve nice meeting you."

They chatted all the way to the yatch. there the crew had their cabin ready. The crew came to welcome them again, the girls that Dave and Peter had fun with, immediately embraced them and lead them to their cabin as if to show them but they had other intentions.

John: "Steve, these girls that went with them are the habitual girls for you, not taking into account my finance and Kathy. The rest are yours, they are Bi-sexual and love sex. It is rare when men come aboard to stay. So you are a rare bird in here,

by the way, you see these five girls there. We call them the sisters, don't try those, they are very different, you want like them."

Steve: "They are beautiful John, what wrong are they lesbians?

John: "Let's say you and the of them in dark room, you might count six dicks."

Kim, Kathy and John expoled in laugh.

Steve: "You mean tranvasty?"

John: "Hemaphrodits."

Steve: "You mean they have both, really. I never seen one before interesting"

Finally looking toward Josianne and Gladis they were blonde 5' 10" gorgeous curve and Gladis 5' 8" red hair, her shorts marked her sensual curves like a glove and the short T-shirt showed her lovely stomach and belly button. They both looked at him smiling "Can we show you your quarters sir?"

Steve:" Hi I am Steve, Johns brother, How are you doing ladies?"

They also introduced themselves to him and took him to their quarters.

John looking at them leaving with the girls said, "My dear friends. I am glad that they are here. Tonight we will party. At that moment ..."

"Hum.. Hum ..." they heard behind them. They turned:

"Oh Helena how are you my dear?"

John extended his hands, but she managed to kiss his lips, and then Kim's cheek. She didn't pay any attention to Kathy.

Helena: "Finally, I found you my dear. I had very important news for you."

She was with a gentleman, in his 30's looked distinguished and well mannered." This is the Baron Henry of Liverpool, England. They shook hands then John said, "It's a pleasure making you acquaintance sir. This is my fiance Kim, Kathy is my protegee."

Baronn Henry: "At your service sir." taking Kim's hand, he held it longer and was like hypotized by her "A pleasure madam." Then released her hand.

Helena: "Can we go to your office?"

John: "Of course, please forgive my manners. I was surprised to see you. I just got company from the states. Please follow me."

Kathy excused herself and left, Kim tried to leave too, but John held her arm tight.

In the office Helena spoke first: "Baron came in company of 15 more couples, all royalty and top not riche people from many countries. They form a consortium to be able to buy large quantities of many different items, from Commodities to Military hardware. They are here in Monaco and would like to meet with you as soon as possible. The Baron is the key person in this possible deal and you will have to appreciate his personal cooperation and of course."

John: "That will constitute a problem?."

Henry couldn't get eyes off Kim as hard as he tried. Kim was aroused and flattered.

"Can I ask you a question Baron?"

With difficulty he took his eyes off her and said: "Of course."

John: "What is the buying power of your consortum per anum?"

Baron: "20 billion dollars give or take ten percent."

John: "Now, well let us say we meet tomorrow 10 a.m in my office building."

The baron looked at Helena, she said, "Okay, tomorrow it is."

They stood up shook hands and then said: "Oh, I forgot this Sunday I have a party for my guests, would you grant us the honor of your presence and Kim of course?"

John: "we will be glad too."

John was about to say that he had guest but she went further.

"It will be very private party, just 15 couple mine and you two. I'll see you tomorrow."

Henry shook John hand and bent to kiss an honor madam, and they left. After they were far enough for them to hear.

John: "I didn't punch him, because he couldn't help it. It wasn't his fault you are beautiful. And you can charm anyone, even me."

She wrapped her arms around his neck and said: "Even you? I don't know about that."

And gave him a kiss that also burned the air of his head from so much heat.

"Oh my lord, Kim one more kiss like that and I will be your ex-fiancee, dead!!!!!"

She giggled: "Oh you!!"

John said: "Let us see what is going on with the guys."

First he stopped at Davids cabin. He opened the door slowly. David was in the middle of a tornado, juggling with three girls all naked on the carpet. Kim and John smiled at David and left. Then later, he was with Gina, and Graciela sandwiched between both. Then they went to Steve, Josiane was laying in

bed naked. Gladis kneeled her vagina and Steve on her butt fucking her, his hands on her hips.

The baron and Helena left

The Baron: "Helena I want that angel."

"You're crazy she is his fiancee."

Baron: "I don't care we have to do something. She liked me too, I know it."

Helena: "I wish we could, I would take him for me. I love him very much."

The Baron: "You mean the money. The girl must want his money. He must be at least 20 year older than her. But I have youth money and royalty and I am good looking. I can take her from him."

Helena: "I will see what can I do."

The Baron: "You better see well, remember how much you owe me? I could take all your estate.but I will cancel that dept if you succeed and to show my gratitude, I'll give you the 14 karat pink diamond that you are crazy about."

They left chatting of their devious consipary, mumbling something 'all happy.

John held Kim by her waist and lifted her against him "I would be in trouble if my crew were man. They will all conspire to kill

me, to have you, remember, "No men. Women I don't mind, or the sisters in the mean time. Agreed?"

Kim: "Of course my adorable one. I don't want any man, I want you and only you."

Toward seven p.m. David, Peter, Steve, John and Kim were dinning in the top deck in the fresh air. It was a beautiful evening. All Monte Carlos was illuminated, the yacht arround them too. John was talking about the consortium and the meeting the next day.

David: "Do you need us?"

John: "Of course guys, all off you. I want your input and Steve I want all of them investigated."

Steve: "That is exactly what I brought with me. I have access to all secret services of the world through a special program I invented. I can break any code or decipher encrypted codes or text. Plus the newest technology I got from good friend of mine a very special directional microphone with 80 heads. Meaning I can point each one at one direction and record what it is said from the distance up to 10 miles and record 80 conversations at the same time in eighty recorded conversations of course. We will have to connect it to your satellite in the yacht. Then through a special gagget we will be connected to a space satelitte that will give us all the directions and boost that we may need."

John: "See my love, where will I find a better electronical engineer than Steve. He can do miracles. David and Peter also do daily miracles. They had found you for me baby." They all laughed.

David: "20 billion is big money to deal every year, even with a 10% mark up. That you normaly double. It's 2 billion dollar with one group. That is fantastic."

Peter: "What do you say if we prepare for tomorrow?"

Steve: "That is a good idea Pete, we should go to your office and work a few hours if needed what do you say John?"

John: "I don't mind, but I thought you had plans with your ladies and wanted to party tonight?"

David: "John, let's party when we close the deal, okay?"

John: "Great, I think it is appropriate. I didn't want to be the one to spoil your fun. You are my dear friends, your friendship mean more than money."

Steve: "Thank's John, we know that, but as your friends, we have to care for your business as if it was totally ours."

John said: "Thank you guys. You see baby, they are real friends. They were my friends in really bad times, so in good times they are hundred fold better."

Kim: "I see that my love, remember David convinced me to come to meet you. He is your friend, I can tell you that."

She kissed John's neck making him shiver. When they had finish to dine, John said "Princess the best thing for you is to stay with Kathy."

Kim: "Okay my love. I'll be here warming the bed for you."

Her expression was promising wonders. He kissed her, holding her lovely face in his hands. She returned the kiss passionly.

She looked at them leave chatting and jocking toward John's car. David said "So John, how is your love life?"

John: "It will be better soon but it is going in the right direction. I am following the agrement of the transaction. It's working."

They departed in the Austin Martin. Kim could follow the break lights of the car until they completely disappeared in the darkness of the night.

Kim felt a pair of arms girding her from the back, a mouth kissing her shoulder. "Hi, Kim are you sad?" It was Kathy.

Kim said: "I like his friends, they are sincere. They will guard him from anything wrong ..." They spent the night together making love. Toward 1 a.m. John arrived. He looked at both of them. They looked like sisters than lovers.

He couldn't take his eyes of Kim's triangle, her thighs slightly spread. He was drawn toward it, as if hypnotized.

He sat next to her and was about to kneel and kiss her when: "Hi boss, you're back? I didn't hear you coming. Let me help you undress."

Kathy came around and helped him out of his clothes. She saw his eyes fixing Kim's vagina and said, "You desire her badly, big lover. Go ahead why do you hold, she loves you very much and desire you too."

Kathy caressed Kim's between her thighs and took his hand to put in her. He reacted by saying: "I'll be alright. By what I see you two must have had a good party, were you two alone?"

Kathy: "Yes boss, she is incredible."

CHAPTER 15

Kim awakened first. Kathy was in his arms, as she could see they made love last night. He was still in her, she looked at them for a while and caressed his face. He finally woke-up.

"Oh, hi love! What time is it?"

Kim looked at her watch:" 8:30 a.m. Did you arrive late last night?"

"About 1:30a.m. you were knocked out, Kathy woke-up.

Kim:" You two made love?"

John: "Yes"

Kim: "I am ....sorry. I didn't mean to scream at you ... I was just frustrated, I just want you in me no one else, but you reject me. Instead you make love to her. So, I do anything to satisfy my lust. Can you understand that!" Her face was as if in pain. John took her against him and kissed her lovely face and lips.

"Sorry baby, I am also jealous of anyone making love to you. Even this kid Kathy …" Kim suddenly rose her head and looked in his eyes.

"Really, you are jealous? it means that you love me?"

John:" What kind ofquestion is that, of course I love you. Why would you be here, with me in bed. Not having you, makes my love greater than you can even imagine."

Kim smiled: "I know my big bear, I know even though I can't imagine, it must be a powerful reason …?But I learn how to wait. She lowered between John and Kathy's legs, pulled his manhood from Kathy's vagina and get him a kings treatment making him shiver, moan in ecstacy flooding Kim's mouth with his wrath. her after love treatment was as great as during love.

They had sex for another thirty minutes and they got dressed It was 9 a.m. He had less then an hour to the meeting. The others were ready too. They had a good breakfast.

John: "My love would you like to join us. We will meet all this interesting people from various countries?"

Kim: "Really you want me to come?"

She said joyfully and sat on his lap. Dave, Steve, and Peter were amazed by her sudden joy and childish expression.

John: "Of course you're my angel, and you bring me luck baby more than you can imagine. And of course you will charm everyone. Go hurry up and wear something nice."

"Kathy help her". They both left in a hurry.

David: "She is really something. I have to hand it to you, you were right."

Steve: "Does she have a sister?" he said laughingly.

John: "The matter a fact, she does have a younger sister, Jenny. By the way take with you your special suit case."

Steve: "I know the one that I let each one touch the special figurine fet their appreciation, and their fingers prints are recorded in my computer, this we will have and know everything about them, even their D.N.A. without them noticing the lose of a particle of their skin. I will take care of it."

Peter said: "Who is this diver there." Showing a man in a diving suit about to jump into the water.

John said, "Oh, he is a fag … He takes care of scrubbing the bottom of the yatch from barnicles and algae. I use his service once a month.

Kim returned, she was a knockout in her red dress. It enhanced her blonde hair, and melded her, hinting the treasure that she is covering. "Wow!!!!all said, a true bomb. They will sign the contract without even reading it."

Kim giggled "Really?"

John took her in his arms and said, "Eat your hearts out." and kissed her delicious silky lips. Which she coresponded with all her heart. They all departed toward the office. John drove and Kim sat next to him. The three sat on the back seat.

They arrived at the office at 9:50a.m. all there were waiting for them. Their girl friends or wives were there too. They were seating in the conference room.

John said, "Good morning ladies and gentlemen. It's a pleasure to have all of you here."

They all rose to shake hands. Helena made the presentation and John said: "This is my fiancee Kim, and my associates Mr. David, Mr. Peter, Mr. Steve, all from the U.S."

Everyone looked toward Kim appreciating her rare beauty, one of a kind John invited all to seat down. Two secretaries entered bringing refreshments. The customers were all together sixteen couples ages ranging from mid 30's to 40's all very elegant. It was easy to recognize their title in their ways of speaking or gesture. The ladies were between their late 20's to early thirties, all beautiful. But the man and the latters had something in common they were all snobs.

Their eyes rolled from time to time to look at Kim directly. The women included, making Kim feel uncomfortable. Henry the Baron was pratically staring at her, not even trying to hide his obvious gaze. John felt about to punch him, but he

was a gentleman and business is business and on top of it, he understood him for being mesmerized by this unique gorgeous blonde. John made the presentation by video of the many lifles of products that he beats any competition in the world, plus he could get most of the other products at equal or better price.

So it is better for you to deal if with one supplies, this eliminating headache. All under one roof. The meeting lasted 5 hours. After all had agreed to the terms David and Peter prepared the contract; and went to the secretary's office. To dictate the contracts when you done, let me read it and then make 20 duplicates said David.

They were all chatting, Steve opened his brief case and took out what it looked like a modern piece of art object and all the present touched it. Looked at it, appreciated and commented on it. In the mean time their finger prints were transmited the computer in the suit case to then the latter connected it to the main computer in the yatch. This will give them more info on all of them.

The couples came and practically surrounded Kim. Saying you are so beautiful, nice skin, gorgeous profile. Do you execerise? What kind of Diet? etc.. .etc. .

Henry was practically breathing in her neck. Helena the Baronesse was chatting with John separated from the others. So Henry should get one percent of all the consortium purchases and I ½ percent. Does this is agreeable with you?

John: No problem, I will draft a contract between you, Henry and I."

Helena made a move and came closer to him, putting a hand on his face "you have something here. Hold on let me take it off."

She was rubbing her finger against John's cheeks. Kim was looking at her doing and wasn't so happy about it. She knew that she tries everytime something to touch him or kiss him. Kim excused herself and came and girded John with her two arms putting her head on John's chest, which John kissed tenderly. "So how are you Helena, you look wonderful."

Helena:Thank you dear. ... I hope to see you both on Sunday no excuse. This is a golden opportunity for John."

John saw Dave making him signs to come. He had a stack of papers in his hand. John said, "If you excuse me ladies ..." Dave is calling me. Love, keep Helena company. I'll be right back. Kim did not like the idea much, but she obliged ..."

Helena: My dear you and I should be friends, even though you were the lucky winner of the richest man in the world. But since we are business associates we should be friends"

Kim: I would like that Helena. When I'll come to the party, I have a present for you. It is a special lotion, at you rub your sexual parts as nipples, clitoris, vagina and ass, then he comes and kisess you everywhere he will not resist you. He will be your sex slave.

Kim: He is addicted to me already. I do not need stimulants.

Helena: you are wrong. The moment he taste you with his lotion on, he want leave you not even for a second. She continued talking and Kim was thinking that maybe with this product he will make love to her finally and tell her why was he holding. Helena continued then he will be so in love that he will look at you differently. Not like today. I feel that he has a little coldness with you. this product came from India."

Kim: Why not!!! I'll try it when I get to your party. Thank you.

Helena: know you'll appreciate my present my dear. John had returned and they all at down to sign the contracts. Everyone present signed not including the ladies that only Helena signed. They were all leaving. Saying their good-byes. Henry bowed taking Kim's hand to his lips. It is a great pleasure seeing you again. I hope to see you in the party on Sunday. John felt like beating him in the balls, but smiled. We will Baron.

After they were all gone. David, Steve, Peter, Kim, John sat to talk for a while and then left for dinner, first stopping the yatch to get a girl each. Kathy was invited too. She was delighted. They had a wonderful evening together until returning to the yatch and 1 a.m.

They all said their good-nights and retired to their quarters their respective compagnon. Kim, Kathy, and John went to their cabin.

Kathy said: "Don't move. I'll undress both of you. She began first with Kim, leaving her totally naked, standing in the middle of the room. Then she undressed John. Then both undressed Kathy kissing her gorgeous firm body all over. They went for another round.

CHAPTER 16

The next day John got up without disturbing the girls. It was 8a.m. he had a long day of work with the guys. He looked at the sleeping beauties and smiled. They had slept in a 6-9 position, Kathy on top of Kim. Even though John never liked Bi-sexuality. But two woman together made a beautiful picture. Two gorgeous woman pleasing each other. He met the guys in the third deck, waiting for him to have breakfast.

"Morning guys, so how was your romances last night"

Dave: "They killed me. They thought that I was a cow. They at least took half a gallon from me!" They all laughed ...

Steve: For me it was nice, not to much, not to little. Perfect for me.

Peter: Oh, after a while, I fell asleep and they continued. I am not so young any longer, I am 16 years older than the elder here. So you guys have to acknowledge age.

"Yes, grand pa ..." they all said at one time.

After having finished their breakfast, they went to the computer room. Where Steve had installed the new equipment.

Steve: By tonight, I'll be completely hooked-up including into your satellite."

John: "Great.." that is good news, now guys let us prepare our battle.

David: Well, I am leaving tonight with Peter, we will research everything we can about the people. By the same token, John I need you to sign a bunch of papers for me … He opened his brief case and pulled several files. Steve was busy working on the computer. he hook-up the special attachercase that he took to the meeting.

Steve: Hey guys here we go. Their prints were showing and at the same time, the screen will roll on one window, until one point was recognized then to the second. This will take probably most of the day.

Peter was reviewing the files with John and David.

In the meantime. Kim and Kathy were still asleep. The sisters were anxious to see Kim. Seeing the boss busy with his friend They decided to take the chance and go to their cabin, they found them the same way John left them.

Michelle: Oh look how delicious they are together, it looks like the boss had both of them. They locked the door behind them, all five undressed and pulled Kathy from Kim without

awaking them. Very gently they began kissing them all over, devouring, licking their gorgeous vagina and butt.

Michelle, Gladis, and Janice went with Kim and Antoinette and Debra took Kathy. Kim and Kathy became excited in their sleep moaning feeling the girls.

Kim pulled Michelle penis from her and said, "what's going on here. Stop that now!!!!! She was upset, but she was subdue by the three sisters. Michelle putting her penis back in her mouth, caressed her face.

"Please baby, please we can't be without you, we need you, please don't stop now."

John had to go to his room for his phone book. Opening the door, he saw the strange scene, all fucking each other. He stayed there dumdfounded by the spectacle. The girls did not notice him. Until they were all reaching an orgasm and stretching, kissing, ejaculating, coming, moaning to finally rest in each other's embrace without moving.

Kathy was the first one to see him, she was petrified and jumped. "Oh boss, I am sorry …" All jumped too. The sisters covering their penis. Kim on the contrary was calm. "Hi darling … We had a surprise awakening." John could not avoid noticing the beautiful boobs of the sisters. The silly thing out of place was their penis.

Their breasts looked like from a painting.

John finally said, "So all you ladies having a orgy in my bed.."
They were petrified, even Kim was now worried. Michelle
stood up covering her virility, but still naked said "Boss, it is
our fault. We found Miss Kim and Kathy asleep and we were
attracted by their beauty and we lost our head. I apologize. If
anyone is responsible it is me sir. If you want to fire me and my
sisters I'll understand sir".

John lifted her lovely face with his finger and finally said, "I
didn't say that I will not fire anyone ..." I just got shocked. I
didn't expect this. I appreciate that, the next time you girls
have an orgy, do not do it in my room, or in the next. He
opened a door and showed the contiguos room. Kim stood up
in her wonderful nakedness and girded him with her two arms.
She was hot, burning hot from sex. She kneeled before him
unzipped his pants. He tried to stop her, but she rejected his
hand, pulled his penis that was already erected from watching
the scene and began kissing his virilty all the other watching.
Until Kathy rose next pulled his short and shirt and came
behind him and caressed his chest. He began moaning from
Kim's mouth on his penis.

Antoinette and Gladis came and gave their prominent breasts
for him to suck, he was confused but he did and massaged their
asses with the other hands. Michelle came behind Kim lifted
her lovely derriere and spread her cheeks. John was looking at
her erects penis penetrating Kim's lovely ass. Debra came and
penetrated Kathy's butt and began fucking each other.

John couldn't utter a word, seeing Kim fucked in front of him by a beautiful girl with a penis. Coming and going in her lovely extremely exciting ass. Janice took Kim's head lifted it and came penetrating her from her vagina, and pressing her own butt on his penis. Until he was inside Janice moved on him. They were all connected. Janice's butt was round and delicious. His hands went to Michelle's breast first they were incredibly exciting.

Michelle lifted Kim's leg all the way up, leaving one leg on the parquet. Then tilting her head to the side. Debra came and put her penis in her mouth. Kim was now penetrated from three side and moved on her with grace. John's hands kneading all their breasts and went from butt to butt and fucked all the sisters, ending in Kathy's vagina and one of the sisters in Kathy butt sandwishing Kathy in the middle. His hands reached for Kim's hands which they held each other.

Until he felt his throbbing he pulled everyone and went to Kim's mouth ejaculating in it. Which she gladly sucked making him shiver and moan the only one that could it her way. All the girls came and kissed him all over. kathy sucking his testicles, he was all in heat, with so many mouths, hands, breasts and sex. Kathy had an idea very appropriate, she pulled John down to the floor and kneeled on his face for him to devour her young vagina. She made signs to Kim and take care of him, she immediately understood and kneeled between his legs and began sucking his manhood in order to revitilize it.

Antoinette sat on John chest and penetrated Kathy's lovely butt, lifting her groins, so he want feel them on his chest. Then Michelle came layed under Kim's and took John's testicles in her mouth licking them then making Kim sit on her erected penis. Then Gladis came behind Kim and penetrating her incredible sexy ass. Janice came to Kathy in the mouth and made her suck it. the last one Debra came behind Janice and nake her bend and penetrated her vagina. They were all in motion.

Kim felt his awaking in her mouth. She quickly freed herself from Michelle and Gladis and came and sat on John, taking his virility totally inside her vagina. She began crying and moving up and down, her face bathed in tears. Pushing his testicles in her derriere. Michelle came put her sex in Kim's mouth, but Kim rejected her harshly. Janice also tried to come to her on the back, she also repulsed her.

Kim took his hands putting them on her beautiful tits which he massaged and teased her nipples. She was overjoyed, so many times she desired him, finally he is in her feeling him up to her entrails. Her gorgeous angelical face flooded with tears enjoying him to the up-most, moving endlessly until she felt his throbbing and warm ejaculation, extinguishing the fire in her.

She pressed her vagina to extract every bit of him. Then she kneeled again and proceeded to revive him with her silky lips and great mouth again. The girls came to her and penetrate her both ways.

She was too concentrated in reviving him, to allow their doing interupt her ritual. kathy wouldn't budge from his mouth turning and offering him her delicious butt which he loved to devour. It was cute and well formed even though small. He kneaded her butt cheeks. Attoinette took her from the vagina and Debra through her lovely mouth. Kathy also cried when she saw Kim in ecstasy her beautiful face really crying not just tears, but in esctacy. Kim finally succeeded in reawaking John's member.

This time she again freed herself and put his virility member in her delicious ass and slowly sat on it, enjoying every bit penetrating her very slowly as if in slow motion. Until she felt him lower stomach against her cheeks. And she moved him up and down, making her shiver from head to toes. It was his, not the girls. She now laughed loud then cried.

Kathy took his hands from her butt and put it on Kim's breast. Michelle and Gladis again tried to join her, but she rejected them. Kim took one of his hands and put it in her vagina making her arch her back roll her had back. She wanted to throw everyone out and lay on him and kiss him all over.

Her hands massaged his stomach and his testicles behind her. "Oh my love … I am crazy about you."

She was lifting herself on her knees almost letting his penis out of her. Then seating back feeling his penetration up to her entrails. his fingers masturbating her vagina, without knowing that it was hers. When she felt him throbbing, she moved faster and faster making him hold by strangling the bottom of

his penis very hard to finally releasing it and feeling the strong ejaculation filling her hot derriere.

Then massaged slowly his testicles making him discharge the rest of his contentment. She finally rose from his penis kneeled and then layed the face on his penis kissing and caressing his lower stomach and thighs.

Kathy seeing that her friend had finished. She stood up, the other too. All looked at Kim subdued and holding his virility kissing it with passion. Kathy made sign to the sisters to leave. She left too. They needed to be alone. John rose his head to see Kim, he stood on his elbow and saw Kim in a position holding into him and kissing his manhood. He caressed her lovely face and said, "What's wrong baby?" are you mad because I didn't hold you? I was sure that I had your breasts in my hands, did I?

Kim: "Yes my love. You did. I was just behind Kathy holding her and you held my breasts. I loved it."

John: "Which of the sisters took my thing in her, once in her front and once in her butt?' I know that each time you reawakened me with your delicious mouth. Her heart beating hard.

Kim said: "It was Michelle then Gladis," Why?

John said: "I … .the truth without wanting to upset my princess, it was incredible …" I couldn't even talk or perform with Kathy. was possessed by a strange desire, tearing my

inside. Please don't take it wrrong my love." Kim was all smiles, but she hid her joyfull face and said

"Yes, I know they are all very good my love ..." Do you want her again?" John was quick to say, "Oh, no, no ... .it was great, but that it no more ... " I enjoy you more, just like that holding me this way my baby ... Come here my queen. He pulled her toward him, caressig her face, and show her with kisses., and kissing her lovely breasts. Opening his mouth to allow as much as he could of her bounty in his thirsty mouth. She pressed his virility and they rested in each others arms for a while.

The phones rang: "Hello" Oh Dave I am so sorry Kim was a little sad, so I stayed comfort her. I'll be down in ten minutes." he kissed Kim took a quick shower, got dressed and left. Kathy was waiting outside when she saw him leave. She rapidly entered the room. Kathy all excited said, "So how was it???" Kim stood and held her in her arms.

Kim: "You're my angel baby... It was incredible. I couldn't hold tears or stopped from crying. It was marvellous" she danced with her. He asked me, who was on his thing. Kathy looked suddenly concerned. So I said, it was Michelle then Gladis ... So I ask him Why? I was worried then he said that she was incredible and then he felt something very strange that enetrated his whole being. I felt like dying when he said that. He loved it too, and was very concerned for me, that he liked it, So..I ask him again, would you like to do it again?

He jumped and was defensive when he said:" No! Of course not. I prefer you, like this kissing me than her doing. I had to hide my face from joy and I was also laughing, happy!"

Kathy was happy too, for both of them. She really loved them both very much. I am so overjoyed for you two. He also felt what you felt even not nowing that it was you.

Kim: and also massaging my breasts, he knew that it was mine. He recognized them, incredible!

Kathy: Because he loves you too much. She suddenly felt an anguish that she didn't share with her. The day they will be together finally. They won't need her any longer. Kim saw her sudden change and knew what it could be the reason she smiled bugged her, you are part of us babe. I will never let you go. Kathy looked at her and like a child, put her lovely face between Kim's wonderful breasts and hugged her with passion.

In the mean time at the computer room. They spent the whole afternoon, til the time that Dave and Peter was suppose to leave for Miami. Dave and Peter after saying goodbye to Steve that was staying. They left with John and Kim for the airport were they took the flight in John's plane to Paris and the concord to Miami.

John didn't feel like returning to the yatch right away. So he took Kim for a ride. Holding her by her naked shoulder. Kissing her lovely blonde hair. Kim was happy, happy to be alone with him. Happy to have felt how love will be with him.

"Oh my love. I am so glad to be with you. We owe our happiness to David, for choosing me to be your compagnion. I really fell in love with you my prince. I don't want to make love to anyone but you."

John looked at her: "You really mean that princess? How can you know baby? You never really made love to me direct my sweet queen of hearts."

Kim was taken by surprise, but she said, "I know that ... even though I am crazy about you. I imagine making love to me, it will be hundred fold. Kathy told me how wonderful you were, even Michelle and Gladis. They are totally possessed by you."

John: "They really said that. After we had sex?

Kim: "Yes, love they did. If you want we can arrange another party like this one, would you like it?"

John: "No, my love. I already feel very incomfortable to have done it, and they are my employees."

Kim caressed his face and said, "As you wish baby, you're the master.."

They returned to the yatch around midnight. After having walked hand in hand for an hour, kissing talking and learning more about each other. Kathy was waiting for them, in bed naked until she fell asleep.

Once in the cabin, Kim said, "Oh poor baby, look how cute she is. We became best friends darling."

John: "It really makes me happy to see you two together. She is a lovable and marvellous child."

They both undressed and went to sleep

CHAPTER 17

Sunday morning 9 a.m. The phone rang making a great effort John opened his eyes. At first it seemed that the ring was in his dream, but when it insisted he finally awakened. He looked at his watch, "Damn 9:00 a.m. ... " They had a wonderful night the three of them, "Hello..?"

Steve: Hi, John sorry to wake you up, but it is imperative that I see you in the computer room immediately.

John: Something wrong?...

Steve: Well, yes, but it is good for us or it will be guess!!!

John:I'll be down in 15 minutes just the time to take a quick shower. See you, and he hung up.

Kim and Kathy were all over him. Kim had her gorgeous exciting butt against his. He felt a burning heat travel all over his body sweating heavily. Her beauty roundness of her cheeks and their proeminence affecting him tremendously. He had to make a superhuman effort to disconnect their carnal contact as if it were a powerful magnet without looking at her, he went to the shower.

Ten minutes later he was ready. His eyes avoided looking at Kim's exciting butt and he covered both with the silk sheet, kissed them in their nose and left. He met Steve in the computer room,

"Morning Steve!.. Why are you awake so early on Sunday?

Steve: "Who said that I awakened early.. I haven't slept since last night. When I have something to do, I can't leave it for the next day. Anyway, I searched on all the consortium and about their buying power. They can buy as much as they said even more. They belong to 15 different countries. B) They own the bank you banking with here, C) This girls? are they wives and some are their fiancee, but to five of them they have wives in three different countries. None knows about the other, meaning biggams. D) Two of them belong to a Masochist club. E) listen to this one Henry the Baron and this one, and this are from an Arian brotherhood. Does he know that you are Israeli?

John: I am sure he does.

Steve: Well you have to be careful with this four guys. They don't know that we know about them, it's an advantage for us. The rest are more or less normal. Now about your friend Helena the Baronesse. She is in deep financial trouble. She lost millions in gambling and owe almost everything she got to … I give you one guess"

John: Henry?

Steve: Bravo!!!!now I wouldn't trust her either, because she is subjugated to Henry our dear nazy boy.

John: Hum anyway I never trusted her or liked her. Even though she is a real beauty, but somehow I know that her soul must be as dark as your shoes.

Steve: I don't mind trying her (they laughed) by the way she is heavy in afrodisiacs and pot. The matter of fact all of them. I won't be surprise if they have orgies between themselves.

John: Who cares, they could explode if they want. What else?

Steve: Henry and seven of them have many dark secrets to hide. They are fucking their own sisters, "INCEST" Can you believe that?

John: Where did you get all this info? I connected to all the secret services of the world. So I guess since they are Royalty and all kind of titles. They must know their every move, probably even about us now!!

John: To knowing all this might help us in the future. Keep up the great work. Now I am starved, sex makes you hungry let's have breakfast.

Steve: Me to. They went to the third deck, next to the pool and sat. Josiane came to take their order. Steve held her by her lovely butt and said, "Sorry about last night ... " I stayed working till this moment, but I take a rain check for tonight, if you want me then? Josiane blushed, because John was there.

Yes sir of course, she quickly changed the subject." what would you like for breakfast gentlemen?

Steve:Can I have coffee, toast, and sunny side eggs..?

John: I'll take the same. Thank you Josianne."

She left Steve and John looking at the ass of her exciting butt while she walked.

John: She is a lovely girl. how is she in bed?

Steve:Wonderful, but I have a feeling that she prefers women.

John: you're right she is.

Steve: I know it I am never wrong with woman.

At this moment Kim and Kathy showed up. They wore tight white short pants and pink blouses.

They looked like twins.

Kim: Morning Steve. Hi my love you left without me noticing. She came and sat on his lap, offering her silky pouting lips to him. Which he took between his. Kathy stood there a little shy.

John: "come here girl!!! He made her sit next to him in a chair, but not before he kissed her lovely lips.

Morning boss!!!

John looked at her cute face and said, "You two almost killed me last night … " she giggled. Josiane had came back with two trays.

Oh Miss Kim is here. Can I get you something?

Kim: please Josianne for Kathy too. We will have the same. "Josiane left. At that moment Michelle came and said "Morning ladies and gentlemen!!!!!" John felt a little embarassed but said "Morning Michelle"

Michelle: sir, I was watching with my binoculars around as I do always and noticed someone was watching us too.

John: Do you know who it is?

Michelle: yes sir, it's the gay guy that cleans the bottom of our boat.

John: Well good to know, check him also. I won't be surprised if he is a detective or informant for the local police, who knows?

Have a eye on him, good work. Michelle looked at Kim, but she didn't look back at Michelle. She felt something strange in Kim some kind of indifferences and not the excitement that she was always in. When she was around her maybe she is just tired.

Enjoy your breakfast and she left.

Kim noticed John's embarassment with Michelle. She smiled to herself thinking He still thinks that it was her he made love

to. She was proud of her doing, but all the time he doesn't fall in love with Michelle, that will be very funny.

When they had finished eating Steve said: "Well i am going back to my work.

John: Do you need me?

Steve: I always need you, he said jocking but not for now. Are you going somewhere?

John: No, I will probably just enjoy the pool with the girls, you should do the same.

Steve: Thanks, but I would like to finish all this new things, so I can have a report for you for tomorrow morning. You need it, Okay Steve as you wish.

They all left. John came back to the cabin and they wore bathing suits, so they could return to the pool to enjoy the sun. They all stepped into the pool. The water was luck warm pleasant. John: love don't forget tonight we are invited to Helen at party.

Kim: How can I forget, I wish that we didn't have to go.

John: I know that you don't like her, but try to be friendly we are business associates and she brings me many deals. So we have to go, princess. She loved when he called her princess. Kim came and Melded to John and rubbed her lower stomach with his. Hum my lover. I wish I could have you now, here. John smiled at her, "you are incredible princess."

"We had sex all night."

Kim plunged under water, lower his bathing suit and began kissing his manhood. Kathy laughed. Kim someone might come baby!'. He told her pulling her head out of the water.

"So? They can join us if they want too."

She returned to her doing, this time engulfing his virility in her mouth. Coming out for air every minute or so. Her hands massaging his testicles. Kathy was kissing his shoulder and chest.

"Boss, am I behaving as your wishes?"

John: "Of course little girl, you are a good kid. Come here." he lifted her in his arms with his mouth pulled her bra away and sucked her small but firm breasts teasing her nipples with his tongue. She moaned.

I love your kisses boss, especially down there, showing her vagina.

You do? we can remedy that, He pulled with his hands her bathing suit totally. She felt embarassed

"Someone might come boss!!!

John: So are you ashamed to make love with me?

Kathy: "Oh no my big lover ... I was thinking about you, not me.

He lifted her by her butt and put her legs on his shoulders face-up. She spread them offering him her delicious cleanly shaved vagina, which he kissed gently at first. His tongue teasing her clitoris then penetrating her, licking her inside. Making her moan, his hands massaging her breasts.

Kim came out of the water, and saw them. Oh what about me guys She put his penis between her breasts and moved up and down her hands on his derriere pressing him against her breasts. She was dying to do it again and make love to him, but he might get upset. She also took her bathing suit off and pressed her stomach against his penis. He suddenly released Kathy from his arms and looked at Kim rubbing herself against his manhood. Ho...Kim don't, not yet baby, soon I promise soon … .She looked like a scorned child, which she was taken her candy from.

Kim:I just want to feel you against me, if not Inside me. Kathy seeing the situation between the two and took his errecttion to her butt and embraced Kim, kissing her and blinking an eye. She understood and played along. Kim was kissing her lips and breasts. John had penetrated her cute butt hole, holding her by her hips, moving in and out of her.

Suddenly Kathy turned around offering him her appetizing vagina, which he penetrated too, continuing his doing. She took his hands to her breasts, leaned to him making him put his head on the deck, kissing his lips in an inebriating kiss. She moved in a way that John couldn't understand where her lower

body moved. Kim moved pressing her vagina against his penis, rubbing it. She was about to take it in her.

"Good afternoon!!!" They all jumped, it was Helena.

"Sorry to drop on you without notification and also interrupting your tete-a-tete. I have to talk to you about the contract between us."

Kim had moved away from him, turned over and pressed her butt to cover his virility. Kathy moved and cover her breasts with her hands. Helena couldn't help but admire Kim's gorgeous body. She felt a wetness between her thighs.

John: No problem at all. He put his bathing suit on, but she didn't miss admiring his virility. Kim felt like pulling her by her hair and pull her onto the pool fully dressed. John came out of the water took a towel and dried himself and sat at a table and invited her to sit. Kim said to Kathy in a way it's better we didn't do it. He might have recognize my vagina or the way I do sex and might have put and together and known that we tricked him last night.

Kathy: "You right."

On the other end John and Helena were talking.

Helena: "I need the comission contract addendum, So Henry will feel safe, before we move to open the letters of credit. Not that I do not trust you. G-D forbid but it is him."

John:" I have no problem with that Helena. I'll bring it tonight at your party. Is it soon enough?"

Helena: "Perfect. he will be happy. You are lucky John. Kim is lovely a real gem. She doesn't mind sharing you with her?"

Her is Kathy and no Kim don't mind. Helena jockingly said would she mind if I share you too, dear? John felt like saying maybe she doesn't but I do. But he didn't want her as enemy, she could be dangerous. Why don't you ask her? John said smiling.

"I would if I saw that you are serious, but you like to tease me my dear. Anyway I have to go. I have a whole crew working in my home preparing for night. So, 7 a.m. my dear Ta ... Ta ..."

She gave him a kiss and left, when she passed by Kim she said:

"I'll see you tonight my dear you have a great body. don't get too tired so we can enjoy you tonight, bye love" and she left. Kim felt like jumping on her and punch her or mud-restle her, immitating her. So we can enjoy you tonight!

. Toward one p.m. they had lunch, joined by Steve and Gina. After lunch John wanted to lay in the sun and have a massage.

Kim "I'll give you one my love if you want."

John: "No baby, I want you to get one too ... Then we will take a nap. Josianne, Carla, Kristine and Mimi are professional masseuse. They will give both of us a great massage.

Kathy: I'll go get them, where will you get the massage here or in the sauna?

John: I guess, better is the sauna.

Kathy smiled: yes boss. They will meet you in there in? ...

Ten minutes cuty, she left. Kim came to him.

So is this the same type of massage I got in the plane here? She said rolling her lovely eyes.

John: this depends only on you. They will do what ever you desire princess.

Kim hugged him and said: whatever I desire it's you my prince.

John smiled to her: me too my angel, soon I promise.

Kim took him by his arm and put it on her shoulder, he pressed her against him, kissing her gorgeous face.

You're naughty princess, you are, playing with fire, you might get burn. Making a childish expression,

"Me, that did I do now? Oh, I know I pressed my ass against you and your thing is about to explode" she laughed.

Just wait when the day comes you will see that I mean. He opened his eyes as wide as he could.

Kim:you scare me, you bad wolf. You want to devour me. He pressed her again kissing her beautiful green almond shaped eyes and took her whole nose between his lips sucking it.

When the day comes. No one will found you. You'll be in my stomach.

Kim jumped in his arms wrapping her arms around his neck. He laughed and held her like a child in his his arm, kissing her bare stomach. They entered the Sauna. The girls were there waiting.

Kathy to Josianne said: "Please Miss Kim take your bathing suit and lay on this massage table." John did the same. They both laid on the stomach. John saw Kim's incredible sexy and prominent ass like two enaxewble peak of the highest moutains. He swallowed hard his saliva. Kim was looking at him and his confusion, he turned his head to look the other way. She again was puzzled, why was he afraid or feared looking or touching her vagina or derriere so much. He must have a powerful reason.

Josiane and Mimi took Kim and the other two John. Kathy just layed on a wooden bench and looked at them. Mimi did Kim's back and Josianne her legs.

When she got to her heart shaped ass, she siged, her hands kneaded her flesh, feeling the firmness of her butt, Her hands took one cheek at the time they were gorgeously round and prominent. She was pressing her with full open hands to the back of her cheeks up to the top joining her hands, her fingers

feeling the bottom between her cheeks repeating many times each time the tip of her fingers brushing her hole, making Kim shiver. Josianne always desired to have her, but she wouldn't dare.

Kim finally reacted, "Oh my G-D. I ... don't know what happen, Oh lord think I begin to understand you my love John to break the ice of the almost palpable atmosphere.

He said, "Yes, and what is it?"

Kim serious said, "If this two kisses affected me this way, you probably know that I will die in you making love to me. ... It must be that I will even see fireworks. John caressed her gorgeous sweatily face and said, "Maybe the other way arround ... " She looked at him very serious. Let us go take a shower and take a nap. He looked at his watch, we have four hour before the party. Kim was very silent.

They put their swimming suit on and went to their cabin and took a shower before they crawled unto bed. Kathy joined them too. Seeing Kim so sereine and quiet, covering her body with a large towel. Something she never did before. He said; Whats wrong my love, have you lost your tongue?

Kim: "No my prince, I am worried about you ... "

"Are you going to die?"

John: Aren't we all one day? Kim, you know what I mean!!!!

John smiling and brushing her hair to the side uncovering her gorgeous face, said:Why? will you be sad if I did? Kim suddenly exploded in a hysterical cry. No, you can't do this to me, I'll kill myself. Her cry was uncontrolable and sincere. John: wait a minute you think that I am about to die this year. Oh my poor baby of course not. I do not have plans for that, only G-D knows those things. I meant figuratively die of desire and passion not real death. He kissed and drank her tears, her beautiful green eyes turned red. I am sorry my angel I didn't mean to hurt your feeling or anything like that. I adore you baby, he kept kissing her Kathy cried too, seeing her crying and hugged both.

Kim couldn't stop crying. John kissed all of her face, not missing an inch. Then her gorgeous shoulder down to her hands. For me my princess didn't mean to make you sad come let us take a nap. John layed in the middle. Kim at his left, her head on his chest which he kissed endlessly and Kathy on his right. They fell asleep. Then was an insisting knock at the door. Finally they all woke-up.

Just a moment said John. Who is it? It is Josianne sir, I over heard you talking with the Barone that the party was for seven o'clock, it is six thirty sir. John looked at his watch. Oh!Thanks cutty ... he said to Kathy, Help her dress fast ... I'll be ready in 10 minutes. I doubt about you Kim."

Kathy and Kim hurried. Kathy chose for her a two piece metallic red ress. A top leaving her shoulder naked holding on her firm breasts covering to above her navel, her breasts

free and naked under, if she put her and under she could easily caress them. Then her skirt held on her hips eaving part of her stomach uncovered like forming a V shape.

The bottom of the "V, was like below her navel leaving anyone figure-out easily what as under the rest. The skirt covered her up to half her thighs, letting apreciate her beautiful long legs and well formed thighs. From the back, a nailer "V, shaped then top of her skirt the "V" ending just an inch above e valley of her gorgeous derriere raising up to her hips. The skirt also very descriptive of her round curves and lines forming the most beautiful as anyone could have seen before. The top was barely holding by a double chain, leaving uncovered most her lower back.

She brushed her her hair to one side of her face, she wore a red lipstick enhancing the pounting lips, giving a little color to her pale face. The shoes and the purse matched the dress. John looked at her she was smaching. He could barely breath to see her beauty. In other words breath-taking. "Wow! princess. I am sorry my queen you are going for a kill no one can resist you. I have to praise G-D to have made a beautiful creature like you. He kneeled and kissed her uncovered Lower stomach with burning desire.

Kim said, "Oh not again ... I could faint this time. She pinched his cheek. Let's go my King since you raised my title to Queen. He stood up and gave her a box with jewelry. Here this diamond and ruby necklace, bracelet and earring will match you perfectly: He helped her. "Oh Lord, I am dead ... " I see

an angel from heaven. She smiled at her reflecting image in the mirror. She really looked like a Queen, especially now with her jewelry. She also wore a piaget with the same diamond and ruby John held her by her waist and said, "My Queen, would you let your humble servant drive you to your castle?.."

She gave him a sensual smile that made him swallowed his saliva. Kathy kissed both and said, enjoy each other more than the party. They thanked her, and took the red Corniche Roll Royce that John bought for Kim. It was also red and white interior. John was in tuxedo. At the party, all were just chatting, eating or drinking from a bar in the middle of the hall. Slow music was played by an orchestra.

John and Kim arrived. Helena and Henry were nervous waiting for them. They had plans for the night. They were a half hour late. When they finally saw them coming. She smiled and came toward them "Oh my, how beautiful you are Kim" she was completely sincere this time. She brushed her cheeks with both as if it were a kiss. Remember Henry my dear? Henry looked like an idiot with his mouth open.

Until finally he took Kim's hand and kissed it. How are you my dear, real lovely, he said appreciating her crashing beauty. Then he shook hand with John. They entered the hall where the party the crowd in the room stopped even the music, seeing Kim's make her entrance like she was floating in a cloud. After the chock all came and shook hands with John. The men all kissed her hand, by bowing to her beauty.

All were surrounding Kim and John talking, smiling politely. John Kim did not enjoy particularly that type of snob company. John and Kim were served champagne then Helena taking them both by their arms to the buffet to eat something and were chatting. Thirty minute later without anyone seing she poured a power hidden in her ring in a champaign cup and gave to John. Then a regular cup to Kim and all took one.

Helena was about to propose a toast when a valet came to John and did:I beg your pardon sir. Their is a young lady outside that said that she has an urgent massage for you. He tells Helena and Kim I'll be right back that he was outside waiting ... What happened Kathy.

Kathy: I am sorry to have enterupted you, but a young boy brought this envelope for you. He said to find you and give it to you immediately. It was life or death. So I didn't want take chances. Here it is.

John saw the envelope and turned pale. Without opening it he said. Go back to the yatch and stay there.

Kathy got scared to see his face's expression, he looked like someone else not the John she knew.. "Is ... is everying alright" without answering her question he said, Go..now.." She ft.tn a corner of the entrance he unsealed the envelope and read it. His face turned purple.

Containing his decomposture. He entered the hall. Helena and Kim looked at him. Kim got scared Helena for a moment thought that he had drank the cup she prepared for him. John

came and said, "I have to leave now … " Kim said "I'll go with you.."

John:Listen I don't have time to drop you off, Helena can you have somebody drop her at the yatch. Helena, "Is everything alrigth?.." Please Helena can you?

Helena: Of course my dear I will personally

Kim was worried. John left without even kissing her. She turned and asked. "Can you take me now"?

Helena: But my dear you need to represent your place here … The liderships will be offended the party was for you and him.

Kim started to say but..if you leave now they might take it as an offense and the 20 billion dollar deal with him. I am sure don't won't that to happen?!!!

Kim convinced said, "Of course not Helena … " Helena took her by her waist. Don't worry he is a big boy. He knows how to take care of his problems, I've seen him like this, dozen of times …

Kim: really? She felt a little comfort by her words. To Helena the situation was better than she planned it. She changed her tone with Kim.

You know Kim, I know that you don't like me very much but I would like to be your friend really. My way of talking may seem snob to you, but this is the way everyone is around me.

My mother passed away when I was 7 years old, and nanies brought me up.

Then strict colleges of nuns, with crocodile tears in her eyes she continued need a friend like you with real feeling and not like this robots here. All were looking at both ladies chatting in a corner of the hall. Kim whipped Helena's tears and said. .."I would love to be your friend … " Helena suddenly smiling timidely said, "really, oh great Kim thank you.." She kissed her cheek and said, Oh come with me.. .I have a present for you. She held Kim by her arm and led her to the second floor, to her bed room. It was very large and nicely decorated. It must have been at least eighty feet by forty.

Kim looked: it's very big and nice Helena. Thank you! She pulled a jar that looked very old, like made of potery and said, his is five hundred years old. I paid a small fortune for it. It's from the Incas. It is a magical cream potion. As I told you in your yatch that rubbing it on your nipples and ps. When he will kiss you there or in your clitoris, he will make sex to you, as you never imagined probably for 20 hours and he won't resist your arm. Garanteed I tried it on Henry. I confess that before knowing you, led by putting it and have John kiss my tits, he wouldn't touch me. I was frustrated.

Kim smiled I hope you're not angry because I tried? Kim said:no, I know that he is hard to tempt him.

Helena uncorked the jar and put some in the fingers of both hands. Here let me try it on you Kim. Kim blushed, Not now I'll put it at home. Are you afraid of me? I saw you kissing that

little girl, so I know that you are not afraid of woman! Kim in the defensive of course not, without letting her doubt she came behind Kim wrapped her arms around Kim and reached for her breasts under her short blouse. It's alrigth Kim.

We're friend remember? She massaged her nipples that immediately hardened from her touch and began massaging them, rolling them between Helena's finger's tips. Kim felt a heat waive all over her body, She felt her fingers rolling her long pointed niples making her loose control, she rolled her head back resting on Helena's ioulder. A hidden camera behind the mirror in front of them was filming this strange scene.

Helena continued rolling them harder and harder. even exciting herself from it. Kim had her eyes closed in some kind of trance. Helena saw in her mirror her secretary and with the head made sign that now!! She left not 3 minute later Henry entered and approached them. Helena made sign whispperedd not yet, wait. He froze but watch them. Helena stopped with one hand put a finger in the jar and put a small near of cream in Kim's lips and rubbed it around her lips and whisppered Kim's ear: roll your tongue and lick your lips dear. Kim did as told. Kim began moaning sighing. It was working as she planned it. the secretary rejoined with all the guests. Three of the girls had video cameras and began whilming the two woman in front of the mirror.

All the others surrounded them looking at the exciting scene. Helena took one hand and unbuttoned Kim's top letting it fall to the carpet, uncovering the most beautiful and exciting

pair of breast they had seen. Oh!!, how beautiful ... all the assembly exclaimed quietly. Helena continued rolling Kim's nipples between her fingers. Kim was arching her back head still testing on Helena's shoulder. Then Helena took more cream and this time massaged both breasts fully sqeezing them between her hands, with a sweet rage. It was her revenge. They were filming both women all sides. All were getting excited.

Finally she said to Henry, Unbutton her skirt and take her panties off. Henry came to her, whisppered, why did you call everyone. I thought it was for me only. "I didn't call anyone they followed my girls with the camera I think."

Henry was too excited to reason now. He did what he was asked when dress fell first, all again exclaimed Oh my Lord, she is incredible beautiful, looked like a sculptural marle statue. When Henry pulled her pink tiny panties uncovering the rest and best part of her treasure a beautiful shaved tangle, a gorgeous bulge ending between her thighs seeing the beginning of her incredible sexy vagina. Her derriere round prominent all were super excited by vision of this venus de milo.

Henry was about to devour her, Helena stopped him. Not yet. She put cream in her finger again slided between her thighs spreading her legs and captured her beautiful formed clitoris and began massaging between the tip of her fingers; with the other hand she put cream on her diddle finger and finding her butt hole between her cheeks, she penetrated her gently massaging her inside with the aphrodisiac cream, both hands working together. Her finger penetrating her butt hole

and vagina masturbating her with the potion. Some of the assembly had come in their pants and panties already. Now Helena spread more cream in both of her hands stood sideway and with full ended hands rubbing Kim's vagina in and out and between the cheeks of her each time shoving various fingers in her hole and vagina. She did faster faster as if possessed.

Her hands meeting between Kim's thighs. then wellmed down.with more cream bed the rest of her body from head to toes, after having asked Henry to Kim's heads rest on his shoulder. Her whole body was bright from her massage, the reason she wanted everyone to Kiss her, fuck her and they will lose control once they had some of cream in their mouths. Helena told Kim, stand straight, she did, as if was hypotized. You will feel many hands mouths, dicks. they are all John hear me? She nodded Okay, nowall the women seat in the carpet and the undress and let's begin the show. She called the three girls with the camera.

You three will film everything specially zooming each penetration seeeing every bit of it, no sound. Turning to the hungry men standing naked ready to jump on their delicious prey. Now you will follow my instruction, savagery. Henry spread her legs wide enough and eat her pussy. Henry didn't need a drawing. He kneeled in front of her and began eating after having spread her legs. he was shaking of desire feeling the wonderful bounty in his mouth, his tongue licking her inside nervously.

Helena called Charles you eat her delicious ass. he immediately complied kneeling behind her, bringing his mouth between her cheeks licking her from top to bottom. His hands kneading her wonderful flesh of her round ass. Then Michel, John, each suck one of her tits, they went right to it and pressed her breasts and with their hands began sucking it with full mouth. You Jack grab one piece of her ass and Joseph her other. They went and each grabbed her cheeks with both hands.

Daniel you her mouth. Fraco, her neck, Bob and her shoulders Peter and Allen her thighs. Kim was surrounded and kissed every bit of her body. The last 4 men she said, so take her calf and legs and the two one her belly and the other her back.6 men each had of bit of her. They were all new under the influence of the Aphrodisiac.

The woman were excited and were touching each other or masturbating. Women seeing their husbands that goddess of sex. Helena exclaimed: Now stop. they did but without releasing Kim from their lips. Release her and you play by my rules or nothing. They against their will, released her, bring Kim standing in the middle of this hungry horny men. Helena continued Henry you will masturbate her with one finger only your middle one, you and you and you and you, The 6 of you, each insert a finger also in her so just under Henry's and so on and so on they all did the last two had force their finger's in her stretched her gorgeous vagina.

Eight hands in one finger in it looked a grotesque picture. Helena continued the five you, each finger in her ass press it as

much as you can to fit. The five on the back all penetrated her delicious ass. Now the other free left two squeeze her tits and the last stick your fingers in her mouth and make her suck it. They all did. Each time they forced their fingers in they lifted her of the ground. The girls were filming the cruel scene. Kim as under a spell the guys too. They did this for 30 minutes. All ready to burst. Helena stopped them "flow the good part you all were waiting for, and stay carefully. When you're about to ejaculate pull your dick, let some it spray on her outside then plunge of' the rest, understood? All nodded like robots ...

Now girls with the camera zoom and film each penetration. They approached the woman were looking at Helena, hell bent in Kim. You suck her pussy go easy that's it. He spread her vaginal lips the camera was coming on her and filming Henry's dick penetrating pushing her flesh pressing. Now Henry hold until every one is in place. You Charles fuck her ass hole. He did you hold and spread her pussy to allow the camera to zoom the penetration.

They did pulling Kim's incredible sexy cheeks to the side, uncovering her delicious hole. Charles moved and pressed the tip of his penis in the hole and began penetrating her the zoom showed every detail of her flesh being pressed and spread when he force his penetration frnlaring her gorgeous hole. Kim had both in her up to their groins. You two you will fuck each one her butt wet your dicks with cream here! She gave them another regular loisterizer, they did. Now you two her thighs, but lay on the floor Charles md pull her on top of you and your will follow him. They again obeyed.

She had one on her butt two on her cheeks and hips two pulling her thighs wide tread had their dicks against her thighs. Henry inside how you and you each will masturbate your dicks against one breast. You will lay sideways and rub your dick, on her belly. That makes now the last five you that you have a large dick kneel on top of her head facing her and lay her and put your dick in her mouth and fuck her mouth up to her throat.

When Kim lay down don't put the weight of your stomach on her face, Now you two fit me on each side and take her hand to your pricks. They did, now Kim close your hands on them and masturbate them. Kim obeyed and began masturbating them. Helena screamed, "ready GO!!!!" They all began fucking poor Kim every bit of her body was rubbed or penetrated with their penis, fucking her. It was an incredible scene to watch. The women all exclaiming, "OH WOW ... " She is a sex machine.

They did this for the next hour. The camera girls captured first Henry's ejaculation. He pulled the camera, zoomed and filmed his throbbing then splashing his first drops on her vaginal lips, from penetrating in one shot all his dick and moving frantically in her, until convulsed. The next was Charles in her ass. They did the same by as ritual. Henry and Charles slid out and the two in her, and two others took their place. Henry and Charles rested on the ground not far from them breathing hard.

The other two also finished fast, then replaced by the two in the thighs. Then the two in her hands, then the two in her

tits and the last one were the ones in her mouth and finally in her belly filling her belly with sperms covering her belly buttom. Kim was fully covered with sperm all over her body. The one that was in the mouth also ejaculated showing in camera, spraying on her gorgeous face then plunging his dick all the way to his halls in her throat unloading the rest, his dick throbbing inside her beautiful sensual mouth. Kim was like this dolls that you inflate and suck. She rested alone in the middle of the room. She was ejaculate in and out 32 times.

The camera girls filmed Kim with sperm all over her body from face to legs. Helena to her servants, bring a bucket and sponge and clean her right here. Hurry-up. They did and in 5 minute they were almost washing. "Now since you are sixteen. She can fuck five of you at a time. Five first. Henry you get her ass this time. Charles her pussy. So Charles lay on the floor. Kim like robot layed face to face with Charles and took his dick to her vagina and began moving on him frantically moaning like she was madly excited.

Henry kneeled behind Kim and penetrated her in one bounce and began moving on her lovely butt. She told the other two, you two lay on the floor and grab one f her tits to your mouth, and put her hands on your dicks. You Kim will masturbate them. They all complied. Kim began masturbating them with all her strength moving her vagina pressing it when she had him all the way in and then release and moved her butt and when she had Henry all the way inside her butt hole, she pressed her butt squeezing his penis on and off both of them.

Then the fifth. You sit in front of her face Kim suck his dick fast and hard all the way to your throat. She did. Now Kim's body was too on the move, the men cursing and fucking her until they were about to ejaculate, the camera zoomed on their dicks and capturing the moment ejaculation. The vein of their pricks could be seen throbbing, then brushing splashing Kim outside of her and then penetrated her. Henry began spranking hard Kim's beautiful ass turning red. Exciting themselves and the audience. When they had free totally ejaculated in her and bad their last convulsion. They retrieved their dick from her, was sitting alone. Helena said don't. Suddenly Helena said, what are you fags, your Charles fuck her pussy hard with all your strength like a man slam your dick in her cunt in one push. You Henry fuck her asshole hard she likes it hard isn't it true Kim? Kim nodded like a robot. You go in her in one bounce. then Charles each one his turn with all your strength. You in her mouth, fuck her mouth all the way in up to your balls and you two on her tits, squeeze them on and off and suck her nipples as you wanted to milk her, until you taste her juice and Kim.

Suck until that dick dry hard press those lips and also masturbate those two dicks with all your strength squeeze them hard. Helena was getting a kick talking dirty. "Go now fuck all of you ... They began slaming their penis in her very hard smashing her beautiful Body time they penetrated her, her beautiful breasts squeezed like milking a cow. Their mouth sucking hard her teeth pressed on it made the man on her mouth winced with, but it did not stop him. All their bodies

moved like a machine in Kim's wonderful and beautiful body was totally filled wih sperm..

When the last five finished she said to the first five return and change positions with the other and vise versa. They did this five time each, group making the total to have fucked Kim 107 times each had her 5 times and twice at the beginning. They were all laying on the floor inanimate, drained of sperm and Kim totally sullied with it. Helena called the last one Now you can fuck her let say from now one hour.

He first came to her and began fucking her vagina, when he was done he made her suck his prick when it revived, He got her by the ass fucking her very hard, being as possessed. He was one of the Masochistes. He stepped, took Kim on his lap and began slapping her delicious ass making her beautiful cheeks red from beating. Tears were coming out of Kim beautiful eyes. She couldn't understand nothing of what was going on. She was totally as if hypotized, drugged with this aphrodisiac making her act and enjoy the sex without her full conciessness.

Helena was already her victory with tapes she will give Kim a copy of each and said:Bon voyage! Dear John is mine, even if she shown John the tapes, she doubt that. The last one when he finished slapping her lovely ass. It was red, his fingers were imprinted in the flesh of her beautiful cheeks, he came and continued fucking her in the ass.

When he ended. He again made her suck it to revive it, turned her over spread her thighs completely and began slapping again, this time her vagina between her thighs and pinching

her lower lips then biting them. Helena said, "Not so hard gently ..."

He calmed down and continued slapping and biting her lips, bent and devoured her pussy then plunged and again penetrate her fucking her pussy again, devouring and squeezing her beautiful tits, squeezing them in his hands harshly sucking her nipples. He fell not being able to continue. Helena said Now Kim suck his dick and balls. Kim did until the man puling away from her. Helena could almost ta herste revenge, she has destroyed the most dangerous enemy. She got rid of all her depts from Henry a 14 carat pink diamond and mostly the richest man in the world. She was

Now her final touch, the woman let's taste her all together. The woman undressed and almost jumped on her, each grabbing part of her sucking, masturbating. The woman were more vicious than the men. When they were all laying helpless in the floor. Helena said to her maids:Wash her again and dress her. You and you go make a copy of all the video's now." What Helena forgot to order not to copy the first tape where she was drugging her.

The hidden camera in the wall behind the mirror, they made all the copies within 30 minutes and put it in a bag and gave it to Helena. The maids felt sorry for Kim, but there was nothing they could do. They helped Helena t. carry Kim to her car and drove off to take her to the yatch. As if talking to Kim, were just fucked one hundred and ten time by men and uncounted times by nineteen woman.

You're a real sex machine. Here I made you a copy of the video for your and have a safe trip. She pinched Kim between her thighs. I wish I had time to fuck you, but business before pleasure. She parked next to the yatch waiting for them. John had not returned yet. She ran toward Helen's car, Seeing Kim completely down not responding to her, said. Miss Helena what is wrong with her? not much, she drank to much champaign and I tried to stop her, but she wanted and fucked many of my guests, Let say all of them as if she wanted to break world record to how many men can she handle. Then she asked one of my girls to tape her on video. So she could show him.

Kathy couldn't believe her, "Here this bag is hers, the jewelry is inside this back plus three video cassette of her adventure ... " Kathy pulled Kim and helped her walk to the yatch. Josianne saw them and ran toward them and helped Kathy carry Kim to her room. They undress her, she smelled sperm heavily, she was dripping all over.

They put her in the jaccuzi and filled it with water and soap. Kathy worried remembered that Orly was a gynecologist. She looked in all the dressing drawers and finally found her card. She immediately called her. A sleepy voice answered "Hello" it was her husband. Kathy sorry to wake you up at 2:30a.m. but we need your wife urgently. Hold on I'll put her on the phone. Orly: yes her voice sounded concered. Mrs Orly, can you come to the yatch. Mr. John is away and Miss Kim I think gang rapped by at 15 people off and please bring any tool you need to drain her stomach. She is dripping semen from everywhere, even vomited some, please hurry,

don't tell anyone not even your husband, we have to keep this a secret until the boss comes back and he will decide what to do.

Orly; I'll be there in 45 minutes the most one hour. bye.

CHAPTER 18

3:30 a.m. Orly arrived at the yatch. Josianne was waiting for her in the bridge. When she saw her car parking she ran toward her. "Hi Dr. How are you. Can I help you with anything?

Orly: please there I have to take all this items. She had various boxes, a bassin and cleat hoses, etc ... Josianne helped her and they went hurriedly to the cabin where Kim was.

Kathy opened the door, "Oh thank you Doctor for coming, I am worried for her. She is in there (in the jacuzzi) crying non stop. Orly then saw her, she looked disfigured by pain and an expression that could be anger. When Kim saw her, she hid her face in her hands and cried harder.

Orly: please Kim let me help you. Tell we what has happened!!! Kim raised her beautiful green eyes red from crying and said, "I really don't know." I was in the party, when John left a hurry. The Baronesse promised him to take me home. She convinced me to stay because that would help John. Then she took me to her room to show me something that's it, I don't remember nothing."

Orly: Kathy said that when Helena brought you. She told her that you had many drinks of champaign and then you had sex with all her guestior an orgy. That you were the one to start it and you request to video tape it for you. Do you remember any of this? It's important'."

Kim: Images of men around me, and touching, kissing me are popping in my mind, but I don't know how? why or nothing.. She continued crying.

Orly: "Shush let me help you, let us drain the water of the jaccuzi, Kathy opened the valve and the water began draining. It was totally empty now.

Orly: listen Kim, this is going to be uncomfortable, but it is a must. I am going to this hoses in your vagina and rectum and drain anything in it in this basin then I will send them for analysis. Kim noded giving her the go ahead.

Orly took a bottle and shook it well and said: first drink this don't worry it like a schwepps limon-lime that will help clean you completely. Kim drank it that tasted good.

Orly: Please Kim spread your legs as wide as you can. Good.." Orly took the hose and began penetrating it in her vagina very slowly until she couldn't any longer, good she said. The other end of the hose, she put right leg bend it. That's it, don't move. She took the second hose and inserted it in her rectum, pushing it all the way into her intestin. Don't worry about just relax. I am use to this I did this hundreds of times in the emergency rooms, when I was an intern.

She had inserted most of the hose in her, and when she just put the other end on the bassin, a flow of excrements and liquids that looked like sperm, came in large quantities mixed with some food she had in the stomach from the afternoon meal.. When the liquids stopped flowing, Orly took the bassin and covered it, thus elimated the strong smell of sperm. Kathy sprayed the room with an aerosal. Orly took two more bottle and made her drink still having the hose inside her. Then took two containers that had some kind of medicated cleaning solution and connected one to one hose and the other to the second hose and ask Kathy to hold one high enough and the other to Josianne.

Orly stay laying like this so it will hold the liquids inside you, then we will drain it. Fifteen minutes later, she lowered the hoses disconnected the container and put the end of the hoses to drain on a new bassin. This time the liquids were coming out, wett cleaner. She repeated the same operation three times, in the last time, the liquid coming out was totally clear as water.

Orly:good now there is nothing left in your body, everything is out. Kathy make her a chicken soup, a big bowl. I will go to the hospital lab, and I will be back. Kim held her hand," thank you Orly you're a good friend".

Please believe me I do not know what has happen. Orly taped her hand, smiled and said, don't worry everything will be alright and she left. Josianne left with her to help her carry

the three basins to her car and before leaving she said. Kathy, I'll do the soup, stay with her.

Kathy washed the jaccuzi and then filled it with soap and perfume. Took a scrubbing sponge and said, let me clean your skin from their touch and filth. She began scrubbing her lovely face, her neck, arm, shoulders all down to her toes. Kim took then the sponge from her and began to scrubb her vagina and derriere endlessly, still crying until Kathy stopped her. "You are hurting yourself, you are one hundred percent clean now."

Kathy embraced her, and cried with her comforting her. Don't worry everything is alright now.

Kim: John will not believe me, that I had nothing to do with it.

Kathy: Don't worry he will understand. Even Kathy was doubting now, knowing Kim's thirst for strange sex and her fantasies about having six dicks in her, or breaking world records. Helena mentioned that and those are Kim's words as she told her that night with the sister and her.

Kathy heard the door, she looked, it was John. He was livid, his face as if drained from blood. His hande was bleeding, his suit dirty as if he slept on the ground. It was 5:30 a.m. Kathy looked at him and got scared.

"What happen boss? John looked at their faces, he saw that they have been crying. Nothing much. Where you girls crying? Kim lowered her eyes, she was still in the jaccuzi. Kathy looked

at him and said; Kim had a little accident.. .John's eyes widely opened, "What, whats wrong princess."

Kathy: she is alright now. Helena brought her she said that she drank to much. John seeing that this was not the whole incident said: So? She tried to avoid telling him Kim spoke:

"Helena said that I fucked all her guest! that I started it and that I request to tape it to show it to you. John; is it true? Kim's eye filled with tears her lip trembling cried, I do not remember a thing, not even drinking just the cup you gave me before you left and I didn't even finished it.

John: you remember nothing? Did she give you a pill or drugs? or something?

Kim: I don't remember, I told you. I remember vague scenes of men besieging me, but like a dream and not reality.

John: Kathy help her, dry her and put this bathrobe, he handed Kathy a bath robe. John was upset very upset. Josianne came back with a bowl of soup. She gave it to Kim, Kathy made her drink it. "The doctor said to drink it."

John: A doctor was here? Kathy told him all the happening that night until now.

John, Kim, kathy and Josianne went to the bed room.

John: Where are the video tapes? Kathy handed him the bag. They were numbered one, two three. He switched the T.V. and video on his heart was beating hard, all of them were.

The first tape began there was no sound. Helena took care of that, so he won't hear her voice giving orders. The first image were when Henry kneeled and began devouring her vagina; then Charles. Kim looked like semi-concious and enjoying the sex, her face showed intense excitement. Then they were all over her, all her body covered by their doing.

The girls were crying watching the horrible scene. Kim looked from time to time at him. he had tears flowing endlessly from his eyes, reddened. She had never seen him this way, alway cool and in control. He looked down in pain tremendous pain: seeing him like this, she even cried harder. When no one was looking at him, he took a marble statue that was behind him and threw it to the giant T.V. screen, causing it tremendous explosion they all jumped ... "What, what was that turning toward him ...

He spoke with a trembling voice from the emotion, "I see that you enjoyed it. I do not see you inconcious. You had to do it, but why? Why? I asked you not too the whole world fucked you but me!"

Kim, crying without looking at him: "I didn't, I didn't."

John: I beg of you, give me something, a proof. I need to believe you. I am dying to believe you my life depend on it. Give me something to defend you. You have chattered my dreams fret me and you.

He covered his face with his hands, "Oh G-D why? why? In a rage he threw everything that was on top of the dresser, breaking everything in it.

Kathy was hugging Kim. That hid her face between her arms that were in her lap. Kathy trying to help both, shaking: Boss I don't trust Helena, she is very tricky. You know that!!!

John yelling said; "But look at her in the video in ecstacy, enjoying, moaning, laughing. No one is forcing her. Suddenly, very calm Kim stood slowly and said, "Don't suffer any longer..

I'll leave now. I am going back to my parents. I'll send the money back that you transfered to my parents. Kathy please help me pack and call for a ticket for the reservation.

John was dumbfounded. He said: "Let us not hurry or make difficult decisions in a moment of anger. Let us wait for Orly to return with the lab results.

Kim: No, I want to go. I can't stay here any addittional minutes. She took a box that had the jewelry and gave it to him. He did not take it, she threw it in the bed.

Kim asked: "Where is the jewelry I were yesterday. I don't remember taking it off."

Kathy said:" it's in the bag where the tapes were." She took the bag and took the jewelry. Hold on there is something in the bottom here. She pulled a video unmarked. There is another tape.

All looked at her, John grabbed the tapes from her hand and ran toward the living room, because he broke his room t.v. They all followed him, but Kim.

She began getting dress to leave. John told Josianne to return to the cabin and stay with Kim. Kathy and John the heart beating put the video on. This tape was copied by mistake, by the camera girl that took the tape that was behind the mirror and had all the beginning.

John's face changed expression, when he saw Kim and Helena discussing about the present Helena was giving to her, to excite John then when she rubbed her nipples even though Kim didn't want, then the whole scene massaging her body with cream the aphrodisiac. This tape had sound and he could see and hear Helena telling everyone what to do.

After 15 minutes he stopped it and ran to his cabin. Kim was dressed. He smiled at her, kneeled, lowered his head and said

"Please princess forgive me for doubting you, I was in pain seeing these people having you. I wanted to die!!!!! She made a mistake and the other tape show exactly what she did to you, and the cream an aphrodisiac. She rubbed your nipples with, then your lips. Kim said "Yes I do remember part now."

She suddenly exploded in a hysterical cry, shaking from head to toes. He stood and embraced her. She began fighting him, beating his chest with both hands, yelling and crying... "I hate you!!!!" I hate you!!!!! I want to go home, I hate you!!!! and continued crying trying to free from his embrace.

He said.: "shush ….my queen, shush … Hit me, more. "Which she did screaming slapping him very hard. "I hate you!!!!" until she got tired and fainted in his arm.

He lifted her: " Kathy quick bring me water." He took a strong perfume and made her smell.

She moved: "Oh, my head." John gave her the water to drink. She coughed …

Kim: I want to go home, I want my mother." She cried like a little girl. John held her hands to his lips. "Please princess.. How can I say this. I can't live without you. Please forgive me. I.was blinded by jealousy, hurt to see you taken this way. Please forgive me."

He put his face against her chest and was actually crying. The Iron Man, crying for her. He loved her. She raised her hands then caressed his hair, very gently crying. Kathy and Josianne cried too, then left them alone.

Toward seven a.m. Orly returned from the hospital lab with the result. Seeing John, seating in the couch with Kim in his arms rocking her gently in his lap, caressing her hair, kissing her face.

"Oh Orly, please come in, thanks so much for taking care of my Kim" and he told her about the videos and what had transpired

Orly: It does concide with the lab results. There was powerful Aphrodisiac, and in large quantity. What I was worried about

was anyone of her attackers had diseases that could have been transmitted to her. But thank C-D there wasn't and Kim's blood and body are clean now. No doubt." John took Orly's hand and kissed it.

"Thank you my dear old friend. I owe you my life, because she is my life." Orly looked at his hand. It had a large cut, "What happened to you?"

John looked, his face changed expression, "Nothing. I put my hand somewhere and it had a sharp edge. "Let me attend it. She took a desinfectant from her bag and cleaned it with alcohol, put some antibiotic cream then wrapped his hand with a bandage. "Voila! you two are in good shape now. I have to run. I left my husband with the kids. They will drive him crazy."

John: "Please Orly send me the bill, and thank you, dear friend … "

Orly: "Don't worry she will be alright she needs peace and calm for a while … I and you don't owe me nothing. "She bowed and kissed both in the cheeks and left. Josianne went with her.

John took a shower after having left Kim in the bed in Kathy's company. When he finished he layed next to Kim. He could feel that Kim was still hurt from his suspicion when she most needed his support. Kim had her back to him and he knew she was awake.

John: "My love. I have no excuse but the love I have for you, I was dying … I was chattered while watching those horrible pictures. If anyone had put me a knife in my heart and bled to death, I wouldn't have suffered as much. He was playing with her hair. You see princess, very soon you will understand everything about me, even how big is my love for you. Please give me a chance, do not leave me. I need you more than meet the eye. I adore you." The last words strangled in his throat. He turned the other way and slept.

Kim heard him, Her heart was beating hard, he loved her, even seeing her being ravished that way. Maybe she should continue being disappointed to make him talk more and more open. She remembered the images of the videos she frowned.

This bitch of Helena will pay her dearly. John will surely take revenge, that she doesn't even doubt it and she was more than right.

Kim couldn't sleep she stood and went out to the deck. Kathy was there she couldn't sleep either. The kid that brought the news paper passed by and tossed the papers to the deck, "Bonjour" Kathy also said "Bonjour, Merci" Kathy picked up the papers. the face of a young girl 18 years old blonde. From Cannes a city not far from Nice, where they have the annual film Festival of Cannes. She was found with her breast and vagina totally taken out with a surgical knife. The description was.

Kim: What happened? Kathy showed her the french paper and said another girl was murdered and mulitated taking her

body parts and breasts and vagina. Both at the same time, turned pale, "Oh my G-D"

Kim said "Are you thinking like me."

Kathy: "I think so, but I can't accept it."

Kim:" Me neither. But if analyze it. Each time he leaves mysteriously and comes back, dirty, sometimes with blood cut. The next morning a girl is dead. Maybe he needs help, maybe that is the secret he said he will share one day with me."

Kathy: "I am scared Kim, what should we do? This also happened many times before you arrived here from America, and everytime he had gone for the night."

Kim: "I think he has some dark secret in his special room that none of us is allowed in. I can't imagine him as a murderer, he is so sweet and polite. The only time got scared looking at him was when the incident of the 2 Italian couples, saw murder in his eyes. His jaws clenching as if he was about to break them."

Kathy: "What should we do? Should we call the police? I don't think I can, I love him too much."

Kim:" Me neither, maybe it is circumstances. Let's not judge him without asking him, but not now. We are all under shock."

Kathy: "He ask last night, not to make sex to you, unless you request it. He will probably tell everyone else, meaning the sisters."

Kim: "Talking about the devil."

They came around her and said: "we are sorry, we heard what has happened you. Are you alright now?"

Kim smiled poorly: "I'll be alright thank you." Michelle saw that she wasn't in a talkative mood.

She said, "I am glad, at at least you look alright, be well, bye!" The other also said bye and left.

Kim: "Kathy, don't leave me alone with him at no moment, even if he wants, say that I asked you too, at least until we find out more of this. We have to find the opportunity to see what is in that secret room. I hope it is not what I think."

"Me too."

They returned to the room, Kim and Kathy looked at him with fear and also respect for who he was. They were whisppering seating in the sofa. "Why are you two whispering?" John said. Kim and Kathy jumped.

John: "I am sorry I have scared you."

Kim:" It's nothing we are just in the edge after all this mess."

He put his shorts on, and stayed without t-shirt. They could notice his trong muscles and wide shoulders. He sat in front of them, looked at Kim in the eyes: "Listen, I am about to call Helena and apologize for your behavior." Kim wanted to interupt." Trust me.

What ever you hear is part of a plan to revenge your honor." His eyes were sparkling again, that fire that scared both of them. He picked up the phone and made her sign not to talk. He dialed. "Yes, Hello, this is Mr. John I wish to speak to the Baronesse" "please wait a minute."

"Hi, this is John"

Helena: "Good morning my dear. I have a feeling that I know what you are calling." He had connected the speaker phone.

"Well yes, see I would like to apologize for my fiancee's behavior" a silence on the other phone.

"Are you with me Helena?"

"Yes, please you were saying apologize?"

"Yes my fiance loves attention. I forgot to mention it to you. So I know what she was about to do, So I left her so she won't be embarrassed by my presenve." Kim and Kathy looked at him not believing what he was saying. There was still silence then:

"Please proceed."

"Well she has done that before, but she wanted to beat the record, I guess seeing all young and good looking men, she was excited about the party, even if she hide it well."

Kim and Kathy couldn't understand were he was leading. Finally Helena broke silence:

"Can I ask you a personal question … very personal?"

"Yes, please."

"Are you gay? and get a kick seeing your fiancee being attacked by many?"

John: "You are right it is a very personal question" and didn't answer. Then he continued apologize." I decided to throw a party for all of you in my castle called the Dungeon."

Helena: "yes I beard that you brought it … great when?"

Now Kim and Kathy understood where this was leading.

John answered: "Let us say, today is Monday, so let us do it Thursday before your guest leave, I understand they are leaving next week. So it will be a good bye party and celebrate our business deal."

Helena: "They will like that. Does Kim intend to celebrate too?"

John: "Of course, I think she is reserving them special surprise with all kind of toys, that she bought from the states."

Helena: "Will you watch this time?"

"I talked to her, she agrees letting me watch but not join. So I won't miss it for the world."

Helena: I didn't know that you are so kind of pervert, anyway I like perverts. See you on Thursday night. I love you "and hung up.

Helena was happy, but sad that she didn't get rid of her yet. But she will find something for sure. The guys will be very happy to participate knowing they will go fucked for real this time, no drugs and the future husband watching. Great!!!

John hung up without looking at them, dialed another number.

Kim asked: "You are not going to kill them are you?"

John still looking very cold and said "There are things that are worst than killing that can be done …"

A cold feeling ran along both girls spiner. Thinking about mutilation, then alive, like the poor murder girls.

Kim: "But you will loose 20 billion dollar deal, every year."

John clenching his teeth again: "The revenge of the hurt they caused you, and me (without thinking) my love. For you is worth more than my fortune. Hello. Please pass me David. He isn't; this John, match me to his cellular, I'll wait."

Kim felt a sudden heat wave, "he will give all his fortune for my love loosing 20 billion yearly business for me? I don't understand." she thought to herself, looking at Kathy for an answer. On the phone:

David: "Hi, John. What's up?"

"Remember the article we both read about Brazil, the last time I was there?"

"Yes, it is ......" He stopped him "Exactly. I need the five for the latest, let us say Wednesday pay any price they ask. Charter a plane today and have them here as soon as possible."

David:" You sound bitter, what is going on?"

John:" I can't explain on the phone. I'll see you in a couple of weeks. You don't worry, it is nothing I can't handle."

"Thanks Dave, I'll see you. Oh and more, tell them to bring every equipment they need or give them my fax number to send me list. I'll buy it here. I think it will best. So I don't have problems with the customers. Bye thanks." He hung up. Kim and Kathy now couldn't understand shit of what he was bringing or who he was bringing from Brazil and for what. Still with a severe ice look:

"Kathy go get me the sisters, here, now!!!"

She said:" Yes, right away boss."

John harshly:" Stop calling me boss."

Kathy made a very sad face:" I am sorry sir" with a calmer voice.

John said: "No, I am sorry kid, please forgive me." He took her in his arm and kissed her nose. He felt her shivering, he didn't

know that they were very scared of him now. "Please go, tell them that I need them immediately."

Kim waited Kathy:" I'll go with you."

They both left in a hurry.

Kim: "I was scared to death you heard what he said."

Kathy: "Yes me too." They knocked at the sisters cabin.

"Come in"

Kathy opened the door. "The boss want to see all of you in his cabin, right now!!!"

Michelle was worried: "Any trouble for us?"

Kathy: "I don't think so. Hurry."

The five girls left in a hurry. They knocked, John opened the door "Come in girls, thank you for coming. Please sit and listen carefully. Do you know what has happen to Kim?" They all nodded. "Good so we won't waist time. I want you girls to go and get me all the dirtiest homeless people you can find, even with diseases. They must have a minimum of a 10 inch dick, I need them for two weeks. As many as fifty by tomorrow night, rent a bus that you will drive, take as many girls that you need. You offer them $1000 per day per person, food and drinks on the house and accomodation and take them by tomorrow night to the castle, the Dungeon the one I bought

three months ago. Take with you as much booze and food that you can and money hold on."

He opened the safe and took a bunch of french banks notes. Here is one million nouveaux francs about $200,000. The other girls will prepare a feast for 40 people. The best possible lock the people that you will have in the lower flat, so they won't be roaming in the vecinity. See how he is doing there. Okay?"

Michelle smiled: "okay sir, understood."

She took the money and put it in her purse and left. Outside Michelle told Gladis, get Josianne, Mimi, and Gina, that will be enough. We will drop them first with the food that we will buy, plus we have plenty of tables and chairs there anyway. I'll purchase all the whites uniform for us and prepare all the room for them. Go and rent a bus. I'll be back. Get all our tools. Be ready."

She left in a hurry. Kim and Kathy looked at them running everywhere.

She said: "Something big is going on, it looks like war. Do you believe he is doing all this for me and we are afraid of him, but … I love him very much. He said he will be killing to give all his fortune for me!"

Kathy:" yes, I heard it too … Let him give us the answer.. Shush.here he comes."

John came toward them:" Kathy would you like to help them too?"

Kim Jumped to her rescue: "No John I need her, just in case you have to leave. I am afraid to stay alone, especially that another girl was murdered last night." John had a strange expression looked away and left. His cellular rang. Kim had it in her hand,

"Hello.."

David: "Hi Kim. Where is he?"

"Hi David, hold on he is there, I'll catch him for you. "She yelled: John, Dave is on the phone.." He came running and took it from her hands.

"Hello Dave"

David: "Hi, John they are faxing a list to you within the hour. They want 500 grand each, no question, asked anything you want."

"So it's 2.5 million, good... Pay them anywhere they want, give them half now and half after the job. When will they be here?

"Tuesday night to set up everything. The fax will go to your office. Satisfied?"

"Yes dave, thank you again you're a friend, bye."

He hung up and dialed another number: "Hello this is John I'll be receiving a fax from Brazil. Take it and go and get me

everything in it and deliver it to my castle "the dungeon". He can use our corporate credit card. I need all of it by the lastest tomorrow afternoon. In the castle, and tell him not to worry about prices, just buy them from anywhere, understood?"

"yes sir ... " he hung up ...

Kim approached him, "Can you tell me, what is all this? What will you do to this people?"

John had an expression that was meant to be a smile, but it was terrifying. "Trust me princess, no one fucked with me and less with my future wife ... "

She looked strangely at him, his future wife he said. He took her in his arms and tried to kiss her lips, but she turned her face and he kissed her beautiful cheek. His lips were cold as ice:" Still angry with me!!!"

Kim:" No it's all the happening. I am afraid to be kissed or touched for now, give me some time."

"Sorry princess, I won't touch you again until you tell me to." He was sad. She felt a pinch in her heart to have denied him a kiss for the first time even through he said that he loved her more than all his fortune or anything and that he intended to marry her. He turned around and left, his shoulders down and sad.

Kim, "I don't know why I did this, I hurt him badly ... " Even through he is or he could be the murder, I love him ... I am confused, terribly confused!"

Kathy caressed her face, "Don't worry Kim all will be better soon.." They didn't see John until night fall. He was out all day. When he entered the cabin, very la evening, he didn't kiss either of them. "I had to go shopping and to the office. Tomorrow morning we will leave for the castle. We will spend there a few days. So take at least one gala dress each and regular clothing for let's say a week."

Kim: "Alright, I'll pack now."

Katy me too:" I'll go to sleep in my cabin."

John:" No Kathy, you stay with Kim. I'll sleep in the next cabin."

Kim: "But, I.."

John: "It's alright.. I understand that you are still angry about me accusing you and the harsh words I told you. When you needed me the most. I feel ashamed of myself, but what is done is done. We can't turn the wheel back. I would have being ready to pay it with my life if it were possible. Good night."

He left her again dumbfounded. That was the third time he expressed himself in such magnitude. She whispered:" I can't believe all the beautiful things he is saying to me. Since this

morning he is very sad. I would jump in his arms, but I am afraid of a part of him. His dark side, he gives me the chills."

Kim went with Kathy, took her lugage and returned to her cabin. She prepared her lugage too. She knocked at this door and opened.

"John, do you want to have dinner?" Without looking he said, "No thanks I am not hungry. Good night."

She closed the door. She had tears in her eyes, He is hurt, he is suffering. What should I do? Kathy: let time give you advice. Let's sleep we haven't slept for 48 hours. They fell asleep. They both had nightmares, Kim saw John with a knife trying to cut her breast and vagina and butt. She screamed loud, "Oh G-D No … No!!!" Chilling the air, John came running from the next room. What is it princess? He tried to hold her in his arm, but she screamed." don't, don't hurt me!" Kathy was looking at them. She was awakened by Kim's scream of terror from her nightmare.

John: What are you saying? Me hurting you?"

"I'll dye first, realizing what" she said.

Kathy said first: "she had a nightmare."

John: "I was hurting you in your dream. So angry are you with me. I see hate in your eyes. I am sorry but if you hate me, I won't touch you again. You are afraid of me, of my touch. I hope that this is from the shock of what the people have done

to you. So I won't try to dissuade you. I hope that time will heal you."

He took a sheet and a blanket and went out the room.

Kim: "Where are you going?'I'll be in the top deck, I need some fresh air. Lock the door. So you won't be scared. Good night." He left her dumbfounded again. Kim and Kathy could barely fall asleep. The yatch was very quiet half of the girls were gone to the castle.

Kim: "He is outside feeling miserable. I will go and talk to him. He won't hurt me. I know that he loves me too much. Stay here. I'll be back."

She put a robe on her and left. The night was cool. It was 1 a.m. She found him laying in a long chair next to the pool. She sat next to his chair. "Can I?" John looked at her beautiful almond shaped green eyes then her pale face, beautiful as the full moon, "yes, please."

"Listen John. Please forgive me if I said those things I was hurt terribly. I feel empty inside, sullied by this bastards. I am not angry or hate you.just need time, can you understand how I feel?"

John had tears in his eyes. Sadness was written all over his face.

"I blame myself for failing to protect you twice, when you are priceless for me more than my own life. Something is wrong with me..."

She put a finger in his mouth "Shush.." She whipped his tears, took his hand and kissed it. "I'll be alright, just give me a little time. Everything will return to normal, Okay?"

John gave her a poor smile. "thanks for coming. It was sweet of you to reassure me that you do not hate me" He brushed her face with the tip of his fingers. This time she felt his touch burning her, as it always did. Then with the back of his hand gently caressed her cheek." I love you princess …"

Kim smiled back at him and left, "Good Night". John went to Steve and told him everything that had transpired and what he was planning to do. "Please Steve take care of the yatch and the girls here. find out how can we crush these bastards, any stock of their campagnies, I need to brake them.

CHAPTER 19

In the morning, Kim and Kathy were ready when John returned to the cabin, said "Good Morning."

John: "Morning., I'll take a shower and I'll be ready in ten minutes."

He came out in boxers, took clothing from the closet and dressed in a pair of white slacks and a dark blue polo with short sleeves. He had his suitcase ready." Let's go ladies. Do you have everything you need?"

"Yes" were the answers. John took their suit cases from their hands and left. John locked the door behind him. He saw Marianne in the deck and called her. She came running: "Listen, call the captain for me, would you?"

"Yes sir, right away" she ran. 5 minutes later the captain showed up. She was in uniform.

"Good morning, are you traveling sir?"

"Yes captain, I'll be at the dungeon for the rest of the week at least until Sunday. Please watch the yatch."

He took a card from his pocket. Here is my cellular number, the other is the castle, Okay? So any emergency, please call me. If anyone sends an anonymous message, take it and call me. it will be urgent, bye."

John went ahead with the luggage to the car.

Kathy said: "He said about anonymous message. I also brought him one the night of the part that is the reason he left in a hurry and left you there. Maybe someone is blackmailing him or certain girls. So he kill them?"

Kim:" Let's not think about it now.."

John opened the door to both said, if you want Kathy can sit in the front with you, there is plenty of space in the Austin Martin.

Kim said: "Okay.." So both sat in the front seat. Kathy in the middle. In the road they didn't say much. Until he stopped at a gas station that had a coffee shop. "Let's have breakfast. I forgot to offer you breakfast." They stepped out of the car and went inside the restaurant and sat to eat breakfast. There were two ladies and three children asking for money to eat, theywere poor.

John and the girls were seating at the table. He saw the waiter chasing them. He stood and stopped him. Come in ladies and sit at any table you want. (talking to the waiter) bring them anything they want plus food to carry out and bring me the bill.

"Yes sir, please ladies sit anywhere you like." John discretly took a pack of money from his pocket and without anyone noticing he put it in the older lads hands." Buy something for the kids, some clothing and rent an apartment for them okay?" The ladies without looking at the amount he inserted in her hand.

"Thank you sir. G-D bless you in our name and the children, thank you sir."

Kathy was saying, He is so kind, he does this all the time. How can he be a murder."

Kim: "He does this all the time?"

Kathy: "Yes..shush..here he comes." He eat without a word. He began sipping his coffee. Suddenly, the poor lady this time it was the younger one probably in her thirties. "Sir, I beg your pardon!"He turned his face seeing her he tried to stand up as respect, but she said:" please don't sir. I just wanted to tell you" showing a big roll of money in her hands," It is too much money sir. We can't accept it." He smiled at her" No it's not, take it as a loan, one day you will back on your feet. You'll find me. For now take it for the kids." She was very well spoken she said: "I … don't know what to say. You see two months ago, my husband ran away with his mistress and took every penny we got, even the furniture. When we arrived home the house was empty. He even cleaned our account. She had tears in her eyes."

John slided to the side and said: "please do sit down, this is Kim and Kathy. I am John" seating down. "We've been going from place to place, I even had to sleep with a man to give food to my children …" She broke an cry. John put his hand around her shoulders and gave her his handkerchief to wipe her face. He didn't care about her clothing being dirty, he hugged "talk to me. What you did, you do not have to be ashamed of. You did it in desperation and love for your children, anyone with love would have done the same. Some do it for pleasure, you for survival. The money is not a problem for me. I have more than I can spend for a hundred life times."

He took a card and wrote a number, "Call this number tomorrow … It's in Monte-Carlo Monaco. I will leave instructions for you. There is a way you can repay me. Take care of your kids and don't feel embarassed for the money it is my pleasure, good luck...Take a cab and go to Monaco."

"G-D bless you sir." She took his hand and kissed it, "Thank you, good day ladies." She returned to her table happier this time …

John had tears flowing freely over his cheeks. He turned his face toward the window, looking outside. Kim and Kathy saw him. Kim took his hand and kissed it. He whipped his tears away discretly.

"How can a person like you, tough that make the biggest fortune in the world, is so sweet and sensitive inside, pure marshmellow. John looking at her wanted to play tough, "That's business. I'll get her to work in my office, so she can

pay me back." Kim's pulling his face, to look at her. Who are you trying to fool. I saw your tears and the tenderness you held her, not caring of her dirty clothing. There is so much I have to learn about you and know you" Dismissed the complimented. I do everything that will make me money. Don't think I am stupid."

Kim decided not to insist. He was humble, that she knew. John excused himself and went to the bathroom, but it was to call. He called the secretary. "Listen a lady by the name of Yollande will call you. Get her one of our appartments for her, her kids and her mother. All furnishes and see what she is good for, secretary or anything that work on the second floor. Okay?"

"Yes sir, by the way Felix the buyer bought all the equipment that was written in the fax. You received a fax from Mr. David that the will be arriving Nice, international airport tonight at 7 p.m."

John:" Good have someone rock them up at the airport with a sign that will say, Brazil, then bring them to the Dungeon."

"Understood sir. bye!"

The girls were talking when he left.

Kim: "It's hard to picture him as a killer. He has a good heart, humble. Maybe he has Multiple Personality syndrom.. who knows, but one thing I know I love him more everyday. If he is in trouble I'll be there for him, that I promise."

Kathy: "Me too, shush..here he comes."

John paid for him and the ladies and were leaving. He looked at the family eating hungrily. He greeted them, "Enjoy and please call my secretary. She knows already about you calling. Do not pay the food, I already payed it." The ladies had risen when he approached the table.

"Please sit down and continue eating. Good luck to you all." He stroke the children's heads. They were probably 4, 6, and 8 years old. Yollande and her mother. "G-D bless you sir, thank you again."

They left John had a new light in his eyes. He felt happier. This time Kim sat in the middle next to John. She held his hand between hers, on her laps. He was happy. She noticed it and kissed his hand warmly." I know you hiding many secrets from me. But what ever they are bad or good, even very bad. I will love you always and will help you with all my heart to resolve them. When ever you are ready to tell me. I will be waiting and ready." She took his hand to her lips and kissed it tenderly.

John:" Thank you princess, I feel better now. I was devasted when I saw hate and fear in your eyes. Your beautiful eyes that usually reflects paradise."

Kim: "forgive me my love. I was confused and still am, but I trust you all the way." He took her beautiful face in his hand and caressed her chin his thumb brushed her nose that he adored and cheeks." I love you princess. One day soon you will know everything. Then, you will decide of our future

together." He pulled her and put her face against his neck and hugged her. His hand on her shoulder. He extend it to Kathy which grabbed it and kissed it tenderly. Kim fell asleep on his shoulder and Kathy fell asleep too. Holding his hand to her face, her head rested on the back of the seat.

The Austin Martin wasvery luxurious and comfortable car. They had finally arrived at the castle. Josianne was there to help them with their suit cases. John whispered: "take care of the car, call the other to help with the suitcases. Ill take Kim to our suite." He took Kim in his arms. Kathy was still asleep. They were both forty eight hours without sleep. John too. He found the door open, and layed Kim on the bed and went back for Kathy.

She was still asleep, he carried her to, and layed her next to Kim. The bed was a King size bed. He went down to speak to Josianne "So what is going on until now?"

Josianne: "well we bought all the food, table cloth, licors. By the way Felix your buyer brought a whole truck full of hospital equipment. He is setting it in the North Isle of the castle, close to the Dungeon. On the underground floor, we have prepared the cells with beds eight in each. Then prepared the big hell that use to be the prison, just under the dungeon. We made it a dorm for all the people that Michelle will bring."

"Did you prepare 5 guests suits for the doctors that will be arriving tonight?"

Josianne:" I did not know about it."

John: "please do it soon, they will be here sooner. By the way is the cat in his cage?"

Josianne: "Yes sir, she is being fed, just about now."

"Good Josianne, thank you. You're great", he pated her butt and kissed her cheek. She blushed.

Josianne: "Does Mister Steve will be coming?"

John:" Not today, he is doing a very important work for me he will be here on Friday for the weekend. I am going for a nap. Thanks again for caring for Kim. He pinched her chin. Josianne, we all love her sir, she is great." John knew that she was in love with her and who wasn't?

John: "If there is anything important wake me up, okay don't hesitate."

Outside he looked around him, he was in the court of the castle, in the middle of it. It was an 11th Century castle in the times of the crusades. It needed repair, John bought it as a bargain, from the government of France with condition to restore it and allow in a an historical sight. He had 150 acres of land surrounding the castle. No one can transpass an accompanied with a guide predetermined periods. John fell confident, of his plan at the North End, there was the tower called the Dugeon.

It is said that ghosts haunted it. They use to torture and decapitate people. John was yawning. He decided to go sleep so

he will be awake when the doctors come. In the room, the two layed as he had left them, he first looked at Kim beautiful face.

She was like a dream, he kissed the tip of her nose and barely brushed her lips. He felt aroused just touching her. he went to his side. Kathy was in the middle of the bed between them. He began caressing her, she was facing Kim. He put his hand between her thighs, it was hot and exciting. He unbuttoned and took of her shorts leaving her delicious cute ass naked.

Than took her shirt too. Leaving her with the necklace she had and her shoes. He undressed in a hurry wet his finger and inserted it in her cute succulent pointing the tip of his penis in her rear entrance, and put his left hand under her enable him to emprison her breast, then the other on her well formed triangle and vagina. He pushed himself in her, flatening her in the bed face down, and mounted her feeling his virility engulfed slowly in her hot derriere until her lovely butt cheeks were against his groins and lower stomach. He was all excited, he began moving in and out of her, his hands knowling her breasts and invading her wonderful moist paradise with all his fingers. His mouth devouring her silky neck that smelled like a flower. She was delicious, he was very excited by her body heat and cute young figure that excited him tremendously just looking at her childish face.

She moaned in her sleep, her cheeks turned red from love. Each time he penetrated her, he exhaled savouring all her little body, until he felt the eruption, that cramped all his body on top of her, flatening her lovely butt cheek against his lions. He

was in ecstacy, and reached an early orgasm filling her young well of his flow of desire, electrical currents running through his body until he stopped moving.

They layed on their side one against each other, he fell asleep holding her tight still feeling the heat of her butt against his lower stomach. It was soothing. Four hours later, Josianne entered the room after knocking since no one answered. She had to wake him up. She saw John with Kathy in his arms. She felt a warmth between her thighs. She looked at Kathy burned in his huge arms and his leg covered her thighs. She then looked at Kim's incredible figure, she was a dream. She was totally in love with her.

She approached her I sat on the bed next to her. She just looked at her and felt the urge to make caress her. She did but Kim and all of them were exhausted. She inserted her hand in her shirt and felt her gracious breasts. She pressed them slightl, Kim couldn't feel nothing. She unbuttoned her shirt and freed her proud firm breasts, beautiful as if cut in marble. She felt them in the palm of her hands, emprisoned them and pressed gently and with her lips captured her nipples, sucked them with passion.

She didn't say anything and let her continue. She was all burning kissing her inside. She felt her tongue explore her vagina, her tip touching places that made her shiver.

She shyly looked at her, her lovely nice wet with Kim's excitment.

"You too are in love with me? Tell me the truth don't be shy."

Josianne: "Yes Miss Kim since the first day you came."

She freed Kim. Now they were facing each other. Josianne couldn't look at her incredibily beautiful eyes. Instead she put her head between her breasts and layed on her, her hands caressing Kim's hips and thighs. Kim caressed her back and soft hair. "You are a sweet girl. I like you too. But I acceeded to your desire this time but we can't be doing it again. I awakened aroused from your kisses. Lately I feel differently even though I enjoyed your passion on me." Her finger were caressing Josianne scalp between her hair.

Josianne timidly: "You want me to go now? "

Kim: "you can stay a little while longer if you have more desire or that was all your fantasy?"

Kim pressed Josiannes head against her breast. Then Josianne kissed Kim all over her beautiful face, thank you again. She rose got dressed. She was happy, she looked at Kim's beautiful face and body one more time, blew a kiss with her lips and left in a hurry to return two seconds later. Oh!I forgot why I came. The Doctors have arrived Mr. John asked me to wake him up. The Doctors? exclaimed Kim. She did not know yet what was going on. Yes Miss Kim. I showed them their suites and are waiting for him. Showing John with her finger, then left. Kim turned and looked at Kathy hidden between John's big arms and legs. She was about 5' 2" and John 6' tall. She put a hand between Kathy's legs and felt his penis in her butt.

Kim thought he loves her too, I know. I would have loved to be in her place, exactly like this, feeling him in we and also I fear him. I fear his dark side, but how a man that holds her like that with so much tenderness could harm a woman. I can't figure that out yet.

She better wake him up. she shook him. Kathy woke-up instead. How did I got here?

Kim: "He carried us probably." Then feeling his penis in her butt, she smiled "oh he made love to me in my sleep. Hum … I love it. He still desire me. Kim continued shaking him, but he wouldn't wake up."

Kim:" Kathy move please let see if he reacts to my caresses. Kathy moved against her will. He is so delicious. I would love to stay all day like this. Kathy sat on the bed and Kim moved against him, pressing her vagina against his virility, she moaned "Oh! I want you so bad." She took it inside her layed on him and took his hands to her butt cheeks. "Oh! John I want you so bad …" She felt his lax penis pressed between her lower lips and began moving on him, then she pulled him on top of her feeling all his weight on her, his hands still on her ass.

She felt his penis awakening and his hands pressing her butt. She thought that probably he thinks that he is on top of Kathy. His penis was in her now, slowly erecting in her she moaned. He began moving in her slowly, Kim felt that he was about to wake-up. He was pressing her butt and penetrating her more, moving. She closed her eyes. He was saying with his eyes still closed. "Oh G-D!!, am I dreaming? am I in paradise. I never

felt so excited with her before ... "He was pushing himself up to her entrails. Kim and Kathy were now worried, but kept their mouth shut and faked being asleep. John moaning he was afraid to wake-up and the wonderful dream will end.

Kim had her orgasm already, her cheeks were pink from love and ecstacy. He finally opened his eyes and petrified, "OH LORD!!!What did I do ... " He immediately retrieved from her and pulled his hands as if he was burned. "OH!! oh!!!! I took her in her sleep, but how? Oh I hope she did not notice. Kim felt his breath on her hair, and heard everything" he said she was satisfied and totally engrossed from making love to him. He stood up, got dressed and covered both girls. Kim opened her eyes.

"Hi, my love. Did you sleep well? Oh before I forget your guests are here. The Doctors!..Josianne gave them each a suite and they are waiting for you! John looked at her puzzled, did she feel him? Hi princess, thank for the message ... how do you feel? your mental? Kim can't function without a kiss.

John came and bowed to kiss her succulent lips. She wrapped her arms around his neck and kissed him with all her being and then said, I feel great this morning, wonderful. I just had a dream that you were making love to me. It as so delicious. Why did you wake me up, you stopped my fantasy!!Kathy was laughing her heart out. what an actress she thought. John breathed heavily, "Oh you dreamed of me making love to you.. And you loved it?

Kim: "It was incredible. I wish I was still dreaming. I can even feel you anoide me, incredible as if for real" she was teasing him and seeing his convulsion smiled. Do this excite you, I mean my dream?

John: I ... have to go welcome the guest I'll see you later, bye.

He stole a kiss from her and butled out, leaving Kim and Kathy laughing their hearts out.

Kim: "Did you see his face, his confusion. He was afraid that I would know that he actually licked me a little. Oh Why did he wake-up so fast. Hun...i can't still feel his penis inside me. I don't care if he is the serial killer, we know only his good side. Kathy yes you right, we have no reason or proof to be scared of him i love him too."

John asked Josianne which room she assigned to the Doctor's you look very happy today. I am, thank you. Please follow me, by the way Michelle arrived with a bus full of strange people. She said that shivering, showing disist. John laughed at her remark and face expression. Good girls ... They are very reliable. They arrived in front of the rooms. John knocked the door opened to middle age man, 5' 6" tall, thin wearing glasses.

He looked very latin, I am Mr. John welcome to my humble castle. Thank you I am Dr. Rodriguez collegues are next door, let me call them. He rushed and in 5 minutes all them came to John. He presented his collegues, Dr. Decarlo, Dr. Nonsante, Meriaga y Dr. Praga. John shook hands and invited them to follow him living room.

They entered the spacious room accomodated a living room. It must be least 150' x 100' ... More of a party room.

Josianne: "Can I offer you anything drinks? Coffee? or are you hungry?" The suspicious looking.

Dr. Rodrigued since he was the one that made the presentation asked. Mr. John can you give us an idea of what you want us to perform?

John: "Of course, you see I want ...." he told them exactly what he wanted. The Doctors had as stone face. He couldn't read their opinions. Finally Dr. Carlo asked, If I may ask, what terrible things this people have done to this to them?

John: "My future wife and I were guest at a party one this people. They have ganged raped my fiance 110 times sixteen people in one time."

Dr. Praga:" So what make you think that this people will show up on Thursday night, especially knowing that you are aware of it.

John: "Simply, because I told them, that I apologized and that my Kim or my fiancee likes orgies, but since she was drunk which she was not she was given powerful Aphrodisiac. I have the proof of it plus video tapes filmed during he whole sessions, by them. At least the that her main. If a Doctor friend of mine didn't come to my yatch in time. She might ave been dead. I know that this is very unusual but it is my desire and it as the reason I did not argue the price.

Mariaga: "we have no problems morally with it. The getting an eye for an eye. But as you know we are not licenced in this country. So we must keep our identity secret."

John:" Your names will not be mentioned at all. I guess am really the only one that knows all of your names. I have cards printed with completely different names."

Josianne returned with the coffee and some cookies. Josianne, please hold on (turning to the doctor,) Please write the names that you want in your business cards from Caracas Venezuela."

John hand them a piece of paper and each one wrote a name easy to remember, and a fake address in Venezuela. John took it from them and said. Josianne have this business cards made for all of them. I need them by tomorrow.

Josianne: "Understood sir." She was very efficient and never asked questions. She disappeared closing the doors behind her when they had finished their coffee.

John said:" If you please follow me, I'll show you the small hospital that we accomodated." They did and entered the pavillion. They were all surprised. It looked like a real hospital with everything in i., each door they entered had a certain equipment, but all had each a suregery equipment..

Rodriguez: "Very impressive, how did you do this in one day or two days."

John smiled:" with money." they all laughed.

Dr. Mopsatto: To spend all this money on us here and much more I imagine you must love your fiances."

John's look darkened "Yes, more than my eyes or my life. They destroyed me, especially I watched every bit of it. And this people had just signed a 20 billion dollars yearly contract that I will make two billion profit a year. If I don't care for that kind of money, so putting two and two together. You can calculate how much I love this woman!!!"

They were all impressed with his love declaration said, "We will do the countest job that very few could do, please dont of us 100% … "

"Thank you, would you like to rest now?" John asked.

Doctor Rodriguez: "No sir we have to worry.with this particular equipment, plus we will each need a nurse to assist us or anyone that could understand what we ask from them."

John: "No problem. I'll have you five girls this evening if you need anything. You call me. Thank you … leave one of the girls with you."

She John told Josianne to assigne Mimi to them and to call the yatch to his five additional girl immediately.

Josianne:" yes sir" and she left. He returned to his suit. On the way he met.

"Hi Michelle"

Michelle:" We have exactly what you asked, It was hard to make them believe who pat our offer is real. So we as you said got whiskey and votka. Then they allowed us to the bus, would you like to see them?

John: "yes, please. He looked at her ass. Thinking that it was her that he fucked the other night with the girls, he was still confused about his feeling regarding her.

"Michelle, I would like to ask you a personal question?"

"Yes sir" ...

"Regarding the other night your girls, Kim and Kathy and I. When you, Kathy and Kim were on top of me. was I in you?"

Michelle blushed, but seeing his embarassement, He didn't know, Kim must have told him that, I was the one on his dick, she probably doesn't want him to know that it was her. So I won't change that.

"Yes sir, it was me. Why, may I ask?"

"No, nothing special, just never before had ... you know ..."

Michelle: "Yes sir, I know, was it alright?"

"Yes very nice. I liked it."

Michelle without looking at him: Anytime you want me sir, I'll be there or for Miss Kim.

John: Th..Thank you Michelle you're sweet." He was still impressed by the way she made love, and the sensation he felt almost like this morning with Kim, but the surprise he had seing himself in Kim's arm didn't let him feel properly her incredible paradise. He could still feel her body heat and the touch of her lovely derriere. Just thinking about it, made a bulge in his pants. Michelle looked and smiled thinking it was for her.

They had arrived at the dorm. It was locked with keys. Marianne was at the door:" Good evening sir", she opened. John entered, the people were walking around. John called in french:

"Please listen all..." They converged around him. They looked dirty and disgusting and smelled urine and dooze. They must be at least forty to fifty. He continued: "I am your host Mr. X".The reason I have brought you here is the following. The men and women that will come here on Thursday have molested my wife, they have raped her sixteen people at one time. So what I expect from you is ......"

He explained every detail what he expected from them. "Does any of you have a problem with that? Two hands raised.. "You!!!"

"How much do we have to pay you?"

John laughed:" No I am the one to pay you. You will leave here with, let us say you stay here for fifteen days. So each one will receive $15,000 dollars plus cases of whiskey, and food and

brand new clothing that I will give you in your last day. then turning to the second peddler, you!!.

"Well do we have to stay here all the time?"

John: yes until Thursday night they will meet the people in the other place, and live there with them or the rest of the time. You will have to work hard at it. In the mean time. Tell my girls what would you like to eat drink and she will bring you three T.V. so you can watch. Do you like porno movies? all cheered,

"Yes ... Horay!!!!" all applauded.

John: "Okay you'll get everything you desire it's in the house, enjoy my hospitality. One more thing, you do not touch none of girls that work for me, understood? anyone even trying will be punished very, plus each of this girls is an expert in martial arts.. Good, we understand each other. Food will be served soon. Good night ..." They all said good night and John, Michelle and Marianne left. the latter locked the door.

John said to Michelle, give them anything they want.

Michelle:" I will sir remember if you need my services, I'll be glad to."

John confused said.. "Th ... Thank you Michelle and he left in a hurry."

Michelle watched him walk away. "Oh I wish he did really have me that tight, I know what he felt in Kim. I did too. She is addictive."

John arrived at the room. He opened the girls were still in bed chating. Kim looked at him. She felt a heat wave in her heart. She knew now for sure that she loved him more then she thought could be possible. Hi my love, did everything went well?

John: "Yes princess, everything is in order. Michelle and Josianne are very efficient. Let us say they all are. Well chosen the st crew?"

Kathy: "But I am not doing a thing lately" John approached her and held her lovely face between his big hands:" You have the most difficult one, to take care of the personal needs of your bosses. Kim and I. That is simple to you?"

Kathy rose naked in the bed. He was still standing on the room and dressed in short. She approached him, and put his head between her breasts. He felt the warmth of her delicious breast in his cheeks. he kissed them, she embrassed him and kissed his head. Kim said, "What about me guys, I am forgotten? unloved?"

Kathy pulled her hand to lift her, John took it from her and easily pulled her totally naked also putting her breasts also against his face and kissed both pairs, gently sucking their hardened nipples. He held Kathy by her butt and the other hand he held Kim by her waist.

Kim got upset … "Why do you not hold me like her? Are you afraid that i will bite you!!!She pushed his hand down to her sensational derriere. He had the wonder of wonders in the

palm of his hand. She felt his heart beating in his chest and sweat dripping from his temples. She liked his touch: "Love, I need so much your touch there and everywhere you have me in, prove me that you love me. Caress me properly." John obliged gently caressig her exciting ass cheeks. His breathing became heavy, his mouth engulfed the half of her breast, tasting it, sucking it with passion. His other hand released Kathy's and held Kim's ass with both open hands.

Kathy moved and now John was facing Kim, kissing her breast and caressing delicately her sensual ass, his fingers between, brushed her deep valley. His heart was beating very hard even Kim got scared. She made sign to Kathy to come and rescue him. She came behind Kim took one of his hands in, put in her ass and then the other in her vagina.

He probably recognized them and calmed down gently stroking her inside the places. Kim caressed his head, pressing his face against her breasts, satisfying herself with his kisses." Poor darling, you are afraid of me, at least that's what I feel", John was too aroused. He released both, undressed in one bound and said," Okay princess you won, I'll take you now until whatever end will come. I can't resist you any longer."

He stood naked in the bed, approaching Kim. He kneeled and kiss her stomach his hands emprisoned her gorgeous ass that drove him crazy, Kim felt his lips burning her stomach, his hands touching tearing her soul to pieces, desir him to the outmost, he was going down in slow motion kissing and licking

her stopping at her belly button, his tongue serveying it she felt trail of burning desire that his lips left in it's path.

They were both enraptured, lost they are semi-closed in ecstacy. Soon he will be reaching er paradise. Kathy had to do something. If he wanted to wait before he made love to her He must have had a powerful reason or reasons. She stopped took one of is hands from Kim's butt. It was like opening the frozen hand of a corpse. hen she succeeded she push herself between them, putting her vagina against is lips.

She broke the enchantment..A.1Soory guys, I worry for you two. John ou said various times that doing this before a certain time that you have determined could brake the rest of the future between you two, is it still true?

John:" thank you little girl, it is true, you see how important you are!!

Kim had tears flooding her gorgeous face from disappointment and desire. She was in paradise and suddenly she fell in a free fall straight to earth.

Kim: "I was there, it was beautiful, but I fell so hard that every part of my body feel it.

Kathy: "Where were you?"

Kim: "In Paradise, John with his touch only and has elevate me to sky, I ... never felt this way before ...

John: really princess? I ... am glad to hear that I was too, I thought my heart was about to leave my chest and run after you princess. One thing I know now for sure that soon we will join without frontiers or restriction. I'll be able to tell you all. If you then still love me. Then we have succeeded. I felt something similar the other night with Michelle. I was very troubled, I thought that other women in the universe could make me fell that way, but you."

Kim and Kathy looked at each other and exploded in laugh.

John surprised said: "What did I say funny?"

Kim suddenly turned serious: "No sorry ... It's the way you said it. You were like somewhere else."

Kathy said: "Let's do it again tonight."

John said: "No ... not tonight

CHAPTER 20

Kim woke up around 9 a.m. All were asleep. She had John manhood against her face. She smiled and gently bit it and kissed it. "I like to be awakened this way" John said emprisoning her head with his thighs.

John said, "let's get ready today is your day my love. I can promise you one thing, this bastards won't be able to do it once again."

Kim and Kathy looked at each other, but did not say a thing they got shower and got dressed in a hurry. John took Kim and Kathy, his hands holding them by their waist and said, "Tonight everything you see, do not question it ... On top of this when you two see me coming up to this room with Helena, give me ten minutes then come up. Don't be shocked if I make love to her, you two will join in."

Kim suddenly serious said, "What do you mean, you are going to fuck her?"

John: "The three of us are, but don't worry it is part of my plan."

Kim with a suspicious face: "I don't like this plan already … I don't want you to fuck her, you never did before, why now to thank her for raping me?"

John forced her against him and said: "Look in my eyes princess, do you trust me?"

Kim couldn't resist his gaze, deep she felt he could see into her soul: "Yes, I trust you, but I … am jealous, anyone but her."

John kissed her nose: "I love to see you jealous, your gorgeous (talking to Kathy) look this beautiful face. I am crazy about her, jealousy makes her more irrisistible." He bite both of her lips: "Okay girls let's go have breakfast." They went to the patio and had breakfast outside.

Michelle came: "good morning everyone. To John, she made a special facial expression. "How are you boss, did you have sweet dream?"

They all said "Morning … "

John: "Thank you Michelle that was a commemorable night. Have you seen the doctor this morning?"

Michelle: "Yes sir, they are in the hospital preparing everything."

"Good thank you Michelle."

Michelle said bye and left. Moving her ass in a way to awaken John desire.

John semi-convinced said: "Maybe, whatever." Kim felt relief.
When they had finished breakfast John rose and said:

"Let's go, Kim I want you to meet he doctors."

Kim worried ask: "For what? Well I told them that you are
my future wife, so as the host you should know them." He
pulled her hand then Kathy's: "You too come with us kido."
He grabbed both asses with a hand between their thighs.
They both jumped Kim laughed: "You thought that you can't
touch my ass baby? Well with clothing it's not so dangerous."
he laughed.

Kim:" What do you mean so dangerous?"

John continued laughing: "To me you are princess, you'll give
me a heart attack."

Kim: "So that was your secret? You have a heart problem?"

John this time grabbed her harder, holding a moment of her
cheeks his gripp. "Yes, my heart problem is you. I see you and
my heart begins playing lune-tunes crazy about your gorgeous
face and body." Savagely he took her in his arm lifting her
from the ground and kissed her with all his might. eying
her breathless, his hands squeezing her lovely butt...When
he release her, she said taking a breath, "Oh my!!!Oh my!!! I
think he is in love with me" Kathy was laughing real hard, Kim
continued: "A few more seconds and you would have taken all
my air from me, leaving me lifeless, but(she put a finger in his
mouth) I like it."

She kissed him again tenderly this time, wrapping her arms around his cheeck, still having her emprisoned between his big paws. "I love you princess more then words can express." He said those words with a serene expression looking her in the eyes. She felt a very deep warm feeling penetrate her being. She looked at him as if she just discovered him anew, a feeling that as like just having made love again in one instant.

They looked at each other without talking for a long minute Kathy looked at them moved by the tremendous display of love, in those simple words, but she could feel the power of his love.

Kim closed her eyes as if an ecstacy he burned his face in her throat gently brushing it with his lips." Oh John, I love you so much. The way you said those words and looked at me made me come, as if you had made love to me. I love you more by the day." He kissed her chin and lowered her to her feet still very serene. "That rejoices my heart princess, very soon we will be as one my queen of hearts!"

Kathy felt out of place." …… That was beautiful you two." She had tears of emotion. They hugged her and kissed her cheeks warmly.

John: "Okay let us go back to business." They walked the long corridors of the castle until they arrived at the make shift hospital. Dr. Rodriguez was the first one to see them:

"Good morning … Mr. John and Mrs. Kim"

"Good morning doctor this is my fiance Kim and Kathy my protege."

Kim: "It's a pleasure Dr."

The the other doctor joined too, and met Kim.

Dr. Rodiguez:" I understand now everything you told me yesterday, we will do everything you ask 100%. No wonder you value her more than your fortune." Kim upon hearing this words pressed his arm.

John: "Is everything alright? Do you need anything?"

Dr. Rodriguez:" The only thing we need will be the nurses."

John: "They should be here anytime now!!! Did you have breakfast?"

Dr. Rodiguez: "We all did thank you. Well we have to go back to work."

John Kim and Kathy said bye and left. The moment they stepped outside, Kim stopped John and said: "Did you tell them, that you prefer me than your whole fortune?"

John:" Yes I did."

Kim: "Do you really mean it?"

"Look at me ", he looked into her gorgeous almond shape green eyes. She could read him clearly, "You do mean it. I can see,

Oh my love. I do not know if I deserve you and so much love", she began crying and hide her lovely face between his neck and shoulder. He kissed her nose. "Baby you became my reason for being you have enslaved my soul princess." Seeing Kathy alone, he aproached her and kissed her." And you little girl I love you too. Let me tell you something, Kim and I will never leave, until you yourself want to leave or a new love, but I will never ask you to go, you are part of me baby." She had tears rolling her gorgeous childlike round cheeks with frekels. He stole a kiss from her.

Kathy: "I'll never leave you either. I love you both."

John: "Okay, okay!!!enough sentimentalism let's enjoy the day."

Josianne showed up: "Morning everyone. Boss the 5 girls have arrived. They are unpacking and they will go to the hospital."

John: "Good." He brushed her face with his finger." Take us to see the cat."

Kim:" The cat? you like cats?"

John: "This is a special cat." Josianne was looking at Kim with admiration. Kim felt it and said:

"So Josianne how are you? "and she kissed her cheek.

Josianne was elated: "Oh thank you Miss Kim, I am great this morning." Kim was amused and also elated by her love and devotion. They walked up to a basement and went down a staircase.

They heard the roaring Kim and Kathy got scared:" What's that?"

Josianne opened the door. They saw a beautiful tiger of Bengale a wonderful specimen: "Oh, Lord. A tiger what is it doing here?" exclaimed Kim. It was in a giant cage. John said: "Oh!!!He work for me too. I bought it last year. So I am using it tonight!"

Kim and Kathy jumped: "You are not going to throw them in the cage?" they said petrified.

John laughed: "Oh No, I don't need too. He is just going to make them do what I want."

Kim and Kathy shivered. "Okay girls let's go." They went up. She did not care that the boss and Cathy was there. Kim John said: "Okay girls let's go to our room. It's noon now. We will have lunch and must and be ready for tonight. We have a long night, let's go girls Josianne you can come with us." I think the girls and I would like to enjoy you for the rest of the day, would you like that?"

Josianne looked happy: "Oh yes boss, if you all want me!"

Kim: "Why not ... I think the boss loved your ass very much isn't darling?"

She wasn't smiling anymore." I am yours forever my prince." She kneeled and put her face against his stomach. Holding him tight, he lifted her. "Oh little princess. I know that you

love me, but when you know everything after me and you still desire me the same way. I'll be yours for life my Queen hearts. Let us go it is 6:30 they should be arriving any minute now. Come love." He put his tuxedo jacket and they both went down. Hand in hand Kathy ding him by his right arm. They all look royalty. Josianne had returned to room to get dressed.

The doctors admired Kim's beauty. They bowed and kissed her hand. John smiled to Kim in front of all the girls and doctor.

He took her hand "Your majesty, would you grant me the honor of this first dance." A valse was playing Kim had tears, fell to her knees and hugged him "My Love … I do not deserve so much love. I adore you John." He stood and raised her. "Let's dance your Majesty." He held her one arm on her waist and one held her hand, and they danced. Looking at each other in the eyes, saying a million love expressions out a word.

The guests were arriving. A girl dressed in vallet announced. "The Baronesse" she began citing names and title each time she knocked her staff to the ground. John and Kim approached them. Helena couldn't believe at Kim's elegance and beauty, the last time she left her, she was all humiliated and destroyed smelling terribly.

Helena was dressed in a long black dress, making her look thinner and taller. She was a knock out, her red hair braided rested on her very well pronounced ass. Her blue eyes were sparing. John came and took her hand. "How lovely you look

Helena." He kissed her in the lips. She shivered, it was the first time. She was always the first one to attack him.

Kim: "How nice to see you again, Helena. I am so sorry to have passed on you the other evening, but I enjoyed it very much." She held Helena by her arm and kissed her in the lips too. Helena got aroused "Wow!!! I didn't know that you two have a new passion for me."

All the other couples were mouth open appreciating Kim's elegance and beauty. Just looking at her, created a bulge in their pants. Thinking of how they fucked her and how they will tonight. Henry took her hand and kissed it. John and Kim were playing the game well, but it was very hard. They allowed them to the middle of the hall were music was playing.

Helena: "You prepare your parties, all the way." All the men were behind Kim surrounding her. Kathy was assigned to watch over her.

Henry: "You look smaching. I tought about you all this day. You were magnificent the way you handled of us. The real Venus de Milo." He inserted his hand between her dress on the side and squeeze her bare cheek. She jumped "Hey not here and we have guests. Later I have a great surprise for you, we will enjoy each other very much more than you can imagine without drugs this time. So we can fully appreciate sex to the fullest. We were all already very excited just the idea." John was with Helena, he held her by her waist." You know Helena I never told you, but I always had a fantasy with you."

Helena: "You mean a sex fantasy?"

"Yes, you are very beautiful but for some reason your title bothered me."

Helena's eyes and ears were totally open: "And what kind of fantasy?"

"Oh, i don't dare tell you. I'll blush from head to toes."

Helena: "I'll do your fantasy anytime even right now."

John: "Really? The truth I think even now that beauty is not everything, the reason I went for Kim it is, because she doesn't mind libertinism, but you would have been very strict and jealous."

Helena: "Me, you must be jocking I love liberatinism and I am not jealous or old style."

"You mean if I were to marry you, you won't mind having Kim as a mistress? or have...you know?"

Helena smiled "Oh really you would marry me?"

John made himself as if embarassed "Would you have accepted me like that?"

Helena: "Of course my John" he kissed him her, arms wrapped on his neck.

John: "Wow!! that's a kiss. Come let's go to my room and I would fulfil a part of my fantasy."

He pulled her by her arm and they both went up the staircase to John's suite. Kim and Kathy saw it and looked at there watches. It was 7:30 they will go up in 10 minutes. All men and women were touching her, not missing an opportunity to pinch her breasts or her charms. Once in the room John closed the door behind them.

"Oh Helena I waited so long for this moment" she was about to kiss him. He pushed her to kneel he opened his zipper taking his penis out and directed to her mouth. Helena shocked "But ..." he didn't let her finish and pushed it in her mouth. She finally decided to comply and sucked it, he was pushing her head against his loins, making her take all his penis in her almost shaking.

"Helena, you have a great mouth, oh your lips are exciting." he was moving in her mouth as if it were her vagina. She was so well dressed and kneeled sucking it seemed degrading to her, but that was the idea. She was stroking hard the bottom of his shaft to make him come fast, he did. She wanted to retrieve it so he will ejaculate outside, but he held her head pushing his nuts harder to her throat, unloading his sperm in her mouth. She almost threw up, but he made her close her mouth and slowly moved sporatically releasing his sperm in her. Making her swallow it. When he was done he kissed her face. "You excited me so easy. You're great." She felt elated, making her

forget her bad adventure. He came behind her and wanted to undress her.

Helena: "But John what are you doing?"

John kissing her neck: "But you told me that you wanted to grant me my fantasy, don't you?"

Helena: "Of course, but …. "he did not let her finish and slipped her dress leaving her almost naked. She only had pink panties which he kneeled and pulled it with his teeth.

He really appreciated her gorgeous body. Full firm breasts, beautiful small oreols, and long nipples. She didn't have a body that bones could be seen. All her body was fully covered of firm fresh not showing heavy or skinny, her ass was full round and exciting. Her triangle formed a nice bugle and vagina's well defined lips, he put a hand of each side of her between her highs lifting her from the ground, his mouth devouring her breasts and sucking her nipples. She began moaning: "Oh you naughty you." At this moment Kim and Kathy entered "John. … "they stopped short seeing them. Helena was first embarassed them seeing her face she was happy.

John: "Oh honey, come you too Kathy. Helena is a real delicacy, see her body. She is a real royal fuck."

He undressed and put a finger in her mouth "Suck baby suck", she did. "Look how she makes love baby." He took his wet finger and put it in her ass hole and masturbate her to suddenly pushed his penis in it with all his strength. She jumped and

winced from pain. He held her by her hips and smached her big round cheeks against his lower stomach. Kim and Kathy were astounced, but John made an eye sign to move on her. Kim came and kneeled between her legs," Oh what an exciting pussy my dear. It demand my mouth." She began by sucking her triangle with all her strength. Helena moaned and held her head. "Oh my Kim your hungry for me too?"

"Yes you don't know how much. "Her tongue spliced between her vaginal lips. Kathy so attacked her breasts sucking them hard, her hand kneading her gorgeous.

"Helena how beautiful tits you have you are a real jewel." John lifted Helena's legs up to her hip. Leaving Kim devouring her cunt with rage bitting and sucking her lips and her well developed clitoris. John fucked her hard and dry. His mouth made some hickies, in her neck. He then let himself fall in bed with her on top. She felt his penis penetrated hard in her ass when she fell on him. Kathy came took her panties off kneeled on top of her face and said "suck baby, suck. I love your lips and your tongue, go baby go" she obliged and devoured Kathy's young vagina.

Helena: "You have a cute pussy Oh how lovely." Kim was on Helena's vagina. John pressed her breasts with all his might making Helena scream:

"Oh my tits you are doing it to hard my dear."

John continued and fucked her harder. He said:" Helena you have a great ass. Oh what a great fuck. Missed so much of

you." He flipped and was on top of Helena, and moved faster on her ass, harder, his hands squeezed hard her tits slamming his lower body each time he penetrated her hole. Kathy was under and had her butt in John's mouth and Helena's mouth on her lovely vagina. Kim also was under sucking and biting her vaginal lips, until Helena felt John throbbing in her ass and then a strong warm flow.

"John you came, you love my derriere." Kathy came into her mouth, she pressed her vagina hard on her mouth. Helena wanted to avoid her fluid but Kathy hold her mouth open, all her flow boded Helena's mouth. She rubbed her vagina in her face and mouth, "Helena I loved your mouth."

John then took her and turned her around and came to her vagina and again fucked her with all his strength. Kim layed on top of John's s and rubbed hard her vagina against his cheek. Her hands squeezing hard Helena tits. John was in rage fucking her so hard that Helena screamed, "Oh John it's too hard."

John: "That's the way I love to fuck by. You've a great one." His hands kneaded her ass with all his might squeezing her flesh in his fist. Kim had Helena's legs under her arms lifting them all the way and Kathy on her mouth again. Kim was excited to be on her vagina bare against his cheeks. Her hands on Helena's tits. Each time he penetrated Helena and lifted his penis to re-enter. He will lift Kim on top of him. Finallly he finished ejaculating in her..

"Helena I love to fuck you. Kim go you and Kathy and ask everyone to be ready and undress we are partying now." Kim and Kathy got dressed and left him on top of Helena.

John asked: "So dear did you enjoy?"

Helena: "Oh yes" she pressed her vagina on his penis on and off to revive him.

"Helena you are exciting me, I am now going to fuck your mouth", before she could say a word, he rose and went up to her face and put his dick in her mouth and began moving in her mouth. "Suck baby, suck hard" and he did until ejaculating again in her throat mouth and splashing her face with his sperm too... "Oh babe your so good." He went to her ass and begin biting her leaving mark of his teeth in her lovely ass." I want to eat you." He masturbated her pushing three then four fingers in her butt hole, making her feel pain, but was enjoying his excitment until he finished and rested his head on her.

"Helena it was wonderful. Do you think you can handle sex like this everyday if we get married?"

Helena exclaimed: "You really mean it? You want to marry me?"

"Of course I enjoyed your sex very much and I would do it day and night."

"Oh John finally you are reasoning. I didn't imagine that you fantasized about me."

John: "Yes Helena I did and you'll see the rest of my fantasy after the party. Let us go my dear." They got dressed. Helena fixed her hair and was cleaning herself.

John said: "Don't worry we are going for a giant orgy, we will be naked anyway."

Helena: "Yes, but I like to be presentable anyway.."

They finally left. Outside Kim took the microphone. "Well ladies and gentlemen follow the young ladies in white uniform. We are going to the place where the real party is, I have games that will excite all of you."

A loud cheer "Hooray Kim!!!!" John came down with Helena that was Queen of the party." Let's go and have our Orgy ", another cheer this time even louder. They all followed Michelle and Gladis down the staircase leading to a hallway. It was spooky, they walk for a few hundred yards until they got to a more illuminated area.

Michelle said: "Please everyone undress here put everything in a bag with the suits on the hangers, so it won't get wrinkeed, and remember your number."

Some hesitated, Kim approached "Well anyone that wants me, you better hurry." She showed a breast, and everyone was undressing in a hurry to get there first, men and woman. When they all naked, Michelle said: "Please follow me." They did. They looked ridiculous walking in line naked. Michelle opened a big door, that led a giant room, that had 2 rows of

large cells in both walls and in the center there was old torture equipment. They all got chills, but John spoke, "We are going to play like medieval times. Kim will be tied to a different torture machine each time, and you guys will be the bad guys that will torture her and of course fuck her."

All cheered again, eliminating the fears they might have had. Who wants to be the first five to torture and rape her." I " all lifted their hands. John said to Kim: "My love all of them want you, you chose the first fives, then the second, then third." Kim remember from the videos who they were. So she chose the same one. "You Henry, Charles and you, and you two." Henry and Charles were delighted to be first.

John said: "Okay, you go to the first room." he called it room and not cell. Kim chose the others and John said:" Five at each room." The last one was one of the Masochist the same one that inflicted pain to Kim, he put him a cell alone. All the cells had Barres, no doors like old times, each cell had five beds all with white linen very clean.

John had Michelle lock the doors with a chain. It worried them a little, but they didn't let it show.

John: "Now the women will be all together in this big room." It was a cell of 50' x 100' and had twenty bed. All women entered and Helena wanted to stay with him.

John said: "No you too my dear. There are no exception to the game!" He put a finger in her ass and accompanied her to the room. She blushed and entered the room with the others

all naked from head to toes. Gina passed them soft material shoes so they don't be bare-feet. When everyone was locked down, their faces between the bars. John stood at the center of the place, in the middle of all the cells, so everyone can see and hear.

John said: "Come my love ..."

Kim came to him, put a pedestal and asked Kim to step on it, he whispered: "Please do no question what I am doing and do it, okay princess?" She acknowledge with a smile.

Once on top of the pedestal John said "Should I undress her?"

All screamed "yes"..John took her dress, he noticed a slight hesitation from her. she was naked in her splendor only having her tiny blue panties. John took them too and handed it to Kathy that was next to him. All were whistling she was incredible beautiful.

John said "Who wants to fuck her?" All raised their hands and screamed. "Me!!!Me!!!"

John:" Who wants to rape her?"

All again cheered whistle and said "Me!!!Me!!!" histerically.

John:" Who wants to torture her?" again all cheered raised their hands and said "Me!!!!! Me!!!!"

John stood up on the pedestal next to Kim that was totally embarrassed by now. She stood there totally naked and didn't

know to what John was trying to do. He approached her face and kissed her eyes, nose, lips and chin very tenderly. She closed her eyes from the warmth and intensity of his lips. He then proceeded to her beautiful sensual neck. All were looking and were excited by now. He continued to her breasts and sucked her nipples and gently caressed her breasts, barely brushing them with his lips and fingers. He then kneeled and kissed her exciting flat stomach. She felt a cramp when his lips touched her bare skin.

His hands went to her gorgeous ass and caressed her cheeks. She moaned loud. He never did this before. His mouth continued down and with all his heart in his lips, he kissed her beautiful vagina, delaying his lips in it. Kim was in ecstacy, tears flowed in her gorgeous and divine face. He then turned her and kissed each cheek once and plunged his mouth in between her gorgeous and exciting cheeks and kissed her butt hole.

All were looking, completely mesmerized by this exciting and tender seen. John put a hand between her thighs and retrieved it wet. He showed everyone "You see she came with a few kisses only" he put his other hand and also came out totally wet and displayed it all around. "Do you know why she came so easy just with my kisses?"

All said "No!!! Because I never kissed her in her private parts before."

"Oh!!!" all exclaimed. John had their full attention.

"Do you know why I never made love to her or kissed her private parts? "

All exclaimed "No!!!"

"Because I was keeping it for my wedding night."

All were abstounded looking at each other's face, this time fear showed in their faces. Kim opened her beautiful eyes upon hearing the wedding night. She was all filled with emotion. She thought that Kathy was right. John held her by her lovely butt, his body covering her nudity, his head on her breasts. He continued.

"So all of you know her intimately before me. She is my priceless possession…Sorry love, I meant that you are priceless to me. Not my possession you are not an object", all could hear easily due to the echo, because of the 30' high celling, and also because he spoke loud "So all of you, one by one and all at a same time rapted my princess, my Queen, my future wife. And all of you know my power, this is a death sentence "all were crying by now and, frozen by fear. "But my angel ask me to spare you." All were nodding as if saying "yes, yes"

"Good, so since I am a business man and we are all associats, there is a price to be paid."

All said: "Yes any price, name it."

John first kissed Kim passionately and whispered get dressed my love and go up what follows will not be pleasant to see, go with Kathy.

Kim: "Were you serious the words you said about me?"

"Of course princess I love you beyond limits, go now baby. (turning to Kathy) Kathy cover her with the towel and take her to the room."

Kathy did and took Kim to the room. Six girls were video-taping the whole scene from beginning to end.

John continued: "So how much are you willing to pay?"

Henry screamed: "Any price."

John said: "Good money is not the subject here, but carnal payment. That's what I want."

Helena screamed behind him: "John look at me!!!!!"

John turned toward her. She continued: "You said you loved me, so take me out of here."

John looked at her, his eyes were in fire from anger:" You bitch!!! I fucked you to show you that you are nothing. You orchestrated all this to destroy my Kim."

"No, I didn't she wanted it and Henry too."

Henry:" No!! she is the one that planned everything."

John lifted his hand to put an end to the argument. "I seen also the tape that was behind the mirror and it had sound. I heard everything there is to see, or hear, or know."

Helena was suddenly gripped with fear. Her lips trembling, she couldn't control even the shaking of all her body. John turned to Michelle and said: "Bring them in."

She went out and all were looking with fear toward the door. Their throats dry their hearts pounding rapidly. Finally the door opened and all the drunkards and pedlers their clothes dirty and torn. Their faces with bad ackne some had a nose bleeding, many missing teeth and they smelled urine and alcohol.

The eyes of all the lords and their wives and fiancess, opened round like almost popping out, scared to death. When they saw those dirty men, they were at least fifty of them. They stood in the center of the prison.

John said, "Gentlemen, this snobs think that you are not human, that you are trash. They raped my woman. So please take your clothes off." They al did. Most of them looked that they were three legged and not two legs and a dick monstruous. "Now Michelle, and you girls get out here the first five." Michelle Gladis Mimi Janice Antoinette and Debra opened the first cell to bring the men.

They refused to get out, but they were no match for the girls. They twisted their arms pulled them by their hair and took them out in the middle of the group of drunkards.

John showing Henry:" So Henry you volunteered to be first to fuck and rape and torture my Kim. So we will start with you first!"

He began screaming "No!!!No!!! I'll give you all the money you want. You can't do this, I am the Baron."

John approached him and slapped him so hard that he quieted down. "Good now let's proceed. This two guys here are going to fuck your ass and your mouth and you have to masturbate, this other one is gay he will suck your dick." Henry was moving his head from right to left as saying no, no way. The other were dying in fear. John continued, "If you cause trouble or don't suck his dick showing the phenomenon in front of him. All their bodies had blister wound seven their dick were with all kind of bloody blister and infected wounds.

Turning to Josianne, "Bring the cat … " Josianne left to return 5 minutes later with the tiger chained and had a muzzle on his mouth. All froze from scare. Michelle brought a maniquin and put a condon with a piece of meat in it and put it on the manrain as a dick. Josianne attached the tiger's chain to the wall and the muzzle off. Michelle approached the maniquin to the tiger and immediately the tiger snatched in one bite the condon with the meat in it chewing and swallowing it in two second. All were shaking dead scared.

John said, "If any of you don't suck a dick, we will tie you to the wheel and the cat will eat your dick in a second. This I guarantee, go ahead" the five first took Henry and the one

with the biggest prick spit in his finger stick two fingers in Henry's ass making him scream.

Then he masturbate a little, when he was all erected he spread Henrys cheek, the others held him straight pulling his arm and in one push penetrated Henry's asshole. His eyes almost popped out. He scream "Ay!!!!Ay!!!!Ay!!!" John approached him: "So how does it feel to be raped? But wait you are going to have a good time." The other took his mouth with his fingers pressed his mouth open.

John showed the tiger. He opened it wide. Then the other put his prick in his mouth. Henry almost vomited. Michelle came fast and spray his throat." This will allow you to swallow deeper." The other pushed his dick in his mouth and ask him to suck. He was frozen and looked ridiculous. The one on the back was fucking him hard his hand holding his hips. The man at the mouth slapped him "hard suck bitch." He began sucking closing his eyes, but the other made them open. One went under him and began sucking Henry's dick. He had a few teeth left in his mouth. The other two sat on the floor, lubricated their penis and took Henry's hands and made him masturbate them.

"That's it very well Henry, good, now you will feel what my Kim felt. "Turning to the others," Each five of you take one of this pricks ", they were all crying.

The women were terrorized seeing their husbands raped. It was a big orgy. 25 men fucked 5 the first group. John made the second group, "come you" and told the others to do the same.

You could see 50 men raping ten high society lords. The men in their asses were enjoying forcing their dick that were 12' totally in their ass, and then other forcing them in their throat.

The scene looked gross and disgusting. The women watching horrified some fainted. Helena was crying and praying for this nightmare to end.

John said loud: "All men listen when you are done, trade places with your partner until everyone of you has sucked him everyway possible. Then the second group trade with the first. So each of this asshole is fucked 5 times by each X 50 men. Two hundred and fifty times. But we will do 50 times per day per person." Everyone of the raped people and their friends were crying, "John forgive us, we are very sorry we will give you any money you want."

John: "you think you can buy my honor and of my wife's with money? Michelle take the rubber stick and spank everyone in the ass very hard ten times in each cheek."

"Now I want you all to beg, fuck me please, fuck me, make me a woman, then maybe I'll change my mind."

They all began screaming yelling, "Fuck me please fuck me, make me a woman."

It was so ridiculous, they looked great for the camera they looked begging to be fucked and made them woman. The drunkards said: "No problem will fuck you and make you like a woman, suck bitch." And the new guy on his ass will began

"Michelle give them a few sprays for their throats." He called the men in the other cells. "You I want to watch your wives been fucked. If anyone of you closes his eyes or don't look. We will take some of the men to fuck you all night. So watch!!! As I watched the videos you fucking my wife, go.." They all rushed to the bars and with open eyes watched their wives been fucked. Their eyes wide of afraid to be raped them selves again.

Helena screamed: "You can't do this to me …… John. No!!!"

John chose the 5 ones that had the biggest and dirty dicks, and said "She is the most beautiful and dangerous one. Fuck her hard all night. She can be fucked only by five at a time, you hear all of you? "All nodded." Go ahead."

They roamed in the cells, they took Helena first and two immediately penetrated her in her pussy and asshole. They layed on the floor her face up screaming and one came and sprayed her throat and slapped her six times. She stopped screaming. He said, "I am going to give you my dick to suck. If you bite I'll brake all your beautiful teeth, so you will look like me. Suck bitch!"

When she saw his prick all with infected wounds, she fainted, he slapped her so hard that she woke-up, "suck bitch." He put his dick up to her throat and made her suck, the other two layed next to her, and began chewing her tits and made her hands masturbate their dicks.

All women were crying and being fucked harshly. Their flesh kneaded and chewed by the mouth and bands of the drunkard. It was a humble scene to watch five men in each woman being raped, their dicks were forced up to their testicles in one push. The men were enjoying the gorgeous delicate women.

Some cried: "Please don't leave us here."

Helena: "John please no, don't "And the man put the dick back in her mouth. She had a gorgeous body. They were having a feast with her.

John said, "well ladies and gentlemen have a pleasant night and girls better enjoy the fucking and don't fight it after two days you will beg for it." Turning to michelle: "give a shot of tosteterone to each of the men every 8 hours. Feed them and give them to drink. Don't let them sleep until at least 4 a.m. Okay?"

Michelle: "yes boss..." She caressed his penis on top of his pants, "I can come to you when ever you desire sir."

John looked and smiled at her. She said: "Boss, I am 100% with you this bastards deserve what they getting."

John: "Thank you kid"

He kissed her, and went up. It was 1 a.m. He went to his room. Kim and Kathy were in bed naked and asleep. John came and kissed Kim's face and breasts. She opened her eyes: "Oh my love. I missed you. I was dreaming with you. The beautiful

words you told me there, and I didn't want to take a shower. I still feel your kisses there (showing her vagina and derriere). I didn't expect it my prince. Does this mean that now you can have sex with me?"

John: "Not yet my beloved, let's wait until I'll tell you. It's very soon. Now, what I did downstair was to show them how much they have inflicte pain, to me and you. Let us go to sleep baby."

Kim looked shyly at him and said: "I need a favor from you before I can go to sleep."

"What is it baby?"

Kim: "I just want your kisses in my pussy, I was waiting for you for that, I need it as a drug, please love one time only."

He smiled, bend between her, held her hips very delicately and placed his lips on her triangle. She moaned: "Oh!!!Oh!!! my prince, I am in fire." He continued down and kissed her vagina, holding her lower lips against his. He felt her flow of contentment in his lips. She was exhaling, feeling his mouth burning her lower lips, then his tongue licked her three times between them and stopped.

"That's it my love, let's leave it for a better occasion."

She had her eyes semi-closed in ecstacy her mouth open. He kissed it pushing his tongue inside her mouth and savouring the honey that flowed in it. Encountering her tongue, that they exchange on and off. He held her in his arms and fell asleep holding and kissing each other until morning.

CHAPTER 21

J osianne came to wake them up at 5:30 a.m. They were exhausted. She shook John's shoulder, he opened his eyes: "Yes Josianne, what is it?"

We have all the men in the operating tables and anestheside, the doctors want you. He dressed up rapidly and left the room. Josianne stayed looking at Kim with adoration. She saw her face last night when John kissed her vagina in front of everyone.

It was full of passion, she even felt her intense excitment. Kim loved him very much she knew that. She put her hand on Kim's stomach and was looking at her triangle which she caressed with the tip of her finger, then kissed with her mouth. She was warm and sleeping." Oh how delicious you are princess", she spread her legs and gently kissed her vagina, her tongue penetrating totally in her, then sucking her clitoris between her lips.

Kim satisfied continued asleep. Josianne left her and went back to the hospital. She saw John there.

Dr. Meriaga:" Well we are ready. When they wake up they will be exactly as planned."

John: "How long it will take to for them to be ready for action?"

Dr. Megiaga: "Well with the special herbs that we have. I guess one week. The most 10 days."

John: "Good so please go ahead with it. I'll see later if you need me just have any of the girls call me. Thank you Doc" and he left.

wedding if we hold a little longer. I can't expand on it now, but soon. I will know when you are ready to hear me my beloved angel."

They hugged each other with tenderness and total dedication, he could feel her heart beats against his chest. "Oh G-D I don't know how can I hold without making love to you day and night. Burning everything around us from our fire desire for each other. That day will he my most memorable day to be united with you, be one feel your entrails. Oh princess I am so afraid to lose you."

Kim: Oh baby, you will never loose me ever, even if you have the darkest secret. I love you beyond comprehension." They sealed their declaration in an enabriating kiss.

Toward 6 p.m. John went down to the prison and see what was going on. The orgy was on, men fucking all the women, anyone was inactive. As John requested Helena was taken care by five drunkards. She looked pale, probably didn't sleep.

She had so much semen in her that she vomited. Her usually lovely body looked like a tramp. She saw John and manage to pull the dick from her mouth. "I beg you John, stop them, please stop them. ... I am dying." The one in her ass was spanking her cheeks and pushing his member in her up to his testicles. The same in her vagina. They looked monstruous.

They were slaming their organs in her. She probably felt it up to her stomach. "Please John" she begged "have pity on me." She didn't care about the others, just her. The one in her mouth pushed his dick back in her mouth and slapped her face twice "Shut up bitch."

John finally acceeded to her cry." Okay men when you ejaculate this time, let them rest for a day. Go back to your dorm, eat and sleep, watch T.V if you want tomorrow you will continue your fun."

All acknowledge and fucked them faster and ejaculated. John was looking at Helena specially. The two in her ass and pussy, ejaculated at the same time, squeezed her, their hands two on her ass, squeezing so hard that blood did not circulate. The other on her gorgeous breasts also squeeze closing grip on them and sucked very hard her nipples.

Finally the one in the mouth came, and shoved half of his dick on her mouth, ejaculating. She looked like being without air, sperm was coming out of the inside of her mouth. He pulled and closed her mouth. "Swallow bitch every bit of it" she had too.

Then the two she was jerking off come to her ass and mouth to finish in her.

They took her hard and shoved their prick and were moving faster and faster until they reached their point, and ejaculated in her and the one in her mouth splashed in her face then shoved the rest in her mouth and made her suck it to the last drop. John was looking at the grotesque scene. John told michelle to let the men out.

They all followed Michelle to their dorms pick-up their clothing in the way, putting them in without even washing, it was real disgusting. John entered the large cell where all the women laid naked, filthy smelling a very strong odor of sperm and urine. Some urinated on them too. Their faces and tits were all smeared with sperm. Helena raised her head and said, "I beg you John no more, I can't please have mercy on me … "

John: "Did you have mercy on my Kim ; she is my life you wanted to destroy her. So I won't love her, but you did the contrary because I love her even more. You put 16 men on her at one time. You almost killed her bitch, that is what you deserve. I'll let all of you rest until tomorrow. The girls will give you a shower and food."

Helena: "I didn't let Kim have sex with dirty people like this with diseases. "

John: "Your people and you are worst. Your soul is black as a cauldron. This poor people is their exterior that is dirty, but their inside is cleaner than yours. Your disease is a million

times more mortal than theirs. You want to destroy people, but the poor people just want to fuck to enjoy that's it. You smell terrible Baronesse."

He called Gina: "Take the big hose and wash this dirt bags."

Gina approached with a firemen hose and released the valve and washed the 19 girls, the jet was so strong that the girls were pushed against the wall. Turn over they all did feeling a relief, some vomiting scrubbing their skin as if to take the contact of this dirty people from them. Gina gave then bars of soap which they used gladly. She then provided them towels and robes. When they were all done. "Okay ladies you can use the men's cells they won't be needing them for now." They all rushed out from this horrible smely place. When Helena passed close to John, she threw herself at his feet.

"Please I beg of you, let me go. Have mercy on me." she cried loud. "You made love to me, just yesterday, how can you be so indifferently to my mercy?"

John released his foot from her grip and said: "This was the reason I made love to you. To show you that I do not give a fuck for you bitch, did you have mercy on my beautiful Kim. She hasn't done nothing to you and you almost killed her. She is a queen you are a demon, even after all you have done to her. She begged me not to punish you too hard. Take her to the cell with the others." She was thrown in a cell.

John: " You better rest ladies tomorrow the party continues."

One lady rose her voice: "What has happen to our husbands? Did you kill them?"

John: "Oh no that's too good for them. They will live a long life, but as whores like you."

John felt bad to treat ladies that way, but they were not ladies but Demons. They almost destroyed his dream, his reason for being. He will let them suffer more to learn to respect everyone in life even these poor men, to beg them not to fuck them so hard. They even made them lick their wounds. John returned to the room and took Kim and Kathy to dinner, to Cannes. They enjoyed the evening quietly.

Kim asked: "What is happening with the 15 couples and Helena?"

"Oh they getting a lesson and what they deserve. They might learn to change their ways."

Kim: "What I am afraid is that they might accuse you with the authorities of kidnapping and rape."

John had a sarcastic laugh: "Oh no, not when I finish them, they will beg me not to tell anyone and our business will continue as planned, believe me child."

Kim: "You scare me John, what are you doing to them? Why this doctors?"

John took her hand and said: "My princess you don't want to know, believe me. It is better for you, not to see what happen to my enemies."

Kim looked at each other and felt a cold feeling along their spine. John dark side, they suddenly were afraid of him again. They returned to the castle toward midnight and went straight to bed. John wanted to make love to them, but they found excuses of headaches. Kim made herself asleep but he took Kathy:

"What's wrong, you do not want to make love to me now?"

John opened his eyes. He was wrestles. He looked at Kim's beautiful face, she seemed tormented by something. Maybe she didn't like his revenge, but he was doing it to save her honor. At that moment she opened her eyes, their gaze encountered each other. She was very serious and not as always romantic or playful.

"My love I can't sleep, would you come with me to see a movie?"

Kim: "Now at this hour?"

John looked at his watch: "It's only 10:30p.m. We've been most of the day in bed, let's go you and I."

Kim didn't look enthousiastic but acceeded: "Okay …"

Kim wore a short and blouse and John a pair of jeans and T-shirt and they left. They went around many movie theaters until they found one that was open.

John said: "It's porno. I am not so crazy about it, what about you?

Kim: "Whatever you decide."

John: "Okay let's go in. If we don't like it we will leave."

He bought two tickets and entered. They were like 40 people inside mostly alone. They sat in a row alone. The movie was of course the type of people having sex every two minutes. One ugly girl with an 8 men orgy. Suddenly John remembered: "Love I have to call the yatch to see if Steve is coming and also I am going to the men's room. I'll be back soon."

He left Kim was very quiet and he felt she was disappointed at him. A young man came and sat next to Kim. He was looking at her beauty. He put his hand on hers. Kim didn't move or looked at him, with his right hand he opened his pants and took Kim's hand to his dick, and rubbed it with her hand. She didn't budge.

He then took her hand to his mouth, wet it with his tongue and put it back in his penis. "O babe strike hard." She looked at his dick and began masturbating it, two men behind then saw the scene. One came to Kim's left and opened his pants too, took her hand, and wet it and put it on his dick. "You can do it blondy", she was masturbating both with no emotions shown in her face.

Now one in the back, opened her blouse and began massaging her breasts with all his strength. Now, most of the spectators noticed what was going on and aroached them one in front of

Kim turned toward her pulled her panties and smelled them. "Oh how wonderful." He put his hands between her thighs under her and shoved three fingers in her vagina, forcing his way up masturbating her. Finally the one at her left, took her head to his dick: "Suck it baby, suck it."

She began sucking it hard. The one to her right, lifted her butt and came to her hole and penetrated it in one bounce and began fucking her, holding her by her hips. The guys on the back tried to keep on her breasts squeezing them. The one she had in her mouth ejaculated and was cursing and holding her head to swallow all of it. Then the one in her ass also came, he layed on her butt unloading his ejaculation.

Now the one in the back pulled her head above the row of chairs to put his penis in her mouth. She began stroking it and sucking it hard. She looked enjoying it. The one that had his hands in her vagina, took her ass and penetrated her harshly and began moving in and out of her burying his dick in her. Everyone in the theater stood up and stood in line to fuck her, their pants down. In the mean time one layed in the floor and began licking her vagina another squeezing her tits and two took her hands and made her mastubate them. Kim was all joyfully moaning and enjoyed the whole theater. Her eyes suddenly encounter John's gaze that was watching the whole scene.

She did not stop on the contrary she began moving frantically and told to all of them, "Fuck me harder, faster" and she

continued looking at him and she smiled at him as saying stand in line. He was next to the entrance door.

The men were lifting her, passing her to other rows, men with their pants down waited to fuck her. Two took her one from the front and one in her ass and fucked her hard at the same time. Lifting her each time of theground. She was screaming.. "yes..yes..fuck me harder, harder you fuckers."

John couldn't hold his tears. He had lost her. He began crying hard: "Why??Why??" A hand began shaking his shoulder, but he will brush it aside. "Why Kim? Why you had to destroy our lives?"

The hand that was shaking his shoulder became more insistant, until he turned and screamed "What?!!!"

"John, John wake-up you are having a nightmare." He opened his eyes Kim and Kathy were looking at him, when he realize that it was a nightmare his exclaimed, "Oh G-D, thank G-D it was a nightmare and not real."

He jumped on Kim and kissed her with all his might, squeezing her body against his, "Oh princess I was never so glad to awaken from a nightmare. Than G-D!!!you are still mine." He kissed her all over her face, her breasts up to her stomach his hands touching all of her.

Kim: "What happened? What was the dream about?"

John: "Oh, it was stupid, I think I am becoming jealous ..."

Kim: "Tell me please …"

John recanted the whole dream. Kim again felt compassion for her lover. "You really love me John!!" She caressed his sweaty face, took a towel and dried him: "You better take a shower love. Come I'll wash you." He went with her, and she took a sponge and soaped and washed his body. When she rose he pressed her against him. She felt his erection against her vagina and both felt a strong emotion. He rubbed his penis on her, both entraptured. His hand reached for her gorgeous exciting ass which he grabbed nervously, "Oh Kim, I can't resist any longer, I want you now!!"

As always Kathy rescured them, by sliding her head between them and sucked his penis. But John's hands were cramped on Kim's gorgeous cheeks.

"I need you more than ever. I am afraid to lose you before even haven the opportunity to have you my love."

Kim kneeled and together with Kathy kissed and sucked his penis sharing it and massaging his testicles with one hand each and the other caressing his cheeks and thighs. They felt his strong ejaculation and shared him taking each part of his excitment to their thirsty mouths.

John's back was against the wall, enjoying this two girls on his penis, lie then put Kathy between them and fucked Kathy in her vagina but holding Kim by her butt cheek moving on Kathy as if it were on Kim, kissing her gorgeous delicious round sucking them.

Then lowering his head to her breast and devouring them harshly.

They returned to the bed when they continued making love until they passed out. Josianne came in just when they were about to fall asleep. "Boss Mr. Steve has arrived, will you see him now?"

John: "Thank you Josianne. I'll be down in a minute."

Josianne: "Oh no sir, he is in his room. I'll take you to him sir."

John stood up she was looking at his nakedness he noticed and smiled at her. He got dressed in shorts and left accompanied by Josianne he knocked. "Come in."

John opened the door: "Hi Steve finally you showed up."

"Oh John I came as soon as I could. I had so much work. I had a ton of shit on this high society people enough to bath them in it."

John:" Good, because it would help to keep them quiet after we finished with them there."

Steve: "So how is it going on?"

"Come I'll show you."

He took him to the prison, the girls were all deep asleep snoring, he told him what had happened and showed him one of the tapes.

Steve: "Oh! Shit! look at the Baronesse … She got more than what she bargained for. Look at those dicks in her. How many times they bad her in one day?"

"About 50 times. I feel pity on them, even though they don't deserve it. Let's go to the hospital and see what the docs have done."

To their surprise the Doctors were still working. Dr. Meriaga came toward them: "How are you Mr J.?"

"Well, thank you Doc. This is Mr. F my associate."

They shook hands.

Dr: "Come, I'll show you, we have finish all of them. Tomorrow we will take care of the women."

They followed him and showed him the first one. He was still under the anesthesia. The doctor uncovered him. John and Steve couldn't contain a laugh that send them to the floor. After having laughedn enough.

John said: "I am sorry even though I was expecting it, but seeing particularly him like that I couldn't contain my laugh, sorry.."

Doctor: "Don't worry, I understand, come I'll show you the rest."

He took him around and showed him the sixteen men. They were all asleep. John wished the Doctor good night and went to sleep.

Steve: "I'll see you tomorrow."

"Josianne and Gina are waiting for you."

"Yes, I know, I need some good treatment after so much work. I hope I won't fall asleep in the middle." They both laughed and said good night. In the room, the girls were asleep. John undressed and joined them in the bed, falling asleep quiet fast.

CHAPTER 22

T he week went by fast. John did not go down to the
hospital. It's been a week since they had taken care of
the women. It was Monday. John woke-up at 6a.m. Everyone
was asleep as always Kathy in between. He looked at them,
Kathy looked like a child and Kim like sleeping beauty more
beautiful than ever.

A real princess. He was thinking, looking at the ceiling
reviewing all the events. Today was the day that all will know
the extent of his vengance. All sixteen couples were kept under
sedation until now, today they will be brought back to the cells.
The drunkards rested, enjoying the week, eating, drinking and
watching movies, they wanted sex.

So they were promised that today they will have a feast and
will go back to where they came from, eleven thousands dollars
richer, and take cases of whiskey, food, and a suit case of new
clothing. All was ready for them. They will leave this night
toward 10p.m. They had the whole day to fuck.

John stood up and looked through the window. Kim that had
awakened came behind him, girded him with her two arms
and kissed his shoulder. He felt her warmth and an incredible

contact of her body with his feeling her lower stomach against his derriere.

"Hi princess did you sleep well?"

"Hum. Yes big lover, I rested enough this week, are we going home tonight?"

"Yes darling, today beginning 9 a.m the party begins. It is your vengance day."

Kim: "Can you give me a hint what you have done to them?"

John: "Be patient curious, I don't won't to spoil the surprise."

She captured his penis and began stroking it with her two hands.

"Are you trying to excite me little girl?"

"Hum ...I want you to make love to me."

John: "Soon my love, I know it will be soon. But in the mean time come here." He pulled her around and made her kneel. She knew what he wanted. She took his virility that was already erected and first began kissing it and rubbing it against her face. Kissing his groins, licking his shaft up and down, her tongue drawn. He was moaning with her and watching her. "Oh my little princess. I had many women but none can do this better than you."

Her lips and tongue were burning hir penis. Her hands massaged his testicles. Her mouth enveloped all of it, she felt his throbbing, He bent his upper body, covering her. His hands massaging her hips and up to her breasts. He convulsed in pleasure releasing his strong ejaculation which she mastered and made shiver his whole being, her lips and the rolling of her tongue in the head of his penis.

She was happy to make him feel so excited and then his moaning gave her the tune of the extent of his orgasm. "Oh princess you're so good. I can only imagine your paradise and your butt". She kissed his relaxed member and press it between her wonderful proud firm breasts.

Kim: "I am happy that at least I can satisfy you with my mouth baby."

John: Every bit of your body is a source of excitment. Just give me time and we will have our night, Queen of my heart."

She kissed his thighs. He lifted her and carried her in his arm at the same time he stole one of her breasts in his open mouth.

"Don't eat me now. You won't have nothing left for later."

She rolled her head enjoying his continued and unlimited desire for her. Her beautiful throat arched and stretched back He went for it and licked it all over sucking her Adam apple and her chin.

"Princess how much I love you. When you are mad at me, I feel miserable. I love to see you like this loving desirable."

They heard a voice, "What about me, you have forgotten me?" It was Kathy, she had a sleepy face, cute like a little girl, beautiful.

John came toward her, he had Kim in his arms he said:" Jump in pumpkin on top of Kim and hold my neck." She did she was hot, just waking up. "Oh kid, your so hot and exciting you are making me horny again."

He took both to the shower and made love to them as always Kathy being the separation between them. They went to breakfast, they found Steve, Josianne, Gina already there waiting. When they saw John, Josianne and Gina tried to leave, but John stopped them: "Stay, don't leave because I came. You are with Steve, so you are his compagnions and his guests."

Josianne said: "Well let me bring all of you breakfast."

Kathy said: "I'll help you Jos …"

Steve: "So today is the day and three million dollar plus later."

Kim said: "I feel bad to have caused all this."

John: "You didn't cause a thing, it's my fault and I let you down for not protecting you from this vipers."

They had breakfast and were ready for the V-day, they went downstairs. Michelle and the sisters were there ready. The

other girls had the six video cameras ready to roll. Finally all the 16 couples were brought in wheel chairs and put in their cells, still half conscious. Dr. Rodriguez came followed by the other doctors.

He said: "Hell all, I hope this will make worth for all the money you spent. They will be completely awakened in ten to fifteen minutes."

John: "Good (turning to the girls) I want one camera directed at each cell filming when they discover the surprise." All the couples had hospital gowns on. They were all awake. The women in their cell and the men in the smaller cells.

John cleared his throat and said: "Listen all of you" all aproached the bars of their cells, still tired from so much sleep." I collected enough for raping my wife. Today you will enjoy a party until 10p.m. Then you will be all released to your homes. All men come out of your cells. They were happy that they will be leaving this place alive. Once they were out."

John had a box in his hand." This is what I charged you for my Kim." He took a glass case from inside the box. First no one understood what it was, until John with a glove on, pulled one from the box. Suddenly all uncovered their bodies and looked, the screaming was horrifying. "Oh No!!!!it can't be." Kim and all the girls were dumbfounded, looking at them.

The men had a well defined vagina instead of a penis. They had tits and a round ass.

They tried to jump on John, but the girls stopped them and Josianne attacked them with the tiger. Their wives couldn't utter a word. They also touched themselves and screamed. They had their clitoris removed. So they can't get excited any longer.

They screamed and cried. John threw all the human parts to the tiger. He ate them under the horrifying eyes of their previous owners.

John continued," Now you won't flick or rape anyone. I have tapes of you begging to be fucked by the men that you're been fucked by and also begging please make me a woman. Now if you go to authorites to complain. I will denied any wrong doing, because you asked for and by some miracle this video tapes will be shown around the globe. So take your punishment graciously and fuck-off and you will find yourself new husbands. Michelle bring the men let the party begin."

They tried to hide in their cells, but the girls had closed them. The men aroused horny. When they saw the men with cunt, they didn't try to understand, they jumped on and each three took one ex-man fucking him in his cunt, ass and mouth.

They screamed their heart out. The sixteen men were being raped again by the 50 men under the eyes of their horrified wives. John turned to Helena "Now bitch you have no clitoris to get excited. I bought all your debts and your friends too. I ruined all of you. I own you now.

If you behave well, I'll leave you were you are with your title including your friends, the contract will continue as we signed it. But this time, I'll control all of you and profit, I'll let you live like you do now. I'll give you much to survive nicely. The first trick and I'll put you on the street to work like a whore, understood?"

Helena: "Why? Why so much hate? Why so much revenge?.."

John: "What a stupid question. You have destroyed my dream. You had 16 men sullied my Kim penetrate her, fuck her. Something I was keeping taboo for myself. From now on, when I'll tell you to jump, you'll ask how high? .understood?"

Helena nodded her head down.

John: "I'll send you a file of how I own everything you ever had, even your jewelry, that was declared stolen 5 years ago and you defrauded the insurance company out of 14 million dollars. I can send you to jail for 15 years, but I won't. All the time you behave. One more thing all the girls, your pussies stink from now on no one can lick of eat your cunts. Now you reflect what you really are devils. Kim and Kathy couldn't believe their eyes. Seeing the men look competely like women. They needed long hair and make up and shave their bodies and they would have looked like brodes. the scene of the formers men being raped was too much for them, they ran out of the prison disgusted and scared. John turned to Helena: "When they finish fucking the men or former men they will began with you, enjoy as much dick as you can, because no one in his right mind will fuck you outside. So enjoy."

She tried to beg him not to but he didn't listen. He turned to Michelle: "Take care everything, pack around 9p.m. Give the cars back to the ladies and send them home. I'll leave now. Kim is very upset from all this."

Michelle: "You can count on it boss" he squeezed her butt and she liked that.

He turned to Steve: "Let's go." In the way to their room.

Steve said: "Wow!!!that was a terrible revenge John. I didn't know that you could go to such an extend one thing is saying it and one thing is seeing it."

John looked at him: "I know that it looks terrible, but that's what i felt when I saw Kim raped by 16 men at one time. Spanking her, biting her private parts. Here 50 beautiful and delicated. She is the reason of my strength. Fuck those bastard. They should be happy that I haven't killed them. In two days we will have a meeting with them in my office. Well get ready, we will leave in 30 minutes."

Steve looked very impressed and shocked with what he saw.

John entered the room. He found both Kathy and Kim pale and crying.

"What's going on?"

Kim looked at him with a rage he never seen her in: "How could you? How did you have a heart to do this, you destroyed them for life."

John: "How could I? Do you know how I felt seeing you raped by all this fuckers? I promised you that no man raped you, but women. You didn't understand me then, now you do. "He approached Kim to hold her and calm her.

She screamed: "Don't touch me, i am afraid of you." He felt his heart break to pieces.

He turned toward Kathy: "You too?"

Kathy didn't look at him, and did not respond.

John said:" Okay now you both hate me. I understand. Are you coming with me or staying..?" They didn't answer. "Okay!! You can go with Steve in his car. I am leaving bye." He took his suit case looked at them one more time and left. He stopped at Steve's room.

"Steve take Kim and Kathy with you, they are very upset."

Steve: "Don't worry in a couple of days they will forget. Go ahead I'll take care of them."

John took his Austin Martin and departed in one bounce, squecking his wheels in the gravel, leaving a trail of dirt. He was very upset. Kim and Kathy saw him leaving through the window.

Kim: "He is very upset what I said, but I am really afraid of him and you and I know that he probably is the serial killer. I can't stay with a man that I am afraid of. I am returning to the states."

Kathy: "I'll be probably return to Sweden. I am also afraid of him."

Steve came and they departedr towards 3p.m, almost 5 hour after John. When they got to the yatch it was 4;30p.m. John wasn't there. Steve convinced Kim not to leave now, and wait a week at least. Kim acceeded to Steves request. John didn't show up until two days later. He looked feverish. Kim and Kathy slept in Kathy's cabin. They saw him arrived toward 8:30 p.m.

She rejoiced to see him back. She really worried for him. They been reading the papers to see if there were new victims. But none were announced. Not seeing him come out of his room. Kim and Kathy decided to go and see him. They had to break the ice. Kim knocked at the door, but no answer

She opened with her key and found him laying in bed all dressed. She tried to touch his face. He was burning of fever. "Oh my G-D Kathy he is burning with fever, call the doctor." Kathy took the rolodex and looked for the number and called the doctor. He was on the way to the yatch. He said: "I'll be there in 15 minutes."

Kim and Kathy suddenly felt passion for this man laying in the bed. He was talking delirious: "No, no my love don't, don't."

Kim was worried: "Kathy I am worried for him. I hurt him with my words, look what I did." Steve came and helped them take his clothes off and cover him with a blanket he was shivering, his teeth vibrating clacking against each other.

John was still talking in his delirium. "No, let me go he is going to kill her, let me …" He was very agitated, sweating, Kim was trying to calm him, whipping his face and body.. caressing his face." It's alright my love, I am here next to you relax … shush …"

The Doctor arrived.

Kim: "Doctor, thank you for coming so quick, he is burning with fever."

The doctor took his stetoscope and cheeked his heart. Then his pulse checked his eyes. After a good check-up, he took a serynge and injected it in his cheek.

"Madam, he is very agitated, probably under a great stress this caused his high fever, wash his body with alcohol and water and put ice bags on his head and feet. So it will lower the fever." He took a pad and wrote a prescription." Here this are antibiotics, send someone to buy them, 3 tablets per day with food, with the injection I gave him he will calm down, and rest. Just keep an eye on him at all times, did he have an emotional problem lately?"

Kim looked away and said: "Yes doctor I am probably the cause."

Doctor: "I understand, he needs rest and calm, good night."

Kim: "Good night doctor, what about the bill?"

Doctor: "I bill his office, bye …"

Steve: "I'll get the medicine, where can I find a place open at this hour?"

Gina: "I'll go with you Steve, I know where to find one, it's quite far."

Steve: "Thank's Gina, let's go." They left closing the door behind them. Kim and Kathy took a bassin and mixed water and alcohol and washed John's body with it, then filled up 2 ice packs and placed them one on his head and one on his feet. He was shivering from cold. They covered him with two blankets, Kim was worried:

"Oh Kathy I am probably the reason of his illness."

Kathy took his pants and folded it on top of a chair. A bundle of keys fell from his poket to the floor causing a metallic noise.

Kim looked and picked up the keys. There was a gold key. She looked at, and touched it.

"I think that is the key of the special room." She whispered in Kathy's ear, "I think that we should see what's in it." The doctor gave him and injection, so he will sleep for a few hours. It's our only opportunity. You want to come?"

Kathy: "Yes...let's go." Kim turned toward Josianne:

"Please Josianne stay with him until we come back, would you?"

Josianne: "Of course Kim."

Kim followed by Kathy their hearts beating hard, went to the room. They stood in front of the door with fear of what they will find in there. Kim, finally put the gold key in the lock and turned. It was the right key, it opened. There was a small light inside, but they couldn't see much.

She found a switch and lite the lights.

The first things they saw was many partitions and had many pictures of children and next to each pictures there was a stack of letters. On top of the wall was an inscription in large letter, "My Goals." They approached and read the letters of a little girl.

"Dear Mr. Benefactor:

I want to thank you for saving my life with the money you send to the Hospital. I today have a new liver and can live like any other girls, play, pray, and study. Oh also thank you for sending money every month for my education.

Every night before I goto bed, pray to G-D to look over you and keep you from harms way. Even though I do not know your name, I call you Mr. L for love. At the beginning I did not understood why you kept your name secret but now I do my teacher explained it to me. I imagine you are big and beautiful with shining armor, ready to rescue every orphan, because I know that your the same that helps all in my orphanange. One thing I also pray that one day G-D will send me a daddy like you. I Love you always, Melisa …"

There were thousand of letters like that, each little girl was writing to him, almost every month. No wonder the mail bag was deposited in his personal mail box and never allowed anyone, to pick it up for him.

And when he answered, he locked himself up in this room for a whole day. There was thousand of pictures, each with various letters. It looked like an Kim and Kathy had their faces flooded with tears.

Kim said: "Look at all this. Do you believe? he does so much charity and given hope to all this orphans and keep it so secret." She cried loud. "Do you believe that he could be a murder, but how? I am so confused. We knew so little about his private life."

They continued looking through the various partitions until they arrived to the last wall. Kim suddenly froze and screamed, "MY G-D!!"

CHAPTER 23

K im couldn't believe her eyes. Kathy also was with her mouth open. The whole wall 20' by 7' was Kim's picture, laying on a fisherman's table, the tiny dress lifted on her hips leaving her incredibly beautiful derriere totally naked, and the shirt of the same material of the dress.

Holding on her arms living her breasts, back and stomach naked. Beautiful as a dream. Her arms folded holding her gorgeous head up straight on her hands. Her long blond hair brushed to one side, leaving her Angelical face to be apreciated, her almond shape green eyes looking at anyone that will look the picture following him with her gaze.

Her jaw, the most gracious well designed as if painted by Michel-Angelo under the picture there was a large bronze inscription "Desire of my desires." Kathy and Kim looked at each other "Oh my lord, when did he make this giant picture of me?" It is the one David put in the internet, looking for her. It was from an adult magazine two years ago.

Without noticing she was telling Kathy a secret that she did not know. She was dumbfounded. There was a gold pedestal and a book in it. There was an inscription on the cover "My

beloved." Again they looked at each other and Kim said "But..I ... did not know him eighteen month earlier, I just know him three months now." Seeing questions on Kathy's face she said: "I am sorry, but I'll tell you all later." She turned the first page, it began like this:

"Today I found a picture from a magazine, she is the most beautiful girl I ever seen in my life. Something told me to keep it. I borrowed it without my friends knowledge. She is incredible."

A second inscription, the next day:

"I can't understand but I dreamed with that girl. I can't understand but I dreamed with that girl. I do not even know her name. She looks like an angel. Oh I wish I had money, I lost all my fortune 400 millions dollars because of government agents. Now I am penniless. I wish I was rich, I'll look for her anywhere in the world."

"I can't figure out, I dreamed with her again. Am I falling in love with the picture of a stranger? She popps out in my mind even during the day, working, praying, or eating. I am restless. How could I become so hooked-up to a stranger from a picture?"

Kim's heart was beating hard. She was reading it so Kathy could hear it. There was various pages of the same retoric, until the one page "I must be crazy but I am in love with the stranger. I do not even know her name. I'll call her Desire of my Desires ... She is in my mind day and night. One thing I

am sure. I have become rich again and I look for her." Kim was overcome with tears of joy.

"Oh dear Diary, how can a man in my age 45 years old, with so much experience in life, can fall in love this way, she is probably 20 to 24 max ... and just a picture. That's crazy, but she has rekindled a fire in me, I have to become very rich. For her I feel so much in love like a child, I even feel younger, even my friends do not understand my new looks. I look happy, ready to chalenge the whole world. Incredibly or not I am in love."

Kim was smiling and crying, the tears blurred her eyes. She had whipe them out to be able to continue reading.

"The way I fell for her reminds me of a short story. There was a kid next to a lake, he was as if talking to G-D 'Oh G-D, I want to be a King ... ' by coincindence the King was behind the three and heard him. He came behind him and by surprise took his head and plunged it under the water and held it for a minute. The kid was battling to lift his head out of the water. Finally the King let him go. The kid turned and saw the King and he bowed 'I am sorry your majesty.' The king said 'Tell me child, when I held your head under water, what did you wish the most?'..The child without thinking said 'To breath for air, your majesty.' ... The king then said: 'If you wish to be a king as hard as you wished for air, you will be King one day' ... So the story tells exactly how much I wish to meet the desire of my desires, my misterious blonde. I need her as air to breath. I feel like 20 years old in love. It's crazy, but it's true."

Many more inscriptions of the same type were for hundreds of pages until:

"I finally succeeded in closing my first big deal with the bonds. Thank to the desire to meet her. She has been the impulse behind it.

G-d I have not the necessary means to look for her, but I'll wait a little longer and prepare a base in Europe. I want to repurchase my yacht. I would like to meet her there. Incredibly or not, the business with my bonds haven't stopped. I am a billionaire in six months, all for her."

Various months inscription have passed. The next one was: "Believe it or nor, David just called me to tell me that we closed the deal that made me the richest man in the world. I am now in my yacht. I told David to look for my desire, my angel in disguise. I am excited like my first time that had a date."

"Finally David was connected by her, Oh G-d for real this time. Her name is Kim. I've been telling everyone about her as if she was my fiancee. I didn't want any one but her, I couldn't make love to anyone else but her. I sit in my secret room for hours and watch her beautiful face. Well not just the face, but her incredibly exciting butt. She drives me mad. David, Peter think that I lost my mind, but Steve believes in it like I do."

"G-d she is coming tomorrow. Oh, Desire of my desires, I am finally going to see you too, actually talk to you. Before I did talk to you, to your picture and response was forthcoming,

but now you will be in flesh and blood. My plane is bringing her to me."

Kathy: "Well I do now, with your craves for weired sex."

Finally. She read. That a big intitution made a bet with John, that he should withhold sex with her until he gets married, if not he will loose all his fortune. That was the bet, mostly pushed by his old aunt. No wonder he was holding.

Kim continued reading about their encounter in the plane. Then he wrote of that evening: "Oh how gorgeous she is, even more that her picture my heart almost raced out of my chest. I am crazy about her. Would I be strong enough to resist her if she likes me, and wants to make love? Poor Kathy she is paying my lust for Kim. I made love to her before, but very ocassionally, but since Kim arrived. I do everyday three times to aliviate my need to have sex with Kim. In a way I have a certain love for Kathy. She is my cry pillow. She's been there everytime I felt anxiety, need for tenderness or just morose. She doesn't ask for anything. She just want to be with me."

"Oh G-D last night Kim slept in my bed naked. When finally I have her next to me, I can't touch her. She must think that I lust be gay. It is so hard to see her beautiful nakedness, her gorgeous derriere at the reach of my hands and not being able to touch her, to make love to her. It was easier to become the richest man in the world that holding myself from making love to her. It's crazy but I am madly in love with her, she might after a while be in need to find more loving parties, harder and harder. She tempts me at every opportunity. Her beautiful

Angelical face reaps me to pieces, when I refuse her. Every part of her body excites me. When she kisses me, my heart wants to leave with her, exiting through my mouth."

"Oh today she gave me a blow job. Oh lord, I couldn't last even two minutes in her. Her lips were tearing me apart. I couldn't stop that she has me enslaved to her. Poor Kathy I pour my wrath in her. She is lovely and I feel for her. Her young body and childish face excites me very much. She helps me cope with my every minute of the day dilema. Kim. I enjoy very much sex with her. Kim is jealous, I know it. I feel Kathy part of me already. I don't think I could leave her. Oh!today I've surprise the sisters making love to Kim. I thought I would die. I am so jealous, but what else can I do? At least they are girls not men. I have to follow the bet, and continue making believe that is doesn't bother me. I am even hurt or jealous when she makes love to Kathy or Josianne."

"I am behaving totally to the contrary of my moral principles. All this to sooth my desire for her, I never made love in so many different ways thant I am doing now. But I feel that rage of desire tear up my whole being each time. I see her naked or kiss her body. I think that I am losing my mind for this girl, she is in my blood, under my skin and in all my thoughts."

The rest of the journal she knows most of it. She hugged Kathy: "Oh Kathy he is crazy about me. Everything he does is for me. It's crazy but I do feel what he feels. I am madly in love with him. Who else can love me the way he does." Seeing

Kathy quiet "He loves you too and I do too." She kissed her. Kathy kept looking at her. Kim said: "What's wrong?"

Kathy broke silence: "We came here believing that we will find something else..There is still no explanation for his special nights and the next day a girl is murderred. We haven't seen or read a clue of that part."

Kim: "What I think is that he might have a split personality and one doesn't know about the other."

Kathy: "Maybe, who knows? If he does how can we help him?"

Kim: "I don't know, we will give him enough love."

Kathy: "The time we went to Iatly, no murders happened, the time you and him went to Paris, nothing happened. When we spent almost two weeks in the castle no murders. Now he again disappeared for two days. I am afraid to read tomorrows news."

Kim: "Let's go back before Steve comes back."

They went back to the cabin. Joasianne was asleep in the arm chair. Kim undressed and enter under the sheets and melded to him: "I want to give him my body heat, so he will heal."

She felt his body against hers. She felt a strong emotion, whe his penis pressed against her vagina: "Oh my prince, I couldn't know how much love you had for me." She moved on top of him and began rubbing her body against hers. She was getting excited. Her mouth kissed his chest and face, her hands on

his derriere. Holding him with all her strenght, feeling his manhood between her thighs. She moaned and kissed his throat "My love, how much I desire you."

At this moment Steve knocked and entered "Oh!!I am sorry."

Kim: "Don't, I am just giving him body heat. He was shivering."

Steve gave Kathy a white paper bag. "Here those are the antibiotics. He has to take one every 6 hours."

Kim: "Thank you very much Steve."

Steve: "Oh you are welcome ..." He could appreciate her gorgeous face and naked shoulders, and part of her breast that was uncovered.

Steve: "Good night ladies ... keep him warm."

Josianne had woke-up and left with Steve and Gina. Kathy undressed and entered the bed eclosing on him, caressed Kim's butt, then took John's hand and put it on Kim's lovely ass.

Kim was moaning and rubbing himself against his penis. Kissing him, she felt an awakening between her thighs. He is reviving finally. She took his penis to her vagina and pushed his penis in her. Closing her eyes and moaning, "My love want you so bad, awake and making love to me all the way. I don't want no one else just you my love."

Kathy wet her fingers and inserted it in Kim's butt whole, and gently masturbating her at the same time. She was moving

on him, felling his penis almost completely in her, and feeling Kathy's fingers in and out also exciting her. They made love, but he was out all the time and even though his erection was under his inconsciousness Kim felt her orgasm send shock waves over her entire body making her break down in cry of happines.

She had more love and respect for him, especially after having read the childrens letters and all about her in his dry. then kathy made love to her, but her mind wasn't there. She let her do all she pleased to satisfy her lust. But Kim was thinking of him only.

CHAPTER 24

Kim stayed all night awake caring for him attending his fever. Until early hours of the morning when she fell asleep at his side her arms wrapped around him as if protecting him. Kathy woke up and checked his temperature, his fever was down. She looked at Kim, she looked different, more mature, she held him protectively as a mother her child. But his child was bigger than mama. She smiled at herself.

She put her bath robe and went out to breath fresh air. It was a little cool at 7a.m. She stretched and saw the newspaper on the floor. She took it and went to the kitchen to have coffee. She opened the front page and she got the shock of her life, three young woman one 19, 21, 24 years old were found floating in the harbour, their sexual parts cut-off as all the 23 women were murdered, the police had no clue what ever. The police said that he changed patterns everytime, and wasn't following a certain order of the things, sore a certain timing.

They never knew where to expect the next. He was nickname The Surgeon ...... due to his use of a scapel to cut the young women's parts.

He never left a finger print nor any clue as to why he was killing these women.

She left her coffee on the table and ran to John's cabin. She shook Kim's shoulder various times until she awakened. She made her sign to follow her outside. Kim put a robe and followed Kathy.

Outside she showed the paper and explained what was written in it and the picture showed three young beautiful girls.

Kim: "Oh my G-D, it can't be him. He is too tender, loving, careing for thousands of children, and also how he treat us. No, I can't accept that."

Kathy: "It is hard for me too. I love him very much. But again he disappeared, but this time two days. Three women showed up murdered and mutilated. How can we explain that. I think we should call the police."

Kim: "No, not yet let's try to investigate. Let's look for clues everywhere. Let's get dressed and searched the cabin and everywhere he is use to sit, maybe in the safe."

Kathy: "We don't have the combination nor a key?"

Kim: "Will see … They got dressed and looked all over, he was still asleep." Kim was trying to open the safe trying his keys and looked for the number.

"Do you want the jewels Kim?"

She jumped surprise and scared. Hitting her head against the picture frame that served as a door and cover of the safe.

John jumped out of bed and held her." Oh I am sorry princess, I scared if you, are you hurt let see your head." He looked and said, "You have a little scratch." Kathy that was behind him froze and was scared to death. Kim couldn't utter a word.

He continued: "Here this is the number of the safe, for when you need it, and this a copy of the key. I am sorry for not have given it to you before."

Kim finally reacted and managed to say: "I am sorry to have awakened you. I needed money to go buy your medicines and other things."

John: "Forgive me baby, I didn't pay attention you needed money, how stupid of me."

Kim changed the conversation: "You scared us a lot you disappeared for two days and came burning with fever, the doctor was here last night, you were deliric you talked a lot."

John's face expression became serious. "What did I say??"

Seeing his sudden face change, she said: "Nothing.. Nothing that we could understand."

John turned and saw Kathy: "Did we receive the newspaper?"

Kathy: "I ....don't ... know I'll check outside."

She rushed out and returned a minute later with the paper rolled and tide as he usually receive it. He tored the wrapping paper and Opened it. He saw the three girls and read. His face turned pale and his lips turned blue, his eyes closed and passed out. Kim and Kathy rushed to him and began crying.

"Oh G-D. He looks bad." They gave him mouth to mouth ressucitation and massaged his heart afraid that he was having a heart attack.

Kathy said: "You see, he has to do with the murders."

He was coming back to his senses after Kim made him smell an essence.

Kim: "John you scared us again, you fainted when you read the paper."

John was confused for a few second and finally said: "When I was reading, I felt deasy and I don't recall a thing. I am sorry princess to have scared you."

He tried to kiss her, but she moved away as if she did not notice that he was about to kiss her. But he knew that both girls were behaving strangely.

He took his clothes he was still weak and got dressed.

Kim: "But you are sick ... Where are you going?"

John:" Oh don't worry, just to my study room."

Kathy: "You should eat something first."

John: "I'll go to the kitchen and grab a bite."

Kim: "I'll get it for you."

John: "No thank you. You both are acting very weird toward me lately. So don't worry I'll manage. He left slamming the door behind him."

Kim had tears: "Now what do we do?"

Kathy couldn't answer. But Kim continued: "He knows that we are afraid of him. I can't go to the police. I love him, i adore him. I'll help him even at the cost of my life."

Kathy: "Me too, we can't forget all his done for us. Let us keep watching him and try to make him realise of his other personality."

John went to the kitchen. He met Josianne and the sisters chating.

Michelle: "Hi boss, good to see you better. Do you need any thing?

John: "Yes, just a tuna sandwich or anything else that is ready."

Josianne quickly prepared him two sandwiches, "Thank you girls, I'll take it to my study room."

John went opened his room and locked himself in it for most of the day. Toward 7p.m. Kim became worried: "I am going to see what is going on, "she went and knocked various time. "John please answer". He opened the door, he looked pale.

"Yes what is it?"

Kim: "My love, please don't shut me off talk to me, confied in me. I love you."

John: "I am alright I have to go, I'll be back late."

Kim: "Not again please talk to me, trust me please." She was crying.

John did not respond and left. He seemed very disturbed. Kathy came late and saw her crying and took her to the room and tried to calm her down hugging her.

Three hours had passed, the phone rang, Kathy picked it up.

"Hello?"

John: "Kathy! Good that I found you. I need you to do me a favor, take money from my drawer and go buy me twelve bottle of champaign. We have a business meeting tomorrow at the office, could you do this for me?"

Kathy: "Of course boss, I'll go immediately."

Kim was trying to ask who it was. Kathy hung up.

Kim: "Was it him?"

Kathy: "Yes, he ask me to go and buy twelve bottle of champaign for a business meeting tomorrow." She took the money from the drawer and left after taking a jacket, it was cool.

Kim was very nervous and anxious, maybe he will call back. She tried to lay down and rest, but she was too nervous. One thousand thoughts came throlig her mind. Thirty minutes had passed since Kathy left, when the phone rang, she jumped and picked it up. Thinking it was John: "John?"

A voice she didn't recognized answered: "Miss Kim?"

"Yes, this is she."

"My name is Jean, I am outside your yatch. Mr. John had an accident."

"How? Where? Is he alright?"

Jean: "Well he is wounded, he doesn't want me to call the police, nor go to the hospital. He asked me to bring you to him. I am outside in a black Peugeot."

"Let me put a jacket, I'll be there in one minute!" She hung up, took her jacket and hurried out. She had tears. She prayed G-D for his well being and to help her to be able to help him out of this madness.

The man was blonde 6'2" thin, on his early 30's blue eyes, and pleasant face. He came toward her "Bonsoir Madmoiselle ...

I am sorry to be the bearer of bad news. But he gave me a lot of money to take you where he is and not call the authorities, I didn't."

Kim looked at him: "Thank you, please hurry-up is he alone?"

Jean: "No my fiancee is there with him." he spoke English with a heavy accent.

He drove fast. She didn't even look at him. She was very worried. She didn't even know how or what she will react or do when she sees him. He will probably will confess to her everything. She wished Kathy was with her.

She asked: "Are we still far?"

Jean: "No Miss, five more minutes."

They arrived at a big house on the suburbs of Monte-Carlo it was a modern villa. She opened her door and followed him. He walk fast and her behind him trying to be close to him. Her heart was beating hard, he opened the house.

"Please come in." She followed him to a back room. What she saw there, made her scream. Three young women naked were tied each on a table. There was a fourth one empty. She didn't realise what was going on, until she felt her heart twisted to her back and an arm enclosed on her gorgeous and frail neck. She couldn't move, the guy said, "Don't even try, I'll brake your neck.." He was too strong for her. Her legs were shaking, scared.

He pushed her to the empty table and tied her hands first than her legs each to one side of the table. Kim began screaming. I Ie slapped her.. "Shut up! ... American bitch." The slap made her recover her calm. She looked at the naked girls next to her. They were all young and beautiful. Their eyes red from crying and scared to death.

The man: "So finally I have his favorite girl. I beat him everytime, not even his money can buy you out of this nor this three girls here. They will be passengers to hell with you. Let us see what you got for me. He took a type of knife. Kim's eyes opened wide, she was so scared that no sound came out of her gorgeous mouth. He put the knife between her legs and began cutting her dress up to her breasts.

He tore the whole thing leaving her almost totally naked. Just her pink panties on. He cut it on both side and pulled it uncovering her beautiful sexuality. Hum:" He really got himself the best merchandise." He caressed her vagina, then put a hand under her, moved her to the side to see her derriere: "I like that very much." He then continued to her breasts, surveyed them with his hands. "Very good ..."

"Well I will take all of this for me.. I collect them. Tits, Asses, and pussies. Yours my dear are the best until now, Kim was crying, "No, no..please don't kill me, please ... " he put his hand between her thighs and squeezed her vagina hard. "Don't cry again or scream, because no one can rescue you ... And again your lover has lost this time too." He took a video camera and placed it on a tripod and put it on record.

"Now scream loud, the four of you. I am recording. I love screaming, it's an art that you have to understand. I am going to cut all your parts with the knife without killing you first. I'll trust you'll die alone." His eyes were of a mad man. He laughed scarily.

He turned to Kim first. "I'll start with you, you are the best of my collection!". He first caressed her vagina. "Thank you for saving me time and work. It is well shaved I like that." He pointed the knife above her triangle and was marking the line where he was to cut. "Yes this is the perfect spot.." She saw the knife getting ready to cut, she closed her eyes and prayed. She didn' feel the knife, but heard instead a strong noise of struggle, "You son of a bitch … finally a found you … " She couldn't believe her ears. It was her beloved's voice, John.

She opened her eyes, John and the murderer were fighting. John had no weapon, the murderer had the knife, they were circling around each other until John jumped and held his arms. They struggled, the knife was getting closer to John's shoulder. She could see the knife touch his shoulder, then his white shirt colored red blood. He was wounded. Kim screamed, "No, no John!!!!" Finally John smached his armed hard against one of the cabinet probably breaking his wrist, he winced from pain.

John twisted his arm in one bounce braking it at his elbow. The man screamed from so much pain. John then lifted him with two hands above his head, bent his knee and smached the man's back, braking his spine leaving him inanimate on the floor. He rushed to Kim and cut off the straps that was

tying her to the table. She cried, held him, shaking in his arm, kissing and crying, then the blood on him. "My love, you are wounded." She was hysterical.

John calmed her … "Shush ….princess, it's nothing.. Everything is over. Let me free the other girls." He did, the poor girls kissed his hands, face …"

"Oh Merci, sir G-D bless you … " They saw death very close. John took rags and said to all of them.. "Cover yourselves with this, am calling the police …" Each took their torn clothing and covered themselves as best as possible. John was calling the police, he asked one of the girl to see outside what address they were ene knew and told him.

Kim jumped again in his arms and was shivering, hiding her face in his neck. Then again realised his wound. She took part of her rag and tied his shoulder, the police arrived, the sirenes broke the silence of the night. There were at least 30 police cars and five ambulances, the detectives recognized John. He told them the whole story from the beginning. Kim could understand a word. They spoke in french.

A paramedic attended his wound. It was just superficial. The girls were taken in an ambulance all shaken; but very happy to be alive. A doctor checked the serial killer, he wasn't dead, but paralised from head to toes. The police invaded the house, and found everything that puzzle them up to now. All the women's parts were preserved in fermol. Some were discated formed and placed as a trophy on a placque in the wall.

Kim fainted. A medic took care of her and she came back to her senses. John carried her in his arms her head on his left shoulder. He put her in the car and they left. He had to drive with her in his lap. She wouldn't let go of him.

CHAPTER 25

At the yatch all the girls were looking at Kim. When they finally saw them arriving they rushed toward them. Kathy and Josianne were crying. Once inside they all sat in the living room. And waited for explanation. John stood up and left Kim on the sofa, holding onto Kathy.

He said: "Well I know that most of you suspected me of being the serial killer.."

There was a faint protest, but they all felt ashamed and looked down. He continued: "I don't blame you, because each time I disappeared for a night or two, I came dirty. Some time with blood and the next morning the newspaper published a new victim. This had started three months after I had arrived to this country. I thank you for your loyalty of not going to the police. Each time before a murder, I was receiving a message that said, "If you don't try to find me and my hostage i'll cut her parts without killing her, and let her suffer … Don't try to contact the police, because I know your every move. I can hear and see everything you do or say. Then he will write a riddle, that I could never discover, because I do not know the country. I faxed the notes to the police chief who is a friend of mine with

a note. And he also investigated but to no avail until tonight. I found a note under my door that was placed that same evening. This time, I knew that he intended to kidnap Kim. So I made myself leave and returned in another car and watched the yatch until I saw a car stopping near the yatch and Kim coming out five minutes later. I followed them, to try and save the other girls, you know the rest."

Kim stood up, letting the rags fell, naked came to him. "You mean you used me as a bait?"

"Well darling, he would have killed those three girls, plus one day he would have succeeded in kidnapping you without me being around."

She slapped him twice. "This is for using me for bait and I almost died from fright ...."

All looked at the scene enable to say a word then she continued "And this is for saving me and not being the murderer.."

She jumped to his neck, wrapping her arms around it, and kissed first his cheeks that she had slapped, their kissed him with all her essens. All smiled and slowly left the room, leaving them alone.

Kim: "Oh my darling, I am so happy that you are not the murderer ... "

She continued kissing him. He finally lifted her in his arms naked and took her to the room followed by Kathy. Once in

the room John put her on the floor and undressed, behaving a little cold toward her and Kathy. He said: "I'll take a shower …" They both looked at him astonished. He finished his shower and put a shorts on and stayed without shirt.

Kim finally spoke: "What is wrong now, you are behaving strange with us …"

John: "How could you two, that I thought knew me so well, could have thought that I could murder young ladies … That usually would risk my life to save any human being. Now I understand all your strange behaviour, especially you Kathy that known me for so long. Good night." He left them both mouth open and left the room torso naked and his shoulder bandaged.

Kim: "He is very hurt, Oh my G-D. We betrayed him.."

Kathy: "We did, and me the one he saved and took care of, Oh lord, I am so ashamed..I couldn't look at him in the eyes any longer."

John returned 5 minutes later. He put a T-shirt on and left again.

Kim looked at Kathy and said, "Let's go out with him and comfort him.."

They went out, but they saw him leaving in his car. He departed before they could say one word.

Kim looked at Kathy and said, "I have something I could try … "Hide in the corner of the room." I'll wait for him. I know how he might forgive us."

She rushed to her suit case in the next room and brought something from it and wore it.

Kim: "What do you think?"

Kathy: "It might just work … " both had a mischivious smile in their lips." I'll be in the sofa. I don't think that he will switch the lights on, in order not to wake you up. Leave the night stand lamp, so he can see you."

Kathy was laying flat on the sofa and Kim positioned in the bed waited. John returned an hour later. They heard the door open. John entered and didn't pay attention at Kim, nor could see Kathy. He undressed and went to the shower. Took one and came out drying his hair. Suddenly he saw Kim, his eyes almost came out of their sockets, Kim was naked, with just two rags, one above her hips leaving her derriere bare.

The other leaving her shoulders and breasts naked. Her face turned toward him, smiling at him mischiviously holding her head and upper body up resting on her elbow. She was slighty sideways so he could see her lovely ass and her breasts, exactly as the picture that he fell in love with …

John: "Oh lord, why are you doing this to me, I can't resist any longer, I am sorry even though I love you above all. I … can't."

He kneeled just behind her, his hands barely brushing her wonderful ass cheeks as if it were a vision. His heart pounding almost as if he could hear it. "Oh ... how gorgeous you are my love, I desire you I can't hold any longer ... "

She said, "I know prince charming, I want you, all of you now!!!"

He plunged his face and burned it in her deep valley in between her prominent round and exciting ass cheeks. His hand were shaking from so much excitement. His lips kissing her inside, and licking her deep well of his long, waited fantasies.

Kim could feel his heart beats on his lip that were kissing and licking at the same time between her cheeks and her rear entrance. "Oh ... finally ... " She exhaled, feeling his hands caressing her ass tenderly. His lips and tongue surveying all her valley in depths.

Kim came already.

His mouth was just kissing her vagina, which she just had lifted her incredible derriere to his mouth, feeling her flow of passion. He drank from it, savouring every bit of it. But the flow continued non stop with his hands, he wet all her ass with her contentment over her vagina and triangle and licked and kissed all of her bounty, trembling ... His body shaking uncontrolably from the intensity of his excitement. Kim moaned loud, her head was down on the bed, bitting the sheets and her hands gripped on them.

"Oh my love, yes, yes … " he kissed and licked all of her ass, every bit of it tasting the potion of love that flooded from her paradise and that he smeared all of her cheeks and thighs with it.

John's heart was racing in his chest. In a small break he said, "I hope I am not dreaming, I'll die if I am … Oh my goddess of love, I am enslaved by you.."

These words made Kim reach a third orgasm in his face, he felt the pouting of her vaginal lips and felt her throbbing, her lips and clitoris swollen. He let it flow in his face as if it were blessed water from a fountain of youth. He rubbed his face face between her thighs smearing her elixir on her thighs then licking every bit of it. He did the ritual for three endless hour that seemed to both as a minute.

He pushed his face in between her thighs, after having tilted her sideways. His mouth reached for all her vagina, triangle and back to her ass. Chewing her bulge, her lips, her clitoris, then plunging his tongue in her vagina surveying tasting enjoying her sweetness in depth. Then to her rear gate he plunged his rolled tongue in her, biting her cheeks gently.

Kim cried, moaned very loud, sighing as if complaining. Kathy had an orgasm just by hearing her and seeing the extreme passion of these lovers. Kim continued having orgasms one after the other, which he drank, also took some with his hand and massaged her breasts with, teasing, rolling her hardened nipples between his fingers. All her body was smeared with

her flow of excitement and John was chewing licking her flesh kissing.

He lifted her thighs to slide up to her breasts and suck one at a time. So intense that he felt milk coming of her breasts, they were both totally enraptured in the seventh heaven, surrounded by singing angels. Kim had her eyes semi-closed her tongue drawn in between her teeth. Her face painted by her excitement, reflecting an immense joy, happiness that no one could penetrate or disturb. John feeling again her orgasm, returned between her thighs and put his lips against her vaginal lips, feeling her lips throbbing about to come. He pressed his lips, teased her inside with her tongue making her come faster in a strong flow into his mouth.

He took every bit in his mouth without swallowing it, close it and rose in between her thighs layed on her and put his lips against hers, waking her open mouth and shared the potion of love with her.

John: "Taste my love, taste how sweet you are inside, this is how bless me with each time you come, princess ... " She drank her own potion. It excited her more, he made her open her eyes, his were almost glued to hers, face to face, body against body. His penis against her triangle making both shiver, trembling as if they were cold, but it was from so much desire for each other.

"Look at me in the eyes my love, open your eyes ... They were half closed I want to see paradise in your gorgeous green eyes my love when i come to you my queen. I can't hold any longer."

He held her gorgeous face in between his large hands their eyes fixed on each other.

She could see deep into his brown eyes, discovering the real meaning of love and how deep were his feeling for her, hungry as a wolf, ready to devoure a sheep after having not eaten, for a whole month, his heart pounded heavily against her breast. Their lips trembling, saliva was dripping from the side of his mouth, from so much thirst he had for this angelic being as he were enraged. "Look at me angel, i want you now."

He began rubbing his penis against her triangle. Kim lifted her legs to feel him against her swallen vagina, pounding wanting him finally in her, willingly.

He moved and rubbed more and more, looking straight in her eyes. She guided him forcing him in her. She felt his tip between her vaginal lips, which he rubbed against her clitoris, she was all shaken, exhalting looking at his memerezing eyes. "Come my love, penetrate me, now.. (she cried) I can't hold any longer … Ah!!" She was convulsing her back arched. He penetrate her, feeling electrical currents rock her entire being, rocking her soul.

Her warm reception was burning his penis, feeling her wetness as if he plunged in a river, she had a instant orgasm.

She felt also his instant throbbing still looking in his eyes, when he ejaculated deep down in her paradise. He also exhaled, his face had an expression of tremendous excitement. "Oh my princess, Oh … I am sorry, I couldn't hold, Oh!!!"

She smiled at him tenderly, moaning in his mouth that he was kissing, her tongue drawn from the excitement and captured between his lips and sucked it … "Oh princess, I can see paradise in your eyes. I waited so long for you, for your love, to unite together as one, feeling you entrails swim in deep of your pleasure chambers. Oh love of my life. I don't mind dying in your arms now that I have reach the pick of my desires you my beautiful angel, my adorable girl."

He licked the shining liquid gems coming out of her eyes, expression of love, having reach the ultimate. He also had tears of happiness. He kissed her lovely face, endlessly, savouring her lips between his. She finally able to control her trembling lips, she said "I never knew what love meant, master of my being, your love is endless … I feel you inside me … The moment you entered I came too, it was too much excitement, too much desire and too much waiting for this moment."

"Make love to me again, love me … I want you now and forever." She began moving her lower body, moving her vagina on his penis making him sigh. He semi-closed his eyes, "No love, don't, look at me.." It was her now that wanted to see his excited eyes and face, exciting her by the same token. This time, love making became more intense, his hands grabbed her fantastic round, proeminent and sexy ass, and began moving in her. She felt his penis deep in her, then retrieving to replunge deeper with more desire and passion, moving faster still looking each other in the eyes, his mouth devouring hers, sucking her lips, her tongue, drinking the honey that flowed from her mouth which he drank in desperation.

Then they rolled in each other, moaning.

Kim crying openly from joy. She stretched her body, rolling her head back. He sucked and kissed her neck, her adam's apple with full open mouth in desperation. Kim arched her back complettly offering him her firm, exciting breasts which he sucked in a sweet rage opening his mouth totally, engulfing as much as he could of her bounty to then suck her nipples and repeated on.

He moved his penis on her vagina in and out faster and faster, shaking his powerful hands clenched on her ass cheeks, his finger penetrating her rear entrance in and out up to his knuckles pushing as he wanted to force all his hand in her for a treasure called sublime ecstacy, this pushing her agina against his penis. She girded him with her long silky leg with all her strength.

Kathy not able to resist any longer, came and joined them, she was about to come, she sat on her mouth, at the moment she reached an orgasm just by seing them. Which Kim acknowledge by devouring her cute young vagina, one hand penetrated her ass, and the other her breasts.

"Eat me Kim my love eat my pussy ... " She layed on Kim's face, her back to John. He ate her ass with thirst. Kim felt her flow in her mouth, flooding her. She drank it like a very special liquor. Kathy felt their mouth devour her pussy and ass together in unison. It was incredible to feel devoured by the mouths of people she loved the most body and soul.

Kim felt his throbbing about to explode like a storm or a volcano. She pressed her vagina, crossing her legs under him on and off. He convulsed and exploded like a volcano, releasing his burning lava, washing away in her paradise, burning everything in it's path. Kim's esctacy reaching it's peak, felt her orgasm and flow extinguish the brush fires in her, caused by his powerful ejaculation. They both held each other shivering, convulsing enable to control their muscles. Kim and John were breathing hard, almost breathless in sweat.

John kissed her beginning from her forehead going down, licking her sweat away, kissing every bite of her body sucking her breasts in the way, belly button and vagina up to her toes. Then turned her over and kissed again from her feet, up to her mountain of love, crossing her deep valley of her exciting ass, up to the top her head a process that took him a whole hour.

She enjoyed every bit of it. All her body was covered by his lips and tongue. Until he finally rested next to her.

Kim: "My love, that was wonderful..I feel like your mouth was giant and all my body fit in it." Kathy came around and layed between John's legs, kissing and holding his penis against her face, feeling his testicles on her chin.

Then she began sucking it. John's hand caressed Kim's exhilarating body, making her shiver each time he brushed his finger between her ass cheeks. She was laying her face down. She turned her face toward him, looked at him intensly, her eyes shinning, smiling a new light was.

Kim: "I know that you loved me, but not like this, you have showed me a new vue at life … I can see life through your eyes and I love it."

John: "My love, I am totally in love with you. I am crazy about you, love me always, never doubt me. I love only you, no one else."

John put his face against her, nose against nose. He smiled with a sigh.. "You know princess, my life since I knew you, has been a fable, a dream, you are as beautiful as a full moon, and replendent as a sunrise. I melt with your smile or cry. When you moan, I am lost. I hear it as the sound of mermaid, a sirene trying to trap the sails unto the depths of the ocean forever."

"Now that I made love to you.. I was lost completely. You could have do anything of me. I know that hard times are ahead of us, you are too beautiful to have you for myself, like a rare jewel that i have to keep in a safe with all the alarmin the world." She had tears of joy in childish expression of her marvellous Angelical face.. "But I trust you to judge the situation in proper time. If you find yourself corner in a sexual situation, If there is nothing you can do to get out of it, don't just go with it, even enjoy it with thinking to how or what, just think of me. To fight it or suffer from anxiety could traumatize you. When you see me, i want to know all of it, I'll do the rest, I'll collect. But no one will stop me from loving you. Only you can, by betraying me volontary. That will be a knife direct my heart."

Kim caressed his face tenderly: "I love you John, that is the only thing I can tell you my love."

John: "You're so beautiful princess, my heart aches when I do not see you for a second or feel you next to me. I feel very fortunate, I am almost twice your age, we look like the Beauty and the Beast, my favorite compassion."

"Don't say that again, never, never, inside you're the most beautiful human being ..." she almost told him about the secret room's the kids letters. Kim looked at him and continued: "My love, I know that you are dying to make love to my ass, that excites you the most in my body. I love to be taken by you this way, conquer me again, come my love. I know you waited too long to feel my depths in there, I want too my darling come penetrate me all the way, love me deep."

The words alone affected John's sexual desire, lifted himself above Kim's back, slowly releasing his body weight on her. The moment his penis touched between her cheek, he had a violent ejaculation all over her ass and back, exhaling and feeling embarassed ... "Oh I am so sorry my love, I don't know what happened to me."

Kim giggled, "Oh I know what happened, my butt scares you, it excites you too much."

Kim moaning.. "Oh John, don't hold my love, penetrate me, don't make me suffer any longer, nor yourself, come stay me with it ... Come my love I want to feel your penetration."

He moved one more time rising on his elbows.

make a effort to go up. Then she relaxed her cheeks pressure to let.

Their eyes were saying a million words. Kim felt his erected penis, move faster and faster inside of her gorgeous ass. Having all her entrails on the move, she loved it. She was biting his lips, until he bled a little, but they did not pay attention. They continue their struggle to an infinite happiness. Kathy heard the door, she opened it was Josianne. She was pertified by the lover's act. Kathy asked, "What is it?"

"To my beloved John. The Hero of the year.."

All said "To John."

Steve was happy mostly, because he was surrounded by gorgeous women..The whole restaurant looked at them recognizing John from the morning papers. They joined in the cheer. John thanked them, then they sat down. John whispered to Kim, "I will have my revenge.." She giggled like a little girl that has done a mischivious act. John excused himself to the bathroom. Kim said, "Hold on my love, I'll go with you..!" She held his hand and followed him. The restaurant was very fancy.

When they arrived in front of the restroom, John looked inside, seeing no one, pulled Kim's hand and both entered the men's room. She didn't care. They fell in each others arms kissing with thirst. He pulled down her panties and lowered her dress to uncover her breasts. She wet a finger of hers and penetrated her rear entrance hole wetting it. He turned her

over, and penetrated her lovely ass in one push and made love to her with all his might. Squeezing her breasts.

He knew that men will eventually show up. Not even five minute had past that a man in his late thirties entered. He was shocked at first to see the sex scene. Kim had her dress up to her waist line and the tops too lowered her divine nakedness. She had her eyes closed and her head rolled back on his shoulder.

She looked at John, he made himself that he was mad..Kim laughed, she cleaned herself and John too. The fixed their clothing and left. Two men were just about to come in and saw them leaving the men's room. John said in English, "Sorry we need the telephone.."

They looked at them. One said, "this Americans are idiots.." They were back at the table. They had a great dinner. It was 11:45 when the phone rang.

"Hello?"

"Oh hi Dave, Peter, please just listen to all of us for a few minutes!"

John had three phones. The second one also rang then the third.

All looked puzzled, mostly Kim. The second phone was John's daughter and each of them had a phone extension. He also said hello and asked them to hold the line. He gave the third phone to Kim to answer,

"Hello, yes?"

"Hi, baby its us"

"Oh Mom? Jenny? Oh my G-D how did you know that we were here?"

The mother: "Mr. John told us to call at this hour …"

Kim looked at John dumbfounded, all were. He pulled Kim to the the table and Kathy to let her sit down. She did. He put the three phones on the table, and kneeled in front of Kim, his mouth close to the phones. Took Kim's hand, and taking a little box from his pocket and pulled a gorgeous diamond ring of at least ten carats. The whole restaurant was at their feet, watching the romantic scene.

John said: "My angel, love of my life, I would like you to be my wife forever."

Orly, Kathy, Josianne even Steve all had tears in their eyes. He was saying it loud so everyone could hear. Mostly the phones Kim was totally speecheless.

Then she managed to say, "You really want me to be your wife? Marry me?"

John: "Yes my princess? I want you to be my queen and give me many little princes. I love you my angel, you are in my every thoughts. Loving you is dreaming awake. I think of you every second of the day or night, sleeping or awake, just looking at

you, my heart races after you. You have illuminated my dull life!"

Kim had tears bleuring her gorgeous almonds shaped green eyes.

He continued, "Your tears are like liquid diamond to me..Your mouth flows the exlixir of love. It's taste honey. I want you with me every moment of my life."

At this moment a whole band of musical entered, a beautiful romantic music. Twelve young ladies brought each a bucket of roses of different colors. Kim could barely see him with her eyes clouded with tears. She kneeled in front of him. He kissed her tears away and said, "So what do you say?, would you be my queen forever?"

Kim, "Yes, yes, yes, I want to be your wife … "

All cheered in the restaurant. John picked up the third phone. "Would you grant me the hand of your daughter in marriage?"

Even Kim's sister. Then he took the phone with his daughters and he spoke in hebrew, smiled and looked happy. Then he took David's and Peter's call.

David: "Congratulations that was a surprise.."

John addressed the three phones: "I'll send my jet to pick all of you up. "The wedding will be in two weeks ",another round of applause. John yelled: "Champaign for everyone.." He took Kim in his arms and kissed her with all his essence after

putting the ring on her finger. John lifted her from the ground, she jumped and girded him with her legs in an inebriating kiss with her strength.

She didn't notice that her ass was a little uncovered. Orly covered her. Everyone came to congratulate the hero of the year and the richest man in the world. Some asking for his autograph. Kim wouldn't release him not eve for a moment. Her marvellous face was radiant, she really looked like a queen, they finished the party it was 1 a.m. Kathy and Josianne were still crying from the emotion.

Orly: "That was a spectacular love declaration and request for marriage ... (turning to her husband) You should learn from him"

They all smiled. The cars took them to the airport, to return to Nice then Monaco. They arrived at 4a.m. at the yatch, and they were so tired they fell asleep. Kim on John's arms and Kathy next to them, hugging each other. They had a great night sleep.

CHAPTER 26

John woke up at 9:45a.m. He had a meeting at 12:00 noon, In the office with the Consortium or what was reduced to. He picked up the phone and called Steve:

"Hello?"

John: "Morning"

Steve: "Oh I feel so tired.."

John: "Don't tell me you fucked the girls when you came back.."

Steve: "I didn't, they did, I think my eyes must be out of orbit. What's up?"

John: "Don't forget that we have an appointment in my office with the Consortium..They will be there at 12:00 noon. Do you have a file with their records copied?"

Steve: "Yes everything is done.. I'll be ready at 11:30 am."

John: "Good enough, see you.."

John looked at Kim on top of him. He immediately got aroused. Her body heat was incredibly exciting. He had his hands on her incredible ass. He made love to her in her sleep. She was deliciously exciting. He was all in heat, burning of desire for her, his hands penetrated her gorgeous derriere feverish, moving his penis and hand in and out of her, kissing her nose and lips, her eyes. She felt it and semi-opened her eyes.

"Oh my love is fucking his bride to be in her sleep. I am very pleased ", she said, the last word in suppens and imitated his movement. She was all excited, feeling his manhood in her vagina, moving frantically. His hands in her ass cheeks and his finger planted in her inviting hole. She rose her breast to his mouth to make him sucked them. He didn't need a picture to tell him what she wanted.

Kathy awakened by the emotion, became aroused. She came around and put her cute ass on John's mouth and her vagina in front of Kim's face, but the latter did not go for it. But Kathy pushed Kim's head to her pussy and held her mouth in her. Kim kissed her a little but did not continue. Kathy that was aroused said, "please Kim, do me ... " She finally did gently teasing her clitoris and kissing her lower lips to please her.

Kim felt his throbbing.

. He stood up and got to the shower and followed by the girls. When John found himself alone with Kathy he said,

"Well done..She is actually changing. Now go to plan B. Do you have everything ready?"

Kathy unhappy said, "yes boss. Are you sure you want to do it?"

John: "It is hard for me, but we have too, are you up to it?"

"Yes everything is ready. Okay, I have a meeting that will last until 7 p.m. It gives you seven hour and a half from the time I leave. Remember anything goes wrong, call the sisters. They know about it."

Kim came back with a towel wrapped around her." So whats going on a conspriacy?"

John kissed both and went to look for Steve and left for the office. At 12:00 noon they arrived at the office. As expected all were there. No one looked at John in the eyes.

"Please sit down, let's cut the formalities."

The Baronesse was the closer to him. She looked different, she had pimples in her face, and finally he pinpointed what was missing in all of them "Arrogance".

"Well let's go directly to the point."

Steve passed a copies of the file to each one that had their name on it. It was very personal..

"I know that you are all frustrated, for what I've done to you, but I don't give a damn. You have gang drugged and raped my future wife. There is no man alive that can do that and live to tell about it. So thanks to Kim I didn't kill you. Today I own you totally. The files about each of you is in front of you.

So I agreed to let you keep your fortune and titles enjoy the best you can under the circumstances. You can buy yourselves dildoes if you want. Their are many ways you can satisfy each other. Now back to business, we continue as planned … "

They continued their dealing for most of the day. In the mean time in the yatch Kathy and Kim.

"I have a tennis game with some friends from Sweden. We need an extra player. Please join me."

Kim looked at her and said: "Well I have nothing better to do, why not.."

Kathy "Great, let us be ready we start at 12:30pm!"

They put their tennis outfits took their raquet balls and left in Kim's Rolls Royce convertible, when they arrived four young guys in their late 20's early thirties came to greet Kathy. They were all great looking all blonde, over 6' tall and very atlethic. They kissed and hugged her.

Kathy said, "This is Kim a friend.."

They all shook her hand … "Nice meeting you."

Their eyes were undressing her. They went in and began playing three against three. They played until 2:30pm. They were exhausted and all in sweat.

"Okay guys, go take a shower and we meet outside for a drink okay?"

All answered "O.K."

The men's shower was next to the women's shower. Kathy and Kim undressed and entered the shower. It was so cooling and refreshing. They heard noise behind them. They turned and saw the 4 Sweedish standing naked watching them. Kim was surprise but Kathy said, "what's wrong guys?" One of them answered," there is no water next door. Do you mind if we wash here with you?

Kathy said: "Of course not." before Kim could object. She explained "In Sweden we shower together. Do you mind?"

Kim was embarassed, but said "No of course.."

She did not know how to behave. She never showered with strangers. She looked at their exgerated size penis. All huge. She turned her gaze from them. Kathy played with them, and slowly it turned to a love scene.

The younger kneeled and began eating Kathy's pussy. Take pressed himself in her ass until he penetrated her. Holding her by her hips and moved on her. They all had their dicks erect. One began devouring her breasts.

Kathy was moaning: "Oh, guys it's been so long since we've fucked together"

The one on her vagina lifted her legs and stood up and penetrated her pussy. Their penis could not penetrate all the

way, they were to big for her. The other kissed her, his hands on her breasts and fucked her on and on.

The fourth spoke to Kim, "She is a great kid. She can manage easily this big guys."

Kim nodded politely trying to avoid looking at him.

He said: "You are very beautiful … I never seen a beauty like you before."

He approached her, she could feel his breathing on her neck. He stood now behind her, his hands barely brushed her shoulders, slowly going down. She was petrified, but excited. He caressed her hips down to her thighs.

Then went back up this time caressing her breasts, making her nipples hardened. He circled them various time. Kim was tense. His left hand lowered to her stomach gently caressing her shaved triangle down to her vagina, he played with it, brushing it with his finger:" You are so smooth. Your skin is exciting. Relax you are tense let me just massage you."

His hands now massaged her breasts and her stomach down to her vagina. She couldn't breath. He kissed her shoulder and necks. She felt his penis pressed against her ass. The guy that was kissing Kathy came to her from the front and caressed her nipples then teased them with his lips. His hand then went one to her breast and one to her vagina, gently masturbating her. She was petrified. She couldn't move or say a word.

Now both pressed her between their bodies feeling their enormous dicks pressed against her stomach and between her ass cheeks and began rubbing their dicks on her.

Kim was enable to defend herself from their advantes. They took her to massage table and layed her in it face down. Each took one of her legs and massaged her up to her vagina, one hand massaging her cheek.

She felt their fingers and hands, brushing her vaginal lips and also passing by her rear end touching her hole. A third guy joined and did her back. She felt the guy on the right massage her between the vaginal lips slowly penetrating her, the other on the left wet his finger and began circling the hole of her derriere, then pushing it in a little then retracted and repeated each time penetrating more, both were doing the same.

The guy on the right lifted her from under her triangle and began kissing and devouring her pussy with full tongue. The other kissing her ass and his tongue replacing his finger on and off interchaning. Kim was totally lost in their hands.

The one at the front lifted her face and made her kiss his giant penis. The fourth one approached Kathy was looking at them, but couldn't do a thing, until she rejected them. The fourth one took her hand to his penis and made her masturbate him.

Now she was totally in heat. The one on her right lifted her and slided under her. The other layed on top of her. They both pointed their organ in her vagina and ass. The other was pushing his penis in her mouth. It could barely fit. They began

penetrating her. It was tight for them. The one on the bottom devoured her breasts and began fucking her until he penetrated his whole dick in her. Then the other her ass, pushed more and more lifting her ass to make it easy penetration.

He pulled out, put some soap in his finger that he penetrated her massaged in it up to his knuckles. Then soaped his penis and this time penetrated her all the way in.

"Oh, Oh it's too much ", she tried to say taking the penis out of her mouth, but the other put it right back.

They were fucking her hard, squeezing her tits, devouring them. The other had his penis up to her throat moving in and out. It was an incredible scene. Kim was encasted between this two gentelman. She felt their penis up to her stomach. Their throbbing made her feel an incredible sensation.

They followed by a volcano's eruption filling her completely. But they continued fucking her. Then they turned her over and did the same, just changing positions. This time they lifted her legs up the one on her back fucked her ass and the one on top her vagina. She was in ecstacy with 5 big dicks around in her. The guy she masturbated layed on top of her head and fucked her mouth. The last one sucked her tits and she masturbated him.

They turned each other on and on. They finally took her two at a time. Standing and fucked her squeeze between both. She called:

"Kathy, Kathy" but Kathy did not answer. Again "Kathy, whats wrong, answer. It's time to go."

She finally opened her eyes. They were still at the yatch and she had dosed off. Waiting for Kim to put her tennis outfit. "Where you dreaming?"

Kathy: "Yes … I was thinking about my friends. I haven't seen them in 3 years from high school." They left thirty minutes later and arrived at the tennis club.

All went as she had dreamed up to the shower. When the guys came to the shower. Kim saw them and yelled:

"Get out of here now.."

She took a towel and wrapped herself and said to

Kathy: "Let's get out of here.."

Kathy: "But Kim don't over react … In Sweden, it is a normal thing." Turning to the guys. "Sorry guys."

Kim saw their big penis and turned her gaze and said,

"Please give me a minute to get dressed, then you can have the shower.."

Kathy stayed and the guys began kissing and slowly turning to fucking as she dreamed it. One guy stayed on the side and came to chat with Kim:

"I am so sorry we didn't mean no disrespect … For us it is a normal thing as making love, we do it anytime of the day any place."

Kim apologized, "I am sorry but I am tired after so many games.."

She chated, looked at Kathy. She was in full swing with the guys. they cheeked for a few moments. She felt more relax now. He said:

"I am a massagist in Stockholm … Come by my guest, lay on this massage table … "

Kim: "no, thanks I am alright now."

"Do not be afraid of me, I do not bite. You will remember this massage as the best you ever had"

He didn't let her argue and made her lay in the table face down. Kim could see the love scene. The guy took a lotion and rubbed her feet first. The pressure points are in the feet. They can relax most of your body. He massaged her pressing in certain points of her feet making her relax. Her eyes were getting heavy. His hands went up to her calf, his large hands wrapped them easily. He continued to her thighs, his fingers coming close to her vagina and down. She felt his fingers as if they were leaving a trail in her flesh.

He continued each time higher, until the tip of his fingers brushed her vagina she frowned. She didn't say anything, he

did the same a few more strokes. Then he moved to her next. She saw Kathy looking at her. He lowered the towel to her waist. She liked his hand, they were of a professional. His thumbs went along the spine down to the beginning of her cheeks.

His two hands spread covered the width of her back. It was very relaxing, but she could feel a little excitement between her thighs from his previous touch. His hand were reaching the ass, and hips. his hands penetrated under the towel covering her gorgeous sexy monumental derriere.

She shivered up to her waist to return a little further. He stopped and unfolded the towel. She jumped, but he calmed her down "Shush ... this is what I do every day. I massage people, I see."

She herself began spreading her thighs each time further, until she was completely spread waiting for his fingers to caress her hole first. He could see her hole completely defenseless and un by the height of her delicious cheeks. She continued moving her ass from excitement.

He put his finger in it circling around the hole, feeling her soft stretchable skin. She was in ecstacy, burning. He put more lotion in his middle finger and began penetratin her hole. She moaned, "Oh, Oh, yes ... "

He had the tip of his finger in her the walls of her ass hole. He looked at his finger penetrating her, his penis was completely erect. He push his full finger in her, and with the other fingers

he massage the hole around it. She was pushing her butt up to feel his finger further. Now with the other hand, he massaged in between her thighs, pressing her lips each time his hand went from her ass down to her triangle that was shaved.

He felt her flow of juices on his hand. She had come at least twice. He looked at the others. They understood and came toward him. Even Kathy came and looked at Kim in total esctacy. He had his finger plunged in her hole pushing hard in, then when he returned. He pushed a second finger. Then a third she was convulsing from excitement. His other hand also, he had a finger in her vagina and the others massaging her gorgeous vaginal lips.

The skin there like a little girl. A second guy stood at her side and took over her ass. He lifted her to her knees, she was completely spread. The first guy could see inside her pussy. It was pink and beautiful to see. Now the one on her ass, began massaging her butt, and shoving his thumb in her hole, and with it, he massaged her interior. The other hand massaged her thighs up to her left vaginal lip pushing his fingers in tomassage the left wall inside her. The first guy did the same, shoving a second thumb in her ass, forcing it, thus enlarging her gorgeous orifice.

Second hand on her right thigh, and also put two fingers to massage her vaginal right wall. Kim was moaning loudly, possessed by convulsion. Kathy caressed her head thinking: "My poor Kim, you won against the Baronesse and everyone … Now you can lose John fighting yourself."

The other two guys one took her head moved it up to reach out of the table. he spit in his hand and lubricated his penis. Then made her open her mouth, and he brushed all his length between her lips. It was an emormous penis. It looked bigger than the three others. He was moving in her mouth sideway, when she got to it giant head. He tried to shove it in her. Her mouth totally open, stretched, she could barely suck the head wetting it and repeating the same operation. He put her hand on his testicles, to massage it and rubbed then against her gorgeous face when her lips reached the bottom of his penis. The fourth one layed next to her and sucked her breasts. His hand squeezing it and sucking as much he could fit in his mouth. He took her other hand and put it on his dick to masturbate him.

Her hand barely covered a quarter of his length. Her hand closed around the penis could not circle it. She stopped from licking the other guy to put the fourth guys penis tip in her mouth, wetting it with saliva. She felt like putting a whole orange in her mouth. She had plenty of saliva on it, and began masturbating him with all her strength. Her mouth returning to the other penis. The first two guys were contemplating her beautiful ass and pussy.

They were mege. They roll to her side and lifted her leg all the way up and asked Kathy to hold it. She did. Now the guys had a clear view of her deliciou assets. They shoved each two fingers in her ass hole and vagina. Masturbating her non stop. She was moaning. Fluid flooding their hands. They spread

the liquids in their hands and smired all her ass and vagina and thighs.

But the fluid kept coming more and more. They also wet with it her tits. Now both began eating one her ass and one her pussy that was completely spread. Kathy could see their drawn tongue lick her inside, sucking her vagina lips one at a time, pulling each stretching it to the max. Then pulled bath her lips with his two hands and plunged his tongue licking all her inside dry, as it were liquor. The other was biting her ass without hurting her pressing her cheek to be able to bite her.

His fingers playing moving inside her asshole. Kim was also screaming with her moaning, her gorgeous body was possessed by this four giants. her cheeks pink from so much excitement. They were devouring her. Kathy was excited seeing her beloved totally possessed, eaten licked in and out. But she cried because she knew that John will not marry her now. And it was her doing, following his orders. He was crazy about Kim, but wanted that if he had it, to suffer now, that he is strong, better than latter that it could be too late. The two first guys, stopped from kissing and etaey her pussy and ass and layed next to her. Kathy still holding Kim's leg all the way up.

They began rubbing their giant dicks against her vagina and ass touching their balls against each other between her thighs. The one on her mouth, stretch her head backward, and made her open her mouth completely. Kim had finally broken the spell she was under and realised the situation.

"Oh, no, no don't no … "

The one in her mouth forced his penis in her, her jaws totally stretched to the max. She couldn't move struggling, but he pushed further, and further. The position of her head put her mouth in allignment with her throat. He pushed more and more. She struggled. Kathy wasn't paying attention to her resistance. He had three quarters of his giant dick in her mouth and throat.

He caressed her lips to relax, she was breathing with her nose very heavily. He pushed more until his whole dick was in her. He layed sideway facing Kim put her between his thighs and enprisioned her lovely head between them and moved in and out of her throat, this way also neutralizing her. The other guy's head was just under his ass, sucking her tits, and tolding her two hands gripped on his enormous chaft and made her masturbate aim holding her hand in place. She wanted them to stop, but couldn't.

The two others one spread her vaginal lips to the maximun and blocked her vagina with the head of his giant dick. The one in the back, spread her ass hole with his fingers and also put the enormous head on it. Kathy seeing this said, "Hold on let me lubricated your dicks, you could hurt her ... "

She took cream and massaged their penis a few times. Not seeing Kim's face, she couldn't notice her desperation.

They both pressed their dicks in her and began penetration, causing convulsion to Kim from so much pressure, not so much the enormous length but the diameter. Their were pushing until they were completely in her. The one in her

mouth retrieved, the two retrieved and the other plunged all the way in her throat totally, just seeing his huge balls slam her chin and then repeated on and off for 45 minutes as if they waited for each other. They began throbbing in her and erupted lake giant volcano's filling her ass, pussy and mouth with a giant flow of sperm.

The last one was ejaculating between her tits splashing her gorgeous throat and his friend ass. They were convulsing her. The one in her ass held her by her hips and moved faster slaming his ball against her ass. The other also slaming his balls between her thighs.

Until they cramped on her. Kissing her back and hips.

He said, "Isn't she the greatest fuck ever?"

All said "Oh yes, she is a beauty, Kathy was right … "

The one in her mouth was still throbbing and ejaculating. He had her mouth full coming out from the side of her mouth, and most of it in her throat. He exclaimed:

"Oh what a sucking queen she is. She is the only one that could swallow my whole dick, the damn thing and also drinking elixir all of it."

They finally freed her a little. Kim almost vomited from so much sperm in her mouth, she said: "Kathy help me, please help me..I was rapped.."

Kathy jumped, "What do you mean rapped?"

"Yes, they did they shut off my mouth and held my hands so I won't move or scream. Help."

Kathy tried to free her, but the one on Kim's tits rose and emprisioned Kathy in his arm and turned her on her stomach and penetrated her ass hole forcing as much as half of it.

She yelled ... "Your crazy, her fiance will kill of you. You don't know who he is."

But the one fucking her turned her head and emprisioned her mouth, and her tit between his large hands and began fucking her. She tried to fight, but he was too big and too strong for her. Kim also tried to fight, but they stretched her on her stomach on the width of the massage table and the one that was before in her mouth came to her ass and spread her cheek and plunged in her hole up all the way until she felt his balls slam in her ass.

The one that was in her vagina went and grabbed her mouth and forced it open and penetrated her to the throat, and began fucking her mouth she could feel his dick up to her sternum. The third one layed under her on the table across from her and told the guy on her ass, spread her legs totally, "So I can fuck her cunt too."

The guy forced her legs and lifted her by the hips and let his body penetrate her pussy sideway. And again they fuck her tremendously hard. The one in her mouth squeezing her tits on and off as if milking her. Seeing that at three it was hard. They did it two at a time.

The third only sucked her tits and they sucked her two each time. Until they all rested without strength next to Kim and Kathy. They were both holding hands. Kim was incredibly calm, even smiling. The first guy noticed. "Did you enjoy."

It nodded smiling back at him." You hear guy she finally liked our dicks, she knows how to appreciate. Let's give her the final fuck of the day the 4 of us? "turning to Kim:

"Would you like that angel. You want us to give you a last fuck."

She barely answered: "Yes, please fuck me hard."

These words revitalized the 4 guys, Kathy was crying thinking poor Kim, she is at square one, back to her nymphomania. Kim's body was very lax, the guy that layed under lifted her, all her limbs lax, not even trying to keep strength. She looked like a rag doll all flask. He lifted her and land her ragina to his dick. He penetrated her without any resistance. The one that same to her ass said,

"Maybe she is num from so much real dick, let's revive."

He began spanking her until her gorgeous ass turned red. He spread her cheeks and put the hcadAon her ass hole, and pushed penetrating her in one bounce. They began fucking her franically, hard. But she was still very soft. But she was smiling and moaning, "Yes fuck me harder push harder.."

The guy in her ass said, "I can't believe that she wants more.. She is the first to say that."

They fucked her harder each time. They could feel their dicks touching each other through the flesh separation. The other two stood in front of her their dicks erected. She first sucked their dicks head each at a time, wetting them enough. Then masturbated both. Then sucking each at a time, up to his balls and with one hand masturbating the bottom of his dick, and with the other hand the other giant dick. Kathy looked at her being revished, there was nothing she could do or say but cry.

"Oh Kim I am so sorry, I am so sorry … "

She felt a voice behind her.

"Kathy, Kathy, Kathy … "

She turned, Kim was dressed in her tennis outfit.

Kim said, "What's wrong with you. you fell twice asleep … "

Seeing her crying, "Oh sorry my little girl why are you crying.." I am sorry Kim, that I let those 4 rape you."

Kim puzzled said, "What four? what rape?"

Kathy just had realised that she had a dream a second time. She rejoiced and jumped on her neck.

Kim: "I love you. Thank G-D it was a nightmare?" She kissed her lovely face with all her strength.

Kim smiled "Oh so much affusion of love..What was the nightmare about? Oh nothing just a stupid nightmare."

Kim said, "Okay I am ready let's go."

Kathy jumped, "No, no let's forget about the game … Maybe dreaming twice the same thing it was an omen."

"Don't be silly, let's go, I am ready."

Kathy had no choice but go this time. They arrived the four guys were waiting. Kim barely paid attention to the four hunks. They were offended by indeference usually the girls were crazy about them. They played three against three. They had three full game, taking two hours. They went to the shower.

Kathy was scared. She knew that they will come. It was a nightmare releaped three times. She went to the back door that led on the men's shower and blocked it with a locker. Kim couldn't understand what as wrong with her, is she afraid of her friend. She was acting weird.

She then returned and undressed and both took a shower. As her nightmare he guys just entered naked from another door. Kathy had blocked the wrong door. Kim seeing these 4 guys with their giant dicks. Ran and covered herself with the towel.

"Get out of here, are you crazy." and the story tried to repeat itself with the same bullshit.

Kathy said, "Leave her alone.."

The guys smiled thinking that she was acting good, but she wasn't.

The tallest one approached Kim and said the same talk about him being a massagist and so on.

Kim smiled and said: "Thanks, but no thanks … I have a loving future husband that can give me any massage I may need. I don't let anyone touch me. I have everything I need at home and by the way I know this trick already ending in a fuck frenzy. I have been there."

The guy looked at her as if ofended and showing his humongous dick said, "But you don't have one like this at home … "

She smiled: "How do you know have you seen my fiances dick? And let me tell you something. Quantity is not quality and there is a study that said bigger the dick smaller is the brain."

She laughed. He pulled her towel violently leaving her naked, grabbing her against him. Kim not losing control said, "Oh you want to play! And also fuck me that's it?"

"Yes, I like you bitch, I want to fuck you."

Kim took his dick between her hand and said, "It is impressive, she did as she caressed it squeezing it between her two hands.."

He was happy, "Oh yes baby you got it."

Kim: "You right I got it."

He had his hand on her ass pressing her against his dick. The other looked at the strange scene in one move she twisted it, she heard a crack as if she store up a muscle and followed it by slamming her to his balls. He couldn't breath, he bent holding his dick and testicles face wincing in pain.

Kim rubbed her hands in a towel and began getting dressed. Let's go Kathy. Kathy was pleasantly surprised, she rushed toward her, kissed her and also took her clothing without drying herself. The other three realized the shock how this gorgeous blonde broke their buddy in two minutes. They grabbed her, and took her clothing from her hands and each held her arm. Kathy began screaming, they didn't care. Kim for some reason wasn't afraid. She said "so the four of you against me a tiny girl … how courageous. So you want to."

"Yes bitch" said the one that she hit on the balls. He held her by her waist, spreading her legs with his and had his dick against her pussy. The other two pulled her arm, Kathy was beating one of them but he lifted her like kid neutralizing her. They were a plus and very strong. Kim was strangly calm.

"So big fucker, you think that you are a man, because you are four big, I am not afraid of your dick I can take all of you in, but my finacee can kill you, go ahead fuck me you bastard."

He said: "Look at this bitch the think that she is going to scare us. Put her on the table, her ass is mine. He seemed to be the boss."

They put Kim on the table her feet on the floor and her upper body stomach down. He came behind her and put his dick in her hole. Kim was waiting for him. She lifted her leg between his legs and kiked his balls with her bare heel. He released her, the other taken by surprise didn't see it coming. She ran naked to the street screaming, "Police, Police".

The guys hearing her screaming police, released Kathy and ran away putting their shorts at the same time, one fell. Kim returned seeing just Kathy. She ask her, "Are you alright?" Kathy as if looking at an extrateresstrial said, "Yes I am alright. You were fantastic, you overcame all those bastards by yourself, you were marvellous …"

She jumped on her neck and kissed her. Kim smiled at her. We better get dressed, the police might come. They got dressed in a hurry and left. In the car Kim looked at Kathy with a serious expression.

"Kathy, I want to know what is going on … everything you dreamed, don't hide anything from me …"

Kathy told her everything about John then continued: "John does not now that we read his diary about you. So he wants to be sure that you want all for something like that when you two get married in two week."

Kim looked and a mishivious smile appeared in her lips:

"Okay Kathy it's pay back time. Listen."

She told her of her plan. They both laughed. They arrived at John's office building. The door man rushed recognizing her car and opened the door. She gave him the keys to park it. They took the elevator to John's office at the penthouse. The secretary greeted her. Kim and Kathy recognized the young lady that was with her mother and children in that restaurant dressed in rags. She looked very elegant now, she worked as a secretary.

She recognized Kim too, and began to thank her.

Kim entered John's office. She could see him behind the one very mirror. He was talking to the whole consortium. She remembered their faces when they saw they had no dick but a vagina. The horror they felt.

Kim said, "So Kathy you know what to do.."

Kathy went to the conference room and said: "Hello." and whispered something in Steve's ear. Steve followed her and left.

He saw Kim in the office, "Hi Kim does he knows that you are here?"

Kim: "No, it's a surprise."

Kathy explained that she won't feel comfortable if he stayed, because she respected him and asked him to take her to the yatch and tell the secretary not to interrupt.

Steve: "No problem Kim, don't make him suffer to much, please. He adores you."

Kim smiled, "Don't worry. He just needs a lesson, I love him too."

Steve and Kathy left. Kim waited a minute. Then she entered the conference room, "Good evening ladies and gentlemen ... "

All rose shocked to see Kim, the way she stood there naked as the day she was born. John was speechless. She came and melded to John's body kissing his neck. All the consortium couples were full of fear, thinking that this was another trap for them.

John finally recovered his speech. "What is the meaning of this?"

Kim continued kissing his face, "Oh my love, I was just aroused and i thought that we could have sex right here in this table. I am sure they will appreciate."

She opened his pants, but he stopped her." Enough Kim get dressed now." He said upset. He tried to cover her ass with his hands and pressed her against him. The sixteen couples were dumbfounded afraid of a possible additional retaliation. Having his hands on her butt covering her, she succeeded in pulling his penis out, she kneeled and captured his penis in her mouth and began sucking it. He was completely confused. He didn't know what to do. She released his penis and said, "My love they know me well and you yourself undressed me naked

before them, you did.." She made a sign showing John's penis as if a knife cutting it. They all frowned, "So my love, this is my fantasy, I want you to fuck me here on the tables now them looking. If you really love me do it."

He didn't know what to do. She opened his pants and took his penis to her vagina. "Please love, excite me.."

She grided him with her legs and began moving on him..

"Oh my prince fuck me hard." he continued holding her ass covering it.

"Please excuse my fiancee, she must be drunk … "

Kim: "Oh no my love, I am completely sober … "

She made him lose his equlibribrium and fall on top of her on the leather paded table. Kim lifted her gorgeous legs spreading them.

"Now my love fuck me hard, I want you."

All were looking at her, 36 people all together. John didn't not know what to do, she took his penis and spreading her vaginal lips she pushed it in and wrapped her legs on his waist. John finally taking control of the situation stood, but she got up still hanging on him kissing his neck. All could see her lovely ass, which he covered with his hands.

"Excuse her, she must be drunk."

All were frozen look at this incredible creature naked with a body of a goddes, that was the cause of their fall and misery now was fucking him in front of all of them. Kim pulled John shirt and began biting his chest." Kim please my love" he calm, "control yourself"

Kim: "If you try to stop me, I'll go to the yatch naked like this."

She looked at him defiance. She continued her doing and undressed John completely leaving him naked, she first gave him a blow job massaging his groins. All began to leave, but Kim sreamed, "No!!no one leaves I want all of you seating there, especially you Helena."

Kim layed on the table and pulled John up too pulling him until they were in the middle of the gigantic conference table. John couldn't resist her any longer and didn't care any longer about the spectators. He devoured Kim's excited pussy. Making her moan loud, "yes that's it, thats it, yes eat me."

John lifted her legs and came to her penetrating her and fucked her with all his might. He couldn't resist her, she was too much for him. So then turned and offered him her fantastic ass that alway made him lose control. He plunged in her delicious cavity fucking her, shaking of intense desire for her.

John came unto Kim's ass, she felt his throbbing and strong ejaculation, flood her wonders of wonders, making her come for a fourth time to falling on the table. John and Kim looked at all the faces staring at them.

He smiled at Kim. John took her both kneeling in the table and fucked her in the ass very hard. His hands on her large and very firm breast. Kim masturbated herself with both hands kissing his mouth. John finally ejaculated squeezing her tits with all his might and kissing her neck breathing hard. Until they stopped.

They all rose and left quietly John said, "I'll see you tomorrow.."

Addressing Kim: "What's wrong princess what is this behavior.."

She released him and went to his office and began dressing up.

"Oh now, I am happy. I wanted to fuck you while they watched us-It's exciting."

John took his jacket and held Kim by the arm and left together.

In the car she was all joyfull and laughing.

"I loved to see their faces. I am sure no one had a hard on me."

She exploded laughing, he was also laughed at her remark. When they arrived at the yatch. John was looking for Kathy. She was in their cabin. Kathy didn't look at his eyes. She hated herself as if ashamed.

He asked "Why is she so happy about?"

Kim: "You are sure that you want to know why?"

John said: "Yes"

Kim looked at him in the eyes and said: "Well, I am very happy. I was attacked by four hunks, blonde 6' 5", 18" dicks as thick as your arms. Oh I hink I am in love with the four. … They fucked my brains out. I never felt o much excitement. I could feel their dicks up to my stomach and one had his pick up to down my throat, they fucked me so hard it was delicious. Oh!! I want them!!"

She began dancing and undressing, he looked at her completely serious. She undressed him too he let her do it..

Kim continued: "My love as you let me have the sisters, let me have them hey are young and cute, big, strong like bulls. They must be lifting enormous weights with their enormous dicks. You will enjoy how they fucked me. So hard didn't want in the beginning ask Kathy, but slowly I loved it … I begged them to fuck me, more and more and harder and harder..I still have their sperm in my stomach, I am filled, would you let me have them here in the next room."

Kathy couldn't hold and turned toward the window to laugh. She was playing marvellously.

"So my love can I have them."

John finally reacted, "So you had enough fun?"

"Not enough my love, I want more fuck."

She turned and rubbed her tits against his dick to excite him. He stopped her and she turned to look at him: "Does it mean, that you do not want me to bring them? So I will go with them to Sweden. I'll pack my stuff now.."

She looked serious. John opened a secret drawer under his side of the bed and pulled a gun and pointed it at Kim: "I'll kill you first. You're mine or nobody's."

Kathy hearing this, turned and paled when she saw John pointing a gun at Kim also turned pale: "But I was joking my love, I was just paying you back with your own game."

John: "I don't believe you, you are saying that because I am going to kill you right here and then I'll kill myself … "

Kim's shaky said, "But my love, you … love me. You can't kill me. I love you more than my life."

John seemed to be thinking and finally said, "You right, i love you to much to kill you, I'll kill myself instead … "

He turned the gun nd put the point of the cannon in his mouth.

Kim and Kathy began crying, "No please don't I swear we were joking to punish you for trying to tempt me and I also read all your diary on me and I saw all in your room, my love. Your the only one I want or love. Please I beg you … "

She kneeled to beg him. Kathy jumped on his arm and wrestled to take his gun from him. Kim joined both trying to open his hand, "Give me the gun"

Their hands were pressing the finger in the trigger, until it fired.

Kim's face was wet, then he turned the gun on Kathy and fired again, wetting her face. It was a water gun, he exploded laugh, falling to the floor.

Holding his stomach from so much laugh. Kim and Kathy looked at each other.

Kim finally said, "You made fun of us, you scared us to death, how could you let me cry … I thought you loved me!!!"

They both jumped on him, Kim put his penis in her mouth and bite it hard, making him yell, but couldn't stop laughing. They wrestled on the floor. Kim couldn't let his penis go.

"Princess your teeth are going to bleed me to death. I'll be penisless."

This caused a round of laugh by the three. Until they ended, kissing each other and making love with intense desire.

Kim was as everytime he made love to her. In a deep trance, moving like a serpent can him, making him scream of passion, burning fromiher touch of her lips all over his body. Kathy and her were kissing all of him head to toes.

Kathy: "Oh my two lovers, I am crazy about you two.."

John said softly, "You are a great kids delicious a great body to fuck. We love you little girl."

John sat on a chair and took on Kim his lap, he said: "So now that I now that you sneaked in my secret room, and saw everything including my personal diary on you … Even after all this, you still suspected me of being he serial killer.

I can't understand how could you? and you Kathy my little girl that I took as my confident and the only one that I made love to, and towing me more than Kim. I am hurt. I thought you loved me too.."

Kathy and Kim had their eyes looking down ashamed, they looked like two little girls sermond by their dad.

Kim said, "I am so sorry my love, but things looked suspicious, but you too suspected me and made these guy try me and they almost raped me and Kathy why did you?"

John: "t we were madly in love and that I saw a change in you.. She told me that this could be temporary and that I should try young and attractive people. So Kathy said that she knew these four friends of hers from high school and that there was no danger of rape. So we did, but if not all. I had the sisters in the locker room hidden and were watching you at all times. They saw everything but were advised by me not to act until the situation was totally out of control. They called me just after you two left.

She told me how you played it calmly and kicked the big bully his balls laughed and was proud of you."

Kim and Kathy couldn't believe their ears.

Kim: "You mean when I came to the office, you already knew all this? And also you let me play all this scene about me fucking them?"

John laughed hard. She put the hand in his neck as if trying to strangle him. John answered, "you were so cute that I let you play and also played with you. The only time that I was really surprised was when you entered my office naked. You shocked everyone including me, then I understood that the little traitor (showing Kathy) had traded me for you. More than me. She loves you."

Kathy hid her face between her legs. John continued, "You excited me."

Kim giggle: "We can do it another day."

They both laughed.

John "Now since you two had been bad girls, you know that you have to be punished. What is tour dislike the most to be punished with?"

Kim put the tip of her finger in her mouth, and looked toward the ceiling as if thinking after a few second she said with a childish expression: "I know I don't like spanking."

Kathy: "Yes master ... We accept the punishment and we won't appeal to be forgiven, we are very proud women " she was cute.

They moved, John sat in the bed, and Kim sat on his lap, Kathy was next to him. She said, "My love all this beautiful things you wrote in your diary about me, are they true?"

"Of course my angel, and after knowing you, I love you even more."

"And was your inspiration to become the richest man in the world?"

"Yes my darlings princess. You know I never made love the way I do today, as we had with the sisters. Josianne, Mimi, Kathy and others. I was always very reserved but with you, I do crazy things. I feel rejuvenated. I found sexual strength I never knew I had in me. I never made love in front of someone else, with you I do."

She squeezed herself against him, her face on his neck, she kissed him. He felt her burning lips on his neck. He also kissed her neck smelling the heavenly scent, which he took a deep breath of her to his lungs.

Kim very serious said, "I love you John ... I want to be your wife forever...I want your children as many as you want. Let me make love to you again, just lay down and rest I'll do everything ... "

Kathy screamed hystrically, "NO!!!..NO!!!! ... Murderers, you killed them",gun pointed at her "Kathy! Kathy! Shush ... Shush ... hey baby were here ... Shush!!"

She looked at the worried faces of her beloved John and Kim that surrounded her. When Kathy saw them, "Oh my G-D your alive, your alive..Oh thank G-D." She kneeled kissed both of them nervously. She put her hand like draying and lifted her eyes thank you G-D for saving them.

John and Kim hugged her kissing her and calming her down. They layed with her in middle and her body between their. She was shivering cold. Their warmth soothed her.

John: "What's wrong baby, you had a nightmare.." Kathy was crying freely, Kim kissing her lovely face whipping her tears. John caressing her body to warm her up.

Kathy: "I was ...." She told them about the dream that she had twice already." I am afraid that this could be an omen that's the third time I had similar dream, but this time they killed both of you." She cried again.

John: "How can they hurt us, if they are on the way to Saudi Arabia sold as slaves at this moment ... The sisters heard that they planned to take revenge. So they Lured them for sex. They kiked their asses, fucked them and handcuffed them, called an Arab friend of Fashir and they sold them as slaves. Some people love white asses over there. It doesn't matter man or woman. Now let's go back to sleep."

They kissed and made love to their little Kathy. She was warming, her cheeks turning pink, moaning her eyes closed enjoying their hands mouth and his penis pounding her in depth in her delicious pussy and then her cute ass. She was delighted by their undidivided attention. She felt like a slice of Salami between two slices of bread with a pickle in her ass, she laughed at that compassion. They fell asleep, her squeezed in between. It was 9:30 am when the phone rang: "Hello?" answered John's sleepy voice.

Steve: "Hi good morning, sorry to woke you up, but you have a press conference with the mayor of the city, to thank you for your act of Bravoury and the princes will give you a medal and so on. You've been postponing for three days."

John: "Okay Steve, I'll be up thanks.."

Kim was all ears and happy to hear of their wedding finally her Cinderella fable has come true. They had arrived to the mayor's building, where all the media, were waiting for John. The Mayor, The Princes and the Prince and three young ladies he saved were there, even the parents of all the 36 murdered young ladies by the evil serial killer. The media rushed toward the car. Flashing their cameras at John's entourage. Finally John and company joined the Mayor and the Royalty. The camera were rolling.

The mayor gave a speech praising John for his bravoury. The Princess pined on his chest a medal and a ribbon his shoulder to across his chest to his opposite hip across. There was a great applause.

The camera also concentrated on Kim. The Mayor continued by giving his condolences to the families of the murdered young ladies. John shook their hand and also expressed his sympathy he gave his card and told them if he could help in anyway, to please call him. Then followed the parents of the three girls he saved. The girls kissed him in the mouth at the surprise of all the present and media.

They all kissed him a long french kiss. Then they kissed Kim. She whispered something in their ears, they smiled and said.. "We will.."

Then the Mayor congratulated John and Kim on their wedding. The press rushed to ask them questions, mostly at Kim. "Do you love him even though he is 20 years older than you?"

Kim answered, "Age is not of the essens, I never met anyone that can equal him in strength and how to make love.." All smiled and laughed, but John blushed from head to toes.

The press: "There is rumors that you are marrying him for his money.."

John jumped to answer, "Kim is the chairman of T.C.N.N. news network and is very rich. She doesn't need my money. Whoever spread this rumor of is welcome to tell us this in my face, it's pure jealousie. We are in love with each other. Thank you."

John thanked the Mayor, The Princess and their entourage. They departed in the car and returned to the yatch. Friday,

John and Kim, Steve, Kathy and Josianne waited at the airport for all the family members. They had rented three buses. The first one to arrived were David, Peter, and their families. They hugged each other. Felicia followed them. She said hello to Kim:" Hi Miss Kim remember me?"

Kim "Of course I do and mostly your massage.."

They laughed." I'll be at your service any time Kim."

"Thank you I'll have it in mind.."

David came to Kim, "So finally you pressed the noose around the bachlor's neck. He seems to eat from the palm of your hand ..."

Kim smiled: "Yes he is in love.. "He makes love to me 20 times day." She giggled.

David: "Anyone with a woman like you will.."

Kim blushed: "Thank you Dave.." The next to arrive were John's parents, daughters and his brothers with their respective families. The encounter was very emotional.

John's daughter Tal: "Oh dad she is gorgeous.."

"Hi Kim I am Tal. Your incredibly beautiful. You are barely a year older than me. My dad is a Romeo." As a gorgeous young lady, she was with her boyfriend.

Then Lyn also appraising and both kissed her.

Kim: "I hope that we will be good friend. By the way I don't know what all the press is saying about us, but I love you dad like crazy, we are very much in love. John parents and brothers with their families each appraised Kim's beauty and kissed her. The chemistry between them was there. They liked each other.

Then were Kim's mother, brother, and sister.

The mother cried, "I can't believe my eyes, I finally see you ... Oh you look like a queen. You were right please forgive me, my baby. By the way I stopped smoking." Kim kissed her mother her brother, began crying and hugging Kim strangely for a teenager he wouldn't release her. Then kissed her sister.

Kim: "Mom this is my beloved future husband John."

John approached and hugged and kissed her. They shook hands with her brother. Then kissed Jenny.

John: "It's a pleasure to finally meet you all ... Before you say anything madam, I love your daughter and my only concern is her happiness. I adore her, she is my jewel."

Mom Iris: "Oh Mr. John I am so happy that my daughter finally has found the right man..I always told her how her ex-boyfriend the lawyer was bad for her, I never liked him!"

Kim and Jenny looked at each other and exploded in laugh.

Mom Iris: "Whats funny?"

Kim: "Nothing mom, just we are so happy to see each other.."

She hugged kissed John in his chest.

"Mom I love him more than life. He is the greatest of all. He loves me beyond comprehension."

After that Steves daughters and parents arrived.

John called everyone to ride the bus. The direct family parents, and John daughters Kim, himself rode in the limousine, and all the other cars and bus followed. Steve drove with the aston Martin with his parents and daughter, David and family with his wife and Kids and his parents in Kim's red Rolls Royce. Peter and family also in an other car, the bus followed them John took veryone to the yatch first.

Kim's mother and brothers "Oh it's gorgeous, beautiful … "

Iris: "Oh Kimmy is this all his.."

John: "No mam it all belong to Kim, even myself … "

Kim kissed him tenderly and melded to him: "Oh moms I love him, he is the best that ever happened to me.."

Iris: "I see my baby you were born to be queen.."

She began crying allowing her nose in a handkerchief. Jenny and her brother were marvelled.

Jenny: "Cool this is the love boat.."

Kim and John looked at each other and exploded in laugh.. Kim took her sister to show her the yatch followed by everyone.

Kim to Jenny, "Oh I never fucked as I was in this yatch.. He is the best lover ever."

Jenny: "I like him already, he look handsome and strong, very respectful. Can I try him too?" She giggled.

Kim: "I'll arrange that tonight."

Jenny: "I was joking, sis"

Kim: "Why not he will devour you like a candy, I have a surprise for him the night before of our wedding..You know, I converted to his religion, so we will marry under a conoppee..I'll do anything for him. I know that he also has a surprise for me to where we will spend the honeymoon..I love him sis, very much ..."

Jenny: "You look different, more serene and like a real queen with all this jewels.."

After the long tour with the crew saluting everyone and giving explanations. David and Steve took the lead and took all the families to the Monte-Carlo few, luxurious hotel which John had reserved totally for his guests for two week. All the guest were marvelled with John's riches.

The party was for 4000 guests including all John's employee with their husbands. Orly and sisters with husbands, John's family from everywhere in the world. President leaders of

other countries. Kings and Princes of course the consortium and ronosse, Helena ... the latter were docile like a pussy cat.

That evening John organized a giant party on the decks of the yatch, champaign flowed like water.

The party was sensational, buffets were layed in his parking lot, with crew of caterers. So the crew of the Sarah III could the party. Toward all left taken by David and Steve to the hotel. John and Kim embraced returned to their cabin. Kathy was there already.

John took a shower when he came out, the light were off, just one single night stand lamp was on. Kim and Kathy were covered in the satin sheet, "What happened my love are you cold tonight?"

He slided under the sheet at their legs, he landed his mouth in a vagina, her legs slightly open. He smiled "Hummm ... its smells good". He began kissing and teasing her vaginal lips. She frowned and trembled, "One of my angels is getting excited, I see."

He spread her soft and tender legs, them all over to end again with full mouth, shaking, shivering pussy, delicious to the palate.

"Hey this is not Kathy, not Kim and is very young ......"

He pulled the sheet, "Oh Lord, Jenny I am so sorry, I didn't know."

Kim: "No my love, I just wanted my sis to feel the way I do when I am with you ... I don't have words to express my feeling."

John: "But it's ... "

Kim hushed his head back to Jenny's delicious recently shaved pussy by Kathy. He could feel her blushing and trembling between his lips. He obliged eating her juicy young pussy. Lifting her legs also devouring her cute smooth ass. Shoving a finger in her after wetting it in his mouth. He sucked each of her swallen lips, and clitoris.

She had come in his mouth. She tried to avoid it, but he held her drinking in her fountain of youth sucking hard in her clit. She convulsed from so much excitement. Kathy was devouring her breasts. John's other hand was on Kim's asshole and pussy, throbing her.

She was wet to see her future husband eating her sister's pussy. Jenny was in extreme heat, having an orgasm after the other. She was moaning with her cute voice.. "Oh.. Oh. ... Kim he is marvelous, Oh!!!"

She was crying in ecstacy. Kim caressed her face, finally seeing her sister so much in heat she said, "Darling fuck her young pussy now she is about to explode."

John rose and began kissing and sucking her triangle, then her soft silky stomach going up his hand on her breast rolling her nipples between his fingers iardening she bads. small oreols and long tips, which he sucked hard, making her scream of

pleasure. He finally arrived at her face, looked at her gorgeous young face.

Then straight in her deep blue eyes, he kissed her lips gently be said, "I am honored to give you pleasure, do you want me to?"

Jenny blushed and nodded: "Yes".

He put his hands holding her cheek caressed them. She had tears of joy and her gaze was full of desire. He gently rubbed his erected penis between her vaginal lips, his finger penetrated her tight ass hole, gently and stroke in and out of her, then pointed his penis in her vagina pressing it against her clitoris making her shiver, moan loud, still looking at each other in the eyes. She was all trembling her lips moving as if she wanted to say something.

She was deliciously desirable, her baby face reminded John his youth.

Kim and Kathy looked at them without moving, finally he put her legs on his arm, raising them up to her hips, his hands returning to her ass and gentl' penetrated her tight young pussy, wet from excitement and pushed until he penetrated her completely making her moan and tremble, losing control over her muscles. He fucked her, making her moan too and move in and out on her pussy, his fingers on her lovely asshole masturbating her. He grabbed her mouth in an inebriating kiss, soft and full of desire. She kissed him, her soul coming out through her lips.

John was getting excited he began devouring and sucking her lips and mouth until she could barely breath, having sucked her mouth dry, he lowered his head to her gorgeous large breasts, firm and silky touch skin. Her breasts were larger than Kim's. He devoured them with full mouth.

He was losing control of his senses. She was a real delicacy, her long gorgeous blonde hair made her as if look like a mermaid. He fucked her with all his might each time he penetrated her, his testicles will slam against her gorgeous derriere. He was in esctacy "Oh Jenny you are a delicious kid, I could eat you alive … " To Kim's surpris she answered "Yes, please eat me again and again…I want you fuck me all over.." that made John reach an orgasm.

She felt his throbbing and he felt hers too. He ejaculated flooding her paradise…She screamed in excitement:

"Yes, yes, I feel you it's warm, I love it, more, more much more, put your finger on my behind."

He did pushing his finger further. It was hard but he succeeded, she was all convulsing and him too, holding all of her prisoner between his large arms until they stopped and finish like serpents on top of each other. Kissing her neck and chin, face, "Oh little girl you are fantastic.."

Kim: "More than me.."

John: "My love you are another league.."

Kim looked at her sister moving her face pink, her eyes closed enjoying the final touch from his lips. Kim said, "Now Sis you give him a blow job, so he will fuck you in the ass."

Jenny, "I never did before does it hurt?"

Kathy: "I'll take care of you.." She positioned Jenny on her knees and her head down began sucking John laxed member. Kathy took cream and put some on Jenny's ass sliding her fingers in her hole and massaged her their, turning her finger around the walls of her inside. Jenny was moaning already, sucking John's penis. Kim brought a spray asked her to open her mouth completely and spraye on her throat.

Kim: "Now you won't gag you can take his whole penis in your mouth … "

She positioned her head in a certain way and showed her how to do it, by doing it herself … Finally Jenny could and enjoyed the new lesson. John in the mean time ate her young pussy with full mouth, making her come three more time, enjoying her elixir. When finally John was about ejaculate he said,

"I am about to.." but it was too late, he ejaculated in her mouth, Kim saw her stopping about to let it out, but she said, "No baby, swallow it, it's good … "

She did at first, then pushing his penis to her throat she swallowed his strong stream of enjoyment. When she sucked him dry. She continued like she was sucking on a lolypop. Kim and Kathy laughed … "Wow!! we created a monster."

Finally John rose and came to her ass and first massaged her cheeks. Spreading her cheeks to see her beautiful ass hole. Which he pointed to it. Kim took his penis and pointed it to her sisters hole. "Push my love..Penetrate her young ass and fuck her."

Her dirty talk excited John. He pushed and slowly penetrated, Jenny was moaning an a little in pain. Kathy put her pussy under her face, "Eat my pussy Jenny … " She did for the first time taste another woman pussy. She did it diligently slowly became expert by the way he did it to her. Kathy squeezed her large and firm tits pressing hard, teasing her nipples.

John held her hips and fucked her in the ass, faster and faster, until he succeeded in penetrating her all the way. Kim squeezed his balls on her sister vagina each time he returned inside her. John releasing one of her hips. He plunged a hand in her youthful pussy and masturbated her at the sam time.

When he was about to erupt. He flatened her on the bed, a hand kneading her vagina the other her gorgeous prominent breasts. He landed on her voluptous round ass, very similar. He moved faster until he erupted ejaculating inside her entrails, cramping on her body, his hands squeezing her gorgeous body against his penis buried in her asshole. Ejaculating non stop.

She was delirious moaning and sighing in Kathy's pussy that also came in her mouth. "Drink me, eat me Jenny.." She did and also enjoyed his grip on her. When he finally released her, Kim asked Jenny, "So you liked it."

Jenny: "Oh Sis he is wonderful I never enjoyed so much.."

John: "Thank you kid, you are very delicious yourself.."

The rest of the evening they had sex the four of them, until exhaustion, Jenny had grown up in one night. She has never shared her sister's lover before. They fell asleep around 4am. John couldn't sleep. He was looking at Jenny next to him, she was gorgeous. She looked in many ways like her sister, she was delicious.

He caressed her breasts very gently feeling her velvety skin. Now he wasn't under Kim and Kathy's scrutiny about the way he or she reacted. It bothered him. He felt her flat stomach his hand going lower until he reached her excit paradise. He stood up and took her in his arm and just scrutinized her looking at her exciting young featured a gorgeous childish face.

Her pointing firm and proeminent breasts. She had a marvellous body. It was awaking a strange desire in him, a new fire. He took her to the next room, and put her in the bed, put himself between her legs spreading them plunging his head to drown himself in her wonder of wonders, he kissed all of it.

He kept looking admiring her beautiful vagina. Her lips were pink like rose petals. He teased her clitoris with a finger when it swallowed a little, he grabbed it between his lips and began sucking it.

She wake up and saw him between her legs, she caressed his hair. "Oh you still desire me!!!"

"Me too. I wasn't sleeping I was waiting for you. I want you too very much eat me more many more times, I want you.."

He encountered her gaze. She was holding herself in her elbows looking at his sucking her clitoris, she approached more, seating and bent more, to look closer how he was sucking it. It excited her more, his fingers massaged her lips, making her shiver, moan.

"Yes, yes..I..love it"

"Your tongue please inside" he held a while until she begged, "please now your tongue.." He lift her ass in his arms and sucked each lips, chewed them, then when she was hot red plunged his tongue inside her thirsty burning paradise. She cried moaned, "yes, yes, oh it's delicious.." He could feel her intense desire. His tongue brought more fire.

She was like a ticking bomb, she was biting her lips, licking her lips He was savaging her delicious pussy with full mouth, plunging in her burning inferno hurrying his face in her, feeling a continuous flow of dew. Then devouring, bitting her triangle and bulge making it disappear in his mouth and sucked and chewed it. It was incredibly tasty and exciting.

She was moaning loud, "Oh!! Oh!! please come to me now fuck me please now I can't hold any longer. It's burning inside my pussy, please extinguish my fire … "

She was convulsing under the grip of his mouth making her lose control of her muscles. A continuous flow of excitement,

flowed into his hungry mouth. Her lips throbbing each 5 minutes announcing a new flood of pleasure. Her clitoris was swallen, he sucked it hard between his teeth.

He then took all her vagina in his mouth and bite it harder each moment as if he was about to eat it, she was in total esctacy surrendered to his desire. When he saw her whole body convulsing with muscle spasms, he rose grabbed her ass in his hands under her and penetrated her vagina in a rage, and fucked her with all his strength.

She wrapped her legs around his waist. They looked at each other in the eyes and continued fucking her on and on. His hands masturbating her delicious ass.

She said: "I love you.." he answered: "I love you."

A very surprising expression. He released her ass to hold her head, clearin her lovely face from the hair, stretching it behind her head, caressing her gorgeous youthful face. He ejaculated in her still fixed in her beautiful blue eyes she cried of joy and esctacy. He licked her tears away and kept fixing her gaze and moving in and out of her. She was shighing, "I love your sounds of excitement little girl..They excite me, release everything you got don't hold."

She did, cried and moaned very loud, his eyes hypotizing her but she loved it. He rested on top of her. He said, "You love to see how I fuck you, is it true?"

"Yes I love to see."

He lifted her in his arms, switched on the main light, and stood in front of the large mirror. He put her on top of the dresse next to the mirror and devoured her breasts. She looked in the mirror and saw her being ravished by a real man. He was squeezing her tits with both hands. and sucked them hard, allowing a big chunk of it in his totally opened month.

His right hand masturbated her, he sat her, her legs folded, facing the mirror. She could see her spread vagina. He put a hand under her and forced two fingers in her. She could see his fingers disappear in her hole.

Then his second hand came from the side, without obstructing her vue, he began massaging her vagina, then penetrated her and masturbated her. She looked with curosity and sighed undlessly. She already wet his hand: from bif flow of excitement. She was breathing hard as if she was short of breath seeing herself being masturbated in the mirror.

She came many more times. Until her head rolled back, her back arched from so much excitement. Her mouth looking for his. He emprisoned her lips and sucked her tongue dryloffering her.

When he felt her relax. He put her on the floor and stood sideway to the mirror. His penis totally erect, "Kneel girl and suck my penis ..."

"Oh I see you two are having fun without me?"

John turned arounded and saw Kim with her sleepy face.

"So you enjoy fucking my little sis, how does it feel to have a young lady"

John: "Well it brings me memories of my teenage years. Yes, she is delicious, we couldn't sleep. So we enjoyed each other. Come in."

Kim entered and she sat on the jaccuzi edge.

"What would you say if I told you that I need to fuck a teenager myself?"

John said, "What kind of question is that?"

"So John from what you are seeing, how do you judge me?"

John broke up the silence. "I don't judge without asking for an explanation.."

"Well for you Jenny and I are sisters, and you don't fuck a sister right."

He nodded, she continued, "Well we are not sister, not real sisters."

She is the daughter of a different father and mother..Then her dad married my mother. Does this make things different for you?"

John: "Yes it does, even thought you shouldn't do it between let say half sister ... "

One night she was already awakend and was kissing and sucking my breasts and masturbating me. Slowly it became normal to us. I know that it wasn't right, but it all happened by accident. Then i became a convinient habit and his in a way kept us more at home and did not have to go have sex with boys until much later."

John felt his orgasm and cramped on top Jenny's ass and emprisoned her large breasts that it was hard to hold due to the oil. They slipped out of his hands. Jenny felt his throbbing. She pressed her cheeks together, but instead of holding him tighter, the oil made his penis slippery and was ejected out of her cute derriere.

Kim: "Good girl Jenny.. So John you haven't answer my question?"

John "Which one?"

"About having sex with a teenager now for a few month only. It's important."

John was getting mad, "Listen Kim I don't know what's wrong with you, but let's not talk about it again."

Kim's: "But John there are things I must do and I'll tell you why, give me a chance.."

John pulled himself out and left the bathroom after a quick shower to take the oil out of him.

Kim: "But John my love, let me explain.."

He took a towel and wrapped himself in a robe.. "Listen Kim, we are getting married on Sunday night...I do not want to talk nonsense now, okay.."

Before she could say a word, he left. It was 9 am when he opened the door to leave the cabin after be dressed, he encounter Kim's young brother just about to knock.

"Good morning, yes she is go in ... " and he left. the brother was 5' 7" he was 16 1/2 years old, but he looked younger. He entered and closed the door behind him. Seeing his sister naked, "Hi sis, I couldn't sleep last night, I wanted you..Why didn't you let me stay with you. I cried all night."

Kim came and hugged him, grabbed her ass with two hands and kneaded her flesh and sucked one of her breasts. Kim caressed his hair, "Come my baby come."

She undressed him, and she layed face down on the bed, the kid had a very large penis for his age, he layed on Kim and rubbed his penis between her butt cheeks. Jenny came and took his erected penis and pushed it in Kim's asshole. He began frantictally fucking her, his hands kneading her breasts under her.

Kim: "Yes my baby, that's it, your penis grew since last time.."

He smiled in acknowledgment and was fucking her with all his strength. Kim caressed his hand on her breasts and was thinking how would she explain to John. He didn't let her talk on the subject. John felt that he has been rude with Kim and

the kid. He should have listened to her story. He decided to return to the cabin and talk to her, he opened the door and was about to talk, "Kim, I … What the hell it's going here!!!"

He saw the kid on Kim's ass fucking her as if he was possessed, Jenny caressing one hand on his penis and the other his butt. All turned toward him. The kid didn't mind he continued his coming and going in Kim's marvellous ass. Kim and Jenny were frozen.

"Can someone tell me what the hell is going in here. The young brother fucking her older sister, my future wife, then Jenny her sister…I must be having another of my nightmare. I am sure I will wake up."

Kim did not stand up and left his brother continued his doing, until he finished. John approached Kim and saw the little guy. He smiled as if nothing wrong, and continued his fucking. He could see his large dick penetrate and exit her fantastic ass. His hands gripped on her boobs, squeezing hard on them Kim was looking at him in the eyes serene but not doing a thing to stop him "I must be dreaming, am I?"

The kid convulsed and ejaculated his load on Kim's ass. Jenny then pulled him to the bathroom.

Kim stood up, "Do you want to hear now, what I was trying to tell you?"

John very cold said, "Yes let's hear what do you have to say.. I am very curious. Oh maybe he needed your ass to fall asleep

when he was a baby, what kind of crazy family I joined myself into?"

Kim slapped him hard, "At least I know that I am awake.."

Kim: "He also, he is not my brother, and I let him do this because he is dying.."

John interupted her, "he is dying to fuck you like half of this town.."

She tried to slap him again, but this time he caught her arms, his grip was very powerful. "You are hurting me.." John realized his strength and released her hand.

Kim: "He is dying from leukemia, he was prognosticated 9 years ago that he won't reach the age of 17 be is now 16 1/2 and he doesn't understand right from wrong … He grew up with us in my room. Seeing Jenny caressing and eating me and slept on top of me. He wanted to, he was then very little.

So I took him like a child but I did not know that children or this age are very curious and sexually attracted. He use to sleep sucking my breast. In the beginning it aroused me, he was 7 1/2 years old. We found out then of his fatal illness. So I use to spoil him, giving him everything he wanted. When he was ten he used to stick a finger in my ass or on my vagina. I use to reprimantl him. He would cry loud my mother without knowing what he wanted she would yell at me, and would say if he cries again you are grounded.

He is also from different parents my mam's third marriage. So the kid knowing that he could do what he wants, was touching my ass all the time and sometimes my vagina … He was ten but had the mind of a 6 years old. He continued growing, we felt sorry to know that in a few years he would be no more. At the age of 12, I was sleeping with Jenny as always. He came crying that he had a nightmare.

So he slept behind me. I was holding Jenny in my arms. I was asleep, and I felt something in my ass. I turned a little and i see him gripped to my hips and his penis was inside my hole. He was moving, actually fucking and had ejaculated in me. I was very upset and yelled at him even slapped him.

He cried his heart out, and was very sad. I remembered that he had less than 5 years to live. So I took him with me and let him do what he wanted, but without seeing it as sex, but as a brotherly love, like a hug or a kiss. He doesn't know that this is fucking. He knows he likes it, like eating a chocolate cake. Take it from him and he cries, even now.

That is the reason I didn't stop him when you came in the first time, nor now. I know that the whole thing is crazy, but that were the reason, I had a psychiatrist, so he grew up, his penis to. It became very uncomfortable for me. My exboyfriend did not know why he slept in my room and why I couldn't sleep out with him. I had, to be home for him. Jenny tried to bring him to her, but in the beginning he didn't want. One night I was at the hospital he couldn't sleep alone. So he slept with Jenny, but cried first then began fucking her too."

"One night I felt him sleep on top of me facing me, he was 15 years old,18 months ago. I felt his penis trying to penetrate my vagina, but did not know how, Jenny was showing him, and he pushed and penetrated me all the way so he liked it and fucked my pussy, his mouth sucking my breasts. He had a large penis by then.

So I was confused because I actually had an orgasm. He takes long to ejaculate, so he rode me for an hour, making me come three times. I was looking forward for him to fuck me, he was like if you want a vibrator that's it not a man who knows that he is fucking.

So everynight he will fuck me awake or asleep. If he found me face down, he will get my ass, if not my pussy. So it was hard for me to get rid of him. But when I came aroused, I found him there, he is always looking for me. So if Jenny is there he will fuck her, but if we are both, he wants me. Since then he wanted to bath with me, shower with me even go to the toilet with me. So he fucked me in the bath tub or in the shower. Sometimes even doing my homework. One day he almost did it in front of mom, but she did not notice. Another time I was on the window talking to my boyfriend the lawyer, he was downstairs. He came behind me pulled my panties lifted my skirt and fucked me in the ass while I spoke to my fiancee. He sticks to me like glue. So I had to see a physciatrist, I had certain fantasies tabo, sex. I felt also guilt to get excited with him. He can't live without me, or Jenny. Since we are now both here. He wants me.."

John: "So he isn't stupid after all he wants the best.."

Kim: "That was what I was trying to explain to you this morning..also it is the reason I pushed Jenny to you to enjoy her. You didn't ask to many question then. You like her beauty and youth and fucked her. I saw you when you took her in your arms and went to the other room, I saw the whole scene.

It hurts me too, because I saw and felt the burning desire you had for her. Even my ex-fiancee was dying to fuck her. He tried but Jenny didn't like him so she slapped him. On contrary she likes you, and I am jealous, because she is not my real sister, she is gorgeous and I saw the way you said to her that you loved her. My love for you has no equal, so I close my eyes, because I know that I am the one you really love and her is only a desire reminding you your 20's and I understand that. Now please John he has a few months to live, two three but no more than six. Please let him stay with us even he fucks me, I don't feel nothing as if he were a dildo, but you are my love. What do you say? Please, pretty please."

Her face was angelical, her supplications were too much for him, to refuse. He caressed her gorgeous face and smiled at her "I don't know how I fall into this weird situation, but I love you too much to fight with you, we are getting married in two days.

What the heck if I let you get fucked by the sister, why not.. It's crazy but with you I sexually experience the strangest and rarest problem I ever faced … So I guess, we have to adapt to another one, the bed is big enough..Now we will sleep Jenny, Kathy, your brother, you and I … But it's not going to be easy

for me, when I saw fucking you, I almost grabbed him from the neck, and threw him overboard. I thought, that I was dreaming..

The kid returned with Jenny to the room. Kim was seating on John's lap still naked, he came directly toward her and grabbed her breast and sucked it. John did not know how to behave at this ridiculous situation. His other hand grabbed Kim's by her vagina and masturbated her. Kim looked at John "It's alright my love, as you see he does not recognize the reality, for him I am a chocolate cake.."

She didn't finished saying that, that he pulled his penis and was pushing it in Kim's vagina … Kim as natural as it can be, she lifted her legs on top of John's lap and spread them, letting the kid's dick in her. He was again fucking her, his hands on her ass pushing toward him. Kim looked at John, "Try to ignore that he is here my love.." She kissed John's neck and face, her hand held him from the back of his neck. "My love, love me now.."

She put a hand under her and opened his zipper and pulled his penis and directed it on her asshole.

"Oh yes my love, yes now.."

She sat on him and felt him up to her entrails.

The kid's dick was moving in and out of Kim's pussy with nervous movements, his mouth sucked her nipples as if he wanted to extract milk from her. He was pushing more and

more Kim against John, seating in the dresser. Kim lifted her legs all the way feeling the kid's penis ravaging in her pussy.

She felt his throbbing she grabbed hid testicles and squeezed them hard. She felt the ejaculation she was excited just knowing that John was there and her kid in her at the same time. She held the kid by the balls keeping his penis erected inside her, she was moaning and John was lifting and lowering her in his penis also feeling his orgasm reach stormic and ejaculated. Moaning sighing and kissing Kim's neck and face. He tried to squeeze Kim's breast but he found the kid's mouth on one and wouldn't budge. Jenny came to the rescue and put one of her breasts in John's mouth which he devoured with thirst.

Kim took her other breast and sucked her nipples. It was a ridiculous situation. The kid was still holding Kim by her ass and fucking her frantically. He seemed upset that John had his penis in her too. He lifted Kim having her legs on his shoulder, extracting her from John penis and put her on the bed and flicked her harder with rage.

Kim looked back at John, "Don't worry my love, he will calm down.."

He began fucking her pulling from her vagina to her asshole and back to her vagina not missing the target, with an incredible strength. It was incredible to see him pulling out of one and go to the other vice-versa fucking her both ways at one time even John had just learned something.

The kid continued for a while longer, Kim "Please John come next to me and kiss me please, I need you..I want to feel as if it were you doing this. That's the first time he fucks me like that. If he is claiming both territories to himself."

John felt compassion for her sincere pleasure and lifted Jenny and layed her next to Kim, kneeled the knees on the floor, spread her cheeks and penetrated her gorgeous ass that still had baby fat.

One hand on Jenny's breasts and the other on her vagina, he stretched his body and kissed Kim's mouth in an inebriating kiss as if they were fucking each other. Kim felt the hard penetration on her pussy then her ass it was exciting. She began moaning in John's mouth, "Oh John I love it when you fuck me like this.."

Her legs were up to her head spread the kid was possessed by a strange force. Jumping like a monkey on her ass and pussy.

Kim cried, "Oh yes, yes.."

She never experienced this type of action before the kid had just invented a new fucking excerise. She cried in esctacy.

Holding him by his ass and pushing him against her, "Yes fuck me more, more," She was delirious. The kid's dick was very large incredible for his age. John didn't even wanted-to understand what was going on, he caressed Kim's face and her lips, she bite his hand, he let her.

Kim felt his third ejaculation, still jumping on her and did on both pussy and ass spraying some outside each time he traded places. Kim was having a second orgasm. He pulled out of her and released her legs, took Jenny by the hand to go clean him. Which she looked at John as saying, "Sorry I have to go.." John let her go. Kim needed more sex, she asked John to continue the same way, "Please" she said, "fuck me the same way.." John cleaned her and came to her after pulling his clothes out, and held Kim's legs up and began the same exercise, fucking her both places at one time.

It was exciting but hard to do for long. Until finally Kim moaned, convulsed and cramped on him, but he didn't finish so he continued for twenty more minutes until he ejaculated in both places, holding without spilling outside. He fell on top of her after releasing her legs that she put under him.

John finally reacting, "Kim get dressed before he comes back and fuck you again.."

Kim laughed and got to the bathroom to clean themself. When they opened the door. The incredible scene that they saw, the kid was fucking Jenny the same way he did Kim. John whistled. "I can't believe it for sure that this guy will die, but not from leukimia, but from fucking.."

Kim and Jenny laughed, but not so John …

The kid looked like normal playing a game. Jenny's beautiful sexy body was folded in two and the monster jumping on her juicy pussy that she had com various times. Seeing the liquids

on the jaccuzzi floor and her ass. John, "I should be careful at night, he might fuck me too.."

Kim and Jenny exploded in laugh, John also laughed. He put the shower on and entered with Kim and showered together, he was washing her delicious body and was excited again, he caressed her gorgeous ass and penetrated her vagina. "Oh my love, hum ….it's so good. I can fuck all day with you all our lives.."

John: "Did you enjoyed his fucking there!"

"Yes, I did, it was exciting but as I told you I treat him like he was a plastic dick, a dildo. Dildo's are exciting too, my jealous lover."

John was massaging her body. When the door opened and Hi Ho silver entered the shower with his shirt on and came behind Kim and penetrated her ass and began slamming his balls each time he penetrated her. Pushing John against the tiles.

John: "Oh I can't have this all the time, it's too much for me, good bye. I'll see you at the wedding."

Kim held him girding him with all her strength, "No my love please don't leave me. I need you not him."

John: "But I want to make love to you alone, I do not like to share, sex with any other men or youth, I don't care under the reason could be. Especial now two days before our wedding."

Kim began crying, still holding on him tight, "No my prince don't leave me, I need you to much, don't pay any attention to him, he doesn't exist."

John: "Its hard for me to see you being fucked like this and you enjoying it on top of it. It's hard my love, I love you more than life, but don't know how to cope seeing the kid fucking you every minute without stopping, look at him."

Here he was, slamming his testicles against her ass, moving hard on her each time, lifting her off the ground. His hands gripped on her breasts very hard not even let the blood circulate in her breasts. Kim seeing his face, bitter. She cried loud like an uncontrolable child. John couldn't resist her cry and kissed her lips and made love to her tenderly lifting her legs in her arm and very gently moving in and out of her, kissing her gorgeous face, eyes, lips sucking her more, her ears lobes.

They were now alone not paying attention to the little fucker moving on her ass frantically disrupting the harmounious moves of his penis in Kim's paradise.

Jenny joined the party grabbed the kid by the balls and tried to pull him from Kim, but he wouldn't release his hold. She kissed John's chest and neck also.

Kim's face, her hand caressed John derriere very gently going between his thighs and grabbing his testicles and squeezed then on and off until she felt his throbbing she hold it tighter feeling the pumping of his sperm from his ejaculation making Kim rejoiced moan and have her second orgasm in the shower.

The little devil was still in her ass. She was feeling irritated inside from his nonstop fucking, but after two minutes she felt his throbbing followed by a strong ejaculation.

He didn't move any longer and held Kim very tight, letting his load off. She felt the throbbing of his dick in her until it subsided Jenny took him out and washed his penis and made him dress by force. John and Kim stayed a while longer, she was back in his arms enjoying his kisses and caresses all over her body, "I love you my prince, thank you for being patient and understanding."

John: "I am patient and do not understand but I do love you if I had left, I would have cancelled our wedding, but this I couldn't.. It would be like committing suicide. I could easier kill him."

Kim: "You wouldn't do that, this is like his last wish, my poor boy is dying.."

She began crying hysterically. John calmed her, kissing her and continued caressing her. They dressed after that and went out including the brother and Jenny. It was 12:00 noon. They joined everyone that had come to enjoy the yatch. The preparation for the wedding were done by professional caterers. All news media were talking about it as the event of the year. They had brought Kim's wedding dress.

Kim: "I leave you guys, you John cannot see it before the wedding, I love you.."

She kissed him and disappeared. Jenny also followed her. The brother was looking a yatch that was docking, he did not pay attention that his sister had left.

John took the opportunity he needed and said, "Listen kid, now that you and I are alone, let's talk like man to man … " the kid looked arouned, looking for Kim. He was about to run look for them, when John held his arm.

"Listen kid I know that you are very smart and fake your bullshit. So let's talk..Do you want to destroy your sister's future? She loves me, she loves you to like a brother and not a man, you hear me?"

The kid: "It's not true she love me, not you, she is been mine for many years. I love her."

John: "So you do have a tongue and you are not dumb.."

The kid: "You might be the dumb, she doesn't love you, she likes your money, not you.."

John: "So you played the robot all these years, why?"

The kid: "Because I was too young, and she wouldn't let me touch her, or make love to her. So I decided to play dumb, and it because she loves me...and I made love to her a million times, more than you can do in your life time or what's left of it."

John: "I see, so this way you can fuck both your sisters."

The kid: "They are not my sisters."

John: "What about you dying of leukimia, even if you were right and she wants you, and on top of it you are 8 1/2 years her junior. You have just a little while to live, then you want her to stay alone, if you really love her, you should want her to be happy."

The kid: "I was found healthy two years ago, I was the one receiving the mail so when I read it, I store it, so no one knows.."

John was pushing his ego to make him talk.

John "Very good, you are smarter than all of us together. What if I go and tell her what we spoke?"

The kid: "I will continue to play dumb, she can't believe you, she knows me for years. We grew up togther, I slept in her bed every night. I made love to her three to four times a day. She will never accept that she was fooled for more than ten years."

John: "You should be ashamed to trick your sister and destroying her future."

The kid: "You are destroying her future, she was mine before you."

Seeing Kim and Jenny returning, he resumed to play the dumb. Kim arrived and kissed the kid, then girded John and kissed him tenderly, "Oh my prince the wedding dress is marvellous. I never seen one so beautiful, thank you my love. I have to go and try it. I'll see you soon."

John smiled returned her kiss and said, "Okay princess, go ahead, I have to do to ... I'll see you later."

John left Kim worried, he usually was more alive, he answered like a robot, it wasn't like him.

Kim, Jenny and the kid went to the room, were the dress designer was waiting. She tried the dress on: "Oh G-D.." said Jenny "You look marvellous. I envie you, Wow!! incredible."

In the mean time John went to see Steve, "Did you record the conversation?"

Steve: "Yes, it's very clear.."

John: "Good, now please fax this note to the office we have in L.A. I want an answer before tomorrow 12:00 noon. The wedding is at 7pm. I want to have time to resolve this matter that really bothers me a lot."

Steve: "How did you suspect?"

John: "Well the way he fucked Kim first I could barely do it. b) he fucked in front of me, trying to shock me. He almost succeeded in having me cancel our wedding he wanted that. So the mistake was that if he fucked in front of me, because he is dumb, why not in front of Kim's mother and she told me that one time he almost did. Almost and one time, if he is dumb he will be doing it anywhere, any time in front of anybody."

"I'll take care of the hospital files, I'll ask Dave to help me with our law firm there too!"

John: "Good Steve, when we are sure he is not dying, I have a surprise for him!" John had a devilish smile.

Steve didn't ask what was the surprise. John went to see his parents and daugthers, all his brothers and their family. David and Peter went with their wives to buy stuff to take back to the states. Steve went back to work. John went to his room. What he seen again made his blood boil. The kid fucking Kim again. He took Jenny that was standing there, "Come baby lets make love in the other room."

John on the other room had undressed Jenny and himself layed her on the bed and surveyed her whole body with his kisses and licking all of her. Enjoying her marvellous breasts with full mouth tenderly. He could hear Kim's moaning between Jenny's sighing, "Oh John you are a wonderful lover.."

His hands captured her large breasts, his face burned between them kissing the proud mountain of velvety firm flesh. His fingers rolling her nipples between them. "Oh John, I want you, please fuck me now.."

John: "Shush baby soon, let your desire increase more.."

Kim had finished and opened the door to talk to him. She saw him drowned between her sisters beautiful breasts. His body covering hers. John continued kissing her tummy down to her shaved triangle which John licked and kissed tenderly making Jenny moan loud, "Yes, eat me, bite me.."

Kim felt a inch in her heart, she knew that it was jealousy. The way John kissed her full of passion and desire Jenny was melting under his kisses. The same he did to her, the first time he made love to her. Tears flowed from her eyes. She knew that he was hurt, very hurt. But what could she do. Her brother had only 2 to 3 months to live. She can't let him down now after so many years.

John knew that Kim was behind him, "Oh Jenny you are incredibly sexy and desirable. I wish I could marry you too, but I can't. Oh how a gorgeous pussy you have, I want to devoure you and then fuck you."

Jenny: "Yes, yes my love eat me, fuck me."

He lifted her legs spreading them, and very delicately licked her and kissed her vaginal lips. Jenny was in esctacy and in tremendous heat, arching her back, moaning. He put his hand under her ass, lifting her and let his elbows rest on the bed. His hands also were spreading her cheeks.

He licked her lovely ass, plunging his tongue in her rear entrance, probing licking and then very tenderly kissing, until he continued to her vagina sucking each lips delicately. Jenny was pratically screaming in excitement, "Oh lord, oh!, Oh!.." She had come for the fourth time in John's mouth, which he covered her pussy with his mouth to enjoy her flow of elixir.

Kim was aroused, jealous, sad and crying. The kid seeing Kim crying on the scene he pushed Kim to the bed with them, making her lay down next to Jenny and lifted her legs the

same way Jenny was. Kim was dumbfounded. He ever did that before and plunged his penis in her pussy and began devouring her and sucking her vaginal lips. John did not look their way and continued his doing.

Kim put a hand on is head and caressed him, but John did not pay attention to her caresses, Kim was hurt but since she was aroused, let herself go moaning, "Oh John, yes eat me, yes my love, you are eating me.."

The kid became upset hearing Kim calling him. John as he was doing it. He was furious and began biting her pussy harder. Kim "Not so hard baby, not so hard."

He stopped kneeled above her head, his penis all erected and had Kim turned around and took her mouth to his penis, pushing it in her. Kim couldn't understand what was going on. He never done that either. They were just in John's view. He made her open her mouth and take his penis in it. She did and sucked it allowing it all in her mouth.

She began sucking it and her hand massaged his balls squeezing them on and off. John was about to kill the bastard, but that what's he wanted, he restrained and instead took Jenny and fucked her in every way possible. The kid did more or less the same to Kim. But at one moment Kim released herself from the kid and jumped on John: "My love I know that you are mad, please make love to me, please."

John that had finished making love to Jenny said, "I am going to make love to you, kiss you and you are full of his filth. What

do you think that I am a masochist or retarded? Give me some respect."

He took his clothes and left for his room, to the shower and got dressed. Kim came and stood naked at the door. The little fucker sticked to her ass.

"John please we are getting married tomorrow, let's not get upset with each other remember that I only love you no one else. Please my love don't push me away!"

She ran to his arm leaving the kid at the door and hugged him crying, "Oh my love, please don't chase me, you also are fucking my sister, I know that you are in love with her too, I don't complain. But you don't want to understand my situation."

John was now about to explode: "I don't want to understand you have this little fucker here stock to your ass fucking you day and night.

Kim: "Don't call him like that..He is very ill."

John wanted to tell her, but he prefered to wait for the answer from the hospital, because if he is really dying. He won't revele to her what he said, but he isn't the kid will have the surprise of his life.

John: "I am sorry my love, you're right. Its no big deal. I know that you love me, I'll get over it, let this not spoil our wedding tomorrow.."

Kim cried and hugged him. He stroke her hair and kissed her forehead. "I love you baby.."

The kid seeing that, came and took Kim by her ass and tried to penetrate her again to enrage John, he didn't want them reconcile. But Kim stopped him, "Look I am tired, I need to take a shower and rest. Come I'll wash you.."

She pushed him inside the shower not before kissing John and began washing the kid which didn't miss an opportunity in squeezing her breasts or tried to masturbate her, grabbing her ass.

John saw his doing and left.

But the kid wanted him to stay. He let Kim wash him and then she dried him. She then went back to the shower to wash herself. Jenny came: "Hi Kim, oh he is marvellous. He ate me like I was his last meal. And he made love to me, it was just incredible."

Kim: "Don't rubb it on my nose, I know I saw it. Also I ask you to please take care of the kid for this days. He is very upset to see him fucking me non stop even though he understand. But he is not just a kid, he has a big thing you know. So please from now on let him fuck you. Okay?"

Jenny with a grouchy face: "Okay. Okay I'll do it. I had to suffer him all this past 5 month since you left. My boyfriend left me because of him. I was having sex with my boyfriend in our room and the kid came and fucked me in the ass, just on

top of my boyfriend. He also punched the kid. I had to stop him, and tried to explain, but he didn't believe my bullshit story as he called it. He left and never called me again."

Kim: "But this is my wedding tomorrow, I don't want John to cancel our wedding, I love him too much, please take care of him.."

The rest of the day they spent enjoying the family, shopping around Monaco, Kim's mother was elated. Kim showed her Rolls Royce.

"See Mom, John bought it for me the first week I was here." Then she showed her the jewels.

Iris: "Oh my lord, are all this real??"

Kim laughed, "Of course mom. This belonged to Cesar's wife almost 2000 years ago. It cost him 14 million dollar."

Iris: "Oh my lord, and I tried to make you change your mind, I like him, he is very polite..Does he love you?"

Kim: "Oh mama, he adores me, he makes me feel and treats me like a queen. I adore him, he is my prince charming and I am Cinderella. He will be my husband tomorrow night. Oh Mom! I am so happy."

They talked for a while and then she took her family for a ride and showed her mother, John's office building.

Jenny: "Can I stay with you and live here Kim?"

Kim: "It's his decision, I would love too."

But her voice was betraying her real feeling. John spent the day with Kathy going around to resolve last minute thing.

Kathy: "I missed you boss, you didn't make love to me since all this people arrived and soon you are leaving for your honeymoon."

John pulled her by the hand and took her to his room without saying a word. He pulled her clothes and fucked her brains out for an hour, he had missed her too. Falling on her, resting. They were all in sweat. Kathy was happy. "I loved it boss, you're wonderful. How is Jenny? Do you like her?"

John: "Yes she is a jewel and her body is marvellous, she loves sex like there is no tomorrow and she is hot very hot."

"Okay!Okay!Don't get excited just thinking about her."

John looked at her cute face. Kissed her nose and said: "Let's go we have a lot to do today." He took his family to shop around town. Toward 8pm they returned. They were tired from a long trip shopping tour. Kim, her family with John's family, Steve and family, David and family and Pete and wife went all out to a restaurant that John had fully reserved, in Nice, France. It was a beautiful night of August.

They had a fantastic evening. Knowing each other better. Kim was holding John tight kissing his shoulder and neck. He returned her kisses tender. They had returned toward ll

pm. John took everyone to the hotel and only Steve, Jenny, the brother, Kim and John returned to the yatch.

The kid already was hanging into Kim's arm. John couldn't wait until morning to get the answer from the U.S. John went to take a shower Kim joined him. Jenny held the kid, by pulling his clothes and hers. Then kneeled and gave him a blow job, that he liked, but his mind was set on Kim.

Kim caressed John's body under the shower, "Oh my love, tomorrow we will be husband and wife.."

She kneeled and kissed his penis burning his skin then she took his manhood to her trembling mouth, sucking it gently. He loved her lips. They had the touch of silk, her tongue made him shiver and cramped his muscles. He caressed her soft blonde hair holding her head between his hands. At that moment the kid entered. He escaped Jenny and looked at them. He came behind Kim lifting her ass and penetrated her with rage fucking her hard while she was sucking John's penis.

They looked at each other in defiance, the kid had a mocking expression biting his lips and fucking Kim's beautiful ass. He leaned and grabbed her breasts, squeezing them hard with full hand, and was moving in Kim's gorgeous derriere in a vulgar as if she were a whore. John was about to strangle him, but refrained.

The kid then spread her legs further making her hold tight on John's hips. He lifted her from the ground and began sucking her in both, the pussy and ass. His hands holding her thighs.

Kim: "Not so hard kid." She managed to say releasing John's penis from mouth. That was his intention. But Kim returned to her doing. John lifted Kim in his arms, freeing her from the kid and left the kid in the shower. He wrapped Kim in a large towel. The kid began screaming hysterically. Jenny came and tried to calm him, to no avail.

She put her breasts to his mouth to see if he will suck it, but he wanted Kim, John layed down, on top of Kim, covering all her with his body and made love to her, not allowing the jerk come between them. John devoured her wonderful breasts, moving on her, his hands on her exciting derriere. It was incredible, how many people wanted her. He would not have taken the bullshit, for another woman, but he loved her so much to renounce at her. He will fight for her all the way.

He knows that the little devil had fucked her since he was a kid. In a way he understood the kid. He also was fighting for Kim's love and her body that drove crazy anyone that see her. The kid was looking at them, pulling Kim's arm and crying. Kim tried not look at him but his yelling did not permit it. She caressed his face, but took her hand and put it on his dick, thus notifying her of his need.

Kim: "My love the kid is hysterical.."

She freed her mouth and pulled him toward her and gave him a head job, caressing his groins. He calmed down. His purpose anoyed John so he will cancel the wedding. John turned his head not to watch the kid's dick coming in and out of Kim's beautiful mouth, her lips ressing on the young prick.

Jenny came around and layed next to Kim offering her lovely proeminent pale breasts to his hungry mouth.

He released his hands from Kim's derriere and pressed those exciting breasts devouring them, drowning between them. Then his hand reached from her divine pussy and masturbate her. He rolled from Kim and layed on his back for Jenny to come to him, but Kim understood his intention.

She jumped on top of him, kissing his lips and making his penis into her moist paradise and began moving on him. John freed his mouth and said, "Jenny come and seat above my face, so I'll eat you I'm starved of your young and delicious pussy.."

Jenny didn't have to be repeated twice. Kim was terribly hurt but didn't say a word, because she knew hat he did it out of rage of not being able to make love to her in peace. The kid immediately jumped on Kim's ass and spread tile cheeks and pointing his penis in her gorgeous asshole.

He plunged in one push making Kim scream. But he didn't care, he wanted his message to go through. He put his hands on er breasts and began fucking her ass in a rage. John was devouring Jennys delicious and appetizing pussy with full mouth, his hands on her breasts, teasing her nipples and squeezing her breast on and off. His large hands barely could grabbed her whole breast.

Up to half of her bun, Jenny was moaning crying and coming into his mouth. She felt the strength of his jaws and lips. Her head rolled back enjoying her scavenger, he had all her vagina

in his mouth then he will suck her triangle. At the end when her lips and clitoris were swallen. He grabed her clitoris with his lips and sucked it with all his strength making her lose control of herself and her muscles moved uncontrolably.

Kim was watching his hand up to Jennys breasts. She also saw his chin under Jenny's ass and his jaws moving, his adam's apple up and down as if he was drinking. Probably her flow of excitement. She felt miserable. He barely moved in her, the kid was fucking her and moved for both. John felt the kid's hand squeezing Kim's breast his hand against his chest.

He really lost control, stopped his massaged on Jennys breasts, took his hands from Kim's breasts violently. The kid got scared to redo it, he was pushing it to much.

Kim did not say a thing she also was afraid to antogonize John too much. The kid pulled Kim and rolled with her on the bed on top of him with one hand he emprisoned her breasts, his other hand on her vagina, his legs he put them on top of Kim's thighs between them and pulled them apart, having a grip in her, and made her moved on his penis.

Kim's mind was on John and Jenny. She was very jealous, extremely jealous. She could see John's excitement, the kid's dick moving in her ass, broke her concentration, the kid then released her and came to her standing on the bed lifted her thighs, her head laying down, he penetrated her vagina, is hands on her cheeks and began fucking her.

Kim couldn't believe how many new position the kid was doing lately. When he ejaculated in her vagina. He made Kim give him a blow job. Then flipped her the same way he held her before and lifted her legs and fucked her in the ass.

John was making love to this gorgeous young lady, she was like fire in his veins until they fell asleep. The phone rang John, felt like a train had run him down. He looked at his watch. It was 7am. It was Steve:

"John sorry, I got the whole file on this creep. You were right he is a real devil he has fooled everyone. He isn't sick at all. The diagnostic he had when he was a child was error. They found out two years ago when they made him new blood tests. They re-did it ten times. It is believed that the first blood test were mixed up with someone really sick with the disease. This kid is a devil, he fooled the sisters and mother for many years, blackmailing them, playing down and fucking both sisters."

"Steve please prepare me the tape and the file and please call the sisters, tell them that I am bringing the kid for a special treatment all the way. She will understand. I'll be over in a while."

He turned toward Kim She was laying down, and the fucker on her ass and his hands on her breasts. He stood up got dressed and violently pulled him it. He screamed from the surprise, "Come little fucker you and I have a business together."

Kim and Jenny scared asked: "What's going on … release him!!!"

John: "You two stupid girls get dressed with anything and follow me."

He was fuming. Kim tried to free him from his powerful grip. "Leave him alone!!"

John wouldn't budge. "Follow me!!!"

They had no choice but follow him pulling the kid naked behind him. He was scared to death now. Kim was trying to wrap a towel around him, but wasnt successful. They arrived at Steve's computer room. Kim and Jenny were dumbfounded, he called them stupid girls, that is the first time he expressed himself that way.

"Steve play the tape."

Steve did. The girls recognizing John's voice and her brother that very rarely said a word was talking. Kim and Jenny's eyes were widely open, looking each other incredulous to what their ears were hearing. The kid was shaking, still naked. John holding his wrist turning white from so much pressure of John's grip.

Kim: "I ... can't believe my ears.." Jenny said similar expression.

John: "Well if you don't believe your ears, then believe your eyes here is the medical records from day one till today."

Kim was turning the pages one by one, until the final conculsion and diagnostic. She stood pale now looking at the kid. She slapped him violently and kicked him in the balls with

all her strength. Jenny also punched him in the nose making him bleed.

Kim "I don't want ever to see you again, you fooled me, you bastard, you didn't care if you destroyed my happiness, by fucking me like you never did in front of the man I love that i can't ever look at his face now, because of you, piece of shit."

He was looking down. John pulled him and said, "I have a little surprise for you.."

Kim didn't care but Jenny ask: "Where are you taking him?"

John: "Don't worry he loves fucking a lot so I will grant his last dying wish. I'll give him to the sisters. He will learn what fucking is. Come all of you, follow me."

The kid tried to resist but he couldn't match John's strength.

They all arrived at the sisters cabin. Kim knew already laughed hysterical and they all entered. The sisters were there beautiful as ever. Michelle took him from John's hand, massaged his wrist that was in pain from John's grip.

"Comme baby. We will give you a lot of love, you will make love to all my sisters." The kid suddenly felt good. Gladis kneeled and began sucking his dick. He was elated he got scared for a moment. He can fuck all this girls I have plenty of juice.

The four sisters came behind him, and began undressing at John's sign. Steve, Jenny, Kim and John took chairs behind and

watched. Steve and Jenny's eyes opened very wide seeing the enormous dicks of the sisters.

Jenny turned pale. Debra came and began massaging his ass. He has not see girls behind him. Debra took a cream and lubricated her penis spread the kid's cheeks, and played with a finger between his cheeks, and she came pointing her dick on his asshole. She held him by his hips and pressed her dick penetration him in one push.

His mouth opened screamed his heart out. "What's this, what?"

The other three girls came to the front. When he saw their dicks, he turned pale. Kim and Jenny couldn't stop laughing almost shocking. Debra began fucking him with all her strength. Gladis began biting making him feel her teeth.

He was now scared to death. Michelle put him an "O" ring in his mouth, by force, his eyes rolling like of a madman. They made him kneel and Michelle began fucking his mouth. She sprayed the anti-gagg spray, he was trying to scream. John came in front of him and ask the girls to hold for a moment so he understand what he was about to say.

"You see kid, no one fucks with me. You are not 16 1/2. But 19, all about you is a lie. Now you wanted fucking, not my Kim, but you will feel what fucking is. They will keep you here for two weeks. When they finish with you, you will have more respect for women. If it were another person, I would have cut your dick, enjoy!!!"

Before he could say a word, the girls returned to their doing, he looked scared to death, the arrogance had disappeared completely. John left followed by Kim and Jenny. Steve had already left. He couldn't watch this, he was a softy.

Jenny: "But John how would you keep him two weeks!My mother will ask about him.."

Kim wasn't saying a word, she looked down.

John: "I will tell your mother that I found an old friend of mine that is a very renown specialist. He took him immediately with him to apply a certain treatment that had to be done right away. So he could save his life and that he could live to be an old man.."

Jenny: "That might do it. Between us he deserve what he gets and much more. He almost destroyed Kim's life."

Kim: "Jenny would you let me speak to John alone please."

Jenny: "Sure I'll go see Steve."

Steve at this moment came running he looked like he had discovered America.

"John look at what I got from our firm in L.A. from David's friend. The father of this kid before he married Kim's mother and afterwas a professional conman and thief. He did the same trick to other women, he is wanted by many. He has a bunch of kids like our Mike and makes romance to various divorced women, makes a phony marriages, then he bring the

kid, as it were his own. The kid is trained to steal from the host. The husband allgelly travels a lot as a salesman. He goes and collects all the stolen money or property and sells it. In a way it's an organized gang. They play dumb most of the time, in order not to get too acquainted and becomes too human to steal from the person that feeds him. All the bullshit story of leukeumia is fake. They did have one kid that has leukemia. They all have the same name and last name.

So the report is accurate about that child. But he applies it to all his gang. So when he leaves that home, and leaves the child there, the family is already attached to the child. So they don't get rid of him due that the child is terminally ill. But never dies. So he made one mistake, our Mike needed to have a blood analysis. They found out that it wasn't the type of blood of the kid in the chart, and voila brilliant conman."

John:" tell Bashir to arrange a long vacation to Mike to the Saoudis they like a young white ass, and tell them that he is a present from me as a sex slave.

Kim: "Oh my G-D now that you mention, money and various pieces of jewelery has been stolen from us all during those years. Oh my Lord, now everything fits into places, and he deserves what he gets."

Jenny was livid, she looked like a ghost.

She said to Steve: "Can I come to your office to read the whole file?"

Steve: "Sure come in.."

Kim and John went to their cabin. Kim was still pale, her gorgeous silk lips that usually had the color of roses, were colorless. Her angelical face was in pain, she managed, to say: "John, I know that today is our wedding day, but if you want to cancel it, do not worry I'll go back to the states. I do not want anything. I know that the image of Mike fucking me with you and in front of you, will haunt you, please do not feel obligated to marry me.."

John very serene said: "Well since we talking serious I found out that I do not love you." Tears flowed freely from Kim's beautiful almond shaped green eyes, her lips tremble.

"The reason I do not love you is because I...adore you princess."

Kim didn't realise instantly, when she did she covered her face with her long pale hands, and cried hard. John took her in his arms and carried her to the bed kissing her all over in desperation for her, all of her.

"Oh Kim you are the most beautiful being I ever layed my eyes on. I love you beyond comprehension. You have me in love like a kid. I know that my life with you will not be dull. I expect a lot of problems because of your beauty. I'll have to fight the whole world, you excite everyone that sees you or is in contact with you. I am ready for the fight, that will enhance our love. You are worth every bit of it."

Kim was looking at his eyes, when he said all this. She could feel the incensity of his words of his incredible love for her. Tears continue flowing from her mesmerizing eyes. Kim softly said: "I love you John, make me yours now and forever, make love to me my prince charming."

They closed their eyes and kissed very tenderly. He kissed all her face and made love, enjoying each other to the fullest. Stranded in an island surrounded by a sea of love. They had attained a new hight in happiness and esctacy.

He drank from her river of love, breathing her heavenly scent. Which ended in a sighing, laughs and tender kissing. He kissed her all over her sculptured magnificent body. They layed next to each other, just holding her in his arm. Words were not needed. Kim finally spoke, "Oh my G-D it's 10:30am. You have to leave this room now. I have my wedding present coming in at 12:00 noon. Hurry-up my love."

She pushed him out of the bed, making John laugh.

"Can you give a clue??"

"Nope you'll see, be patient."

She had a mischivious smile the colors had returned to her devine face.

John: "I'll never get used to your beauty, I am crazy about you princess."

Kim "Me too my love. I'll give you love ever day of our lives. I wont give you time to become old. You'll be busy making love to me. Bye"

She pushed him out, John laughed. He went to Steve. He was chating with Jenny. When Jenny saw him, she asked "So do we still have a wedding?" John took her chin and kissed it, "Of cours we do, love is not superficial, if we have problem we resolve them..I fought too much for her to let her go. I have to accept that she is too beautiful and I take her with all the problem that comes with it."

Jenny hugged him, kissing his neck. "John, can I stay here with you and Kim? I love you very much."

She forgot that Steve was present in the back, Steve was scratching his scalp. John held her in his arms and said: "I would be more than glad to.

I feel flattered, I am no hunk, nor too young, I am 46 almost tripple your age. Your beauty and youth gives me energy that I did not had. If Kim doesn't object, I don't either. I'll love to have you around little princess. I personally couldn't ask, because it would sound too selfish. But you have my okay go ask Kim. She is in the cabin."

She kissed him, giggled and ran out.

Steve: "John, I hope you survive three beautiful woman.."

They both laughed. David and Peter had arrived alone without the family. They sat and talked in general and also that the deal with the consortium had began. All normal. They were under control.

John: "Listen guys I'll be in my honeymoon for two weeks. You take care of everything. Any decision between the three of you goes. Don't wait for my ok?"

David: "Where are you planning to go?"

John laughed, "It's a top secret but I'll tell you three, you do not repeat it not even to your wives, promised?"

"Promised" the three said.

He told them.

David: "I can't believe it, let me rephrase it, I do believe it, everything is possible with you."

Steve: "How much it will cost you these two week."

John: "About fifty million dollars."

Peter: "That's crazy 3 1/2 million dollars a day."

John laughed: "If I don't do it to have this incredible souvenir with the woman I most love. What do I need this colossal fortune for. So other will enjoy it and not me? No my friend I want her to be the happiest woman in the universe. I am crazy about her."

David: "I see that, go for it, you're right you'll be in the book of guiness."

The phone rang Steve picked it: "Hello!Oh hi Kim." he listened "I will right away."

Steve: "John you are invited to your cabin.."

John looked at his his watch, 12:00 noon. He said, "That's probably my present..she has some a surprise for me.. I am worried."

All laughed: "Go, go, don't worry she wont eat you."

He rushed to the cabin. Kim opened the door. Jenny was there and to his surprise the three girls he saved from the serial killer were there too. Kim held his face between her hands and said, "Darling the three young ladies are here to thank you in person and inside the other room, there is your present from them, Jenny and mine. By the way I don't have a problem that Jenny stays living with us."

John came to shake the 3 girls hands, instead they jumped to his neck and kissed him in the mouth almost burning the hair on top of his head. The red haired spoke, "Mr. John we wanted to show our eternal thanks for saving us, so your bride and us have planned this present for your wedding."

The Brunette "We are going to cover your eyes if you may!"

"Go ahead.." he said smiling. To Kim he said, "If something happens to me, I'll hold you personally responsible."

Kim giggled, "Of course my love."

They covered his eyes with a towel, and came to the next room. Jenny said "Just one moment.." he could hear all kind of noises that he couldn't pin point.

One girl said, "Now!!!"

He took the towel off, "Oh G!!! I am. ... surprised!!!"

There was 12 gorgeous girls half naked just having a tiny skirt that didn't cover their assets and a tiny t-shirt that didn't cover their breasts either. They were beautiful. John felt the 12 pairs of hands on him, teasing down every button of his shirt and pulling his short down leaving him naked. They were all gorgeous, their ages ranging from 18-20.He suddenly felt the burning of their lips all over his body. He entered in an instant trance.

Two were sucking his penis and testicles, two kissing his derrier cheeks, two on his chest, two on his face, two on his stomach and two his thighs. The two last one took his hands to their vagina.

A tornado like began.

John was handled like a fether with the 24 hand and 12 mouths and 12 sexes and 24 breasts. They rolled him on the floor. The three girls he saved were part of the twelve. Kim and Jenny looked at them excited to see him in such esctacy ravished by the gorgeous gang. They wanted to jump on them

and enjoy too. Jenny lifted Kim's dress and put one hand on her vagina and one on her gorgeous ass, and masturbated her. Kim was moaning enoyed her hands. Kim opened her blouse and offered her breasts to her, she devoured too.

Steve, David and Peter came to the room to see what the present was finding anyone, but they heard the noise in next room. They opened and saw the mix of legs hands asses and other. He said, "Oups sorry!!!"

They left as fast as they came. They didn't see Kim that was behind the door and Jenny ravishing her. Kim was moaning loud enjoying Jennys attention, plunging her fingers in her rear entrance lifting her on and off reaching her in depths. Kim also undressed her and did the same to her. John in the mean time, tasted 12 different flavors of all the charm that each girl had to offer, devouring her youthful breasts pussies and asses.

They took turn to have his penis one injected him with a testosterone injection to ravitalize him. He had sex 36 times, ejaculating 9 times, until they all collapsed on top of him. It looked like a war zone. Beautiful asses, pussies and breasts were all over him Kim came and searched for his head. She found one having her vagina on his face, covering him totally. Kim rolled her and caressed his face breathing hard.

John said, "I am having a heart attack.." He made sound like he was gasping for air. Kim began screaming, "Move! move! he needs to breath. They all moved their faces showed worry. Kim gave him a mouth to mouth resustation.

"No my love! answer me! Oh answer me!" He grabbed her and lifted her on top of him laughing.

"You are my air, I need you urgent."

Kim cried, "Oh you vilain you scared me to death."

All the girls laughed joyfully. He took her and made love to her in front of the 13 people present. He kissed of all of her body licked it covering all of her with his lips burning of desire and had the strength to make love to her front and back. All the girls were admiring this odd couple loving like there was no tomorrow. Kim moaned sighed cried.

All the girls kneeled down and kissed both of them, giving them a new trip of happines. Kim and John feeling their hands mouths and breasts all over them. Jenny joined them too. At the end they practically lifted the couple from the floor and took them to the jaccuzi and washed both. Jenny stood on the side a little sad, John saw her: "What's wrong baby?"

"I was forgotten, you haven't made love to me."

"We can remedie that."

He pulled her inside the jaccuzi sat her on his penis penetrating her lovely ass and her back to him and soaped her body and kneaded her fantastic breasts fucking her. Kim and all the girls looking at Jenny moaning in ecstacy.

Her gorgeous face reflected a strange satisfaction being loved by him and watched by so many. A man that was older then

her 28 years, brown hair and deep brown eyes with a silky touch. His colossal fortune and the power he got from it gave him the exact touch that women liked in a man "Success and Power"

The girls seeing Kim watching them took her and ravished her devouring every bit of her body as they had done to John, finishing all completely exhausted. When everyone was dressed and ready to leave, John spoke to the girls: "Have your passports ready, I will send all of you to the United States, then to Hawaii for 2 week all paid."

The girls "Oh thank you Mr. J" they almost raped him again. They departed all very happy.

John finally said holding Kim and Jenny in his arms, "Thanks my love fo this present to end my celibacy.."

He kissed both.

Kim: "You are welcome my husband to be in a few hours.."

John: "So it is alright about Jenny, to stay and lives with us?"

Kim: "Yes my love, I know that you love her, and I do too. We will have menage a trois."

John all smiles: "Even thought I can't offer you the same to have another man?"

"Yes my darling, but what about Kathy?

John looked at her and said, "You tell me.."

Kim: "You know it will be terrible to leave her and I do like her too. What do you say?"

John: "Menage a Quatre?"

Kim "If quatre means four, I accept … lets call her.."

Five minute later Kathy showed up her face looked worried. "Yes boss?"

Kim spoke instead "You see we were talking about Jenny to stay living with us. She will stay and live here in the cabin as his second wife but not officially and the question came about you.. so I would like you to stay also If you want too, we love you! You will be no … 3. What do you say?"

Kathy had tears in her eyes, approached Kim and hugged her

"Thank you.. I thought you didn't want me any longer.."

John came behind her and hugged the three of them and kissed theft heads." All this love makes me feel very lucky and flatered. One thing I can promise you, I'll never ask you to leave, but I can't marry legally the three of you, just in our hearts and bodies. By the same token. I can't hold you for ever. If you fall in love of with another man, you are free to leave anytime. Your happiness is mine. I am even going to assign you each a fat bank account for your use. Do what ever you with it. I love you all girls."

Kim, Jenny and John undressed Kathy and mad love to her posessing all her body. Tears of intense joy flowed in her love face clouding her gorgeous blue eyes. Finally she will stay with him even sharing him. That has been always her worry.

THE WEDDING

T he most important moment had arrived for Kim and
John: The Wedding. It was attended by all Medias
and quoted as the Wedding of the Century. Country leaders,
Kings, Princes attended. The religious ceremony was about
to start.

The organ played the nuptial melody. Kim came out holding
her real father's arm, that had arrived that same day. Kim had
the appearance of an angel. She seemed to be floating on a
cloud. Her illustrous weddding dress's train was fifty feet long.
It was with embrodied in gold. She had the jewels that Queen
will die to own.

A light cloud of fog. Felt to surround her from so much
brilliance of her beauty, a veil of mystery. His heart ached with
so much love he had for her. If not for this solemn moment
would had made love to her in front of all this people. What
he didn't know that his desire was prophetic. When she finally
reached him, her father gave her hand to him. They looked at
each other desire and passion was written all over their faces,
her lips said, without anysound: "I love you husband."

He whispered "I adore you wife."

The ceremony was hair raising. John's family were so happy for John to have found a wife that he loved and that she loved him to. All John's family were simple people. Money did not change their personality like it often does.

John and Kim were hearing the sounds around them. The words said to them by the Haire and the religious man marrying them. They heard them as if from far away. They felt alone in this sea of people. They couldn't brake their eye contact. They repeated the words "Yes! I do!" without hearing the question clearly. John's heart was beating hard.

He gave her the cup of wine to taste, lifting her veil. When the formalities were over all were saying, "Kiss her, Kiss her!"

He couldn't move nor could she. They held hands at first. Then John took her marvellous beautiful face between his hands and very softly brushed her lips slowly increasing it strength until they embraced each other. Kissing up to the point that they had to gasp for air, to breath. All cheered, applauded, thousands of flashes fired. The music began.

All were drinking and eating from the long buffet tables garnished like a King's table. John took her to the center of the dancing ground and danced a valse with her, looking at each other, memerized in love.

"I Love you my wife, my gorgeous bride. You have enslaved me with you love and beauty."

"I adore you my prince. I want your love every minute of the day."

Iris, Kim's mother was dancing with her ex-husband. They looked reconciled, it might end up in a new wedding. All danced, John's dad was the first to take Kim from his arms and dances with her. The line to dance with her was reachin, up to the entrance.

John thought, "Poor Kim she has a long night of dancing."

John asked Iris to dance. She said, "I want to thank you for loving my child so much, you made a queen of my baby.." She had tears of joy in her eyes.

"And thanks so much for sending my son to a specialist to cure his cancer. I don't know how to thank you!!"

John: "Be happy. I'll take care of Jenny too. I have a feeling that you intend to remarry if I am not mistaken."

Iris: "Does it show so much."

John: "That's good, now Kim and Jenny will be delighted. The matter of Jenny is staying here to live with us and I'll take care of her. I'll make he study a good career. The kid too I'll take care of him and send him to a good academy. You two can live your lives to the fullest like love birds. I told Kim that I would like your permission to help you out financialy. Please do not take it as an offence, it is my pleasure."

She had a smile from ear to ear and gave him a wet kiss on his cheek sounding like a champaign being uncorked "You are our good angel. The lord has remembered us finally. G-D bless you."

The next to dance with John was Jenny.

"John you look great in tuxed."

"Don't be a liar by flattering me. I know that I am ugly."

"No you're not. You are very handsome a real man and not a baby face or look like those cute face that spend the day looking in the mirror at their reflection. They are feminine, but you are strong and a real man."

"Thank you little girl and my wife no.2."

Jenny giggled to be called wife no.2.She was so young.

"I feel so feminine when you make love to me, devour me, take me from every angle possible like you do."

John: "Sweetheart if you continue, I will have to hide my embarasseement."

She felt his bulge against her vagina. She giggled, "Oh I didn't know that I could excite you by talking. I love you John. I wil never leave you."

"Never say never, you're too young to know what life has in store for you. Maybe prince charming is just around the corner."

Jenny with a mad childish face said, "Are you trying to get rid of me? You are my prince charming, I'll marry you at anytime any place." (in his ear). "I love when you fuck me hard. I want also to be spanked like you did to Kim and Kathy she told me, it must be exciting."

John pressed her shoulder and hands: "You are exciting me kido. Imagine if your Mom came to dance with me again, now."

They both laughed. Then it was Kathy turn, and so on. John finally get his wife back. He raised her and carried her in his arms and said, "Bye to everyone and thanks to all of you for coming, continue enjoying the party. It will last 7 full days and nights!!Bye.."

All began applauding, cheering whistling. Kim threw her bridal bouqet, it fell in Jenny's hands, she looked at them happy and had tears of joy in her eyes. She felt a pair of hands in her waist behind. It was Kathy.

Jenny: "I envie Kim even thought I love her too."

Kathy pressed her lips and kissed her neck. The kiss was burning and promising a goodnight enjoy. At the airport John's plane engine were running. They boarded and the plane took off a short time later.

They rushed to the cabin, he undressed her and she undressed him, falling both in the bed, trembling with emotions, holding each other their hands shaking with intense desire to make love their first time as husband and wife. They love the whole

trip until the captain announced: "Sir we will be landing in Moscow in 20 minutes."

Kim jumped "In Moscow?"

John: "Yes it's a surprise inside a surprise."

"But love, I thought we might go to Hawaii to the sun, not Russia!!!"

John smiled again, "Don't you trust me?"

Kim "Yes of course my dear husband."

They got dressed in comfortable clothing. After hanging the wedding dress and tuxedo in the closet. At the airport in Moscow the Minister of Transportation and a delegation were waiting for them. A translator welcome them to Moscow and informed them that every thing was ready as planned. John pulled an envelope from his pocket and gave it to the minister. His face lite-up when he saw the cashier check for $50 million.

Kim asked, "What in the envelopp?"

"Just a check my love."

"For how much?"

"Just fifty princess"

"Fifty thousand!"

"It doesn't matter my cute wife. Let us follow them."

They got into the car forming part their entourage. In the car she had a glimpse of the check. She whispered in his ear: "50 million!!! What are you buying baby?"

"Don't be so curious you will see soon."

John told her the conversation with her mom. She was delighted and thanked him profusely with a kiss on his neck that made him shiver.

"You're great my prince, you helping mom and my dad to get together and you brought them a house in Hawaii. I wish I knew the size of your heart. One thing I want you to do when we get back. As proof of my true love for you. I want to sign a contract, that i want nothing from your fortune, just you. I didn't marry you for your money, maybe at the beginning I was fascinated by your power and fortune, but now you have won me with your endless love, what you have endured to have me. How you suffered in silence for all that has transpired since I came to you. You have forgave me everything and loved me even more."

"There is one thing I want from you."

"Yes my love?"

"I want the diary you have about me, that's the most precious of present you can give me."

"Princess you are everything I want or desire, all this fortune without you doesn't mean a thing, if you asked me to give away all my fortune. I will in a blink of an eye."

"Oh John you are a romantic fool, your love encompasses the whole universe. I love you my dearest husband. I hope that I am not dreaming.."

"Life is a dream my angel."

After 3 hours they had arrived at Military installation. All the gate soliders looked at their credentials, saluted and standing in attention and the escort followed a path led by a jeep. Kim was nervous and anxious to see what was going on. After ten minute drive and stopping at two more gates, before continuing. Finally they had arrived to a place that was a giant launch pad. A space shuttle with the Russian insigne was on it, was in launching position.

Kim: "Oh lord you brought a shuttle."

John laughed: "Yes more or less baby look at the name of the shuttle."

Kim cried loud: "Oh G-D, Oh my love, your love for me has no end."

Tears came out of her gorgeous eyes. The name the shuttle had was "Princess Kim.." She hugged him and couldn't speak from the strong emotion "Oh my prince, you bought the right

to put my name for 50 million, so thebwhole world will see it. I don't know what to say."

Her gorgeous almond shap green eyes were blurred by tears.

She kissed his hand tenderly. They exited the car and walked to a building that was nearly, high ranking officer welcomed them, female officer came with bouquets of different color of roses that had a ribbon written "Congratulations to the newly wed" in English. She kissed each of the ladies and took the bouquets from them. Another officer took the bouquests from Kim to safeguard them until they returned. They entered a room that had space suite in it. John said, "They want us to try the suit and go visit the space shuttle."

Kim was excited "Oh darling you're fantastic and excentrique."

She looked like a marvellous child going to the luna park. She was all excited. The lady officer gave her an orange jump suit and one to John. The male officers had left. John undresed sligthly embarrassed. Kim did too, maybe a little shy in front of these female, officers. The women said something in Russian when they saw Kim's almost naked body.

It seemed like a compliment. They made every effort possible to touch her everywhere when they helped her dressed with the jump suit. First being too big, they changed her three times until they found the real size. Kim felt their hands everywhere in her ass and between her thighs up to her boobs. John was amused, the whole world wanted to make love to Kim.

Finally they where in space suits, and connected to an air battery pack. Kim looked so cute and so small inside the suit. They could communicate through an inside nicrophone.

"How do you feel baby?"

"Strange but I am excited to visit a space shuttle. Thank you my love for such a great surprise, I love it."

John smiled to himself. "Wait baby you'll see."

They walked to an elevator that took them to a ramp. From the ramp they walked a long walk in a metallic ramp up to another elevator that elevated them to the shuttle.

Each letter with Kim's name and princess in the shuttle was bigger than Kim and John.

Kim's heart was beating hard she was afraid to look down. Once inside the shuttle four cosmonauts were waiting for them. They made sign welcoming them. They were 2 men and two women. It was hard to see their real features inside their space suits. The official that brought them in, gave John and Kim a tour of the shuttle explaining the different things.

Then he showed them the quarter. The captain blinked an eye at John. When the tour was finished he made the presentation. The captain's name was Boris Nureyev his second was Vladimir Bolchenco. One of the ladies, she looked like a red head was Katherina and the last one a blonde name Irina.

After the presentations, John and Kim took each a seat that was behind the cosmonauts and they connected the speaker to their space suits.

John: "It's like the real thing they will even ignite for us to make us feel the way they do when they are launched."

Kim: "Oh baby I am so excited wait I'll tell moma, Dad, and Jenny about this. Will we be able to watch the lift off on T.V. and see my name on it?"

John "Of course not just us, but the whole world. Look down the T.V. crews and Medias just arriving, when we come down, they will interview us. You will be world famous, babe.."

The people that had come with them left. They were in launching position John and Kim were watching the cosmonauts speaking to the control tower in Russian and switching all kind of instruments. The count down began.

Kim said, "It's like the real thing."

The engine were roaring. Everything could be seen from the T.V. screens inside the cabin. The rockets were fired, the whole shuttle was shaking.

Kim: "Darling it's moving, I swear, look we are lifting off."

"Don't worry it's just an excerise."

When the one and lift off was called on the speaker a cloud of fire and smoke covered all the shuttle and began lifting off.

Kim felt her derriere going up to her chest. "John we are going up I swear."

John was hillarious laughing his heart out.

Kim held his arm, "I am scared John."

He could barely hear her with the noise. Then the shuttle was rising in the sky higher and higher.

Kim screamed "We are going, I know.."

John: "Don't worry baby will be alright please trust me as always.."

This calmed Kim a little. Suddenly they were catapulted front then pressed back to their seat from the speed of the shuttle. Kim couldn't even speak any longer until they react space and the rockets disconnected. Suddenly it was silence. John broke it "Look darling at the earth, look America."

"Oh G-D, is grandiose..John you have actually hired the shuttle for a ride, did you?"

She had a questioning smile.

"No my love, I hired the shuttle for our honey moon, a real one, we will come close to the moon. I want to buy the moon for you my little sunshine."

"Oh John, you did? "

On her eyes blurred with tears. It was too many emotions for her, his love encompassed the whole universe. She could see the earth, it was beautiful, breath-taking. They were told that they could take their suits off. The cosmonauts did first and then helped them, they spoke good English. They were two men and two women.

They were floating in the cabin. Kim held John's arm afraid to release him. The women cosmonaut Irina was a gorgeous blonde blue eyes an incredible body. She asked them to follow her. Floating in the hallway behind the cabin. Kim aroused and scared at the same time.

They arrived at a door which opened to let them in and closed the door behind Kim and John. Inside John grabbed Kim, "My love you and I are the first honey moonering the moon and space in the history."

"Oh my prince, yoy, you ... are incredibly romantic."

She cried and held him tight. They were upside down in the air. John unzipped her jump suit, it came out alone pulled by the antigravitational pull. They stayed naked floating in the air. Kim couldn't control her laugh. "Oh my Lord you're impossible with your imagination, I understand how you became the richest man in the world."

She continued laughing hilarious. John pressed a botton, it was an intercome, he spoke into it.

"How do I switch the video to record?"

"Hold on." said a voice, "I will be over."

Irina that led them to the cabin came back opened the door and showed John the video switch. The camera was in one of on the top corners. So it recorde everything in the cabin. Irina was mesmerized by Kim's beauty. She couldn't take her eyes off her then looked at John's manhood that was very excited and smiled appraising it. John thanked her. Kim smiled at her and was embarrassed by her gaze. She finally left. John caught Kim by her ankle because she was cramped in the ceiling not knowing how to get out of it. He laughed and said, "My love we are the first married couple that comes to space to have their honeymoon. I am going to fuck your brains out.."

He pulled her a little too hard and they were both catapulted against the other wall. They laughed tremendously until John caught her gorgeous face that kept him a thousand nights sleepless, fantasizing being with her.

She was more beautiful than a sunrise an full moon together. He emprisoned her lips in an enabriating kiss. Their saliva floating in their mouth. His hands on her fantastic ass cheeks. He succeeded in penetrating her vagina, then they separated for not knowing how to hold to each other. He finally grabbed her in a 69 position and began devoring her gorgeous vaginal lips that looked like rose petals the most beautiful anyone could have seen.

He began devouring her, tasting her sensitive clitcoris with full mouth. She was already coming. Her flow floated in the air, he grabbed it with his mouth not letting a drop lost. She was

sucking his erected penis, as only she know how. Both were moaning, her vaginal lips were swallen, her clitoris too that he sucked very hard with and incredible speed.

She was all convulsing, crying, moaning. She couldn't hold an orgasm after the other. His mouth feeling her coming covered her vagina with full open mouth to direct her flow of elixir of love directly to his throat making him come too in her thirsty mouth. She sucked harder and harder. So no sperm will get to float around the cabin.

He continued sucking her clitoris in hysteria, his hands on her lovely cute and best exciting ass in the universe. She was all in a trance, her eyes semi-closed enjoying his mouth and his lips tearing her senses apart.

She had renewed the sucking of his penis that was so erect that it was hard as a rock. She wanted him in her, deep inside her vagina. She succeeded in 5 minutes. The situation floating was also an aphrodisiac to their already rich sex lives.

He grabbed her and penetrated her vagina, this time holding her ass very tight and began flicking each other's brains. His hands on her cheeks and finnally gets in her hot rear entrance. They bounced against a different place each time he penetrated her.

His mouth devoured her breasts, kissed her mouth their back to her breasts sucking her nipples making her yell of excitement, tasting the milk that came of her breasts from so much sucking on them. He was happy to taste her like this,

"Oh my love I drank milk from your breast like our future child will when he will be born."

Kim was elated, "Did you? Did you? and did you like it?"

"Oh yes I loved it, but I always loved my milk with cookies."

They both laughed: "My cookie is a piece of your breasts."

He engulfed a big part of her breast in his fully open mouth. His tongue teasing it, then sucked on it undlessly. After that taking one of her lips between his and sucked it then the other.

She was sighing at the thirst he had for her. They had a ferocious appetite for each other. He made love to her endlessly until they cramped on each other, feeling her orgasm triggering his ejaculation. They didn't rest. He then grabbed her and flipped her over, coming to her by her behind one hand and arm on her breasts and one on her vagina, masturbating her nervously and moaning in and out of her mountain of love, her incredible ass. Penetrating her with all his strength and desire upside down, their feet on the ceiling and their heads down.

They didn't notice that they were very close to the video camera filming where their bodies joined just were his penis penetrated her delicious ass. He has conquer the world for her ass and her as a whole, his mouth tasting licking her neck and face by extending his head above her shoulder.

He loved so much to feel her ass against his lion. When he finally ejaculated feeling also her flow in his hand. He held it

tight so no drop will escape. When he rested pressed against her ass. He released her without releasing his hand from her burning and swallen pussy. He turned upside down on 69 and drank her potion of love.

Which she also grabbed his penis on a 69 position thus triggering a new trek in their happiness. 6 hours of love making had passed before they were called to see a beautiful view of the earth and the moon. They were like in between both. Kim was marvelled. The cosmonauts were looking at the couple excited. Kim took her camera and took pictures of both the earth and the moon. They were now in direction to the moon.

Kim: "My love that the best present you have given to me after your love of course.."

Boris the cosmonaut was a typical Russian blonde, blue eyes, he looked strong like the Russian bear, he was at least 7' tall. Vladimir was 6' 6" red head and very strongly built. Katherina looked good but a little on the masculin side, she probably prefered women. Mostly by the look in her eyes. She was red head and probaly 6' 2", Irina was blonde and sweet really beautiful a gorgeous body, blue eyes and was 5' 10".

Irina: "In Russia we don't have any problem for nudity, we are all the same in a way. So why hide our G-D given gifts."

It was easier said than done, then she undressed and was in her birth suit. John looked at her body, she had a great sexy body. Her tits were firm and had small oreals and long nipples as Kim's. Her ass was not as round but gorgeous. A nice pair of

legs. Katherina also undressed not bothered a bit from their gaze. She had nice boobs and wider hips. Strong thighs and legs.

Her triangle was neatly trimmed, barely showing the red crop, leading to her pussy, her clitoris looked oversized almost like a small dick. The men undressed. Boris was very atheltic, white like snow inside he had a huge penis. Katherina grabbed him by it and pulled him to the cabin.

And Irina grabbed Vladimir too and went to the cabin floating in the air. It was only one cabin for everyone. With their excitement, John and Kim did not notice the other beds. Six in total. John and Kim followed them and also undressed. The blonde girl Irina pressed a button to stop the video. They all were floating. Katherina came to Kim and surveyed her body with her hands.

"How gorgeous you are Miss Kim, I hope you do not mind!" before Kim could answer, caressed her gorgeous breasts. John came behind Kim and held her tights. The Russian girl did not care. She continued by sucking her breasts, her hands on her pussy even caressing John's penis pressing it against Kims vagina. John didn't know how come they were so aroused and so fast. But he quickly forgot about it.

Kim looked at him as if what do we do? John shrugged his shoulders. She took his hands she wanted him to caress her boobs, he did. John never had fucked a Russian or one with big breasts. He pulled her by it sandwiching Kim.

She grabbed her pussy and masturbat her, her pussy juice was floating in the air. She was moaning hysterically her hands also masturbated Kim. Irina also came to John from the back and tried to grab his testicles. Boris came to Katherina and began fucking her in the ass, she screamed whe he penetrated her, then calmed down. She jumped on him, "Bite my tits hard I want to feel your teeth."

John: "But Miss!"

She didn't let him talk. She pushed his face to her tits. John obliged, feeling his teeth sinking in her firm breasts, they were like Kim's in size, shape and firmness. Then she wanted him to spank her ass very hard. He put her on his lap and began spanking her hard so she would scream, "Harder don't be sissy, do it like a man.."

He spank her harder, her firm ass cheeks were bouncing and turning red. She roared like a lion, she seemed to love pain. John's strong hand was hurting already, but it excited him tremendously. She spread her thighs "Beat me between my thighs, in my pussy. I want it red hot for you."

He obliged again. Lifting her legs completely above his head and spank her vagina and between her cheeks. Her sexual organs were all red, it excited her, "Now fuck me in my ass hard, slam me against the window, I want the whole world to see me raped.."

He pressed her against the window, overlooking the earth globe and fucked her each time slamming her ass with his penis. His

hands on her breasts squeezing them very hard. When he ejaculated in her she said, "Now I want you to bite me hard. I want your teeth in my ass, my cunt, my tits everywhere."

He began biting her ass first, "Harder I said." he did leaving his clear teeth marks on her beautiful sexy cheeks. It was exciting both of them tremendously. He had never done sex so savagely. He was in nature a soft and smooth love. In the mean time at the quartet, Boris Vladimir and Katherina came down from their bunks and sat on Kim's bed.

Boris began rubbing Kim's vagina and Vladimir her ass. Katherina began kissing Kim's breasts with thirst. Kim was moaning: "Oh!!! my love you excited again?"

She spread her exciting thighs, Vladimir shoved a finger in her ass and gently began moving in and Boris also began masturbating her with one finger and with the other teasing her clitoris. They were as if enraged moving faster and faster.

Then they moved her toward them, sideways and Boris ate Kim's pussy and Vladimir shoved his tongue in her rear cavity. He had an incredibly long tongue. Katherina was now squeezing Kim's breats and sucking them at the same time. Kim had come in Boris twice without waking up totally.

Boris moved along side Kim, lifted her left thigh and penetrated her with his giant penis making Kim scream in her half asleep state. Vladimir rubbed some cream in his dick that was very large too, put some on his finger and penetrated her lovely ass in and out. Then shoving a second and a third finger enlarging

and lubricating her hole. He put the head of his penis in the rear entrance, held her by her hips and pushed in slowly. Kim jumped and opened her eyes.

"What the hell."

She saw both of them fucking her. Vladimir pushed in one bounce making her scream. But Katherina muffled her mouth with hers. She was kneading her breasts. Kim began fighting trying to free herself to no avail. They were enraged fucking her when Boris will penetrate her, Vladimir will retrieve and so on. Kim bit Katherina's lip making her bleed. Katherina screamed, Boris took over and covered Kim's mouth, her eyes were almost out of orbit.

He said "Look, you better be quiet, because your husband is fucking Irina in the cockpit and she is Vladimir's wife and he also fucked my wife. So if you are not quiet and fuck, many accidents can happen in space to your husband, nor if you …"

Scared, Kim noded, he released her mouth up to now they didn't penetrated her all the way. They continue moving in and out of her slowly, shoving more. Kim was in pain, their dicks were very wide and long. She could see half Boris penis still outside. She tought about what John had told her after her problem with the consortium, "If you are in a situation that there is nothing you can do to stop it, let it go and enjoy it, we will present the bill later.."

She relaxed her muscles and felt the enormous penis penetrating in her. Boris was devouring her breast that could

easily fit in his mouth. Vladimir was sucking her ears and neck and moving on her ass, lifting Kim's leg and massaging both pairs of testicles and sucking each at a time. She could see the tremendous dicks forcing their way in Kim's ass and vagina.

Boris said something in Russian. They held Kim tighter and pushed shoving their dicks up to their balls, making Kim scream terribly but Boris expecting it covered her lovely mouth with his. Katherina was very excited seeing this monster in Kim all the way in. They stooped for a second and then Boris retrieved, this time Vladimir retrieving.

Kim felt her inside stretch to the maximum and they fucked her on and on. Katherina when she got tired of sucking their balls. She went at Kim's head and offered her pussy. Seeing Kim not moving she pushed her face agains her vagina and rubbed it on her mouth. Until Kim had to obliged. Boris was sucking Kim's incredible breasts. Vladimir began shoving his finger in Katherinas ass.

Kim was like a sex toy in between this giants. She could feel their erection up to her stomach.

She slowly began enjoying it and was in trance, her hands reached for their testicles and began massaging and squeezing them. She first felt Vladimir throbbing in her ass and explode in a river of sperm deep inside her cavity. He cramped on her, kneading her buns, stretching them terribly and sucking her shoulder. She felt the sporadic releases and slowly she felt a little less pressure in her ass. His member was losing it's rigidity.

He was slowly relaxing. Boris moved Kim on top of Vladimir, lifting her legs and began fucking her faster and faster. Kim couldn't believe the enormity of his penis. He would pull out up to the head and plunged back up to his balls. Kim massaged his testicles that were enormous. She was moaning loud, she could still feel Vladimir moving inside her ass pushing her by her hips. Until she felt the incredible throbbing of Boris feeling his pulsation moving all her vagina and stomach.

Then the volcano erupted flooding her inside totally. He then began to move very slowly at every move, Kim's body will be in complete motion. She felt her inside completely full of his sperm an slowly feeling less pressure his genitals were relaxing. Kim had come six times Katherina came twice in Kim's mouth. Both retrieved their penis from her and layed next to her exhausted. Boris said "You are a great fuck. Come revive our dicks with your mouth and hands.", Until they all layed down without strentght.

NEW CHAPTER

I n the control room. John was exhausted. Irina was a tigress, she loved pain. He fucked her in every way possible, even leaving his teeth marks all over her body, answering her replies for him to bite her. The spanking John gave her, left her ass red as a tomato, exciting both of them to the utmost. Irina even shoved a control stick in her pussy.

They decided to return to their quarters. Tomorrow they had to land on the moon with a special vehicle.

When they got to the door, Irina spoke and laughed out loud in order to announce to the guys that they were coming back. Boris and Vladimir returned fast and went to their beds. Katherina did the same. Once inside Irina went to her bed, completely satisfied. John found Kim sleeping on her stomach. He walked over to the bed and kissed her.

Irina: "Did you enjoy?"

John: "You're still awake?"

Kim waited for an answer that did not come, and so replied, "Please carry me to the shower." John obliged, carrying her in

his arms. He felt that something was wrong, but decided not to say a thing. They left the room toward the shower. With one hand John turned the knob and the water ran on them. Kim wrapped her arms around his neck and started sobbing. John was alarmed. "What's wrong, baby? I am sorry if upset you by going with Irina. I did it so she would let you rest."

Kim then began telling him what she had dreaded to say.

"It … it was all a trick, Irina attracted you so the three of them could fuck me until now. They left when they heard you returning. I feel very sore all over with their enormous dicks."

She proceeded to tell everything in detail. Why she had allowed it to happen. He caressed her nice, and kissed her, then proceeded to wash her, letting her stand and take a hose and put it in her vagina first, making all the semen flow down. Then he shoved the hose in her rear entrance and did the same, until she was totally clean.

Then soaped her body from head to toe, making her spread her legs and washed her vagina and ass shoving his fingers in her with soap and gently massaging her inside. All this he did without saying a word. All he did was repeatedly kissing her gently on her stomach. She looked at him, feeling his tenderness. She knew that he was hurt.

She caressed his scalp. "I love you John."

John: "I love you too. I'm sorry to have let this happen to you."

Kim: 'Don't worry, as you told me before, if you can't do anything about it, enjoy it. However, don't start it. So I did."

John: "Did you enjoy it baby?"

"The truth is ... I did, but as sex and not love. When you kiss me there, I can't help but melt."

John kissed her vagina very tenderly.

Kim sighed. "Oh baby, I love you so much. I am sorry that everyone wants a piece of my ass and pussy."

John: "You drive anyone that sees you crazy, including women. Your name should have been 'temptation' and mine the 'enforcer'"

They both laughed. He continued. "But don't worry, I'll pass them the bill at the end. I know that these two weeks are going to be very active with sex. Just enjoy it and I'll take care of the rest."

He wrapped her in a large towel, and dried her. He then carried her in his arms to the quarters and laid her on his bed. Taking a bottle of baby oil, he gently anointed all her body, massaging her from head to toes. Then lifting her leg, he began massaging, very gently, her vagina and anus. She screamed a little from soreness. He kissed her.

"Yes love, that's better, continue kissing me there."

He did and gently massaged her vaginal lips between his fingers, relaxing them. Then with the other hand massaged her around the anus.

Kim: "Eat me John, please." He lifted her legs and began sucking her clitoris at first, then gently introducing his extended tongue, tasting her insides.

Kim: "While your doing that, put your finger in my ass, caress my inside, that soothes me tremendously. He penetrated her anus with his middle finger and massaged the walls. Kim came in his mouth immediately, and was moaning and pushing his head against her vagina. "Eat me some more."

She was shaking from excitement, trembling between his lips. The fingers in her ass was exciting. Her openings were returning to normal after so much stretching.

The two couples were admiring and watching the tender scene. John was very delicate in his moves. Kim had come two more times in his mouth.

They finally touched ground. Irina had attached each one with a long cable to the space mobile. When they walked Kim stopped hard, and flew at least twenty feet high, she became hysterical screaming. John pulled her by the cable until he held her." Welcome to the room my Princess; we are now having a real honey moon. Since you are my honey and I am yours, and this is ... the moon."

Kim couldn't help but laugh "Oh big lover, you're greatest romantic ever in history." Irina and Vladimir were opening bags in the ground. It looked like a giant transparent plastic boy. It was attached to the space mobile with a long Narvon bag also from the same material like a very heavily plastic. Vladimir pressed a button, and a compressor started.

John and Kim could see the giant bag inflating. Kim wondered what it was. When it inflated all the way, Irina connected her to special stick ups. It was oxygen. It had in the center of the bubble a neatness look alike also inflated. Kim still couldn't understand what was going on.

Irina: "Now you two go inside this door, open the zipper, it has three layers one after the other. Open the three of them, set in sealed the first zipper hermetically, then the second then the third."

John did as instructed and they were now inside a corridor like before the big bubble that was like 12' diameter flat at the bottom. Irina and Vladimir pushed some buttons in the generator when they entered the corridor and sealed back "Now wait" she was checking a regular gravitational atmosphere inside the bubble." Now there is the second door just ahead of the bubble. That's opened it and seals it once you're inside." They did.

Kim's heart was beating hard. Irina was filming every move. Vladimir said "Now you can take your suits off." John helped Kim to take hers, and then his. They were breathing normally without the aid of their portable compressors.

Kim: "Oh G-d we are in the moon, breathing normally. What are they doing now?"

Vladimir and Irina followed them inside and took their suits off. John had a mischievous smile. He came to her and grabbed his lips with her a kiss, he could feel her shaking in his arms. "Okay guys said Irina. You have twelve hours, enjoy your honey moon." Kim finally reacted "What we are going to have sex here until they are filming?"

"Yes my love, we will be the first ones ever to have a real honey moon. Now let me taste the honey that flours from your mouth."

He kissed her and began undressing her. She also undressed him. They were both naked. On the moon, Irina was filming the whole scene with the moon in the background. John was also kissing her gorgeous face. They had forgotten where they were. He kissed her gorgeous almond shape green eyes, her cheeks that were burning hot, her nose he sucked between his lips then her lips, mouth, sucking dry her tongue, then her chin. He licked her long, beautiful, and sensual throat, sucking Adam's apple down to her exciting firm breasts sucking her hardening nipples, taking most of her breasts in his hungry mouth then continued down to her belly button until he reached the crossroads to paradise.

She spread her legs completely allowing his mouth to devour her excitingly dripping vagina, she had her first orgasm. Just when his mouth reached her swollen pussy lips and clitoris he lifted her making her sit on his shoulders, devouring her

bounty, kissing and sucking her lips. She was moaning loud, screaming, crying and sighing, and really cried for reason only she know to this point.

"Oh master of my being eat me, eat me, please."

She rolled her head back letting it fell up to his groins arching her back and reaching his penis in a difficult position. She succeeded in imprisoning it with her mouth, making John moan in ecstasy.

"Oh princess, I love you more than ever."

He devoured her with desire and a sweet rage, taking the bulge of her vaginal lips together in his mouth biting it.

Irina: "This guy is real romantic. To pay 50 million, just for this as a souvenir. And look the way they make love."

Vladimir: "I like him. Boris and I fucked her brains out last night. She told me that she liked it."

Irina: "Don't forget that Boris scared her first; let us say blackmailed her, and he knows that too. He is afraid for her safety and his, so he has no choice to let it go."

John ejaculated in her mouth, Kim felt his throbbing first and in depseration waited for his warm storm, that she wanted to burn her throat from so much thirst she had for his sperm or anything of his.

John then freed her and layed her in bed and ate her pussy first with full mouth, then came to her, lifting her legs to his shoulders and fucked her the same way Mike did, on and off her pussy and ass alternating. She loved it, the other two had never seen such love making but where excited just looking at them.

Kim moaned very loud, her finger nails planted in John's ass, making him bleed a little, he fucked her with all his might. She felt his ejaculation, he stopped it to finish in her vagina until his completely ejaculated. The continued on and on for two hours until he throbbed again, and held his penis in her ass pushing very hard until he exploaded in a tremendous ejaculation.

He moved slow now. He spread her legs further and without exciting her lovely ass, he flipped her over, back to him, and laydown, feeling her burning ass against his loins. His hands massaged her proud and exciting himself. He kissed her face that was hot from so much love and excitement, her cheek pinkish red.

Kim giggled, happy to be in his arms, stranded in the moon. He could see her perfect white teeth, it looked like she was doing a tooth paste commercial.

"I love you princess, I am crazy about you, if you want the stars, I'll buy them for you. You are my sunshine baby. Love me forever little girl."

Kim cried, tears flowed from her gorgeous mesmerized eyes. He licked her tears.

"My love I just drank a flow of your liquid diamonds."

Kim, her lips trembling said: "Oh John, I love you so much that I am afraid every minute to lose you. Hold my hand my love, with all your stranght. I know that you are suffering from what's happenning in there, but don't my love. They are just giant dildoes."

He spread her cheeks with his hands, to feel her better. She lifted her lovely ass a bit to accommodate him.

"Oh darling you are so hot in there. It's burning me."

They began another round of love and ecstacy, again ending in each others arms. She came to him and began sucking his testicles. He loved the warmth of her mouth on his balls. Then, she took his loins and sucked it with and extream desire he never seen in her, and she couldn't stop shaking until he throbbed and ejaculated for the 6 th time.

He then layed on her, and made love tenderly, kissing all of her body from head to toes, sucking from her feet up to her hair, lovely brushing his lips, making her desire him even more.

The moment to return arrived. They got dressed on theirs jump suit then their space suit on helped by Irina and Vladimir, and returned as they came. Outside John and Kim planted a large banner with two sticks at each end.

It said "The first real honey mooners in the universe." Kim and John, Irina and Vladimir were video taping every moment of their bliss including the banner.

John took a few rocks and put them in a zipper plastic bag then onto a stainless steel container. They took all the air out of the bubble and folded everything back to the space mobile and returned to the shuttle. They were to stay ten more days in space.

Back in the shuttle, John and Kim went back to the cabin after first video-taping the panorama as the shuttle was ravishing from the moon. They could see the moon getting swallen by the moment. Kim pulled John by the arm after pilot said that they could take their suits off and went to the cabin, undressing and going to bed, to make love again. Kim invited in, covering themselves with the sheet. John understood.

John: "My love, I see that you are enjoying sex tremendously, would you like to do this at home?"

Kim rose to her albows, looked at him severly: "Why are you offending me? You told me to forget, enjoy as much as I can, and you'll present the bill."

John: "I am sorry my love, I am afraid to loose you. If you turned nymphomaniac as your doctor said. I am crazy about you. To see you taken this way, puts a knife in my heart, and I need you too much."

Kim: "Oh my big teddy bear, I told you, that i take this as dildoes and for some reasons I know that you have profesiced something for them. Are you going to castrate them?"

John: "Me? I won't even touch them!!!"

Kim: "Hum ... for some reason I don't believe you. I predict a lot of pain in their future."

They both laughed.

Irina came and said: "Please come to the cockpit, you have a call from Earth from Steve and David."

John got a shorts on and Kim just John's shirt covering her nakedness and followed him. Vladimir, Boris and Katherina were there. Steve and David were on a TV screen.

"Hi Dave!Hi Steve! Good to see you on TV."

Steve: "Good to see you too. How was the moon?"

John: "Great, incredible, I have all videotaped but for my eyes only."

David and Steve began laughing hysterically. "What are you talking about, I thought that you were an exhebisionist, you taped your first scene on the first day floating in the air and you looked good as an acrobat."

John: "How did you see that? Who else saw it?"

David: "Who else? The whole planet Earth. I couldn't believe my eyes when I saw you two fucking your brains out."

Kim covered her lovely face. "Oh my G-D, oh Lord."

John cursed, he know who did it and why they were so excited when they saw them the first time in the cockpit. He swore to himself.

Steve: "They are selling your tape for porno movies, but don't worry, we have judges all over the world, giving orders of reposession. If a tape is found in any one's possesion."

Boris was behind Kim, he slid a hand behind her, under the shirt, Kim jumped, turned her face and continued watching the conversation on TV.Boris was masturbating her with one hand and the other caressing her exciting ass, shoving a finger in her rear gate. Shoving his fingers deep.

David: "We already confiscated thousand of tapes."

John: "Anyway who cares, now the whole world knows how much I love my wife. They will envie me even more."

He grabbed Kim by the shoulders and hugged her and kissed her face. He couldn't see her face, that something was wrong.

Boris continued masturbating her, she was wet dripping all over the floor and over his hand.

Steve: "When are you coming back?"

John: "In 10 days because they are working on something here, it is a project so they can't stop for us, anyway, say hello to Kathy, Jenny and the others. I'll see you soon. Bye." and the transmition ended.

John looked at Kim, she seemed strange for a moment, the he understood why. Boris now kneeled, spread Kim's legs and began eating her pussy. John noded his head and said: "Please let her rest. She is exhausted."

Boris called John asside: "Look body, I like you two. You are good swingers. Can we meet you next week? We have two weeks of."

John: "Of course!!Why not. Kim will be delighted, but lets keep it a secret from the women. Just you, Vladimir and me. Give me a pen and a paper."

Boris did, he was excited like a kid. John was writing in Arabic and gave the letter to him.

"Next week I'll be in Abu Dhabi. When you get there, give Cheik Ali Kusemach this letter, he will bring you to us. Okay?"

Boris: "Thank you my friend!I like you." He tapped him in the back three times, almost knocking him out.

John said: "Remember, secret!!!Okay? Just you two, we will have a lot of fucking together, I have a lot of gadgets."

Boris: "Promised, thanks!"

John returned to his quarters with Kim. John took Kim and gave her a wash and said: "My love I want to take of you the I.U.D. So you can become pregnant."

Kim: "Oh my love, I want this more than anything in the world. I want your children."

She gave him a kiss that raised the hair on back of his neck.

John took Kim to the shower, spread her legs and with her help and an instrument took the I.U.D off and washed her again. It was evening, John and Kim were asleep covered. The two couples returned for the evening. When they came to the room, undressed and made love to each others wife. John and Kim didn't.

CONCLUSION

In the morning, the crew was preparing for the return to Earth. Finally John and Kim were alone in the quarters. She was asleep on top of him, burning hot, awakening a tremendous desire in him

A week after John and Kim returned to the yatch news paper spoke of two russian cosmonauts that went to Abu Dhabi and presented a letter in arabic to cheik kousamach, it said: "that they came to help you. Since he was gay and impotent, they will fuck his wives for him at no charge." The cheik had them rape by a whole batalion. Then had their genitals cut off and let them bleed to death and just before dying, they were decapitated.

Mike, Kims alledge brother was cured from cancer in a trip to Brazil. He decided to change sex and become a woman by "choice".

Steve married Gina two months later. He stayed leaving in the yatch.

Kathy and Jenny became John's second and third unofficial wives and gave him each three chilrden.

631

CPSIA information can be obtained
at www.ICGtesting.com
Printed in the USA
BVHW07s2108070818
523863BV00001B/5/P

9 781543 746433

John and Kim lived happilly together all the days of their lives and gave him three children. Many were the problems caused by Kim's smaching beauty and attraction, but many were also the castrated.

The End